THE
WIFE
NEXT
DOOR

Amanda Brooke is an internationally bestselling author.
Her debut novel, *Yesterday's Sun*, was a Richard and Judy
Book Club pick and since then she has written eleven further
books. Amanda lives on the Wirral with a cat called Spider,
a dog called Mouse, and a laptop within easy reach.

 @AmandaBrookeAB
/AmandaBrookeAuthor
@amandabrookeauthor
www.amanda-brooke.com

Also by Amanda Brooke

Yesterday's Sun
Another Way To Fall
Where I Found You
The Missing Husband
The Child's Secret
The Goodbye Gift
The Affair
The Bad Mother
Don't Turn Around
The Widows' Club
A Good Liar

Ebook-only short stories
The Keeper of Secrets
If I Should Go

THE
WIFE
NEXT
DOOR

AMANDA
BROOKE

HarperCollins*Publishers*

HarperCollins*Publishers* Ltd
1 London Bridge Street,
London SE1 9GF

www.harpercollins.co.uk

HarperCollins*Publishers*
Macken House, 39/40 Mayor Street Upper,
Dublin 1, D01 C9W8, Ireland

First published by HarperCollins*Publishers* 2023
1

A catalogue record for this book is available from the British Library

ISBN: 978-0-00-843191-4

Typeset in Sabon by Palimpsest Book Production Ltd, Falkirk, Stirlingshire

Printed and bound in the UK using 100% renewable electricity
by CPI Group (UK) Ltd

MIX
Paper | Supporting
responsible forestry
FSC™ C007454

This book is produced from independently certified FSC™ paper
to ensure responsible forest management.

For more information visit: www.harpercollins.co.uk/green

To the Ladies who Lunched

my resilience
heavy as clay
hardened
in the morning light
and
embedded with
my mother's
fingerprints

by Jessica Valentine

CHAPTER 1

The little Yorkshire Terrier darted into the house before Jane had a chance to unhook his leash. She followed Benji inside and was about to close the door when an unexpected draught slammed it shut. Certain that she hadn't left any windows open, she paused to listen to the insistent yaps coming from the sitting room. Between each bark, Benji emitted a low growl. A warning.

As Jane crept stealthily down the hallway, she wished she hadn't been so thorough clearing out her mum's things. She had been going through each room systematically and now she longed for the weight of the bronze statue that had stood on the shelf above the radiator. She caught her reflection in the hallway mirror. Her short brown hair was windswept, revealing grey roots at the temples, and she wore no make-up to accentuate the green eyes she had inherited from her dad. She had never taken after her mum, so the unexpected resemblance threw her. She wore the same fearful expression that had been her mum's death mask. Jane wasn't ready

1

to die either, and her breathing hitched as she imagined an assailant lying in wait.

Leaving one foot planted in the hallway, Jane stepped forward to scan the sitting room, her body tensing for fight or flight, she didn't yet know which. The room was bright, with smooth walls freshly painted a neutral shade of taupe, and minimal décor. There was no place to hide, and yet Benji continued to growl at the white muslin curtains that billowed like ghosts in front of the wide-open French doors. As the little dog shivered, Jane rubbed her arms through the sleeves of her hoodie.

She had used the doors earlier when she had scattered leftover crusts for the birds, and although she conceded that she had been distracted of late, she was sure she had closed them behind her. She was less convinced, however, that she had locked them. She certainly hadn't checked before leaving the house.

Alert to the danger her carelessness had invited, Jane rushed forward and slammed one of the doors shut, but she froze as her fingers wrapped around the handle of the second door. If there was an intruder, he may still be in the house, and she could be closing off a vital escape route – hers, not his. The muslin curtain fell across her face like a shroud, and the hairs on the back of her neck stood on end as she became aware of every possible hiding place in her mum's four-bedroom detached house. Her intruder could be close enough to hear her thumping heart, planning his next move as she considered hers.

With her grip on the door handle slick with sweat, Jane looked down at Benji. The little dog remained on guard, but his focus was entirely on the outside space. 'Bollocks to this,' she muttered and slammed the door shut, turning the lock for good measure. Benji's tail wagged. A good sign. 'Fancy a grand tour just to be on the safe side?'

After unhooking Benji's leash, Jane slipped from room to room and was reassured to find each exactly as she had left it. Her confidence began to build as she moved to the first floor and, after checking the shower cubicle in the bathroom, she shouted, 'Clear!'

Her smile faltered when she approached the last bedroom for inspection. The door to her mum's room had always been troublesome, and as Jane turned the handle, she gave the door a well-practised nudge with her shoulder. She didn't need to enter to see that the room was empty, not only of crazed assailants, but of furniture too. The window blind was rolled up, inviting sunlight to play across the newly laid cream carpet that had yet to be marked by furniture or slippered feet. Above the scent of fresh paint, she was convinced she could still detect the faintest hint of the lavender and chamomile candle that had burned in her mum's final days. Jane had been willing to try anything to ease her mum's passing.

An image of seventy-four-year-old Cynthia Simpkin lying helpless in bed forced its way unbidden into Jane's consciousness. When her mum had suffered a sudden and catastrophic stroke at the beginning of February, Jane had abandoned her husband in Buxton to return home to the Wirral. For two months, Cynthia had lingered in the shadows between life and death, and on the rare occasions when she had been lucid, she had been gripped with a tortuous mixture of fear and hopelessness that chimed against the fiercely independent and protective mother Jane had known.

As Jane pushed the memory away, she scooped up Benji before he could enter the room. 'Your mum's not here,' she whispered into his fur. 'She's gone.'

The only place left to check was the attic, accessed from the landing through a door and narrow staircase. It was the one room Jane was yet to touch, much to Phil's frustration. Her husband didn't understand why it was taking her so long to put the house on the market.

As Jane crept up the stairs, she placed her foot carefully on the third step to avoid the creak, but there was little she could do to disguise her laboured breaths. Reaching the top, she tensed in preparation to defend herself, but no attack came. With limited headspace in the roof, the attic room was relatively small compared to the rest of the house, and the light from the single window was sufficient to reveal several generations' worth of clutter, but no intruder.

Stretching her spine, Jane waited for her pulse to slow. Her exertions had caused sweat to prick her brow, but it wasn't as bad as the cloying discomfort of a hot flush. She puffed out her cheeks and released a sigh. It was entirely possible that she hadn't closed the French doors properly. She knew from years spent renovating her little house in Buxton, that older properties had a biorhythm all of their own. They breathed in and out, stairs creaked, pipes groaned, and occasionally, doors sighed open.

Satisfied with this explanation, Jane's footsteps were lighter and more confident as she returned downstairs. Kicking off her sliders, she stored them away in the cupboard under the stairs along with Benji's leash. She hadn't thought to check this hiding space during her search, and her skin crawled as she imagined an arm with a full sleeve of tattoos reaching out to grab her wrist. She slammed the door shut and was about to chastise herself for over-reacting when she noticed Benji sniffing out an invisible trail back to the sitting room. He remained on alert.

'For goodness' sake,' she muttered under her breath, but she followed him nevertheless.

After double checking that the locks on the French doors were indeed engaged and secure, Jane rested her hands on her hips and surveyed the room one more time. The cushions on the sofa remained plumped, the cashmere throw lying across the motorized recliner was exactly where she had left it, and the charger for her laptop trailed haphazardly from a socket.

Earlier that morning, Jane had been scouring the internet for planting schemes for her mum's garden. Unlike the modernized house, the back of the property had been left languishing since the Seventies, and tidying it up had been a form of escape for Jane while nursing her mum. Phil thought she had done enough, but Jane couldn't bear the idea of an estate agent posting photos of the family home looking anything but its absolute best, and the garden bothered her. There was still so much to do, and she wouldn't rest until she had created a legacy befitting her mum.

Reminded of this much-needed sense of purpose, Jane took a deep, cleansing breath, only to find she couldn't release it. She continued to stare at the computer cable snaking across the floor. Her chest reverberated with the beating of her heart until the breath she was holding exploded between pursed lips. The charger was there, but where was her laptop? She moved the throw. It wasn't there, nor was it behind the armchair, or lurking beneath it.

After turning full circle for another visual sweep of the room, Jane raced into the kitchen. Her laptop wasn't on the kitchen table or the worktops, and now she was checking if anything else was missing. She snatched up the handbag slung over the back of a chair, but found her purse tucked safely inside. Various other portable and pinchable items were in their rightful places too, including her Bose cordless headphones which had been left on the windowsill.

Jane was about to check for any missing jewellery in her bedroom, when she noticed the empty space on the kitchen table where her camera had been. She had been taking regular photos of the back garden to record its transformation, as she did with all her projects, and having spent Sunday jet-washing the paving stones criss-crossing the lawn, she had seen enough visible improvement that morning to deserve a new addition to her collection. She had taken the photos from the attic, which had the best view, but had returned downstairs to upload the images while eating her toast at the kitchen table.

After breakfast, she had taken her laptop into the sitting room, along with the crusts to throw out for the birds, but she had left the camera on the table. This clear and indisputable recollection gave Jane the confidence to rely on other memories. She *had* closed the French doors firmly. They couldn't have opened of their own accord. Nor had her laptop sprouted legs. Someone had been in the house.

The sense of violation caused Jane's stomach to heave. Her mum had fought so hard to make this house a secure and happy home, and Jane needed those feelings now more than ever, but someone had stolen them too.

CHAPTER 2

The clear sky had cooled to cobalt blue by the time Jane left the house again. She reached out a hand to open the gate, only to stop and turn about, almost tripping over the dog in the process. There was no harm checking she had locked the door one more time.

PC Hussein, the fresh-faced constable who had taken her statement, had described the intruder as an opportunistic thief, and as long as Jane was more particular with her home security in the future, she shouldn't let it worry her too much. He suggested she ask her neighbours to remain vigilant, so once she was satisfied that the front door was indeed locked, she set off to do her duty.

It had been a long time since Jane had lived in Oxton, a small village enveloped by the wider conurbation of Birkenhead, and many of the neighbours from her childhood had either died or moved on. Change was inevitable, she supposed – ask any woman in her mid-fifties – but there was one constant. May Jones had been her mum's closest friend to the very end, so after speaking briefly to the next-door

7

neighbours, Jane left the cul-de-sac and headed around to the neighbours that lived in the row of townhouses that backed onto her mum's garden.

As she waited for May to answer the door, yellow and red tulips bobbed their heads from the containers packed into the tight space between the front bay and a set of wrought-iron railings, but Jane's eye was drawn to the doorway directly next to May's. She frowned at the solitary repurposed chimney pot at the side of the neighbours' front door containing a sculpted topiary spiral. The decaying leaves looked decidedly drab compared to May's spring festival of colour.

When May appeared, her face immediately lit up. She was in her late seventies and had ash-blonde hair cut sharp at the jawline which gave her more than a passing resemblance to Helen Mirren. 'This is a nice surprise,' she said, chewing whatever morsel was in her mouth while playing with the fork in her hand.

'I'm sorry, were you having your tea? Should I come back?'

May responded by opening the door wider. 'Nonsense! Do you want to come in?'

'I won't keep you,' Jane replied as she raked her fingers through her unkempt hair. 'I needed to take Benji out for his last walk and thought I'd better—'

There was a rattle of keys from behind Jane, and a long shadow stretched over her. She turned to discover it wasn't simply the low sun that had lengthened the silhouette of their new arrival. The man's height was matched by impossibly broad shoulders and muscular arms, but as Jane tilted back her head, it was his dazzling smile that disarmed her.

'Hello, Evan,' said May, beaming a smile at her thirty-something-year-old neighbour. 'Been to work?'

'For my sins,' he replied, tugging at his red Royal Mail fleece.

'This is Jane, she's Cynthia's daughter.'

There was a flash of recognition in Evan's face, and he turned purposefully to give Jane his full attention. 'I'm so sorry for your loss. I didn't know Mrs Simpkin particularly well, but I know she'll be missed.'

'Yes, she will,' Jane said, swallowing hard. She chose not to correct Evan about her mother's title even though she knew her mum would have done. It hadn't been easy being an unmarried mother in the Sixties and Seventies, but Cynthia had never regretted not marrying Jane's dad.

'I hadn't realized she was a time-served plumber before she retired,' said Evan.

'I've been boring him with all kinds of stories about my Cynthia,' explained May proudly.

'Never boring,' Evan assured them both. 'I can't imagine it was easy for a woman picking that kind of career back in the day. What made her choose it?'

'My grandfather, Henry Simpkin, was a plumber too,' Jane said, and although this was the short answer, there was an even shorter one. *Necessity.* Cynthia had needed to support herself and her baby too, and Henry had made sure his daughter was suitably equipped.

Evan fidgeted as he grappled for some other words to comfort the recently bereaved, and it was Jane who smoothed over the awkwardness. 'Actually, I think we met a couple of years ago, during one of the Secret Garden weekends.'

Oxton held the event annually, inviting visitors into private gardens to raise money for charity. Her mum loved walking around the grounds of the early Victorian villas built by wealthy Liverpool merchants, but Jane took her inspiration from the ordinary gardens that had been nurtured into something extraordinary

'You probably don't remember,' she continued, 'but you and Mum had a long conversation about perennials.'

'Ah, yes, of course,' Evan's smile faltered when he noticed Jane's gaze drift towards the chimney pot with its desiccated display. 'I don't get time to garden much these days,' he admitted. His door keys jangled in his hand. 'Anyway, I'd better get on. Nice talking to you, Jane.'

Evan disappeared into the house before she thought to mention there was a thief on the prowl. 'I should let you go too,' she said to May. 'I just thought you should know there's been a break-in.'

'Oh, no, where?' May craned her neck to look outside. 'Whose house?'

'Mine,' Jane said. 'That is, I mean, Mum's.'

This time, May did come outside, and she clasped Jane's arm. 'Oh, my goodness. Are you OK?'

'I'm fine,' Jane insisted, placing her hand over May's. 'It was an opportunistic thief according to the police, and my own stupid fault for leaving the French doors unlocked.'

'What did they take?'

'My laptop and camera, easily replaceable,' Jane said, playing down the crime.

'You say that, but I know someone who lost all their photos going back years. Holidays, weddings, everything.' She stopped when she noticed amusement play across

Jane's face. 'Sorry, I forgot I'm talking to a computer teacher.'

'I'm an ex-teacher now,' Jane reminded her.

Jane had been working part-time when her mum had taken ill, and moving back to Oxton to care for her had been the final push to end a career that had never truly captured her. It would have been nice if the head had at least pretended to be sorry to see her go, but it had become apparent to everyone that her commitment to the job had been distinctly lacking in the last few years. It was time to go. Her pension was small, smaller still when you factored in a heavy abatement for drawing it early, but Phil had been supportive and they could live frugally.

'Luckily for me, everything can be recovered from my cloud storage,' Jane told May.

'I have no idea what that is, but if you say it's fine, I'll take your word for it,' May said, giving Jane's arm a final squeeze. 'Still, it's a bloody outrage that someone can waltz into your house and help themselves to whatever they want.'

'I don't want to worry you, but it looks like he came in through the hedgerow at the back. Someone's crushed all the chicken wire Mum put up to stop the dog escaping.'

'The little toerag,' May muttered, but her frown softened. 'I remember when you and our Sheena used to burrow your way through there constantly.'

'I'm sure our tunnel's overgrown by now, and actually, the thief came through from next door,' Jane said, tipping her head to May's neighbour. Her mum's garden was wide enough to overlap both gardens, and given that Evan's house was an end-of-terrace with an alleyway separating it from the next row of townhouses, it had provided the toerag in question with easy access. 'Do you think you could mention it to Evan just in case our thief fancies some more garden hopping?'

'Not a problem,' May said as she stepped back into the house. She tilted her head briefly as if listening out for something before refocusing on Jane. 'But what about you? Are you sure you're OK?'

'Worse things happen.'

'At least you'll be scooting back to Buxton soon,' May said, playing with the fork in her hand. 'Are you ready to put the house on the market yet?'

Jane chewed her lip. 'I don't think I'll ever be ready, May. That house has been in my family since 1946. Mum was born in one of those bedrooms.'

May nodded. Neither of them needed to add that she had died there too, as had Cynthia's mother on the day she had given birth to her. 'There's a lot of history there,' she agreed, staring intently at the fork. 'What does Phil think?'

Jane rolled her eyes. 'That I'm taking too long.'

May held off her response as she cocked her head towards a noise. Jane heard it too this time. There were raised voices coming from next door. The high pitch of a woman caught up in anger, or distress, was abruptly silenced by the harsh boom of a man's voice. Evan's.

'Don't worry,' May said, noticing Jane's features cloud with concern. 'They're always at it.'

Jane strained her ears to listen. Evan's wife was saying something about him twisting everything. His response was clearer. 'You're the one who's twisted. Just look at the state of you.'

'Are you sure we should be ignoring it?' asked Jane, as

the row escalated inside. She couldn't recall Evan's wife's name from their meeting years earlier. The willowy young woman with silky blonde hair had remained on the periphery of her husband's conversation, and Jane had been left with the impression that she was a bit standoffish. Or had she simply had her voice stolen?

'Honestly, they'll be kissing and making up in two minutes,' May said. She raised her eyes to the heavens. 'I hear that too. Now, back to you. Have you told Phil about the break-in?'

Reluctantly, Jane tuned back into her conversation with May. 'He'll only want me to come home straight away.'

'I expect he misses you.'

The shouting next door continued unabated. 'He can manage a little longer,' Jane said, her eyes flitting to the dead plant on Evan's doorstep.

'What about Megan?' asked May, referring to Jane's daughter.

'She's far too busy to miss me. Country vets don't get much time off during lambing season, and since she moved in with Greg, all her free time is spoken for.'

'You must be very proud of her.'

May spoke louder than necessary, but Jane's body still jerked when she heard Evan's wife cry out, 'Why are you doing this to me?'

Jane's fingers and toes tingled as blood rushed to her head, and Benji released a whimper as if sensing her distress.

'Jane,' May said, her voice firm. 'You have enough to deal with. I'll keep an eye on them, and if it gets out of hand, I can always intervene.' She raised the stainless-steel fork as if it were a spear.

13

Jane didn't envy anyone who got on the wrong side of May Jones, even a man of Evan's stature. 'Promise?' she asked, shocked at how childlike she sounded.

'Promise.'

'I . . . I should let you finish your tea,' Jane said, backing away so fast she banged her hand against the wrought-iron gate. She swallowed back a sob, and once she was free of May's watchful gaze, she broke into a run, adrenalin pumping as if she were the one fleeing the abuse.

CHAPTER 3

Jane spent the rest of the working week fighting restlessness and unease, but the weekend brought fresh challenges, and there was only so long she could ignore the thumps and crashes coming from the attic. Bounding up the narrow staircase, she found Phil on the far side of the room with his back to her as he broke the seal on one of the few remaining boxes he hadn't already rifled through. Only the dog turned to eye Jane cautiously.

'What the hell are you doing?' she demanded.

'Sorting through stuff,' her husband replied stiffly. 'Someone has to.'

'You were only supposed to be taking a look around. I never asked you to start emptying everything out.'

'You'll thank me later.'

Jane tensed her jaw to hold back numerous expletives. The floor was strewn with items Phil had taken it upon himself to unpack, inspect, discard or dismantle. There were knotted bin bags and pieces of bric-a-brac stacked on top of each other, and Phil was intent on adding more to each pile. He was examining a small blue box with a Royal Worcester logo, and pulled down his reading glasses so he could read the inscription on the inside of the box lid.

'What on earth's an egg coddler?' he asked.

'Does it matter?'

'Well, yes,' he said, only now looking at his wife over the rim of his glasses. The peppering of grey in his beard matched the smudges of dust covering his white polo shirt. 'I've organized everything into five separate groups. Bin, charity, eBay, save, and don't know yet. That's the one you need to go through.'

He nodded towards a relatively small pile which included a large framed photograph of Cynthia as a young child, sitting with her father and his sister. Great Aunt Judith had been a war widow, and became a surrogate mother to her niece after Cynthia's mother died in childbirth. She had eventually remarried and moved to the Isle of Man when Cynthia was in her teens, never imagining what lay in store for her niece.

'I don't know what I want to keep yet,' said Jane, retreating back a step. 'And you most certainly don't. I never asked you to do this. These aren't your things.'

Phil lobbed the egg coddlers onto the charity pile. 'Nor are they yours. Admit it, Jane, most of this is tat.'

'It's not about the monetary value.'

Her husband took a measured look around the room, inviting her to find anything that countered his argument. As head of a private school, Phil was expert at bringing everyone around to his way of thinking, but not his wife, not this time. After thirty years of marriage, Jane was tired of following where he led.

16

'I know it's hard, but you're going to have to let these things go,' he said softly, but no less persistent. 'You've done so well with the rest of the house. This should be the easy bit.'

Phil had no idea how Jane had sobbed over every garment she had taken from her mum's wardrobe, nor had he witnessed the two failed attempts before she had managed to drop off her mum's collection of ornaments at the charity shop. None of it was easy, but she had been in control of each step. That was what helped her push through the pain, not her absent husband.

'I need to go at my own pace, Phil. There's no rush.'

Her husband's only response was to purse his lips before returning to his task. It was as if his wife hadn't spoken at all.

As Jane silently fumed, her thoughts turned to Evan and his unseen wife, who might have handled such a disagreement differently. Instead of withering looks, they were likely to hurl angry words, or something worse. She had asked May about Evan and his wife the morning after they had overheard them fighting, but her neighbour had simply shrugged and changed the subject. Jane assumed that meant she had heard them 'kiss and make up' as predicted, but what about the next time? And what about now? Were they enjoying a lazy Saturday morning in bed, or gearing up for another fight? Weekends were always the worst, her mum could tell you that. Except Jane had never asked. Neither of them had wanted to resurrect old memories for fear of hurting each other, but the buried pain had caught up with her mum in the end.

When Cynthia had been discharged from hospital, she

had been able to sit propped up in bed, but the damage caused by the stroke had left her with limited ability to communicate. If she was awake, her one functioning eyelid drooped in sympathy with the other side of her slackened face, and for the most part her expression was one of vacancy. On the rare occasions when she did recognize who she was, and where she was, her distress was palpable, and Jane never knew which version of her mum she would face whenever she entered her bedroom.

'It's bitter outside,' Jane had told her mum one day in March after a spate of gardening. She spoke loudly as she fixed her mum's pillows, unwilling to accept that Cynthia was completely unreachable.

Her mum's good eye watched as Jane took the seat next to the bed, but it was only as Jane took her hand that Cynthia reacted. Her lips moved, but frustratingly, no words came.

'Sorry, are my hands cold?' Jane asked, rubbing her palms briskly against her mum's to warm them up. 'I was going to plant some bulbs, but the ground's rock hard so I've filled up some of your planters instead,' she continued. 'Tulips mostly, so we should get a nice display in . . .' Her voice trailed off. If the doctors were right, her mum wouldn't live to see the tulips bloom.

Cynthia's body tensed as she made a valiant effort to raise her daughter's hand to inspect her fingernails. Her lips parted again, and the tongue that had once been sharp, worked sluggishly as if talking were a new skill she hadn't quite mastered. 'Dirty,' she said.

Jane leant forward, ever hopeful that this was the breakthrough she had been longing for. 'I've been digging.'

It took a moment for her mum to meet her gaze, but

when she did, there was no mistaking that longed for connection. 'J-Jane?'

'Yes, Mum, it's me. It's Jane.'

'S-s-sorry,' Cynthia said, using up as much strength as she could afford to bring her daughter's hand to her lips.

It was hard to believe that as recently as January, this indomitable woman had been constructing bookshelves in the dining room from an assortment of reclaimed timber. During her working life, Cynthia had needed to fight for every job amidst accusations of stealing work from men with families to feed. It meant she had to be better than anyone else, and more adaptable too. She could do anything she set her mind to.

'Oh, Mum, you have nothing to be sorry for,' Jane said, as she felt her mum's strength give way. She guided their hands back down to rest on the bed.

Bubbles collected in the corners of Cynthia's mouth, and her lopsided expression became one of frustration, quickly followed by anger. 'H-he hurt you,' she said.

Jane bit down on her lip. 'I'm a big girl now.'

Something in her mum's eyes suggested she saw only the child who had suffered much during her parents' troubled relationship. She looked from the door to the window, as if assessing the danger and any means of escape. 'He– He's here.'

'No, Mum,' Jane tried to reassure her.

'Still – here,' her mum insisted as tremors reverberated through her body.

It wasn't the first time since her stroke that Cynthia had found herself caught between the present and the past. Jane had heard this warning often, but never with such clarity.

Her mum wanted to say more, but her words were lost as she became consumed by whatever terrors had overtaken her mind. Only one word was clear. '*Hide.*'

'But I don't have to hide. Not any more,' Jane said, her voice quaking. 'Dad can't hurt us now. We're safe. Because of you, we're safe.'

A shimmering tear pooled in the corner of Cynthia's eye. 'Left it– Left too late.'

'You put up with him for as long as you could, and all the while you protected me.'

'N-no. I didn't.'

'He's gone, Mum. You stood up to him like no one else could,' Jane insisted. The night her mum had kicked her dad out of the house had been violent and bloody, but Cynthia had got her way in the end. Jane had been hiding in the attic when she heard the side gate clang shut as her dad left, but it had taken a long time not to fear his return. It hadn't crossed her mind that her mum had been scared too. 'You were bloody brave.'

Cynthia stared down again at Jane's hands. Had she realized they were grown-up hands, and not a child's? 'Not always,' she said, almost to herself. 'You need– need to be brave now.'

'Don't you worry about me. I can look after myself. And you, too. We're going to get you better,' Jane added, going against the dire prognosis the doctors had given.

'Not– not ready to go. So sorry.'

Jane swallowed back her sob. She had all but given up hope of ever speaking to her mum again, and this was a gift too precious to waste on tears. 'Don't you dare apologize for anything. You're the best mum a daughter could wish for.'

'Not– best for you. How did w-we run out of time?' asked Cynthia. 'S-s-so fast.'

'I don't want to lose you, Mum,' Jane said, dabbing the tear that spilled down her mum's cheek.

'S-s-scared.'

'Me too,' Jane said. It was getting harder to deny her mum's life was slipping away.

Her mum gripped her hand as if sheer will alone could keep the connection open, but with a juddering sob, her body sagged and the grip slackened.

Jane couldn't bear to look at the vacant expression that had returned, and so she leant forward to rest her head on her mum's lap. Finally, she let the tears fall. 'I love you, Mum.'

'Are you OK?' asked Phil.

Jane blinked hard and took a couple of deep breaths, but she couldn't shake the warnings her mum had repeated, not only on her deathbed, but throughout Jane's early childhood. 'He's here.' 'Hide.' 'Be brave.' It was here in the attic that those words chilled her the most.

'I'm fine,' she said, surprised that her husband had stopped what he was doing long enough to pay her any attention. There were times recently when she could have waved a hand in front of his face and he still wouldn't have noticed her.

'You look like you could do with some fresh air,' he said. 'Why don't you take the dog for a walk?'

'I'll take him out later.'

Phil ruffled the top of Benji's head. 'I wonder what he'll make of his new home?'

Jane wasn't buying Phil's enthusiasm. 'I thought you hated dogs.'

'No, I simply thought a dog impractical, but now that you've given up work, you'll have loads of time to spare.'

'Great,' she said dully. 'But if dog walking is all I have to look forward to, I don't see why there's any need to rush back.'

'You can't stay here on your own, Jane. Not after what happened.'

She had put off telling Phil about the break-in until he had arrived the night before, then immediately regretted handing him the ammunition to get her to leave. 'This is Birkenhead, not Basra,' she said. 'Of course I can stay.'

'What does the estate agent think?' he asked, hedging her mood.

'I haven't phoned yet,' she said, forgetting it was the excuse she had used to avoid Phil's explorations in the attic.

'For goodness' sake, Jane. Do you want me to ring them? Or,' he added, in an attempt to be more conciliatory, 'if you really can't face selling yet, will you at least consider my other suggestion? I'm sure we'd have no problem renting the house out on a short-term lease.'

Before Jane could formulate a response, or more likely an excuse, Phil was on her case again.

'Either way, this lot needs clearing. Can you take a look in that box of Christmas decorations over there? There might be something of sentimental value,' he said, a nod to their earlier spat, 'although I'm guessing that doesn't include balding strings of tinsel.'

Jane glanced at the box, not needing to open it to know it contained all the crudely repaired Christmas ornaments she had hung up as a child; family heirlooms her mum had pieced back together after Jane's dad had lost his temper one Christmas. She could still hear the yells and crashes as he stamped on the tree, and the memory made her aware of all the other things surrounding her that bore similar scars. The picture frame with no glass, the lamp missing its original shade. Suddenly, her dad's brooding presence sucked the air out of the room, and she was gasping for breath as she turned quickly to open the window.

In the garden below, the tulips Jane had planted in March added a welcome splash of colour to the vast collection of pots and planters standing on a circle of yellow paving stones. There were paths leading from the garden's focal point in every direction like rays of light around the sun, hence the colour her mum had chosen for the poured-concrete slabs. Jane traced the lines of each ray with her eyes in an effort to ground herself.

Cynthia's Seventies makeover had transformed what had been a beautifully random patchwork of plots, including one for growing vegetables, another for blackcurrants and strawberries, a small lawn, and a mini demolition site where an old Anderson shelter had been. Young Jane had explored each distinct patch as if she were crossing continents to claim hidden treasures. She had never warmed to the sun design that carved her imaginary world into featureless lawned segments that her mum claimed were easier to maintain. What the design did have, however, was potential.

Determined to remain true to her mum's original vision, Jane had cleaned up the paving stones that had aged to varying shades of yellow, but the lawn had to go, and she was in the process of creating a parterre to accentuate the geometric pattern with low-level box hedging. With the right plants, flowers and shrubs, each segment would add colour and variety to the garden all year around. It was going to be quite a sight, and Jane would love to call Phil over and explain her plans, but he would only point out that she wasn't supposed to be staying long enough to see the garden fully established. Yet how could she not?

Resisting thoughts of giving up her childhood home, Jane allowed her gaze to travel to the edge of the property line, over the hedgerow and into her neighbour's garden. Evan was outside sawing wood, his biceps bulging from beneath his T-shirt as he constructed what looked to be some kind of trough. There was no sign of his wife.

'Good grief, not more rubbish,' Phil said with a groan. 'Shall we see what's inside the box?'

Her husband had reverted to talking to the dog, and Jane turned a deaf ear to his one-sided conversation to concentrate on her neighbour. Scanning every window, she was desperate for confirmation that Evan's wife was OK, if only to ease her guilt. She had heard the young woman in distress, and her instinct had been to run and hide rather than help. But wasn't it always so?

'Does this mean anything to you?' asked Phil loudly. 'Jane?'

She turned to see what Phil had found and gasped, the dusty air catching at the back of her throat. 'Where did you get that?'

Phil was holding a plastic snow globe with a red base. The water inside was clouded with age, but Jane knew the obscured scene was a two-dimensional Santa popping out of a chimney pot. It hadn't come from the box of decorations, she was sure of that. It didn't belong there.

'It was in this box. There's a load of other stuff too,' he said, lifting up two yellowed colouring books. They were quickly discarded when he spotted what had been hidden beneath. 'Wow, this takes me back. My dad had an overcoat just like it.'

'Mine too,' replied Jane in a strangled voice that stopped Phil before he could try it on.

'This was your dad's?'

Jane nodded, feeling dizzy and disoriented.

'And the other things?' Phil said, carefully folding the overcoat.

'The snow globe and the books were presents he sent after he left.'

Any other eight-year-old would have been excited to receive gifts from a merchant seaman travelling halfway around the world, but Jane had never played with the snow globe, nor scribbled in the colouring books covered in foreign writing. She hadn't wanted the reminder that he was still out there, and she didn't want to see them now.

'Put it all back,' she choked.

Phil had been crouching in the shadows, and when he moved to add the box to the rubbish pile, Jane reeled at the sight of a gaping hole torn out of the attic wall behind him. It was the long-hidden entrance to a small cubby hole that utilized the space between the eaves and the stud wall. Its door was a piece of plywood that had slotted seamlessly into the gap, but it hadn't been used in decades. From the torn edges of the lining paper that had covered up its existence, it looked like Phil had cut through the outline with a blunt instrument.

'Why the hell is that open?' she demanded.

'I saw the dimple of a little hole beneath the lining paper, and poked my finger through it.' Jane knew immediately what he was describing. The hole had been cut out of the plywood door and served as a doorknob or a spyhole, depending on which side of the panel you were on. 'I did ask why it had been papered over, but you obviously weren't listening, so I used a key to cut around it. I must admit, I was expecting something a bit more exciting.'

'You found the box in there?'

'And a suitcase.'

The attic room walls bowed as Jane's vision pulled her towards the gaping mouth of what had once been her secret den. Her pulse thundered against her eardrums and as she stumbled over a pair of purple velour curtains littering the floor, the shadows shifted. There it was. A small tartan suitcase.

When Phil reached to pull it out for her, Jane lurched forward, her heart in her throat. 'No! I said put it all back!'

'What?' He had his hand around the handle now.

'Will you stop! I don't . . . Just stop!'

Phil didn't have time to react as Jane shoved him out of the way, forcing him to release his grip on the handle. Ignoring his cry of alarm, she grabbed the box containing her dad's overcoat and crammed it back into its hiding place with the suitcase, before picking up the plywood door resting against the wall. Her hands were larger than the last time she had held it, but she slotted it back into place as quickly as she had ever done, then straightened up too fast.

Phil recovered from his shock in time to notice his wife swaying. 'Maybe we should take a break,' he said, reaching to steady her.

Jane rounded on him. 'Leave me alone!'

'It's . . . It's OK,' he said soothingly.

She stared at him. *You have no idea*, she wanted to say. 'I told you not to interfere. Why do you *never* listen to me?'

'I do,' he countered. 'Look, you're overwrought, that's all.'

'*Overwrought?*' she screeched. Her cheeks seared with fury. 'Can't you see you're doing it again? You're not – listening – to – me, Phil.'

'But you haven't said anything!' he snapped back. 'I'm trying to help if only you'd let me. You've been dragging your heels for weeks.'

'And I told you why. The garden—'

'Is a delaying tactic,' he interrupted. 'Come on, Jane. This has gone on too long. You've done enough.'

Her lip quivered. 'I just . . . I wanted to make sure the house was in the best possible shape, that was all. I thought that would be enough.'

Phil's stare was intense as he tried to figure out his wife. 'And now?' he asked, having picked up her use of the past tense.

It was as if a tornado had torn through all of Jane's plans in a matter of moments. Everything was up in the air. Everything. 'I don't know if I can go through with this.'

Phil flung up his hands in exasperation. 'What does that mean?'

'I don't know!' she cried out. 'But it doesn't help with you badgering me!'

'You do realize you're not making any sense, don't you? I know you're grieving. I know this is a painful process, but that's why I'm here. Let me sort out this junk. I'll even sweep the floor when I'm done,' he added with a flourish. 'You don't have to do anything.'

27

'For the rest of my life?'

He looked at her as if she were crazed. 'What?'

'It's not like I have a job to go back to,' she said, feeling her world suddenly shrinking. She had never felt so trapped.

'But you have your family. Aren't we enough?'

She wanted to reply that her family were everything, but how did that explain the decision she was about to make? She didn't understand it herself, but she knew in her gut what needed to be done.

Phil's brow knitted together when he noticed a tear slip down her cheek. 'To hell with this. We can close up the house until you're in a stronger frame of mind. I'm taking you home. Today.'

Jane swiped away the tears to glare at her husband who was inching closer. When he made a second attempt to take her arm, the storm inside her rose up again to unleash fresh fury. 'Will you stop pushing me!' she yelled. 'I'm not going anywhere, Phil!'

'Well, you're not staying here alone in your state.'

'I can do what I damn well like! And I choose not to run away,' she said, her words sharpened by her clenched jaw.

'You're not running away, Jane, but you do have to move on at some point.'

'And you think this is moving on?' She began jabbing her finger at the mess around her. 'Every single piece of junk in this room means something, if not to me, then to Mum, because she made a conscious decision to store it up here. If she didn't throw out that bloody egg coddler, then how can I?'

'Please, Jane. Calm yourself down. I know this is raking up bad memories.'

'You know nothing!'

'Of course I do! Do you think I've forgotten what you said happened here?' They were no longer talking about egg coddlers. 'I can only imagine what you're feeling right now, but leaving you here alone isn't an option.'

'Is that an offer to stay too?' she challenged, confident he wouldn't accept. She didn't want him to, and knowing that almost broke her.

'We have our life in Buxton, and it's a good life, Jane. Better than *here*. I can't believe you'd want to hang around any longer than necessary – given what your dad did.'

'You think my dad defined this place? You think he defined *me*? No, it was Mum who did that! She filled this house with so much love and laughter after he'd gone. She played music and we'd dance to stupid pop songs, all because we didn't have to hide any more. I *was* happy here, Phil.'

'I believe you, but that was a long time ago,' he said. 'And however you're feeling right now, I promise, you can be happy again, back with us.'

'No, Phil, I can't,' she said, her words choked with emotion. She needed to make him understand that this was more than grief, more than her relationship with her mum, and more than suppressed memories. Their problems were very much in the present, and threatened to wipe out thirty years of marriage. She didn't have to look at the cubby hole with its tattered edges to know it had torn a hole in all their lives.

'Jane, please . . .'

29

'You can't make me happy, Phil. I'm sorry,' she said. He looked wounded, but she had no choice but to hurt him more. She couldn't voice her darkest fears, so chose instead to resurrect the more familiar complaints. 'It's all right for you, you have a job that you love. I've just become the little wifey at home with a pinny, a hot meal and a warm bed.'

'I only called you wifey a couple of times,' Phil said with a nervous laugh because he didn't know how else to respond. He was utterly confused by her. 'It was meant to be a term of endearment.'

'And that was fine when it was one of my many labels, but not so funny when it's pretty much the only one I have left. How come we trained at the same time, but you're the one who ended up with the flashy career in a posh school, while I just about managed to keep a part-time job in a school threatened with special measures?'

'You could have come to work for me, and there's no reason why it couldn't still happen. If that's what you want. I'm sure—'

'I don't want to work for you!'

'Then what *do* you want?'

'Purpose!' she said, hoping this answer would satisfy him. Why couldn't he just accept what she was saying and leave?

'You have purpose,' Phil insisted. 'Look at all you've achieved. Maybe you didn't work full-time, but you restored our house more or less single-handedly. I wouldn't have known where to begin on a project like that. I don't understand. Why are we even having this conversation?'

'Because you're listing all the things I've *done*. Done as

in finished,' she said, as old resentments rose up. 'I'm the one who has to start from a completely blank page while your life goes on unchanged. You've never had to worry about fitting in being a father or husband around your career, because I made it work for all of us. That was my job – until I wasn't needed any more, and I haven't been needed for a very long time, not by you, or Megan, and I don't even get to care for Mum now.' She bit the inside of her cheek to stop herself from sobbing. 'What's left for me, Phil, except staying here and looking after the house?'

Phil's face creased with pain. 'I do still need you,' he said. 'Perhaps I hadn't appreciated how daunting it is for you going forward, but can't you see it as a new adventure?'

'A new adventure? Seriously?' It felt more like an old nightmare, but she didn't want to speak of that. She shook her head. 'This is where I'm meant to be, Phil. I see that now.'

'Well, I'm glad one of us does,' Phil muttered. 'Please, Jane, whatever this is about, we can sort it between us. You don't have to be here. Let's go home.'

There was the taste of blood in Jane's mouth as she bit harder into her cheek. She wanted to drop to the floor and sob but she had to be brave, just like her mum had told her to be. There was no way out, and no way to soften the blow.

'I'm sorry. I can't go back, possibly not ever, and you won't change my mind. This is not your choice.' It was barely hers.

CHAPTER 4

1969

Cynthia lay on her side next to Les, her back curving into his chest. Their breathing was in perfect synchronicity, but she knew that once she had fallen asleep, she would invariably wake with a start. It was going to take a while to get used to having a man in her bed, and especially this one.

She had met Lesley Morgan four years ago on a Crosville bus. It was a Saturday afternoon, and he had been on shore leave, whilst sixteen-year-old Cynthia had been out shopping with her friends. They had disembarked at the same stop, and naturally he had offered to carry her bags. She had been flattered by the attention and intrigued by the young seaman with a Scottish accent. Les had seemed so worldly wise, whereas Cynthia had never been further than the Isle of Man. Of course she had agreed to a date.

More dates had followed, but her sailor's visits ashore were sporadic and far too short, which made their time together so desperately romantic. Until Cynthia discovered she was pregnant. Then it had just been desperate.

Cynthia's dad had been furious, but not as much as Cynthia when she discovered Les was already married, a small fact he had failed to mention. He had left her with a broken heart and her reputation in tatters, and the only choice, according to a particularly insistent social worker at the maternity hospital, was to give the baby up for adoption. Cynthia thought differently, and thankfully her dad had agreed. His wife had been too ill to cradle their new-born baby for more than a few minutes, and he wasn't prepared to see another mother and child separated.

'I can give you the shoes, Cyn, but you're going to have to learn to stand on your own two feet if you want to keep this baby,' he had told her, and the 'shoes' came in the form of an apprenticeship. Not that he had been suggesting Cynthia raise her daughter alone, and for the next three years he was a doting grandfather until he had died unexpectedly two months ago.

Cynthia's Aunt Judith had wanted her niece to relocate to the Isle of Man so she could help raise Jane, but Cynthia had been left the family business and she owed it to her dad to carry on. There was also a tiny part of her that had been secretly hoping Les would come back to her, and she had to make sure he knew where to find her.

And Les had found her. He had appeared on her doorstep three weeks earlier with a red tartan suitcase, and an apology on his lips. His dark blonde hair had grown long enough to form curls she hadn't seen before, and he wore a turtleneck jumper beneath a tan leather jacket that reminded her of Robert Redford. The man who had broken her heart had returned to give twenty-year-old Cynthia the happy ending she had been holding out for.

Cynthia felt Les's warm breath against her ear. His embrace made her feel protected, and hopeful not only for her future, but for Jane's too. Her three-year-old daughter was already getting pointed out as 'that Simpkin bastard', and the name calling would only get worse once she started school.

'I love you,' Les whispered.

'I love you too.'

'Good, because one day soon I'm going to marry you.'

'Maybe,' she said.

'You'd turn me down?'

The sadness in his voice made Cynthia turn so they were facing one another. She adjusted the candlewick bedspread so it covered his bare shoulder while giving herself some thinking time. She might be young, but she wasn't a fool. Les had a lot of making up to do before she would trust him again. And of course, there were certain practicalities to consider before she needed to worry about giving him an answer. 'I meant you have to get divorced first.'

He kissed her nose. 'It'll happen, my love. My solicitor says it should be straightforward. Thank God there are no kids involved,' he said with a laugh. 'I'll have you down that aisle before you know it.'

He raked his fingers through Cynthia's hair and drew her face towards his. His tongue forced its way into her mouth before she could speak, and then he was on top of her. She let out a groan of pleasure when she felt him hard against her.

'Do you want me?' he teased.

'Yes.'

'Are you sure?'

Before she could answer a second time, there was a creak of floorboards on the landing. The bedroom door inched open.

'Mummy?' Jane said tearfully. 'Had a bad dream.'

Previously, Cynthia's little girl would have crawled into her mother's bed without invitation, but she remained wary of the stranger who had installed himself in their lives. Jane called Les 'Daddy', but she offered it more as a question than a title.

'It's OK, sweetheart,' Cynthia said, slipping out from beneath Les. She was about to lift the covers for Jane to snuggle up to her, but Les stopped them both.

'Get back to bed, Jane,' he growled. 'Now.'

Their daughter's frozen silhouette was framed in the doorway.

'Did you hear me?' he said. 'Go!'

Jane wailed as she ran back to her bedroom, and Cynthia was up like a shot.

'For God's sake,' said Les. 'Leave her be. She's got to get used to sleeping on her own.'

'She's still a baby,' Cynthia reminded him, pausing at the door. 'And if she's having nightmares, it's because the last few weeks have been so unsettling. She needs me.'

'Right now, so do I,' Les said in what he presumed was a seductive tone.

Cynthia couldn't have been less turned on. She wanted to explain that she would always put her daughter's needs first, but as Jane's father, Les should have known that already. It worried her that he didn't.

CHAPTER 5

The cake was homemade, heavy on the cinnamon, generous with the sultanas, and just enough grated carrot to cut through the sickly sweetness of the vanilla butter icing. It was delicious, or at least Jane imagined it would be if she had an appetite.

'Mmm, this is divine,' Sheena said, giving the teashop owner the thumbs up as she passed their table. 'I might as well give up baking for good.'

Jane gave her old friend an appraising look. It was hard to reconcile the middle-aged woman sitting opposite her with the friend from her childhood, but the mischievous smile was the same if you ignored the feathering of wrinkles at the corners of her eyes. 'You don't bake,' she challenged, before adding, 'do you?' A lot could pass you by when you allowed a friendship to lapse.

'Only if you count Betty Crocker cake mixes,' Sheena admitted. 'I blame Mrs Lyndsey for scaring me off. The only thing she taught me in home economics was how to drift off without letting my eyes glaze over.'

'I've missed this,' Jane said. 'Thank you for inviting me.'

Sheena put down her fork, guilt flickering across her face. 'I was under instructions,' she confessed. 'Mum said you looked down the other day.'

Jane had bumped into May on Sunday morning, and should have known her red-rimmed eyes wouldn't go unnoticed. She had made more of an effort today, brightening her drawn complexion with make-up, and swapping her usual T-shirt and yoga pants for a pale blue linen dress that had taken an age to iron. Not that she could ever compete with Sheena's timeless style, or the fine bone structure inherited from May. 'Then thank your mum, too,' she said.

Sheena wrinkled her nose. 'I would have got around to organizing something eventually, but I didn't realize you'd be sticking around.'

Jane could have picked up the phone many times too, but she always managed to talk herself out of it. The two friends had made noises about catching up at her mum's funeral, but the plans had been vague. And hadn't they said a similar thing after Sheena's dad had died ten years ago? The last time they had got together properly was more like twenty years prior, when Sheena's first marriage had come to a bitter end. Her friend had a new husband now, as well as a teenage son and a demanding job managing a shop in Cheshire Oaks Designer Outlet, and Jane had felt uncomfortable calling in their friendship just because she found her life suddenly empty.

'How long are you planning on staying?' asked Sheena.

Jane prodded her cake with a fork. 'I'm not sure. A while, I think.'

37

'On your own?'

'Just me and the dog.'

Despite the years of separation, Sheena picked up on the deepening lines across Jane's brow. 'I won't ask if you're OK, because I know you'd only lie. It must be hard without your mum. I can't imagine your house without her.'

It was a reminder of how interchangeable their homes had been growing up. They had made friends at Jane's fourth birthday party, and after discovering that their gardens were interconnected, it was as if their friendship had been fated. The tunnel they had burrowed through the hedgerow was in constant use during the summer months, and Sheena's dad had kept the brambles cut back just for them.

'With Mum's constant makeovers, it's not the house from our childhood any more,' Jane replied. There had been at least two new kitchens, and the pantry and an old coal bunker had been demolished long ago to make space for a utility room and a downstairs toilet. The bathroom had been replaced countless times, and Jane was sure her mum did it just to keep her plumbing skills up to scratch.

'It's the same house,' Sheena said, seeing through her friend's attempt to exorcise some ghosts. 'And the hedgerow can still be tunnelled through, I hear.'

'Your mum told you about the break-in?'

'It must have shaken you.'

Jane shrugged. 'It's the inconvenience more than anything. I'm fortunate that I can afford replacements.'

'Even so,' Sheena replied with a scowl. 'And I know you don't like Facebook, but you should join an online community group. I'm in one for Hoylake, and you get to find out if there's anything else dodgy going on.'

'I'll think about it.'

Jane had spent the latter part of her teaching career warning students about the pitfalls of social media, particularly the way tech companies developed their apps to keep users glued to their screens. But Sheena had a point.

'And while we're at it, I'll send you an invite to Wirral Grammar's Facebook page. There are loads of people who'll want to know you're back in town.'

Jane would have to disagree. She had been even less confident as a student than she was now. 'You're the only one I've ever wanted to keep in touch with.'

'Then we should make the most of your time back on the Wirral.' Sheena leant in closer so that Jane had the full benefit of her stare. 'Or are you considering this as a more permanent move?'

Jane blinked hard. 'I don't know what I'm thinking, literally from one minute to the next,' she admitted, mustering a small smile. 'Must be my age.'

'I know how that feels,' Sheena said with a nod of solidarity. 'Bloody menopause. It's the mood swings that get me. Our Jamie literally came out of his bedroom waving a white flag the other week.'

Jane found herself longing for Megan to be a teenager again. She never thought that would happen. 'How old is he now?'

'Seventeen. Can you believe it?'

'Megan's twenty-seven,' replied Jane.

'And what about Phil? How's that going to work if you stay here?'

It was a question that had robbed Jane of sleep for the

last three nights. 'I've told him I'm not going back,' she blurted out. 'I don't want to speak to him.'

'My God, Jane, what happened?'

Jane could manage only a sharp shake of the head. Phil had put up a gallant fight during their argument, but when he realized she wasn't going to back down, he had given in and left, slamming the front door behind him. The sound was one Jane had heard many times in her childhood, and as it reverberated through the house, she had felt old fears rise up through the rafters. Her knees had buckled, and she had sobbed into the dusty curtains, surrounded by the chaos she had inherited.

'Does Megan know you've separated?' asked Sheena.

Jane felt her stomach lurch. She hadn't reached the stage of calling it a separation, it felt too soon, too raw, but there was no denying that was where they were heading. 'I haven't spoken to her yet, and I presume Phil hasn't either, otherwise she would have been straight on the phone.'

There was a clatter of china as Sheena moved their forgotten slices of cake out of the way to reach across the table and take Jane's hand. 'I'm here whenever you need me, lovely. I know how painful the breakdown of a marriage can be, and how important it is to have friends who will back you up, no questions asked. You were there for me, and now it's my turn.'

Jane swallowed the lump in her throat, but still couldn't talk.

'Calling it a day is hard, but it's better than prolonging the agony. Christ, at least you didn't wait for the police to split you up.'

'Who needed the police?'

'The couple next door to—' Sheena stopped abruptly.

Jane straightened up. 'No, go on,' she said in a firm tone that drew upon years of practice extracting confessions from guilty students.

Sheena picked up the teapot. 'Fancy a top-up?' She poured without waiting for an answer.

'You're talking about next door to your mum's, aren't you?'

'The Jarvises,' Sheena confirmed with a grimace. 'Mum told me not to mention it. She said you'd heard Evan and Ashleigh arguing and, with all the kerfuffle with your break-in, she didn't want you thinking you had dodgy neighbours too.'

Even after all these years, Sheena had no idea why Jane would find those raised voices so triggering. Jane and her mum could always sense the thunder clouds gathering above her dad's head, and Sheena would be sent home long before the storm arrived. Sometimes, Jane would go with her, or else take cover in the attic. Whatever happened, Jane had kept her torment a secret from her best friend.

'So who called the police? Ashleigh?' she asked, feeling an immediate connection to the woman she could now give a name to. Ashleigh Jarvis.

'No, it was Mum. She called them out that same day, not long after you'd gone.'

'Good,' Jane said, relieved to hear May hadn't turned a deaf ear to the abuse completely. 'What happened?'

'Nothing much, I don't think.'

Jane took a sip of her tea to wet her lips. 'But it must have been bad if your mum needed to call the police. Did he hurt her? Physically?' she added, although she knew there was more than one way to inflict injury.

'There was no ambulance, at least, and the police didn't stay long. Honestly, it's nothing to worry about. I'm sorry I brought it up,' Sheena said as she noticed the cup trembling in Jane's grasp. 'You have enough to be dealing with.'

Jane set down her drink. 'I'm fine,' she said. But could she say the same for Ashleigh?

'Hmm,' Sheena replied. 'I can see I'm going to have to keep my eye on you.'

It was all Jane could do to stop herself from leaping up and giving her friend the biggest hug. Sheena wasn't going to be fobbed off as easily as some of Jane's friends back home; the ones who had sent messages of sympathy after her mum died and accepted her claims to be 'fine' without question. She could only hope Ashleigh Jarvis was equally blessed.

CHAPTER 6

Drawn back to the attic that had once been her refuge, and might be again, Jane faced either reversing Phil's efforts to clear it out, or finishing what he had started. She chose to be brave, and as her husband had predicted, very little of the junk held any sentimental value, or none that Jane gave herself time to consider. With few exceptions, what wasn't given away, was thrown away, and the remainder was able to fit in her grandfather's old army trunk. Phil would claim vindication if he knew, but their argument had been a symptom of a much bigger problem. Nothing had changed.

It hadn't taken long to transform the room into a little office, complete with a desk Jane had picked up on one of her many trips to the charity shop. The only items left untouched were hidden behind the false panel in the wall. They embodied everything her mum had been forced to endure, so Jane had resealed the door with a roll of lining paper and a splash of paint. They were locked away, along with her memories. She wouldn't think about them. She wasn't that strong. She really wasn't.

Thankfully, there were other issues that demanded Jane's attention, and at that precise moment, these included whether or not to answer her phone. It was lying beside the shiny new laptop she was in the process of setting up, and she watched it vibrate its way across the desk, snatching it up only when it was about to fall off the edge.

'Mum?' said Megan the moment the call connected.

'Hello, sweetheart. How are things with you? How's Greg?'

'We're fine,' her daughter said dismissively. 'How about you? Been up to much?'

Jane detected the note of sarcasm. 'I take it your dad's told you I've decided to stay here.' She could only imagine how Phil might have explained his wife's meltdown.

'He's still in shock,' Megan said. 'Are you ever coming home?'

From her chair, Jane stared out at a gun-metal grey sky above glistening rooftops. The dry spell was over, and the linen dress she had worn the day before was back in the wardrobe. 'I think a separation will be good for both of us,' she said, daring to repeat the word her friend had used to describe the state of her marriage. 'I need space, and there's a lot to sort out here.'

'I can't believe this is happening.'

The pain in Megan's voice pierced Jane's heart. 'Did you know my grandad bought this house after he came home from the war?' she asked with forced cheer. 'Your nan lived here her whole life, and it's only right that it should stay in the family. I think that's what she would have wanted. Don't you think?'

'We all miss her,' Megan replied, 'you most of all, but

your life belongs back here, with us. We were looking forward to having you home again. *Dad* was looking forward to getting you home. Please, whatever he's done wrong, give him the chance to put it right. At least speak to him. He loves you, Mum.'

Jane rubbed her temple. She was making the right decision, and even though she couldn't tell her family everything, there were plenty of truths in why her marriage had been stagnating. 'He might say he loves me, but your dad stopped *seeing* me years ago.'

'He sees the empty space you've left, I know that,' countered Megan. 'I'm not saying he can't be a dick sometimes, and I haven't forgiven him either for screwing up your anniversary plans, but if Nan hadn't got sick, he would have made it up to you.'

'This isn't because of one stupid mini-break to York,' said Jane. She had organized the treat last year because she had wanted them to work harder at their relationship, but her husband had been oblivious to the problem she was trying to solve, and had invited along a group of friends. Despite Jane's complaints, mostly to Megan, she had enjoyed the trip, possibly more than she might have done if it had been just the two of them. 'Maybe there's a reason we struggled to do things together.'

'But you still love him, Mum. And don't say you don't.'

Straightening her legs, Jane disturbed the dog sleeping at her feet. 'It's not enough,' she said. 'I know this is hard, but I won't change my mind.'

'I don't understand. Dad doesn't understand . . . He said you don't feel like you have a purpose . . .'

'And as I told him, that's something I can find here, I'm

sure of it. There's plenty of work on the house to keep me busy.'

'I'm surprised Nan left anything to do.'

Neither of them mentioned the half-built bookshelves in the dining room. It was going to take Jane a while to find the courage to complete the job her mum had been unable to finish. 'There's lots to do in the garden,' she said. 'You won't recognize it when I'm done.'

'I'm sure you'll work wonders,' Megan said, her tone devoid of the enthusiasm Jane had been trying to inject. 'I watched you transform the cottage, inside and out. I know what you're capable of.'

Jane felt the pang of homesickness her daughter intended, but giving up her beloved cottage wasn't the greatest sacrifice she faced. God, she missed her daughter.

'Mum?' Megan said, the silence worrying her. 'Have you considered this might simply be a response to your grief? None of us could have imagined Nan would be taken from us so quickly. There was no time to prepare. And I know it hasn't been easy over the last few years with one thing and another. It's natural that you're struggling.'

'Please, Megan. Don't.'

The drawn-out pause was long enough for her daughter to pick up the sound of Jane's hitched breath. 'OK, I won't push for now, but I'm going to come over for a visit so we can have a proper chat.'

Jane stiffened her resolve. 'As long as you're prepared to accept my decision.'

'It might be too late to rearrange my shift this weekend, but I can try,' Megan continued as if she hadn't heard the warning.

'Why not leave it until the weekend after?'

'Hmm, Greg and I have a dinner date with friends on that Saturday,' Megan said. 'You know what, I'll cancel it. I'll come over then.'

'Don't be silly. Come for the day on Sunday. If you can make it?'

'Sunday lunch?'

'Perfect. Just the two of us,' Jane said in case her daughter had ideas about bringing a surprise guest.

'OK, but if you need to talk in the meantime, you know where I am, Mum.'

Too far away, Jane wanted to say, but instead, she rushed to say goodbye.

Jane didn't dare imagine how much hurt she was causing to her family, and diverted her thoughts back to her laptop. It was going to take some time to upload her photo albums from her cloud storage, so she got up to stretch her spine. Walking around her desk, she looked out onto the garden. She hadn't settled on the exact planting scheme for the parterre yet, but the box hedging she was in the process of adding gave the sun design a halo. It made the traditional lawns and borders in the neighbouring gardens look boring by comparison. Would her mum approve of the changes? Would she approve of what Jane was doing at all?

Feeling a dull ache between her temples, Jane glanced over to the other side of the hedgerow. May's garden was obscured by a large cherry tree that had showered two little girls in pink confetti each spring, but its offering this year had been around the time of her mum's death, and had barely registered in Jane's consciousness. It was heavy with lush green leaves now, which served to emphasize the bleakness of the garden next door. The Jarvises' patch of earth contained a collection of forlorn shrubs, a bedraggled lawn, and the rustic-looking trough Evan had been building at the weekend. He had managed to fill it with compost, but nothing else.

Recalling the neglected topiary on the Jarvises' doorstep, Jane was surprised he had worked on the garden at all. Despite the long-ago conversation with her mum, Evan clearly wasn't a gardener, although he wouldn't be the first man to present himself as something he was not.

Hearing the notification that the upload was complete, Jane returned to her desk. There were thousands of photos, and her heart clenched as she scrolled past albums of family holidays, including ones with her mum. Despite the difficult start, Cynthia had enjoyed the life she had fought to secure, and she had been proud of her daughter's achievements too. Some of those achievements were contained in other albums, including the restoration of the cottage in Buxton.

Turning to the new project she had taken on, Jane opened the album that tracked the progress in her mum's garden. The first photos had been taken in early March when her mum was still alive. There had been much work to do, and as Jane continued to flick through the images, she enjoyed watching winter loosening its grip, and was momentarily distracted by the cloud of pink blossom from May's cherry tree that had failed to add colour to Jane's world at the time. Her finger hovered over the touchpad.

Instead of scrolling forward through the images, Jane went back to the beginning of March again. May's cherry tree was covered in tiny, pale buds, as was its twin in the garden next door. There were two trees, had always been, but not any more. This was why the Jarvises' garden looked so barren. Jane's subconscious had registered that something was missing.

Going through the photos with greater care, Jane noticed how some of the branches from the Jarvises' tree had been lopped off as March gave way to April. There followed a gap in the timeline of almost two weeks when Jane had lost interest in most things after her mum had died, and by the time she took up gardening again in mid-April, the tree had vanished. For the life of her, she couldn't understand why. It had looked perfectly healthy, and it wasn't as if Evan had done anything else with the garden except make that ugly trough.

'Bastard,' Jane said aloud, causing Benji to lift his head.

With a palm pressed against her chest, Jane took in all the other wanton destruction. The spot where Evan had built his trough had once been a flowerbed with bulbs peeking through the ground – until he decided to dig it over. Flicking quickly past an image of her own reflection after accidentally setting off the flash, Jane reached the photos she had taken when she was about to clean the paving stones earlier in May. The jet-washer was out ready for action, while in the neighbouring garden, the ill-fated flowerbed had been replaced by a long, narrow trench.

Jane inched closer to the screen as she stared into that dark pit. Her finger was trembling, and when she tapped the touchpad to reveal the next image, her heart jumped into her throat. She had inadvertently taken a snap of Evan standing knee-deep inside the hole, leaning on his spade and staring straight down the lens of Jane's camera.

She slammed the laptop shut as if he had just caught her snooping.

Taking a moment to tell herself she was being ridiculous, Jane opened the lid again, but her palms were slick as she switched from gallery view to a simple list of files. Her stomach lurched when she read the date stamp. The photograph of Evan had been taken two Sundays ago. It was the day before the police would be called to his house after May reported a disturbance between her neighbours. It was also the day before someone gained entry from the Jarvises' garden and stole Jane's laptop and camera.

She had a gnawing feeling these events were all linked, but she needed to be sure about what she had seen. Taking slow, deep breaths, she reopened the image of Evan standing in the trench. His scowl was menacing, but his foreboding presence gave Jane a good indication of scale. Her blood turned to ice. The hole, and the mound of earth beside it, wouldn't look out of place in a cemetery.

Evan was digging a grave.

CHAPTER 7

Jane came to a stop outside the row of townhouses, her eyes never wavering from the Jarvises' front door. It was early evening, too light to switch on lamps, and the front of the house looked as unoccupied as the back had all day. Jane was longing to catch sight of Ashleigh. All she needed was one brief sign of life.

'Sweet Jesus!' May cried, clasping a watering can to her chest as she stepped out of her house. 'You gave me the fright of my life standing there!'

'Sorry,' said Jane, blinking, and breaking her trance.

'Do you think I've planted these petunias too early?' May asked with a nod to her newly replenished flower pots. 'I always relied on your mum to tell me what to plant and when.'

'I should think they'll be fine,' said Jane. They would fare better than the dead topiary in the chimney pot next door. Did everything that Evan touch turn to decay? She couldn't get the image of the grave out of her mind. Aware that May had followed her gaze, she added, 'How did Evan react after you called the police?'

May rolled her eyes. 'Bloody Sheena. She can't keep her mouth shut, can she?' She set down her watering can and came forward to lean on the gate. 'You'll be pleased to hear that next door has been quieter than it has for a long time.'

Jane wasn't pleased at all. Her mouth was dry. 'I haven't seen Ashleigh. Have you?'

'I prefer to keep out of their way, if I'm honest,' May said. 'They act like the perfect couple, not realizing I can hear them through the walls – or else they simply don't care. For months now, there's been nothing but yelling, crockery being smashed, doors being slammed. You know the sort of thing.' May stopped to scrutinize Jane's features. She may not have known everything that had gone on in the Simpkin house, but she knew more than Sheena did. 'Some people aren't meant to be together, it just takes a while for them to admit it. Thankfully, it looks like Ashleigh has seen sense at last.'

'She's disappeared?' Jane asked, her stomach hollowing.

'Left him,' announced May, as if her neighbour's absence could be construed in no other way.

'But did you actually see her lea—'

Jane clammed up the moment the Jarvises' front door opened. From the corner of her eye, she saw Evan hesitate as he clocked the two women frozen to the spot.

Jane wracked her brain for something to restart her conversation with May. 'I was taking the dog for his last walk,' she finally squeaked, turning her head in the direction of Oxton Fields. She moved as if she wore a neck brace, her body tensing as her gaze swept briefly over their neighbour.

Evan wore a tracksuit with a football shirt peeking beneath it, and was carrying a sports bag. His brown hair was thick and tousled, and his shoulders were broader than she remembered, if that were possible. A brute of a man with a temper to match, he would have no trouble overpowering a woman. Had Ashleigh watched him digging that grave and recognized it for what it was? But why hadn't she run? Or had she escaped?

'A walk does sound nice,' May replied robotically, having followed Jane's example of not acknowledging Evan's presence.

'Evening, May,' Evan said as he locked the front door.

May gave a theatrical start. 'Oh, I didn't see you there, Evan. Are you off to football?'

'Yeah,' he said without stopping. He nodded in Jane's direction as he passed but struggled to meet her eye. 'Hello, again.'

'Hello,' Jane responded with a stiff nod. She couldn't look at him either, fearing there would be a deadness behind his eyes reminiscent of her dad.

Without inviting further conversation, Evan turned away, climbed into the silver car parked at the kerb, and drove off. Jane struggled to catch her breath, but when she did, there was only one question on her lips. 'Did you see Ashleigh leave, May?'

'No, love, but—'

'Oh God,' Jane said, her eyes widening as she looked down the lane again. Evan's car was disappearing from view. 'What if he did something to her, May?'

'Like what?'

'Something awful.' As Jane slipped a hand into her

53

pocket, her trembling fingers wrapped around her mobile phone. She was tempted to dial 999, but an emergency responder could be too late to save Ashleigh now.

'Now don't go putting two and two together and coming up with five,' May warned, stepping closer to lay a hand on her arm. 'Whatever you're imagining, it won't be that bad.'

But May didn't know that, and nor did Jane. 'I've got to go,' she said, picturing the card PC Hussein had left with his contact details. It was sitting on a shelf in the kitchen. 'There's a call I have to make.'

CHAPTER 8

'Hold up, will you,' Sheena said, gasping for breath. 'When I said I'd join you for a Sunday stroll, I presumed we'd be walking, not jogging.'

Jane checked behind her to find that Benji was panting too. They were heading for the Arno, and although the park wasn't far from home, it was uphill. The poor dog had been walked off his feet over the last few days, just so Jane had an excuse to make numerous passes of the Jarvises' house. It had reached the point where Benji had taken to hiding whenever she picked up his leash.

'Right then,' Sheena said, catching up when Jane stopped to pick up the dog. 'Let's start from the beginning. You've reported Ashleigh as missing. To the *police*?' Her voice had gone up an octave.

'I had to,' explained Jane, forcing herself not to speed up again. Why did everything have to take so long?

After calling PC Hussein on Wednesday, Jane had followed it up with an email attaching the photos of the Jarvises' garden. In retrospect, she wished she had asked for a more senior officer rather than the young lad who was still growing into his uniform. If the police would only take the time to speak to May, which so far they hadn't, they would discover that Ashleigh had vanished without a trace straight after they had been called out to a disturbance at the property. The police should never have left her to her own fate. They had failed her once, and now they were failing her again.

'She could simply have left him. People walk out of relationships all the time,' said Sheena, as quick as May had been to dismiss a darker alternative. 'And when it's as volatile as theirs, it's no surprise Ashleigh hasn't been seen since. Mum says her car's gone.'

'Evan could have moved it. Something happened, Sheena, you only have to look at my photos. You should see the way he's glaring down the lens at me. Those eyes,' Jane said with a shudder that made her hug Benji closer. 'There's something wrong with him.'

'You've been taking photos of them?' asked Sheena as if it were Jane in the wrong, and not the predator on their doorstep.

'Not intentionally. I take before and after images when I'm working on something new. Like a time-lapse.'

'Ah, right. Our Jamie did one of those for a school project years ago. He grew bean sprouts,' Sheena said. 'It was quite good. I'll have to show you some time.'

'The point is,' Jane said firmly, 'Evan saw me taking a photo of him. When he was in the garden. Digging a trench.'

'Okaaay,' Sheena said.

Jane gritted her teeth. Why was she the only one that saw the connection between a missing wife and a makeshift grave? Setting a purposeful pace, she led Sheena through her reasoning as to why she suspected Evan Jarvis had murdered his wife and buried her in his garden.

'I can't say I noticed him digging at the time and, honestly, I wasn't aware that the camera lens took in their garden too. I was photographing *my* work, that was all. I didn't even register when Evan chopped down his cherry tree. And it's only because he did chop it down that I was able to see more of his garden. It's not like I was spying.'

'And the case for the defence can rest,' said Sheena. 'I believe you, Jane.'

'Clearly Evan thought differently. You could tell from the photo that he wasn't happy with me. And lo and behold, the next day, my camera is stolen.'

'Hold on, you think he took it?'

It was obvious from Sheena's gaping mouth that she found the entire scenario far-fetched. Had PC Hussein thought the same? 'Whoever got into my garden came through from their side.'

'But they live in an end terrace; anyone could have got through from the side of the house. And I can't see Evan squeezing through the hedgerow. Can you?'

'It's quite woody at the base, and if Evan set his mind to it, I can't imagine anything or anyone getting in his way,' Jane said with a shudder. She wondered what he would make of his meddlesome neighbour. The sooner he was arrested the better.

When they reached the Arno, Jane set down the dog and led the way to the formal rose garden, yearning for some order to counter the chaos inside her head. The rose bushes were contained within a series of island beds cut from the manicured lawn. Each geometric shape looked odd in isolation, but they fitted together to create a perfect circle. A path ran through the centre, and another around the perimeter. Jane took the circular route.

'He would know I walk the dog, and could have figured out when the house was empty. It was a working day, but given he's a postman, he could be out and about without anyone missing him. When you put it all together, not only does he have the motive, he has the opportunity.'

'Sorry, but what motive?' Sheena asked, doing her best to keep up. 'What has any of this got to do with Ashleigh leaving him? Sorry, I mean, going missing.'

Jane swallowed her frustration. She could forgive Sheena because she hadn't seen the photo. The police had no such excuse. 'The hole Evan was digging was a long, narrow trench. You know, like a grave.'

'Whoa,' Sheena said loudly, startling the dog. 'Are you telling me you think he was digging an actual grave?'

'When you go back to your mum's, see if you can look over into his garden. You won't see the hole now because he's covered over the evidence with a big wooden trough,' Jane said, panting with the force of her argument. 'And you don't have to be a gardener to know that if you're building some sort of raised bed, there's absolutely no reason to dig down first, especially if you don't have time for gardening, which is what he told me literally the day after I took that photo. He's covering something up.'

'And that would be?'

Jane stopped so she could lock eyes with Sheena. She waited for her friend to answer her own question because surely it didn't need spelling out.

'Bloody hell. You think he murdered Ashleigh and buried her in the garden?'

'It does happen.'

Sheena scratched her head as they resumed circuiting the rose garden. 'So Evan spends the weekend digging this big hole, sees you taking a photo, then steals your camera the next day,' she said, setting out the evidence in chronological order. 'That night he has a furious row with Ashleigh, and the police are called out.'

'Correct.'

'Which means Ashleigh was alive and well during all of that time. The police wouldn't have left without speaking to her.'

'Alive, yes, but who knows what she had been subjected to. She could have been too frightened to tell the police what was really going on,' Jane said. 'It's hard to speak up.'

'Even so, it doesn't make sense. Who digs a grave *before* they kill someone in a crime of passion?'

'A crime of passion?' gasped Jane. 'We're talking about an abusive relationship that ends in murder. That's not passion, that's psychopathy. And digging the grave in advance proves it was premeditated. Men like that are ruthless. They take their time destroying the person they supposedly love, stripping them of their sense of self over months, if not years.'

'I hope you're not talking from personal experience,' Sheena said with a laugh that caught in her throat. 'Oh, Jane. Is that why you and Phil . . .? Was he . . .?'

'No, of course not,' Jane said brusquely. One day she would have to tell Sheena the truth about her childhood,

59

but she couldn't allow the focus to move away from a far more pressing matter. 'It's Ashleigh we should be concerned about. I don't know why the police haven't started digging up the garden. It's like they're not taking me seriously.'

'They probably have you down as a menopausal woman on a hormone trip.'

'Is that what you think?' asked Jane, feeling the stab of the unintentional insult. 'I know I made that comment the other day about my age, but I was being flippant. My reasoning makes perfect logical sense. To me.'

Sheena looped her arm through her friend's. 'I know you were being flippant, and you've made a very compelling case, but I do think it's time to leave the police to do their job. Why don't you come back to mine for Sunday lunch? Mum's coming, and Chris can drive you both home. It's no trouble. We can open a bottle of wine, or two.'

'Thanks, but I'm fine,' Jane said. She wouldn't insult Sheena by fabricating an excuse, but neither did she want to explain how being thrust into someone else's family right now only made her crave the one she had abandoned. 'And you don't need to worry. I know I have to trust the police to do their job, but Evan can't get away with this, Sheena.'

Her friend pulled her closer as they walked. 'He won't, but I do hope you're wrong about Ashleigh.'

'So do I.'

CHAPTER 9

Jane was perched on the edge of her desk where she had a clear view out of the attic window while remaining somewhat in the shadows. It was the start of a new week and there was still no sign of police activity. What on earth was taking them so long?

If Evan had been interviewed, he gave nothing away. She had glimpsed him in the kitchen a couple of times, and spotted his unmistakable silhouette in the frosted bathroom window once or twice, but the slender profile of his wife was nowhere to be seen. Whenever Jane thought of Ashleigh, her gaze shifted to the dirt-filled trough, its only purpose to conceal a crime.

It was Benji who broke her trance with a loud yap. She assumed he was dreaming, so didn't turn until she heard the scrape of claws across the floorboards. He stood to attention at the top of the narrow staircase, his ears moving like miniature radar dishes, and when the doorbell rang, they both jumped.

Although Jane had been using a scatter cushion for extra

padding during her stake-outs, the edge of the desk had cut off her circulation, and she had pins and needles in her legs as she took the attic stairs one step at a time. The doorbell rang again as she reached the landing, and when she craned over the banister, she saw a dark silhouette on her doorstep who appeared to be wearing a peaked cap. The police had news at long last, and Jane was almost as fast as Benji down the final flight of stairs. Her hand slipped as she pressed down on the door handle.

'Evening, Mrs Hanratty,' said PC Hussein, his words taut, his features solemn.

Jane glanced over his shoulder, expecting another officer, perhaps a plain-clothes detective, but he had come alone.

'Please, call me Jane,' she said, beckoning him inside. Now that she had recovered the sensation in her legs, she could feel them trembling.

The constable declined the offer of a drink and waited until they were in the sitting room before explaining the purpose of his visit. His back remained perpendicular to the sofa cushion. 'I'm following up on the call you made on Wednesday last.'

Jane gripped the arms of her mum's recliner. 'What's happened?' Her eyes flicked to the French doors and the gardens beyond, hers and her neighbours'. Had she turned away from the attic window just as the forensics team swooped in? Was PC Hussein charged with keeping her company while they made their grisly discovery?

'We've located Ashleigh Jarvis.'

'Oh, Lord,' Jane said as she pictured earth being scraped back from Ashleigh's cadaverous face. She didn't understand how they could have found her body without digging up the garden, but the news was no less devastating. 'The poor woman.'

The police officer tugged at his collar as if it were suddenly tight. 'Sorry, I don't think you quite understand. What I'm trying to say, Mrs Hanratty, is that she's been found very much alive.' He took great care to pronounce each word so as to avoid any further misunderstanding.

Jane leant back a fraction. 'She's not dead?'

'No.'

'But how . . .? Why . . .? Where is she?'

'I'm afraid that's as much as I can tell you. As you'll appreciate, any dealings we've had with the Jarvises are strictly confidential.'

'But there is an investigation, surely?' Jane pleaded, as an unpleasant warmth crawled up her chest to her face. 'You must realize that something's wrong over there. Evan had to have been digging that trench for a reason. Aren't you at least going to dig it up?'

'I don't think that will be necessary, all things considered.'

'But you've had dealings with them in the past. You know what he's like. Did you even look at the photos I sent?' Tears of frustration sprung to her eyes.

PC Hussein left a pause as Jane reflected on her response to the good news that Ashleigh was alive.

'I'm glad she's been found, of course I am,' she choked out. She should have left it there, but she couldn't back down completely: what was she going to tell Sheena and May when they asked what had come of her outlandish accusations? Her cheeks blazed. 'But just because Ashleigh is alive, it doesn't mean she's safe.'

'I understand why you were concerned.'

'I'm not sure you do,' Jane said, not liking the sympathy creeping into the young man's tone. Sheena was right, the police did think she was potty. For a split second, she was minded to tell the constable that she had first-hand experience of living in an abusive household, but she wasn't looking to be pitied or excused. She held her tongue.

'I did mention your concerns regarding the theft of your laptop and camera to my sergeant,' he continued, 'but we would need a warrant to search the property, and the evidence isn't there, I'm afraid. We know that the hedgerow at the back of your garden is the most likely point of access, but it would be unrealistic to imagine that a man the size of Mr Jarvis would be able to force his way through all those brambles.'

'It's easier than it looks,' Jane said, lifting her chin. 'My mum would have cut back the old growth last autumn, and the thorns on the new shoots are soft and pliable at this time of year.'

'Even so, given what we now know about Mrs Jarvis's whereabouts, I think you'd agree that he had no reason to destroy evidence of what you perceived to be a crime.'

'But don't you think it strange that my camera was stolen the day after that photo was taken? You remarked at the time how odd it was that the thief hadn't taken my handbag . . .' The police officer's fixed expression stopped her from continuing. He wasn't interested in her theories, and she needed this excruciating encounter to be over. 'Well, thank you for letting me know. I won't take up any more of your time.'

PC Hussein looked relieved as he stood and straightened

his uniform. 'It's good of you to look out for your neighbours. We could do with more community spirit these days,' he offered.

In no mood to be humoured, Jane kept her head bowed as she showed her visitor to the door.

'It's perfectly normal for you to feel a little anxious after having an intruder in the house,' PC Hussein said, still attempting to ease over her awkwardness. 'Did you check the links on home security I sent? I can find you some printed leaflets, if you prefer?'

'I know how to use the internet,' Jane said, a little too curtly. She didn't like the inference that she must be a technophobe, as well as befuddled.

'Ah, yes, you mentioned you taught ICT, didn't you?' he said with a rueful smile. 'Then you probably know what mischief kids can get up to, and an unlocked door is an open invitation these days.'

'Don't worry, I won't be making that mistake again, whoever the thief might be.'

'Like I said, I'm pretty sure we can discount Mr Jarvis. And please be assured that Mrs Jarvis is well enough.'

As Jane closed the front door and slipped across the security chain, she couldn't help but consider what the police officer had meant by Ashleigh being 'well enough'. His choice of words chimed with Jane's continued fears for her neighbour. She hoped that Ashleigh had escaped Evan's clutches, but abusers were as sly as they were persistent. If Evan was anything like her dad, the Jarvises' battles weren't over. The police might have closed the case, but Jane would keep her eyes very much open.

CHAPTER 10

Using her rear-view mirror to check her appearance one last time, Ashleigh wiped away a smudge of lip gloss with a shaking finger. Her make-up was barely noticeable despite the time it had taken to apply. She didn't want Evan to think she was trying too hard. Taking a deep breath, she waited for the tremors to subside before getting out of her car.

It was Sunday lunchtime and although the pub car park was busy, Ashleigh recognized two cars immediately. One was Evan's, and the other belonged to her support team who would be taking up positions inside the pub. Her friend Jess had refused to let Ashleigh go alone, and had dragged along her boyfriend to keep her company.

The women had met five years ago when Jess had joined the travel agency where Ashleigh had been a senior travel advisor. At thirty-four, Ashleigh was two years older and had taken Jess under her wing, although lately, it felt like their roles had reversed.

'It's not too late to back out,' Jess had told her as she

watched Ashleigh pack her sparse belongings into a suitcase that morning. 'There are other options, you know. I don't understand why you'd even consider going back to that bastard.'

Ashleigh had felt a rush of emotion, not all of it good, or healthy. She wanted the crisis talks with Evan to work. 'I still love him.'

'I wish you didn't.'

Her friend's face swam in front of Ashleigh's eyes as they filled with tears. 'I know that Evan and I don't have the kind of marriage you would want, but—'

'You mean a safe, secure relationship built on mutual trust and respect?' interrupted Jess.

'But what about passion?' Ashleigh continued. 'What about loving someone so intensely that it hurts?'

'It isn't love if it leaves bruises,' replied Jess, gently touching Ashleigh's arm.

But Ashleigh's latest wounds had long since healed, and as she stood in the car park, it was as if the terrible incident three weeks ago had never happened, and she couldn't face another night sleeping on the sofa in Jess's one-bedroom flat. When she entered the beer garden, it didn't take her long to spot Evan, who had chosen the picnic bench furthest from the busy pub. The Farmers' Arms in Frankby wasn't somewhere they usually frequented, which was why Evan had chosen it. He had said it was neutral territory, but he had obviously arrived early and given himself time to settle.

Ashleigh's pulse raced as she approached her husband, and she sat down without making eye contact. She concentrated on straightening the yellow summer dress she had borrowed from Jess.

Evan pushed one of the two glasses of lime and soda towards her. 'Ashleigh? Will you at least look at me?'

Ashleigh lifted her gaze but not her head; her blonde fringe a curtain to deflect the intensity of his stare.

'Is there anything you'd like to say?' he asked.

Ashleigh watched the tip of Evan's tongue slide along his front teeth as he waited in vain for her to repent.

'So you're not sorry for all the trouble you caused? Not even a little bit?' he asked, scolding her like a parent might a child. 'What happened to the person I married?'

Ashleigh could ask the same of him. Some might look at Evan and assume he was a thug, but it was his stature that had made her feel protected when they met. If he had cause to show his frustration or anger, it had always been directed at others, and on their wedding day, she had ignored that little warning voice telling her that the more she loved this man, the more he could hurt her. She had thought Evan was worth the risk. For her sins, she still did.

'I was investigated for an alleged murder. *Your* murder,' Evan said harshly as if he hadn't noticed the tears she was blinking away.

'That wasn't my fault,' she said, looking down at her drink. 'I didn't say anything to the police.'

'You didn't need to. The whole street has heard our fights. That neighbour at the back of us jumped out of her skin when she saw me the other day, and even May's been acting odd. Hardly surprising when she has to listen to all our shouting and screaming.'

Ashleigh's head shot up. 'You mean my screams?'

Evan glanced nervously around as though she had yelled at the top of her voice even though her tone had been perfectly level. He had a knack for making her feel guilty, even when she had done nothing wrong.

'Do you think it hasn't been embarrassing for me too?' she asked. 'The police turned up at work, and I've been getting funny looks ever since. The last thing I need is to lose another job, Evan.' She had been made redundant at the travel agency the year before, and was currently working part-time as a receptionist at a beauty salon in Liverpool. It was meant to be a stopgap until she found something better, but for now, it was all she had. 'I don't like that you've had to take the strain of our finances, but imagine how much worse our problems would be if I was out of work. You're stressed enough as it is.'

'If that's your way of saying the demands of my job have contributed to what happened, fine, guilty as charged,' he said, managing to accept culpability without actually admitting he had done anything wrong. 'But we both have to accept responsibility for our actions. Unfortunately, I think you're too scared to admit where the problem lies.'

'Is that what you want? For me to be scared?' she asked, her voice quavering. 'You don't need to tell me that our relationship has become toxic.'

Ashleigh rubbed the back of her neck, turning her head surreptitiously so she could check if Jess and Harry were watching from the pub.

'They're there,' Evan said coolly without following her gaze. 'You didn't need to come with bodyguards, but then I can just imagine what tales you've been telling.'

Ashleigh had been hoping Evan wouldn't spot her spies. 'Jess has been a good friend to me.'

'You mean a drinking buddy,' he said. 'You need people around you who set a better example.'

'She said you'd try to split us up,' Ashleigh replied as she recalled one of Jess's many warnings.

'I'm doing no such thing,' he said, but offered no further reassurance.

Ashleigh jiggled her legs, but she couldn't bring herself to get up and walk. Jess had told her she had options, but her friend had absolutely no idea what it was like to be her. Ashleigh's entire life was a patchwork of tragedies. She had lost her mum when she was nineteen, and her father had died in prison when she was twenty-two. There had been very few constants in her life. In fact, she could think of only one: Evan.

'If I decide to come back, things have to change,' she said. 'I need you to put as much effort into our relationship as I do. I need you to be present in our marriage. I refuse to be the meek housewife who waits at home never knowing when her husband's going to show up, or tiptoe around him when he does. I won't live a life of humiliation or degradation, not any more.' That last bit had been Jess's suggestion when they had been strategizing over a bottle of wine or three the night before. It was a miracle Ashleigh remembered it.

Evan picked up his lime and soda and drained the glass in a couple of gulps. The muscles in his arms twitched. She had made him nervous.

'Do you understand what I'm saying?' she asked, feeling emboldened.

Her husband wiped his mouth with the back of his hand, then locked eyes with his wife. 'I'm sorry, Ash. I still love you, but I'm not sure you should come back.'

There was a sharp intake of breath. 'What?'

'This break has given us both time to think things through.'

Ashleigh didn't understand. She was Evan's obsession. It wasn't like him to give up so easily. An old fear resurfaced. 'Is there someone else?'

Evan rubbed his temples as if he found the whole conversation tedious. 'No, I'm not seeing anyone else, and you either accept that or you don't, but I won't be drawn into another argument about it. We'll only end up hurting each other. Do you want that?'

'Yes,' she said before she could cram the word back into her mouth. Reaching over, she clutched his hand, and was stupidly grateful when he didn't reject her. 'You've just said you love me, and I love you too. The last few weeks without you have been the worst, and I don't want to be on my own. I need you.' Tears spilled as she tugged at his hand to place his palm against her chest so he could feel her heart thumping. 'Don't do this to me.'

Evan went to pull away, but Ashleigh clung on. His jaw twitched, once, twice, and then he was no longer resisting her. His fingers sought out her flesh and his hand moved to her neck. As his thumb caressed her jawline, Ashleigh was aware of how easily he could crush the life out of her. She wondered if Jess was thinking the same from her viewpoint, but Ashleigh had lost sight of everyone except the man she loved.

Evan licked his lips. 'If you do come back, there have to be ground rules.'

'I'll be good,' she whispered.

71

CHAPTER 11

Jane wasn't sure if it was lack of attention, or lack of practice that made her burn the roast potatoes, but Megan didn't seem to mind, and thankfully finished her Sunday lunch without breaking a tooth.

'Are you sure you won't stay over?' Jane asked as she rose from the kitchen table to clear their plates. 'I've made up the spare room just in case.'

'Sorry, Mum, I'm on call tomorrow, and I don't fancy racing down the M62 if I get called out at four in the morning,' Megan said, a sparkle in her eyes despite the prospect of broken sleep. She enjoyed her job as a vet. Jane had forgotten what it was like to feel of value.

Scraping her half-eaten lunch into the food waste bin, Jane was aware that her every move was being watched. She had let slip about her recent run-in with the police, and the afternoon would not pass without the serious talk Megan had been threatening. In spite of this, Jane was stupidly grateful for the company. If it wasn't for May and Sheena, she would only have the dog to talk to.

'It was just a thought,' she said. 'How about some pudding? I've made banoffee pie.' Her daughter's favourite.

There was a groan as Megan stretched. 'I might need to make a bit of space first. How about you show me what's been keeping you so busy? The house looks a lot clearer since the funeral.'

With an excuse to keep her twitching limbs moving, Jane headed for the dining room. After the unfortunate visit from the police earlier in the week, she had avoided the outdoors as much as possible, and it had given her the impetus to tackle the job her mum hadn't been able to complete.

Megan trailed a finger across the smooth piece of timber resting on the Workmate. 'It's hard to believe Nan could take a pile of old pallets and make something so beautiful.'

'I'm not sure the final construction is going to be up to her standards, but I'll do my best,' said Jane, feeling her throat tighten. Handling the timber her mum had lovingly sanded and polished evoked such an intense emotion that she had needed to take it in stages. A yearned-for connection was there every time her fingertips kissed the wood, and yet her mum remained stubbornly out of reach.

'Don't you think the more time you invest here, the harder it'll be to leave?' asked Megan, determined to view her parents' separation as a temporary anomaly.

'Assuming I ever do,' Jane said, and before her daughter could respond, she added, 'shall we go upstairs?'

Jane started with her bedroom. It was pretty enough and sufficient for her needs with a new double bed, the fitted wardrobes her mum had made, and a solitary bedside table.

'I've rediscovered my love of Terry Pratchett novels,' she

said when she noticed Megan squinting at the book next to the bed. 'I hadn't realized how many I'd left here.'

'It's like you want to go back in time.'

Only if I can be selective, Jane thought but didn't say because Megan wouldn't understand. Jane had never wanted her daughter to know about the darker aspects of her childhood. The next generation wasn't going to be tarnished by the past.

After shouldering the door open to Cynthia's bedroom, neither woman felt able to go inside. Megan touched Jane's back. 'Aren't you lonely here, Mum?'

Jane yanked the door shut. 'I'm far too busy for that.'

'But how have you been?' Megan pressed on. 'Truthfully, now.'

Jane wanted to say that she spent long nights staring at the ceiling, her mind yo-yoing between recent events and the dim and distant past, but these were things better kept to herself. 'I'm getting there,' she managed.

'You look washed out. Have you seen a doctor since Nan died?'

'I don't need to see a doctor, I'm fine.'

'You hardly touched your food.'

'I can afford to lose a pound or two,' Jane said, pinching at the muffin top peeking over the navy linen trousers that would be swapped in favour of far more forgiving yoga pants once her daughter left.

'Now is not the time to be cutting back,' Megan lectured. 'You're a healthy weight, and you need proper meals to regulate your moods.'

'My moods?' Jane raised a brow, but she knew what Megan was getting at.

74

In recent years, Jane had suffered with perimenopause symptoms. Insomnia and night sweats had meant she was often too tired or too irritable to go into work, and when she had dragged herself to school, there were other curses to contend with – restless legs to name but one. No wonder the head had been glad to see her go.

When things were at their worst, Jane had made the mistake of telling Megan her woes, and her daughter had bombarded her with advice. To be told what to do by a young, vibrant veterinarian with her whole life ahead of her, had irked Jane in a way that only a woman going through the change would understand. It irked her still as heat rose up through her body to leave beads of sweat tingling on her scalp. She hadn't had a hot flush for some time but could summon one up simply by thinking about it.

'It's not all in my head, love,' she said. Even if recent events with her neighbours had brought her judgement into question, her reasons for giving up her life in Buxton remained valid.

'Then help me understand,' Megan replied as she glanced at the door leading up to the attic. 'Do you want to show me the murder scene?'

If it wasn't bad enough that Jane was struggling with her body's faulty thermostat, she could feel the burn of humiliation to add to her woes. She let Megan go upstairs first so she could waft the cotton shirt clinging to her clammy skin.

'Is this your new perch?' Megan asked, having spotted the cushion resting on the edge of the desk.

'It's for my back,' Jane lied, tossing it onto her office chair before joining her daughter at the window.

75

All had remained quiet in the house opposite, but Jane had spotted Evan planting seedlings in his hastily constructed trough the day before. He had glanced up at the attic window more than once, and if he was doing it to unsettle her, it was working. She preferred weekdays when he was at work, even though she would dread his return home in the same way she had once dreaded her dad's.

'You have to admit, it was some leap to think he was burying a body when he was just doing a bit of gardening,' Megan said, mellowing her words with a smile.

'It's not funny,' Jane said. 'That man has a violent temper, and I still think he's a danger to his wife.'

'I'm not saying it's right, but my point stands. It can't be a coincidence that you've become embroiled in a stranger's life at the same time there's been an upheaval in your own. What if you're transferring your grief onto something you feel you have more control over, or less emotional investment in? And I hate to say it, but the menopause might be affecting your state of mind too. You can't keep ignoring the symptoms.'

'I'm not ignoring anything,' Jane said brusquely. 'If you knew the kind of man Evan was, it would give you sleep-less nights too.'

'So that's why you're so washed out. You haven't been sleeping.'

'What I'm saying is, my menopause has nothing to do with what's happening over there,' Jane said, jabbing her finger at the window. 'I know what I saw, Megan. Evan was acting suspiciously, and I caught him at it. Why else would he go to such lengths to destroy my photos?' Her eyes narrowed as she glared at her neighbour's house. 'He thought I was some dotty woman who'd think she'd simply misplaced her camera. It never crossed his mind that I'd be tech-savvy enough to back up my files. I don't like being underestimated.'

'I know you don't,' Megan said, lowering her head. 'I might not have said it enough, but I've always, *always* been proud of you. When I tell people I have this whacky mum who once got stuck on the roof while pointing a chimney, it's because I'm in awe. You've always had such a belief in yourself.'

Jane blinked back tears as she continued to stare out of the window. 'It's not how I've felt lately.'

'How have you felt?'

As they stood shoulder to shoulder, Jane's gaze was forced away from her neighbour's house and closer to home. Her garden makeover had started as a distraction, but that patently hadn't worked. 'Trapped,' she whispered.

'Here? Or back home?'

Jane turned to cup her daughter's face in her hands. 'Mostly inside a body that refuses to behave like it used to, and a mind that won't rest when it's supposed to.' She swallowed hard. 'It's like I've become disconnected from that person you described. Maybe that's just how it is for women of my age. It's time to find a new me.'

'But why *here*, away from us? Away from Dad?'

Megan sounded like a petulant toddler, and Jane was grateful to feel like a mother again. She would have smiled if she had the strength. 'I want to move on, and maybe my path will lead me back home one day, but I have a lot of baggage to unpack first, and I can only do it here. I know that doesn't make much sense and I don't fully understand it myself yet, but you have to trust me on this.'

Her daughter narrowed her eyes as she cast a glance around the clutter-free room. 'Dad said you freaked out because he was clearing out Nan's stuff, but it looks like you've done a thorough job yourself. What else is left to unpack, Mum?'

'Memories,' Jane said, although that wasn't the complete truth. Thankfully, Megan didn't try looking for the secret cubby hole containing one of the last tangible links to Jane's dad. Phil couldn't have thought it important enough to mention to their daughter, and Jane certainly wasn't going to draw attention to it. She pulled Megan into a hug and squeezed her tightly instead.

'I love you, Mum.'

'And I love you too. So very much,' Jane said, then forced herself to release Megan. 'Ready for that banoffee pie now?'

'Sure.'

Jane couldn't resist one last glance out of the window, but if she had wanted some sign that she could learn to be content with the life she had chosen, it was ill-timed. Standing next to the trough that had evoked visions of a bludgeoned body buried beneath the earth, stood the victim herself. Ashleigh Jarvis wore a yellow dress and had her arms wrapped around her body. Despite the sunshine glinting off her long, blonde hair, she looked as if she were bracing herself for a storm. And all the while, Evan was watching from the kitchen window, which made Jane break out into a cold sweat. This was no symptom of the menopause. Her fear was as real as her body's response.

'Is that them?' asked Megan.

Jane's reply was a croak. 'I didn't think she'd come back. Why did she come back?'

'What you see from up here is only a small glimpse into their lives. What if all that shouting and screaming was out of frustration? You should hear the way Greg and I yell at each other sometimes.'

Her daughter's observations were based on personal experience, but Jane's own led her to a very different conclusion. She had heard Ashleigh raise her voice, but only time would tell if it was determination not to be silenced or a cry for help. Either way, Jane was listening. 'I can't ignore what's going on.'

It was as if the waif-like figure knew Jane was watching over her, because Ashleigh lifted her head. For a split second, they held each other's gaze.

'Come away, Mum,' Megan said, tugging at Jane's sleeve. 'If you're not careful, the next visit you get from the police will be an injunction to stop you spying on them.'

'I don't care. I want her to know she's not alone.'

CHAPTER 12

1970

Cynthia stood next to the stereogram with her hand poised over the arm of the record player. The dining table had been pushed against the wall to make room for a circle of six children sitting cross-legged on the floor. A parcel wrapped in newspaper was being passed reluctantly from one child to the next while Pinky and Perky's helium-pitched singing assaulted their eardrums.

The music stopped and squeals rose up as two boys started a tug of war over the parcel. Cynthia's attention, meanwhile, remained on her four-year-old daughter. Jane leant towards the girl on her right and cupped her hand to her ear.

'Will you be my friend?' she whispered loud enough for her mum to hear.

When the girl nodded, Cynthia's heart simultaneously clenched and melted.

It was the first birthday party she had ever organized,

encouraged by Mrs Lisman, an old friend of her Aunt Judith's who babysat Jane while Cynthia was at work. It had been a challenge finding children to invite to the party as Cynthia had lost touch with most of her so-called friends after becoming an unmarried mother, and Jane wouldn't start school until September so had no friends of her own. At least they had been able to rely on Mrs Lisman's grand-children, who had turned up under duress. More invitations had been sent to neighbours, ten in all, and it had been a relief to see that not all had been tossed into the bin.

By the time the first mother arrived to reclaim her child, the dining room floor was littered with torn newspaper and squished sausage rolls. The woman from the other side of their cul-de-sac declined to come inside and took the slice of birthday cake wrapped in a paper serviette with a polite nod before scurrying away. When the second mum arrived, Cynthia expected another rejection.

'I'd love to come in,' said May Jones. 'I expect you'll need help scraping jam off the walls.'

'I'm just happy to have the chance to talk to someone who isn't blowing snotty bubbles out their nose.'

May was a few years older than Cynthia, but you would never guess she was a mother of two. She had peroxide-blonde hair, make-up straight out of a Mary Quant advert, and her pale lemon dress was short enough to show off her knee-length white boots. Cynthia had seen May's children playing in their back garden, but until now, she had never spoken to her neighbour other than to say hello.

'Can I go to Joey's now?' asked May's eldest.

Steven was seven, and he raced past his mum as soon

as she gave the nod. He couldn't wait to escape, but his sister looked relieved when May didn't send her straight out too. Sheena was the little girl that Jane had taken a shine to, and the two were busy making a Fuzzy Felt farm scene, a birthday present from Aunt Judith, who had been too ill to deliver it in person.

The last two partygoers were Mrs Lisman's grandchildren, and they stared out of the window as they waited to be picked up. One pulled back the net curtain and laughed as she pointed at something. Cynthia had an uneasy feeling she knew what, or who, it might be.

The front door had been left ajar, and when it banged against the wall, little Jane's eyes flickered up to her mum. Cynthia gave her daughter a reassuring wink, but her smile was tight when Les appeared.

'That's good, I thought I'd missed the party.'

Les had a sliding scale of inebriation, and although his speech was slurred and he was incapable of walking in a straight line, he appeared to be on the jovial end of the spectrum. There was an outside chance he wasn't going to make a fool of them.

Cynthia and Les had been living together for nine months, an arrangement that had continued more as a result of inaction than any conscious decision to make their union permanent, in Cynthia's mind at least. She had needed time to get to know Les, and with each passing day, it was becoming clearer that she knew him as well as she would want. She was beginning to see beyond his romantic gestures, and as he kissed her cheek, the only thing she felt was slight repulsion.

Les pulled away, leaving Cynthia with the stench of stale

beer while his eyes roved towards May. 'Lesley Morgan at your service,' he drawled.

May shook his hand. 'I'm May. Nice to meet you.'

'Don't tell me you've got kids.'

'Two.'

There was a knock at the door and someone shouted, 'Hello?'

The new arrival was Mrs Lisman's daughter-in-law, and Cynthia was glad to wave off the last two children waiting to leave. Hurrying back to the dining room, she noticed May's posture had changed. Her arms were folded tight across her chest, and her jaw was set firm.

'Sorry, I was going to make you a drink,' Cynthia said to May, intent on steering her into the kitchen and away from Les. She had set her heart on them becoming friends, and didn't want him spoiling things.

Unaware that she was crushing Cynthia's hopes, May said, 'I should go. The kids might not need feeding, but my husband will.'

'Ah, you can't go yet,' Les said, as he fumbled in his pocket. 'You're going to miss the best bit.'

May ignored him as she went over to Sheena, who needed a tug to separate her from Jane. 'Come on. I'm sure you'll see each other again soon enough.'

Les had pulled out a small, gilt-edged box from his pocket. 'Ta da!'

No, please, not this, not now, Cynthia thought as Les's theatrics gained the attention of the room.

'Wow,' Sheena said with giddy excitement as Les dropped down on bended knee.

'Cynthia Louise Simpkin, will you be my wife?'

With one glance, she could tell the ring was a knock-off from the pub. The box belonged to a pendant and someone had clumsily cut the foam to hold the tarnished solitaire that was more claw than diamond. If it was a diamond.

'You know we can't, Les,' she said as she tried to find the right expression. Disappointment? Frustration? She certainly couldn't show her relief.

'The divorce papers'll be through by the time you've sorted out a dress and all that stuff.'

'So we can wait a little longer,' Cynthia replied, aware that time was running out for her. She had to give him his marching orders soon. Just not in front of an audience.

Les made a show of struggling to his feet. 'She's breaking my heart, May,' he said, turning to their guest. 'I know I've made mistakes, but I'm trying to do the decent thing. It's as if she wants to be the talk of the town. And Jane wants us to get married, don't you, cheeky chops?'

Jane nodded. He had been talking about the wedding as if it were a fait accompli, and had promised their daughter that she would be a bridesmaid, using her excitement to make it harder for Cynthia to say no. Harder, but not impossible. If this was Les on his best behaviour, how would he be at his worst?

May didn't look nearly as impressed as the younger ones. 'We really should go.'

'I'm sorry about that,' Cynthia whispered as she showed May to the door.

'Don't worry. Some men are swines when they've had a few. I'm lucky I've got one that just falls asleep.'

Cynthia watched with envy as Jane and Sheena hugged like old friends, and it took her by surprise when May drew her into a hug too. She had noticed Cynthia's desperation after all.

'Thanks for coming,' she managed to say without choking up.

'Any time,' replied May.

Dragging herself back to face Les, something small whizzed past Cynthia's ear as she entered the dining room. There was a thump as the small box hit the banister behind her.

Cynthia turned to retrieve it, using the time to catch Jane's eye. 'Go to your room.'

'But my new toys are—'

'Now.'

Les was picking at the party food when she closed the door on her daughter's retreating steps.

'You certainly know how to humiliate me,' he said, twirling a cocktail sausage on a stick.

'I didn't mean to, but you took me by surprise. There are things we need to discuss,' she said. She wanted to get it over and done with there and then, but the words stuck in her throat. Les could aim cruel words as viciously as he had hurled the ring at her, and she had grown to fear him.

'You always were a prick-tease,' he said. 'Anyone else would snatch my hand off.'

Except his ex-wife, Cynthia could point out, but didn't. Les needed no encouragement to turn nasty.

'I should be travelling the world instead of pushing hospital trolleys for a living,' he continued. 'I gave up everything for you, Cynthia.'

'I never asked you to.'

'What did you say?' he barked, and in the explosion of

anger, he clenched his hand into a fist, inadvertently stabbing himself with a cocktail stick. 'Shit! Ow! Look what you did!'

As Les continued to howl, he transitioned seamlessly from ogre to baby. This was a version of Les Cynthia could deal with.

'Here, let me look,' she said, daring to approach. She took his hand and plucked out the stick protruding from his palm. 'All better?'

Les lifted his uninjured hand to caress her face. He was smiling lovingly, but in a flash, his features hardened and he grabbed a clump of her hair. 'I'm warning you now, if you don't marry me, I'll find someone who will. And I'll take Jane with me. Your choice, bitch.'

CHAPTER 13

The cellophane rustled as Jane waited on the doorstep. Were the flowers too much? Too little? She shuffled backwards, wondering if she had time to retreat up the lane before Ashleigh answered the door. The twitch of a net curtain from the adjoining house stopped her in her tracks, and she offered May a trembling smile. They were as bad as each other for window-watching. Or maybe Jane was worse. Not satisfied with the restricted view from the attic, she had turned to cyberstalking.

Jane had often demonstrated in class how easily future employers or identity thieves could learn things about her students that they might not want them knowing. If nothing else, it had taught them to tighten their privacy settings, and Jane could only presume that Ashleigh had been served a similar lesson. Her Instagram account was private, and her profile on Facebook was protected too. It wasn't that Jane needed a full background history, but knowing Ashleigh had family and friends to turn to would stop her worrying obsessively. Or at least that was what she had been telling herself the night before when she harvested as much information on Ashleigh as she could find.

She had started with school links, going off the hunch that Ashleigh was local because she couldn't recall an accent that had stood out when they had met during the Secret Gardens event, not that Ashleigh had stood out at all while Evan charmed Jane and her mum. After making a list of possible schools, Jane sent requests to join the various Facebook pages set up by ex-pupils, only to discover it wasn't necessary. Ashleigh had attended Wirral Grammar School for Girls some twenty years after Jane, and access to the group wasn't a problem because Jane had already taken Sheena's advice and joined it. And unlike Jane, Ashleigh had actually posted to the group.

Did you used to be Ashleigh Martindale? someone had asked.

The one and the same.

I remember you.

Yeah, and I bet it's for all the wrong reasons lol.

Not at all. Although now you mention it, is he out yet?

Ashleigh hadn't replied to that last comment, and there was no further engagement, but it was enough to make new links. Armed with Ashleigh's maiden name, Jane followed every potential lead in her Google searches, however tenuous, until she stumbled upon an obituary for a Helen Martindale who had died fifteen years ago, leaving two daughters: Ashleigh and Rose.

As Jane's investigations wore on into the wee hours, she discovered that Helen had been the wife of Robert Martindale according to an archived article in the *Liverpool Echo*. To her surprise, Jane knew of the family already.

Although she had been living in Buxton by the early 2000s, her mum had relayed the information that had rocked the local community.

Robert Martindale, 43, from Birkenhead, Wirral, has been sentenced to ten years in prison after pleading guilty to causing death by dangerous driving. His victim, twenty-seven-year-old Catherine Finnigan, had been using a pedestrian crossing on Woodchurch Road when Martindale ploughed into her, killing her outright. Catherine had been on her way home from Clatterbridge Hospital where she worked as a nurse, and leaves two daughters under the age of five. Martindale admitted that he had been drinking throughout the day of the incident. The judge stated that whilst she noted Martindale's previously clean record and apparent remorse, sentencing reflected his complete disregard for the welfare and safety of others whilst driving three times over the legal limit.

The rest of the article focused on the victim and her family, and rightly so, but the journalist had tried his best to dig up dirt on Robert. There were quotes from so-called friends who confirmed that he liked a drink, and there was a strong suggestion of alcoholism, although Robert was apparently a happy drunk.

Jane fixated on those two words. Happy drunk. It could so easily have described her dad, but he was only happy when he was in the pub and the drinks were flowing. It was an entirely different matter when he came home.

Ashleigh would have been fifteen when her father had

been sent to prison, which meant most of her childhood would already have been spent living with the chaos Robert undoubtedly wreaked. Her mother, Helen Martindale, had died four years after her husband's conviction, so there had been little opportunity for the family to rebuild their lives. By the time Ashleigh was in her early twenties, her father was also dead.

How would these events have moulded Ashleigh's character? It was a sad fact that many children from abusive households went on to experience further abuse as adults. It was hard to establish a healthy relationship when you didn't know what one looked like.

Jane wasn't sure what, if anything, she could do to help, or even if help were needed. She had misjudged the situation once already, and she could be about to make another mistake as she listened to the jangle of keys. Someone with blonde hair on the other side of the frosted glass was struggling to open the front door.

'Sorry, I thought I was locked in for a minute,' Ashleigh said before she spotted Jane peeking over the bouquet. 'Oh.'

Evan's wife was as slender as Jane recalled, but notably less polished. Wearing a T-shirt and jeans, her hair was damp, her face clean of make-up, and her complexion pale.

Jane held out the bouquet. 'These are for you.'

Ashleigh took the gift tentatively, her expression guarded. 'I don't understand.'

'We met once,' Jane said quickly. 'Sorry, I should explain. My mum lived at the back of you.' In case there was any doubt as to where that was, Jane pointed over Ashleigh's shoulder in the general direction of the gardens that connected their properties. 'She died in April.'

Ashleigh stood in silence, too stunned to offer the same platitudes Evan had offered with heartfelt sincerity before going inside his house to bully and berate his wife. He had enough confidence for both of them.

'So, anyway, I'm living there now.'

Ashleigh frowned. 'I know who you are.'

A rush of anxious energy rose up through Jane's body. Ashleigh was right to be cautious, and this could go terribly wrong. 'What you may not know is that it's my fault you had the unwelcome interest from the police. Not the first time they called,' she added, tripping over her words. 'It wasn't me who called about the . . . About the noise. Sorry, I'm making a complete mess of this. What I mean is, I was the one who spoke to the police when you went missing.'

There were footsteps along the pavement, and Ashleigh's eyes darted to the passing stranger in earshot of Jane's bizarre confession. 'Look, do you want to come in?'

Jane hesitated. She had been on a reconnaissance mission earlier, and had it on good authority from May that Evan had gone to work. There was no guarantee he would be out all day, however, but Jane could hardly refuse Ashleigh's offer. 'Thank you.'

After showing Jane into the living room, Ashleigh paused at the mirror above the fireplace to rake her fingers through her fringe. 'I've only just got out of the shower,' she explained. 'If I'd known to expect company, I'd have made more of an effort.'

'Your hair's lovely,' Jane said, realizing too late how creepy that must sound coming from the woman who had been spying on her.

'I've always had long hair, but it can be a pain to dry.

And it clogs up the drains, as one of my friends recently discovered.'

'Good.' It was the wrong response again, but Jane couldn't hide her relief that Ashleigh did indeed have friends.

'Can I get you a coffee while I put the flowers in a vase?' asked Ashleigh, sounding more curious than alarmed by Jane's awkward behaviour. 'I only have decaf, I'm afraid.'

'Water would be fine.'

Ashleigh didn't invite her guest to take a seat, for which Jane was grateful because she was too tense to sit still. She remained at the edge of the room and used Ashleigh's absence to take a good look around. The house was a reverse image of May's, but the Jarvises had sliding doors separating two small reception rooms rather than a wall. The house felt brighter and the décor more contemporary.

The framed mirror Ashleigh had used to check herself was encrusted with crystals, and Jane almost missed the crack in the corner. Something had been thrown at it – possibly the photo frame on the mantelpiece that was missing its glass. Ignoring the enclosed image of the happy couple on their wedding day, Jane continued her sleuthing. There was a burgundy stain on the faux fur resting on the back of the sofa that could be spilled wine, or was it blood? In the connecting room, there was a salmon-coloured patch on the wall, suggesting a replastering job had been necessary to repair damage so violent that a fresh coat of paint hadn't been enough.

Jane jumped when she heard the door behind her creak open. Were the hinges stiff with age, or had it been kicked in one too many times? The clues to a violent past were there if you knew where to look.

'Here you go,' said Ashleigh, offering Jane a tall glass. Jane took a gulp of water.

'What is it you want, Mrs . . .'

'Hanratty, but please call me Jane.'

'I'm Ashleigh.'

'I know,' Jane said. She cringed with embarrassment before adding, 'And I suppose I should start by apologizing for calling the police.'

Ashleigh's features softened and there was the hint of a smile. 'Did you really think Evan had buried me in the garden? It sounds more like an episode of *Midsomer Murders*.'

Jane shrugged. 'Stranger things have happened,' she said. 'I used to be a teacher in a secondary school, and it became second nature to spot the kids trapped in an abusive household.'

'And is that what you see when you look at me? A victim of abuse?' Ashleigh asked as she wrapped her bare arms around herself. If there had been bruises, they had healed well.

'I don't think I completely misread the situation. Unless you want to tell me otherwise?'

When Ashleigh's grey eyes flared, it appeared she was about to eject Jane from the premises, but a beat later, she relaxed enough to respond with a shrug.

'Do you have someone you can trust?' Jane asked. She wanted to add that she knew Ashleigh's mum had died, and that she understood how isolating it felt to no longer have that 'grown-up' in your life, no matter your age. But she couldn't mention it without admitting what a snoop she had become.

'If not,' she continued, 'I want you to know that you don't have to suffer alone. If I've given the impression that I'm some busybody with no better demands on my time than interfering in other people's lives, you couldn't be more wrong.' She paused, acknowledging that she had pricked her own conscience. 'OK, maybe I do have too much time on my hands, but that doesn't mean I can't help.'

'Do you not have family of your own? Grandkids?'

'I have a daughter back in Derbyshire. And I'm separated from my husband,' Jane added. She couldn't expect Ashleigh to open up about her life, if she wasn't prepared to do the same.

'How long were you married?'

'Thirty years.'

'I've been married six.'

'And you have so much of your life ahead of you. Trust me, the longer you leave it, the harder it is to make the break.'

'I think you have the wrong impression of me and Evan. I know one or two of our arguments have been a bit animated, but that's just how we are. It's not as bad as it looks.'

Jane made a point of surveying the room again, aware that Ashleigh could see how her gaze lingered on its scars. 'Are you sure about that?'

'It never used to be like this.'

'I believe you. What changed?'

Ashleigh picked at the sleeve of her T-shirt, giving herself time to decide whether or not to indulge Jane and her theories. 'Evan works for Royal Mail and was an HGV driver until he was offered a management position last year. A promotion is meant to be a good thing, right? But Evan never did like paperwork, and now he's out of his depth. He only took the job because we needed the money after my career took a nose dive thanks to the pandemic. I can only find part-time work at the moment.'

'I'm sorry to hear that.'

'I'm only telling you this so you can appreciate how stressful it's been for us. Evan's a good man deep down, ask anyone.'

Jane wasn't interested in what other people saw. Only Ashleigh knew the true character of the man she was protecting.

'I know we can do better, and we will. There's no one else for me except Evan, and he – well, I'd like to think he feels the same,' she said, not sounding nearly as certain. 'We're trying really hard to make a fresh start. We've even switched to a healthier lifestyle. No processed food, no dairy, no alcohol, blah, blah, blah.' It didn't sound like it was her idea at all.

Jane managed to stop herself asking if it was healthy having your husband control what you ate and drank, but if they had indeed removed alcohol from the equation, perhaps it was a step in the right direction. Evan's last attack on his wife might not have been fuelled by alcohol, but from Jane's experience, there would be a causal effect somewhere along the line.

'He's looking after me,' Ashleigh insisted when she noticed Jane's hesitation.

'Forgive me for questioning your husband's motives, but it was just odd seeing that hole in the garden being covered up, then discovering you'd disappeared,' Jane said, obliged to return to the reason she had become fixated by her neighbour's plight. 'Do you know why Evan would dig so deep, only to plonk a trough on top of it?'

Ashleigh took Jane's glass, a signal that she had over-stayed her welcome. 'I've no idea,' she said, eyes cast down as she gestured for Jane to follow her into the hallway. 'Evan doesn't like me in his garden these days.'

'Why ever not?'

Ashleigh picked up the set of keys she had left by the front door. 'I'm just not very good at gardening. If ever I plant something, you can guarantee it won't thrive, and he's taken to keeping the back door locked when he's out.'

'Is that why you struggled to open the front door? Evan locks you in?' Jane asked, dismayed that Ashleigh spoke of her husband's draconian measures as if it were normal behaviour.

'He's not that bad,' she said a little too brightly. 'He just likes to keep me out of trouble. Obviously, I can't be trusted.'

'Can *he* be trusted?'

'Look, Mrs Hanratty, I appreciate the concern, I really do, but Evan isn't a murderer, and he's not a thief either,' she said, holding Jane's gaze a second longer than felt comfortable. The police had clearly shared all of Jane's accusations with the Jarvises. 'Everything is fine now, so you can stop worrying about me.'

As Jane stepped into bright sunshine, Ashleigh closed the door on whatever secrets she was keeping. Jane told herself she had done all she could for now. The next move was Ashleigh's or, more likely, Evan's.

CHAPTER 14

As the days wore on, Jane couldn't know what tension was building between Ashleigh and Evan, but she shared it nonetheless. She worked long hours to occupy herself by finishing her mum's bookshelves and redoubling her efforts in the garden. She listened out for cries for help as she filled flowerbeds with delphiniums, lupins and hollyhocks, and on her many trips to the garden centre, she made sure to drive past the Jarvis house, just in case she had missed something during one of her regular patrols with the dog.

Her stalking activities weren't confined to the daytime, and after making a mug of cocoa on Sunday evening, the urge to go up to the attic was irresistible. The room at the top of the house had become her guard post, and as she took up position at the window, the world outside was bathed in the amber light of a setting sun. All was quiet, as it had been throughout week.

When her back started to ache, Jane knew she had been standing too long, a timely reminder to look up the advert she had seen for yoga classes at St Saviour's church hall.

It didn't take long to find the details, and the glow of her laptop lit up her face as she tapped out a message on her mobile to Sheena, who had said she fancied attending the classes too. Unless her friend had been showing interest simply out of politeness. Jane drained her cup of cocoa then drummed her fingers on the desk as she imagined Sheena deliberating over the wording of a gentle rejection. All the while, the need to return to the window gnawed at her, and she was about to give in when her phone rang. She expected it to be Sheena. It wasn't.

Phil didn't phone as often as he had when they had first split up, but Jane remained selective about taking his calls. She didn't want to go over the same ground again. She could never give him answers that would satisfy him, and the hour was late. She considered buttoning the call, but she still felt guilty about blindsiding Phil. And if she didn't answer, there was every chance he would phone Megan, and Jane couldn't cope with having both of them on her case.

'Hey,' she said.

'Hey back.'

When Phil failed to offer anything further, it was left to Jane to initiate the conversation she hadn't wanted in the first place. 'How are you?' she asked.

'Keeping busy.'

'How's work?'

He hesitated. 'Do you really want to know? Are you sure I won't bore you?'

Phil spent most of his waking life at his school, and the remaining fraction telling Jane all about the exploits of every teacher, student and parent. His absorption in his work had been one of the complaints Jane had cited for their estrangement, and it had obviously struck a nerve.

'I want to hear,' she replied, surprised that she meant it. It wasn't so much the news she missed, but the sound of Phil's voice; an unwelcome reminder that her reason for not going back to him was because she cared too much, not too little.

She rubbed the back of her neck, aware of the cubby hole that was now almost invisible to the naked eye. How she wished the memories, and everything that came with them, could vanish as easily. She wouldn't drag Phil into this, whatever this was.

'Well, for a start,' began Phil, 'there was a governors' meeting this week, and two parents almost came to blows over the order of service for the graduation ceremony. It's been a nightmare.'

Her husband would be impossible to live with at times like this, and that was one thing Jane didn't miss. These were the faults she needed to concentrate on, but instead she found herself comparing him to Evan. However stressful his job, Phil had never taken it out on his wife, and never would.

As she waited for Phil's monologue to continue, Jane stood up. The sky had dialled down to a deep violet, and lights had come on across the way.

'So what have you been up to?' Phil asked.

The Jarvises' bedroom was aglow and the vertical blinds were open. Ashleigh sat at her dressing table with her back to Jane, her long, blonde hair cascading over her shoulders and down her back.

'Jane?'

'Sorry,' she said. She hadn't expected Phil to turn the topic of conversation towards her so soon. 'Erm, nothing interesting. I've spent most of today gardening.'

'Pete's doing his best here, but it's not up to your standards.'

'Who's Pete?' she asked, only half-listening. The rest of the house opposite was in darkness. There was no sign of Evan.

'The gardener. Remember?' he prompted as if talking to someone suffering with memory loss.

Jane had hired a gardener to take care of things while she nursed her mum, at a time when she thought she would be returning. 'Of course I remember. I didn't know his first name was Pete, that's all. Is he any good?'

'He keeps on top of things, but with so many other gardens to take care of, it's not the best arrangement, not when you factor in my paltry contribution. I might have been a bit lax with the watering. He says some of your plants may not be worth saving.'

'Which plants?' she demanded, forced back into the conversation.

'Oh, I don't know. He's had to clear some of the rockery, and that plant with the heart-shaped flowers you liked has shrivelled up.'

Phil had killed off the bleeding heart plant that had been a Mother's Day present from Megan when she was little. She wished he hadn't told her. He hadn't needed to mention it. He could be so insensitive sometimes. Another fault to note.

'If you're not planning on coming home soon, I was telling Pete it might be best if we simplify things,' Phil continued. 'It's not like I use the garden that much.'

Jane's pang of sadness evaporated as she spotted the trap

Phil thought he was priming. She pulled her gaze away from Ashleigh to look down at her new garden, or at least the one that was slowly taking shape. The design of a setting sun seemed particularly apt. One stage of Jane's life was over. There was no avoiding it.

'You have to do as you see fit,' she said. 'I don't see how I'll ever be coming back.'

'You just need time—'

'No, I've had time,' she said, and as much as it pained her, she couldn't prolong the agony she heard in his voice. 'This is where my life is now.'

The silence on the other end of the line was almost too much to bear. 'I'm sorry, Phil.'

'But you can't mean it. None of our problems are insurmountable, surely.'

'Some things are.'

'Tell me one thing we can't fix.'

As Jane was shaking her head, she caught movement from her neighbour's window. Ashleigh was bent forward with her head in her hands. It looked as if she were sobbing. What had Evan done to her? 'I can't do this now, Phil.'

'Why don't I come over to see you?' he asked, and when she didn't reply, he added, 'Or if there are things you can't say to me, what about Megan? She's a good listener, if only you'd stop shutting down the conversation every time she tries to speak to you.'

'Ah.' Her family had been comparing notes, hence the call.

'She's worried too, Jane. She told me about your neighbours. You called the police?'

Jane touched the windowpane as if she could reach out

101

to Ashleigh and comfort her. 'I had every reason to be worried.'

'It's a bit of a leap thinking he was digging a grave.'

Jane was sick of being told that. She had followed her instincts, and she trusted them more than a half-hearted police investigation. 'You don't know the whole story,' she said. 'Did Megan tell you I think it was Evan who stole my laptop and camera?'

Phil exhaled loudly. 'She did. And I can't say I see a connection.'

'Just because you can't see it, doesn't mean it isn't there,' Jane said as she searched the house opposite. Where was Evan lurking?

There were more sighs on the other end of the line. 'Can you at least consider that your perceptions might be challenged?' asked Phil. 'Grief affects people in different ways.'

'Losing Mum has nothing to do with what's been going on with Ashleigh. You should see her, Phil. She looks like a gust of wind could snap her in two, let alone that brute of a husband. Did Megan tell you Evan's well over six foot, and almost as wide?'

'All the more reason to keep out of it. And if the police aren't concerned, you shouldn't be either. You have to accept that their judgement is more reliable than yours in your current mental state.'

The comment pulled Jane up sharply. 'My mental state? Are you saying I've lost the plot?' she asked, her voice strangled.

'I'm suggesting no such thing,' Phil said quickly. 'But you have to admit that you've been acting out of character. And if you won't speak to me or Megan, I think it's time you sought professional help. I suspect there's a physiological reason for what's happening here.'

'Oh, really?'

'I'm no expert,' Phil began, which was a sure sign that he was about to give his opinion on something he knew absolutely nothing about. He cleared his throat. 'Lots of women struggle with the menopause.'

'Is that so?' Her face was hot with fury, which was a pleasant change from the usual burn of embarrassment.

It was hard to imagine how Megan had broached the subject her father referred to as 'women's problems', and even then only when absolutely necessary, but there was no doubt the pair had been colluding. They had dismissed out of hand Jane's very real concerns about the welfare of her neighbour, and decided she was having some sort of breakdown.

'You've had a rough time of it over the last few years,' Phil reminded her. 'And I can see now that it wasn't simply a matter of your insomnia and the significant blood loss.'

'You mean my heavy periods?' Even after thirty years of intimacy, the reference to bodily fluids could make her husband uncomfortable, but Jane was too angry to spare his feelings.

'Well, yes,' Phil replied.

Jane had been reduced to sleeping on old towels at one point during the perimenopause, and it had horrified Phil. He had expressed concern, but there had been an element of disgust too, or at least that was how Jane had perceived it.

'I assumed, wrongly, that was all there was to it,' Phil continued. 'But that isn't necessarily the case. I've been reading some interesting articles.'

With her curiosity piqued, Jane tamped down her irritation long enough to let him continue.

'I've come to appreciate how hormonal changes can wreak havoc on a woman's emotional state, and I wonder if it's time you considered HRT.'

Jane could feel her jaw tensing. 'I've been on HRT for eighteen months, Phil.'

'I didn't . . . Did you mention it? I'm sorry, I don't remember.'

She had told Phil about her doctor's appointment at the time, and later he had asked glibly if it was 'all sorted'. She had been too angry to give him a proper answer, which she conceded might have had something to do with her mood swings at the time. She felt unable to talk to Phil or to Megan about it because she was the one changing and they weren't, and it was still hard to let go of that resentment.

'It wasn't an overnight fix,' she said, 'and I had to have a scan to make sure there was nothing untoward going on.'

'You certainly didn't mention that,' Phil said, the first hint of annoyance. 'You can't hide things like that, Jane.'

'I didn't want to worry you,' she said truthfully. She would do anything to protect her family from hurt, which often meant going it alone, then and now. 'It was fine in the end. I eventually found the right combination of hormones to control my symptoms.'

Jane had expected Phil to notice the clear HRT patches she applied to her upper thighs at some point, but evidently he didn't look at her body, even when they were having sex. His wife had become invisible to him, and she was surprised he noticed her current absence quite so much.

'Well, that's something.' Phil should have ended the

conversation there, but it was sheer momentum that kept him going. 'But you might be due another review. If there's been a drop in your hormone levels, it could explain why you've been acting irrationally.'

Any remorse Jane might have felt about hurting her husband was swept away by a sudden and unstoppable tidal wave of rage. 'Have you not been listening to a word I've said?' she hissed down the phone 'I'm not irrational. I know what abuse looks like.'

Jane took a deep breath so she could continue berating her husband, only to hold it. Ashleigh had stood up and was dabbing her eyes as Evan stepped into the room. He had a jacket in his hand, suggesting he had just arrived home, and tossed it out of view. It was impossible to tell from his movements if he was drunk, but it might explain why Ashleigh moved warily towards her husband, her satin dressing gown fluttering behind her.

'I know you've seen more than your fair share of violence against women,' Phil replied, in a firm but placatory tone. 'And I understand why the sight of your dad's old overcoat might have triggered you the way it did. But doesn't that prove how tightly strung you are at the moment? Please, Jane, you must see how you're projecting your fears onto your neighbours. Not every heated argument is settled with fists. Not every man is like your dad.'

Phil had been horrified when Jane had told him about her dad. He preferred to see the best in people, so of course he would suggest her current perceptions were coloured by childhood trauma. But if that was all there was to it, why did terror clamp around Jane's heart as she watched Ashleigh place a hand on Evan's chest, her pose painfully supplicant?

'Oh, do fuck off, Phil,' Jane said, cutting the call before her husband could expand on the theory that she was suffering some sort of menopausal mania triggered by grief and suppressed memories.

Jane's reactions were very much in the present, and outrage sparked and flared as she watched Ashleigh tilt her head back to gaze up at her husband. Both her hands were on his chest now, her fingers tugging at his shirt as if she were pleading with him. The pitiful attempts at appeasement were something Jane had seen many times with her mum, and judging by the scars in the Jarvis house, it wasn't new to Ashleigh either.

'Get out of there,' Jane whispered.

For a brief moment, it looked as if Ashleigh had heard her plea because she took a step back. Jane watched transfixed as the younger woman undid her dressing gown and let it slip from her shoulders. She wore nothing except a thong, and her back arched as Evan stepped forward and wrapped an arm around her waist. As they kissed, his hands pawed at her bare flesh, and their passion was tangible as Ashleigh guided him onto the bed.

'Oh my,' Jane said, stepping away so fast she jarred her hip against the edge of the desk.

It didn't make sense. Ashleigh was meant to be living in terror, but it didn't look like she was frightened. If anything, she appeared to be the one in control. Jane covered her face with her hands and pressed her fingers against her eyes. She was mortified, not only by what she had seen, but what it could mean. Had she misread the situation completely? Was Phil right? Was there something seriously wrong with Jane's perceptions?

CHAPTER 15

1971

Cynthia hooked her finger into the hole she had cut out of the plywood and removed the false panel. She had used more sheets of plywood to construct the walls of the secret cubby hole, and there was an offcut of carpet on the floor. 'What do you think?'

Her five-year-old daughter cowered behind Cynthia's legs, her grip on her mum's overalls tightening. She refused to peer into the shadows that were the perfect hiding place for monsters.

'It's your very own den. And Sheena can play up here too,' Cynthia promised.

'But she can't come in when Dad's home,' Jane said, repeating by rote one of their rules.

'No, but wouldn't it be nice to come up here when he's in one of his moods? It'll be quieter,' said Cynthia as she coaxed Jane out from behind her. They knelt down together for a closer inspection.

Jane chewed her lip, and after some considerable thought, she rapped her knuckles on the external wall as if assessing whether or not it would withstand one of her father's rages. It appeared to meet her approval, but her brow wrinkled as she looked from the den to the stairs. Following her daughter's appraising gaze, Cynthia realized the wall with its tell-tale hole was in direct line of sight of anyone entering the attic.

Without saying a word, Cynthia manoeuvred her dad's old army trunk to create a makeshift screen. As an after-thought, she placed the red tartan suitcase, currently full of old bedding, on top of the trunk in case Les ever came looking for it. She wished she had the courage to pack his things for him, but she took his threat seriously when he said he'd take Jane away from her, and he wouldn't be the first to try. A social worker at the maternity hospital had almost tricked seventeen-year-old Cynthia into signing over her baby by claiming they were discharge papers, and attitudes to unmarried mothers had changed little. If Les did find someone fool enough to marry him, the courts would undoubtedly be sympathetic to any claim he made for custody. And he would do it just to spite her.

Cynthia's hope was that one day Les would get bored of them both, but until then, she would do everything she could to protect her daughter. 'We can put pillows and blankets inside to make it more comfortable,' she said, forcing a smile. 'Just in case you want to come up here at night.'

Jane scowled as she considered the prospect of sleeping in a draughty attic after dark, but she was a logical thinker. She would be comparing the relative peace inside her new den to the distress of being pulled from bed by a drunken father insisting they sit around the table while he ate the roast dinner Cynthia would have to warm up for him. It had happened last Sunday, or to be more precise, the early hours of Monday morning.

'Can I have a candle?' Jane asked eventually.

'Maybe a torch would be safer. And you can bring some books and games up here if you like.'

'And sweets?'

'I suppose a few snacks would be OK, as long as you don't gobble them up all at once.'

'Can I go and get Sheena so we can decorate?' asked Jane, setting aside her fears for the moment at least.

Cynthia checked the time. Les was a hospital porter and was working a morning shift. He would go straight to the pub afterwards and stay until afternoon closing. She wasn't expecting him home until three at the earliest, assuming there wasn't a lock-in.

'She can come over for a few hours if May says it's OK. But she'll have to go before your dad gets back.'

'I know, I'll tell her,' Jane shouted, already stomping down the stairs.

Cynthia pressed her fingers to her eyes to staunch the tears she refused to let fall. At least she didn't need to worry about smudging her mascara. She had stopped wearing make-up in a vain effort to appear less attractive to Les, but his determination to marry her had taken on a fresh impetus since his divorce came through. She wasn't stupid. She knew saying yes would mean handing over the house and any means of independence, but the more Cynthia snubbed his proposals, the less inclined Les was to control his anger. He liked to throw things, but at least he didn't hit her. He thought she should be grateful for that.

To the rest of Oxton, it was incomprehensible that a woman with her reputation would reject the offer of respectability, but she had one ally who didn't mind consorting with a social outcast. May had become a firm friend since their daughters started school together, and they had formed their own mutual appreciation society. May loved that Cynthia was a rule breaker, whilst Cynthia listened on with envy to May's tales of when she would sneak out on her lunch breaks to catch the Beatles at the Cavern, then drenching herself in perfume to disguise where she had been when she returned to her boring office job.

May continued to enjoy an active social life, which hadn't been curtailed by marriage or motherhood, but Cynthia refused invitations to join her. Les wouldn't allow her to go out without him, not even to bingo or the pictures, and a night out as a couple was best avoided. If Les wasn't groping barmaids, he was squaring up to anyone who gave Cynthia a second look. It was easier staying at home.

From the attic window, she watched her daughter scoot across the garden that had once been Aunt Judith's domain. Cynthia had tried to keep on top of things, but from this vantage point, it looked like a ramshackle assault course, as was apparent when Jane leapt across the open ditch where the old Anderson shelter had been. Les had demolished it after another of Cynthia's rejections, claiming to be helping, but it had simply satisfied his urge for destruction.

Cynthia continued to follow Jane's progress until she was swallowed up by the hedgerow. May had tried to follow their daughters through it once, but she had been wearing a long, crocheted cardigan, and Cynthia had been called upon to cut her free. They had laughed so hard, their sides hurt.

Returning downstairs, Cynthia spent the rest of the day catching up on invoicing and paying bills before tackling a pile of ironing that included the wide-collared shirts Les wore for his nights on the town. Jane had returned home to show Sheena her new den, and her little friend had instilled a sense of adventure that had been severely lacking in her daughter earlier. Cynthia hadn't heard a peep out of them for hours.

As three o'clock approached, she was on her way up to the attic to chase Sheena home when the phone rang. A fellow plumber who had been a friend of her dad's, had a call-out for a job he couldn't attend, and offered it to Cynthia. She didn't like to be out when Les returned home, but she couldn't turn down work, especially an emergency job where a desperate customer was less likely to turn her away because she was a woman. They needed the money. Les hadn't contributed to the housekeeping in months.

Cynthia was scribbling a note for Les when the girls appeared in the kitchen.

'We need to go out. I have a job,' she said to Jane.

'Can she come to mine?' Sheena asked. 'Mum won't mind.'

Cynthia was about to suggest checking with May first, but the sound of the front door banging open stopped her in her tracks.

'Fine, off you go,' she said, ushering the girls out through the back. To Sheena she added, 'Tell your mum I'm sorry, and I'll pick Jane up in a couple of hours.'

After closing the back door, Cynthia turned to find Les watching from the hallway, making her jump.

'What are you up to?' he asked, leaning on the doorjamb.

'I have to go out.'

'You told me you didn't have any jobs today.'

'It's an emergency,' she explained. 'I've left you some sandwiches in a Tupperware box in the fridge if you're hungry, but I won't be too long.' As she spoke, she kept moving, giving Les less time to consider his next move. All the tools she needed were in her Minivan. She grabbed her bag. 'I could pick up a chippy tea on my way home, if you like?'

Les didn't move from the doorway, and when she approached, he sniffed the air. 'Since when do you wear perfume for jobs?'

'I'm not. It'll be my shampoo,' she said, trying to squeeze past.

Les snatched hold of her arm. 'Do you think I'm stupid? Who is he?'

With her senses heightened, Cynthia's nose wrinkled as she picked up the scent too. She sniffed Les's jacket. He didn't have a monopoly on losing patience. 'It's you that smells of perfume and you dare accuse me of playing around?'

Cynthia didn't see the punch coming. Later, she would recall only the sound of her teeth crunching as the back of her head glanced off the wall.

CHAPTER 16

Pain throbbed behind Ashleigh's closed lids, and she couldn't summon the energy to get out of bed. She had heard Evan leave for work, but wasn't sure if it had been minutes or hours ago. Seducing him the night before had been a pre-emptive strike, but she couldn't help but feel she had prostituted herself. A punch or a kick might have been more honest.

Ashleigh could have predicted that yesterday wouldn't end well when, without warning, Evan had announced he was going out for a quick kick around, followed by an end of season celebration with his teammates. He said he wouldn't stay out late. He said he wouldn't drink. She hadn't believed him, but she wasn't sure which part of his story was the lie, or if any of it were true. Dreading his return, she had gone out for a walk and returned with a bottle of wine to settle her nerves and anaesthetize the pain in her heart.

Peeling open her eyes, Ashleigh blinked away the sting of the morning sun and stared up at the ceiling. Other parts of her body hurt too, but not as much as her pride. She had cried herself to sleep, and if Evan had heard, he hadn't responded. She was scared he was growing cold towards her, but as she turned her head on the pillow, she smiled. Evan had left her a glass of water and two paracetamols on the bedside table while she slept. He knew he had hurt her, mentally if not physically.

As she scooted up in bed, her headache intensified, but Ashleigh didn't touch the painkillers until she had taken a photo of Evan's little care package. She wanted to post it on Instagram so those who knew about the recent police attention could be assured that Evan was very much the loving husband. It was only after downing the pills that she noticed the blinds. She had left them wide open on purpose, anticipating a more violent end to the evening, and despite her blushes, she was comforted by the idea that Jane might be following the confusion of highs and lows in her marriage. Someone had to watch over her, and it wasn't going to be May, who had given Ashleigh little more than a stiff nod when she had returned home a week ago.

Ashleigh considered going downstairs to make a coffee, but with only decaf in the house and an absence of stodgy food to cure a hangover, she slumped back against her pillows. She didn't work Mondays, and there was nothing to do except play housewife. She was considering a trip to the supermarket to smuggle more contraband into the house when her phone rang.

'I saw your post. Why do you need painkillers? Are you OK?' asked Jess. She gasped, then whispered in an undertone. 'Is he with you now?'

'Everything is fine, Jess. I had a headache, and Evan was

being really sweet, that's all. If I'm honest, I had too much wine while he was out yesterday, but he didn't even moan about me breaking one of his—' She was about to say ground rules, but she hadn't mentioned those to her friend as yet. 'We're both on the wagon, or supposed to be.'

There was a pregnant pause. 'So let me guess. He was out drinking all day, but you're the one made to feel guilty for opening a bottle of wine.'

'He can hold his drink better than I can,' said Ashleigh, 'and he didn't have a proper go at me. He was fine.'

'A proper go? Wow, Ash, do you actually listen to yourself?'

Of course she did. 'Please, don't be like that. I'm not saying things are perfect, but we're both learning from our mistakes.'

'You're not the one with the problem, remember?'

'It doesn't mean I'm not part of the solution,' said Ashleigh. Thinking aloud, she added, 'I've been wondering if it's time to start a family.'

'I thought you wanted to put off kids until the very last ticks of your biological clock.'

'Only because I didn't want it affecting my career. Taking time off from the salon will hardly be a sacrifice. And I could become a full-time mum. Why put pressure on myself juggling a baby and a job?'

'And what about the pressure it would put on your relationship? Think about it, honey. If it didn't work out, you'd be trapped. Or is that what he wants? Is this Evan's idea?'

'No,' she said, although Evan had made it no secret that he wanted children. He had pointed out more than once that their chances of conceiving would go down the longer they left it. 'It would just be nice to prove to people that we're not as messed up as they think we are.'

'That's going some way to prove a point.'

'So would you be up for a bit of babysitting?'

'Don't even joke about it,' Jess said, but she was laughing. 'And I'm sorry, but I have to dash or I'll miss my hospital appointment.'

'God, sorry, I forgot you were having that mole removed today. Is Harry going with you?'

'No, it's a simple procedure,' replied Jess. 'But I've told him he definitely has to be there when I get the biopsy results.'

'You shouldn't have to go on your own today either,' Ashleigh persisted. It felt good to see the flaws in someone else's relationship. 'Would you like me to come? I could meet you there.'

'No, honestly, it's fine. I'll let you know how I get on.'

'Make sure you do,' Ashleigh replied, feeling some relief that Jess had let her off the hook. She hadn't fancied sitting in a waiting room with a hangover, but there were other ways of supporting her friend. She had been meaning to send Jess a bouquet of flowers as a thank you for letting her stay at the flat. Knowing Jess, she would prefer a crate of Chardonnay, but flowers would probably last longer. She would put that on the note with a smiley face.

After the call ended, Ashleigh checked to see who else had seen her Instagram post. There were a few likes, and someone from the salon had replied with a rash of love heart emojis. Evan hadn't seen it yet, or if he had, he hadn't liked it.

Her husband didn't share her love of social media, but he had set up an Instagram account so he could follow hers. His first ever post had been one from their wedding, and she was glad to note it was still there. In the close-up of the happy couple, Ashleigh wore a white satin wedding dress, and Evan was in a made-to-measure suit because there was no way he could find one off the rack. Their group photos had been less impressive. The wedding party had been relatively small with most of the guests on the groom's side. Ashleigh's only family had been her sister, and she had been more than enough to deal with.

Typically, Rose had drunk too much, too fast that day, and Ashleigh cringed when she recalled her sister feeling Evan's biceps and calling her then-boyfriend too scrawny by comparison. It had been the beginning of the end for Rose's relationship, and she had been single ever since.

Ashleigh scrolled back to the last photo Evan had posted. It was a scorecard from an amateur football match where he had scored the winning goal. Ashleigh had been sofa surfing at Jess's at the time and had stopped herself from pressing like. It still bothered her that Rose had liked it straight away; if her sister had to pick a side, it would always be Evan's.

Switching to Rose's account, Ashleigh found a grid of photos all on the same theme; lots of inspirational quotes, screenshots of how many steps she had clocked, and pictures of healthy meals that Rose claimed to enjoy with a new sense of appreciation. She was a recovering alcoholic, and although Ashleigh was incredibly proud of her achievement, she was less keen on her sister's fervour, which was reminiscent of a sixteenth-century missionary. As this was one of the few accounts Evan followed on Instagram, it wasn't difficult to figure out who had inspired their current health kick.

Pulling on a dressing gown, Ashleigh went downstairs in search of something to settle her stomach, even if it had to be a piece of brown toast with a plant-based spread. She wondered if being pregnant would make her feel this ill. Jess was probably right about not rushing into a decision. Ashleigh couldn't be sure if Evan had actually been out with his mates the day before or sneaked off to see someone else. Either way, she suspected he had stayed out just late enough to build up the anxiety levels at home.

The games Evan played could be dizzying, and as Ashleigh rested a hand on the worktop to steady herself, her fingers touched a piece of paper. Lifting a silver key, she read the message beneath. There were two words. One kiss.

Sorry. Evan x

Ashleigh felt the weight of the kitchen door key in her hand. Was this another of his tests, or did he trust her? And should she trust him?

CHAPTER 17

'What the hell am I doing now?' Jane said under her breath as she attempted to mirror the movements of the yoga instructor. She had her right foot forward, knee bent, and her left leg extended behind her. Her outstretched arms were meant to be parallel to the floor, but she was waving them about to stop herself from toppling over.

'It's called a warrior pose, I think,' replied Sheena.

'I don't feel like a warrior,' Jane admitted as an unwelcome vision came to mind that made her shoulders fold inwards, unbalancing her further. It served her right for spying on the Jarvises like a Peeping Tom. If anyone needed saving from their foolishness, it wasn't Ashleigh.

Jane lumbered through the rest of the yoga positions with the agility of a baby elephant, and was relieved when they moved on to the guided relaxation. She lay on her yoga mat with her arms at her sides, palms up, and a blanket tucked in at her sides. They were told to imagine sunning themselves on their favourite beach whilst listening to a background track of waves rolling across shiny pebbles.

The instructor's voice was hypnotic as it transported Jane back to Santorini. Dipping her toe into the warm waters of the visualization, she imagined Phil taking her hand, and they laughed as they raced into the crystal-blue waters of the Aegean Sea. His features were youthful, and it would be years before he grew the beard that would eventually turn salt and pepper. When he splashed her, Jane felt the saltwater sliding down her cheek.

'Come on, lazybones. Time to wake up,' Sheena said with a gentle prod.

Jane wiped away the unexpected tears and was quiet as they rolled up their mats and left the hall. 'Thanks for coming with me.'

'No, thank you for getting me here,' said Sheena. 'I actually quite enjoyed it. Same time next Wednesday?'

'Sure,' Jane replied as they approached a line of parked cars.

Sheena had a twenty-minute drive back to Hoylake, whereas Jane was within walking distance of home. *Home.* Now there was a word she had never expected to use again for her mum's house.

'We could always nip into the pub for a quick nightcap,' Sheena suggested when Jane began dragging her feet.

'Even though you can't drink?'

'Even then,' Sheena said, rerouting them towards the Caernarvon Castle. 'Our Jamie's started learning to drive, and it'll be nice to show him that you can go out and have a good time without drinking.'

'How is he?' Jane asked when they were sitting in front of two orange juices.

'A teenager,' Sheena replied as if that explained it all.

'He's started an apprenticeship with Unilever and you'd think he had money to burn. It wouldn't cross his mind to pay for his keep, but then I never gave my mum house-keeping either.'

'Mum took half my wages from my paper round.'

'Ah, but that was different.'

'Only because our mums were different,' replied Jane, but there was no resentment. Or was there? Her childhood wasn't only different from Sheena's, but from every other family at that time. Not that Jane had ever blamed her mum. Once Les was gone, Cynthia had ensured that the remainder of her daughter's childhood had been a happy one, but it was a bit like papering over Jane's old den. You could cover it up and pretend it wasn't there, but if you looked closely, you would see the lasting impression it had left.

'Your mum was ahead of her time,' Sheena said. 'There was so much snobbery back then. Do you remember Iris Rigby, our neighbour? She was always a bit pass-remarkable, if you ask me.'

'She wouldn't let her Jeanette play with me, I remember that.'

'Jeanette was the one who went around saying your mum lived over the brush, and I swear I looked everywhere in your house for an actual brush.'

Jane rolled her eyes with affection. 'I know, you had me looking for it too.'

Sheena went to sip her drink, but another memory hit her. 'Oh God, remember that time your dad got down on one knee in front of us all?' She smiled as she recalled the showman. 'I'm surprised your mum didn't give in eventually, but I suppose if he did a runner when she was pregnant, she must have known he'd do it again.'

'You don't know the half of it,' Jane said. She rubbed the deepening lines on her brow. It was time her oldest friend knew that when they reminisced, they looked back from entirely different perspectives. 'Do you remember our den in the attic?'

The mere mention of it made Sheena's eyes dance, but her smile faltered when she registered Jane's expression. This was not a happy memory.

'Mum built it as my panic room.' Jane paused to give her friend a moment to digest that thought. It paled both their complexions. 'She would send me up there whenever Dad was about to lose it, usually when he was drunk. It got to the stage where I knew to head up there without being told. We'd be chatting like your average family, and then it would be as if the world skipped a beat. Dad would blow up into a rage over something Mum had said or didn't say, I doubt it mattered. I'd race upstairs, begging Mum to come with me, but she always stayed.' Her voice carried a hint of the helplessness she used to feel, seasoned with guilt. 'She knew he'd come looking for us both if she didn't.'

Her friend stared at her for the longest time, making Jane squirm. She was almost ready to bolt, but Sheena reached over to grasp her hand tightly. 'How did I not know that? You were that scared of him?'

Jane could only manage a nod as she rummaged through a trove of memories that held no treasure. She had been conditioned not to tell from a very young age, but once she got talking, she couldn't stop. It felt oddly liberating as she told Sheena about the time her dad made her dance with him in the dining room. She would only have been about six, but she could still recall the panic as her feet slipped off his boots. And the more she panicked, the more she slipped, until her mum came to her rescue as always.

'Even up in the attic I could hear the thuds and crashes of his one-sided arguments,' she said. 'I wouldn't know the extent of the damage until I was allowed downstairs again, usually after Dad had fallen into a drunken stupor, or headed back to the pub with a slam of the front door. Mum would make me a cocoa, and I'd help her clear up whatever damage he'd caused. That particular time, he'd kicked in the stereogram, but most of our things got broken at some point.'

'God, I remember complaining that your telly was never working,' Sheena said. She released a strangled laugh, but her eyes shimmered with tears. She swiped them away angrily with the back of her hand. 'Good God, Jane. How could I have been so stupid?'

'Don't ever think that.' Jane fought to stem her own tears. 'We were just clever at hiding it.'

'And what else did you hide?' Sheena's lips puckered in anger. 'It wasn't just the furniture he took it out on, was it?'

'He hit Mum, a lot. Just not always where it showed,' Jane said quietly.

'What a bastard,' Sheena said, releasing Jane's hand, but only so she could make a fist. 'Of course she would refuse to marry him.'

'He said he wouldn't get so angry if she'd just say yes. I suspect what bothered him most was not being able to get his hands on her inheritance. He would have sold the house from under us given half a chance. He never cared about her, or me.'

123

'Were you ever worried he'd come back again?'

'All the time. I was actually terrified he'd show up at my wedding,' Jane admitted.

Sheena shook her head slowly. 'I can't believe I used to be jealous that you had a dad who travelled the world, sending back all those exotic gifts.'

'Hardly exotic,' Jane said, trying not to picture the cheap plastic snow globe Phil had uncovered. 'And I was glad when the presents stopped.'

'I don't blame you,' Sheena said. She was thoughtful for a moment as she readjusted her view of the past. 'I'm just sorry you went through all that while I was so oblivious. Jesus, I was so sad when we stopped using the den. I didn't realize we should have been celebrating that you didn't need to hide any more.'

'It's why Mum made sure we had the run of the house afterwards. She was always saying we could make as much noise and mess as we pleased.'

'Yeah, I do remember that.'

'You took it more literally than me,' Jane said with a rueful smile. 'I found it harder to break old habits, which was why she sealed the den up eventually.' She spoke as if this were the only reason it was blocked off, but it didn't explain why her mum had used the space to hide away all those artifacts from Les's reign of terror. Jane should have been warned what was in there.

As Jane made a conscious effort to slow her breathing, Sheena fast-forwarded through their childhood. 'I've just realized how all those mad day trips of ours came after Les had buggered off, like Cynthia was celebrating every bit of your freedom. She was one amazing woman.'

'She was, and I can't tell you what I'd give for the chance to tell her that.'

'Some things don't need saying.'

'But what about the things that do? We left it too late,' Jane said, then shuddered as she recalled how her mum had uttered the same words on her deathbed. 'She kept so much to herself.'

'Much like her daughter,' Sheena said wryly. 'But just because you were brought up to be strong and independent, Jane, doesn't mean you have to be like that *all* the time. You're allowed to ask for help.'

'I've cut so many people off, I'm not sure I have a choice any more.'

Sheena arched an eyebrow, waiting for Jane to notice the friend sitting right in front of her.

'I didn't mean you. You are the one shining light in a rather dark world at the moment. I don't know why you put up with me.'

'Because I'm part of your past too,' Sheena said. 'And all my best childhood memories have you in them.'

'Same here,' Jane said, managing a smile that didn't reach her eyes.

Sheena tilted her head. 'What I don't understand is, if your earlier memories are as bad as you say, why on earth would you want to stay in that house?'

'I'm not making it up!' Jane said sharply. 'It was a living nightmare with Dad.'

Sheena's jaw fell open. 'Whoa. Of course I believe you. All I meant was, why put yourself through all of this when it's obviously making you miserable?'

Jane pressed a hand to her brow. 'Oh God, sorry. I know

I'm being oversensitive. It's just that you wouldn't be the first person to question my perceptions.'

'Firstly, I'm not questioning you. And secondly, who the hell would?' Sheena said, raising her voice.

'Phil,' Jane replied. When she noticed the simmering fury behind Sheena's eyes, she quickly added, 'Not about the stuff with my dad. Just everything else. We had a conversation the other night, and I ended up telling him to eff off.'

'Wow, it must have been bad for you to use the F-bomb.'

'Exactly,' said Jane, but she did regret jumping down his throat. She felt guilty about how she treated him in general. 'He'd been genning up on the menopause to show how he could be a more considerate husband.'

'Bloody hell, I can't imagine Chris doing that.'

'Phil's heart was in the right place, but at the time, I was livid,' Jane said, her cheeks pinched with shame. She had been so certain that she was in the right and Phil was wrong, but then she had seen Ashleigh with Evan. 'My family have apparently decided that I'm behaving irrationally, and one of their working theories is that it's a hormonal imbalance.'

'Why is it that once a woman hits the menopause, she can't do anything without it being used against her?' Sheena said with exasperation, only to check herself. 'OK, I might fly off into a rage with only the slightest provocation, but *irrational*? Seriously? It's perfectly understandable, to me at least, that you would need a moment to process your grief, and all the memories it's brought back.'

'You don't think I've gone a bit crazy given what happened with the Jarvises?' asked Jane, her voice quavering.

Too scared to wait for Sheena's answer, she added, 'Phil says I looked at them and saw what I expected to see. And what if he's right? What if, rather than abuse, they have one of those relationships that's simply very passionate and vocal?'

'Mum said it's been quiet since Ashleigh came home,' Sheena conceded. 'Let's hope it stays that way.'

'They seemed to be getting on very well on Sunday night,' Jane said. Unable to look Sheena in the eye, she picked up her drink, but it missed her mouth and spilled down her gym top.

'What have I missed?' Sheena asked as Jane continued to squirm.

'I might have seen more than I should.'

'Oh, wow. We're talking sex, aren't we?'

'Let's just say that whatever is going on over there, their attraction for each other was very much on display,' Jane said, ignoring the smirk on Sheena's face. 'And as far as I'm concerned, I've seen more than enough. I put a blind up in the attic yesterday so I don't have to think about what my neighbours are up to any more.'

'Oh Jane. See what I mean about that house making you miserable? Wouldn't now be a good time to think again about selling up?' asked Sheena. 'It doesn't mean you have to go back to Buxton. I'd love you to stay on the Wirral; in fact, there are some really nice apartments for rent not far from me. You could take one until you decide what to do.'

For a fleeting moment, Jane pictured handing her mum's keys over to a new family, only to quickly snatch them back in panic. 'I can't do that,' she said, responding instinctively. And therein lay the problem she faced. Her reasoning might be flawed when it came to her neighbours, but there could be no debate about keeping the house. She hadn't needed to look inside that red tartan suitcase to know that its contents trapped her. She was as much of a hostage to the past as her mum had been before her.

CHAPTER 18

Waking up from an afternoon doze on her mum's fully extended, motorized recliner, Jane rubbed away the crusted trail of drool on her chin. She had become a rebooted version of Cynthia, living in the same house, with the same list of chores, and the same ghosts. It had suited her mum, who had no end of hobbies to keep her mind and body active, but Jane saw only decades of monotony stretching out ahead of her. It was a blessed relief when her phone rang.

'Hello, sweetheart,' Jane said, answering the call from her daughter. 'How are you? Have you been busy?'

'Oh, you know.'

After a week of swapping brief messages, there should be no end of things to catch up on, but the conversation stalled.

'What's wrong?' Jane asked. 'Has something happened?'

Megan gave a laugh, but there was no mirth. 'Well, my parents have thrown away a perfectly good marriage. How about that for a start?'

'We're still married,' Jane said, surprised at how grateful she was for this. She had been brooding on Sheena's advice earlier in the week about opening up to someone, and Phil was the obvious choice. He was the one person she trusted most and she missed him, but her initial fears remained. Involving her husband wouldn't end her misery, it would simply be sharing it with someone else. But hadn't she made Phil miserable anyway? Her thoughts continued to see-saw. She didn't know what to do.

'How can you say you're still together while having nothing more to do with Dad?' Megan asked, in a perfect summation of Jane's dilemma. 'How is that fair?'

'It's not,' she conceded.

'He's a good man, Mum. And if you can't see that, there are others who will. I don't know what you said to him last weekend, but it hit the mark. He's ready to call it a day too.'

The news winded Jane. 'He told you that?'

'Actions speak louder than words. He's joined an online dating site. He actually asked for my opinion.'

'And you *helped* him?' Jane asked, her voice rising an octave as a sharp pain stabbed her chest. She had never once considered he might look for someone else. Not now, and not ever.

'What did you expect?'

'Which site is he using?'

'So you can stalk his profile?'

'I wouldn't do that,' Jane said, tearing up. She had treated Phil so badly, and he was never going to know why. She tried to tell herself it was for the best, but her heart broke as she forced herself to add, 'You're right. Your dad is a good man. He deserves better than me.'

'Christ almighty!' Megan exclaimed. 'How can two people who obviously still love each other let things get to this point?'

'I know there's no logic to it,' Jane said. Her decision not to drag her family into this mess had come from the gut and she had to trust it. Phil was moving on, and Megan would adapt too. There was nothing left but to lean into the lie she had been telling them. 'We can't make each other happy, love. It's time to accept that.'

'I don't believe you,' Megan snapped. 'Why won't you talk to me, Mum? I didn't even know you were on HRT. What else aren't you telling us?'

Jane took the phone from her ear and pressed it against her chest so her daughter wouldn't hear the stifled sob. There was no choice but to carry the burden alone, and when she was ready, she made sure her voice was steady. 'All I can say is I never meant to hurt you both, and especially not your dad.'

'You know, he hasn't actually gone on any dates yet,' Megan told her, more gently this time. 'There's still a chance.'

When Jane's phone buzzed with an incoming message, she knew she should ignore it, but what else was there to say to her daughter? Phil's life was clearly in Buxton, and Jane was condemned to a future here. In truth, that had never been negotiable. She glanced at the notification on her screen. It was a text from Sheena.

Message from Mum 'It's all kicking off next door. They're screaming at each other again' xxx

Jane's stomach lurched as she checked the time. Six thirty on a Sunday evening might not be the obvious time for a blazing row, but sometimes a losing score or an iron mark on a uniform was all it took.

'I'm sorry, Megan. I have to go,' she said, already on her way to fetch her garden shoes from the understairs cupboard. It was more nerves than urgency that made her breathless. 'I know your dad doesn't need my blessing, but tell him he has it. Bye, sweetheart.'

Jane hung up, and with no time to dwell on the finality of the conversation she had just had with her daughter, she flung open the French doors. The only sound to greet her was the warble of birdsong, and the scrape of Benji's claws across the patio. He jumped over the new box hedging like a racehorse at Aintree rather than weave in and out of the planters pockmarking the centre of the sun design. Jane grabbed a pair of secateurs and quickly followed him to the back of the garden.

As her ears strained for the sounds that had alerted May, she pulled a twig of hazel from the hedgerow, lopping off an inch or two so it didn't look too obvious to the neighbours that she was eavesdropping. Benji scratched noisily at dried earth nearby.

'Shush,' she whispered, glaring at the dog who stared back in confusion, his head cocked.

Jane held her breath, and above the hum of traffic, she thought she caught a woman's raised voice, but in the next moment, a blackbird started to sing. She could see its dark shape in May's cherry tree and was tempted to throw the hazel twig at it, but she wasn't sure it would help. She couldn't hear anything useful.

Retreating back into the house, Jane raced up two flights of stairs and was panting by the time she reached the attic. The newly installed blind was closed, trapping the day's heat and making the air too heavy for Jane to catch her breath. She reached behind the roller blind and opened the window. The fresh air was noticeably cooler, and soon she could hear other noises beyond her laboured breaths.

The traffic noise seemed louder than ever, but at least the annoying blackbird had flown off. There were no other sounds, or at least none that could be attributed to the Jarvises. If they were still arguing, they hadn't ventured outside. Jane raised the blind a few inches and crouched down to peek beneath it.

At first glance, the house that had been the object of her grim fascination looked exactly as she might expect. The vertical blinds in the living room were at their usual angle obstructing Jane's view, and the ones in the master bedroom revealed no signs of life. The kitchen was deserted, although the door leading out to the garden was ajar.

Jane spotted a new swing seat on their patio, which could have appeared at any time in the last week while she had been conscientiously averting her eyes. A more recent sign of activity was the watering can lying on its side in a puddle, turning the hot paving stones dark grey. The large storage box kept against the wall of the house had been left open, and Jane could see gardening tools poking out from it.

Movement drew her attention back to the living room window. The blinds swayed as if caught in a draught from the open kitchen door, but the air outside was still, and

Jane was more inclined to believe the blinds had been disturbed by activity inside the house.

Desperate to hear anything that wasn't the normal thrum of the neighbourhood, Jane gave up being circumspect and rolled up the attic blind so she could lean out of the window. She wasn't in the least bit fazed when she realized she had been caught in the act by her fellow eavesdropper.

May was watching from her upstairs window. She cupped a hand to her ear, which Jane interpreted as a signal that she could hear something. Jane wished she had May's phone number stored on her phone but had to make do with a series of gestures as her neighbour tried to describe what was happening. May drew unrecognizable shapes in mid-air, but then her hand stilled. She pointed down to the garden.

By the time Jane realized it was a warning, Ashleigh came hurtling out of the kitchen. She raced over to the trough, then spun around to face the house again. Jane followed Ashleigh's gaze, but Evan was nowhere to be seen. Not yet.

When Ashleigh looked about as if searching for help, Jane leant further out of the window, desperate to let her neighbour know that she hadn't forsaken her. Ashleigh spotted her, but the connection between the pair didn't last long, and Ashleigh's head snapped back towards the kitchen. Evan had taken his time, allowing the tension to build to intolerable levels, but there he was, a brooding presence that filled the door frame. He folded his arms over his football shirt, his muscles bulging. Fear gnawed at Jane's insides as she waited for his next move.

Keeping Evan in her sights, Ashleigh side-stepped towards the open storage box. She scanned its contents and grabbed a heavy wooden handle. Pulling out the garden fork, she pointed four metal tines at her husband, needing two hands to keep her aim. Evan shook his head as he stepped out of the house.

Ashleigh backed away until her heels knocked against the trough. The frame was only as high as her calves, and if she wasn't careful, she would fall over it. 'Keep away from me!' she yelled at the top of her voice.

Whatever Evan's reply, it was too low for Jane to hear, but it looked as if he were mocking his wife. Jane glanced over to May, who had her forehead pressed against the window, all thoughts gone of giving Jane a running commentary.

'Why do you keep doing this?' Ashleigh shouted again.

Evan jabbed a finger at his chest. It looked as if he were saying, 'Me?'

The strategy was a familiar one. Jane's dad had accused Cynthia of being cruel, demanding to know what he had done to make her hate him so much. Even on those occasions when he couldn't ignore the suffering he had inflicted, he blamed Cynthia for provoking him. He actually believed he was the victim. That was how men like that kept the cycle of abuse going.

Confined to the attic as always, Jane gripped the window ledge. She wanted to scream at Evan to leave Ashleigh alone, but her throat tightened. She was as terrified of Evan as Ashleigh must be. Whatever he was saying had made his wife sob, and it echoed in Jane's chest as she watched the fight leave Ashleigh's body. She had let the garden fork arc downwards and drop to the ground.

Twisting around, Ashleigh grabbed clumps of seedlings from the trough to throw at her husband, but her trajectory was off. Clods of earth flew over into May's garden while others hit the fence behind Evan, disintegrating upon impact.

Evan's face was like thunder, and whatever he said was short and to the point. He was about to go back into the house but stopped to look up at their neighbour's attic window as his wife had done. Jane hurled herself backwards, shrinking into the shadows, but it was too late. She saw him extend a thick arm towards her, his finger pointing in accusation. She let out an involuntary cry, her legs buckling even as she crouched down out of sight. It took a long time to pluck up the courage to stand again, and her heart was still pounding as she peered out of the window.

The Jarvises' garden was deserted and the kitchen door closed. In the house next door, May's bedroom was empty too, and Jane didn't know what that might mean. Had May gone downstairs to continue listening, or was she calling the police? Should Jane phone them? Could she be Ashleigh's voice if Ashleigh was too terrified to speak up for herself?

Before Jane could figure out what to do next, May reappeared in her bedroom. Resuming their game of charades, the older woman flexed her biceps, which Jane took as a representation of Evan. Next, she held both hands in front of her and mimicked turning a steering wheel. Evan had driven off. The tension left Jane's body with a loud exhalation. Ashleigh was safe for now.

There was no need for May to explain what Ashleigh was doing because the wife next door had appeared at her bedroom window. She didn't look across to Jane as she closed the vertical blinds tight. Meanwhile, May drew invisible lines down a sad face to indicate she could hear Ashleigh crying. When she shrugged, Jane shrugged too. The message from Ashleigh Jarvis was clearer than any mime. She wanted to be left alone.

CHAPTER 19

1972

As Cynthia opened the oven door, a cloud of steam bathed her in the delicious aroma of roast chicken. Sundays had always been family time in the Simpkin household. She could remember helping her Aunt Judith gather vegetables from the garden, and they would sit and peel carrots or shell peas together. After lunch, her dad would do the washing up, and later they would settle at the dining table for a game of cribbage. Music would be playing, and they would each have their favourite tipple; stout for her dad, port and lemon for Judith, and Vimto for Cynthia. It was an idyllic scene she had imagined for her own family.

'Is Dad back yet?' whispered Jane.

Cynthia almost dropped the roasting tin in surprise. Her six-year-old knew to contain her exuberance and had entered the house with stealth after playing over at May's.

'Not yet,' Cynthia said. She hooked a finger under her

daughter's chin and examined the fine scratches on her rosy cheeks. 'Those brambles need cutting back again.'

Jane poked her tongue through the gummy gap from her missing front teeth. 'Billy says he'll do it.'

May's husband was as keen as his wife to maintain a safe passage between their homes, and although Cynthia hadn't told them why it was so important, May wasn't blind. Even if Cynthia could hide the bruises, Les's violent temper had left marks all over their home, but at least things had improved since he was given a final warning at work for being late. He had cut back on his drinking, and he hadn't hit her for at least a month.

Cynthia prodded the perfectly browned chicken with a fork, and as she watched the juices run clear, her daughter's stomach growled loudly.

'I'm starving, Mum.'

Cynthia wouldn't dare carve up the roast before Les came home from work, and he had promised her faithfully that he would be back before two. It was ten past, and she was about to suggest Jane eat an apple when they heard the front door open. Cynthia and her daughter held each other's gaze, along with their breath.

'Something smells good,' Les said, sweeping into the kitchen and planting a kiss on Cynthia's cheek.

Her heart sank when she heard the clink of beer bottles in the pockets of his overcoat. It was homebrew from a misguided colleague who innocently assumed Les shared an appreciation for real ale, but at least she hadn't detected the smell of alcohol on his breath. 'I just need to make the gravy,' she said. 'Jane, can you set the table?'

'Come on, let's do it together,' said Les to his dumbstruck daughter. 'You get the cutlery and I'll get the placemats.'

Cynthia tried not to mind that Les's first priority was to take a pint glass from the cupboard, and she enjoyed the sound of giggles coming from the dining room as father and daughter worked together.

Throughout their meal, Les entertained them with stories of his sea adventures that kept Jane enthralled. Cynthia had been similarly awestruck the first time Les had taken her to a Chinese restaurant and introduced her to an entirely new culture. He had seemed so worldly-wise, and it would be much later that she discovered he hadn't travelled further than mainland Europe. Many of his stories were borrowed from his shipmates, but Les was a good storyteller, and Cynthia made sure not to let her anxiety show when he downed his last beer and opened a bottle of rum.

'We need some music,' Les announced, stumbling over to the stereogram while Cynthia cleared the table.

'Come and help me wash up,' Cynthia suggested to Jane.

Her daughter jumped off her chair so fast she almost knocked it over. They both knew that when Les was this hyped up, there would be an inevitable crash.

Les caught Jane's arm. 'I can't have both of you being party poopers. Stay and dance with your dad.'

Jane looked wide-eyed at her mum.

'I won't be long,' Cynthia promised, and hurried to the kitchen.

Water splashed over her dress as she filled the washing-up bowl with soapy water. She could hear the Everly Brothers' harmonies coming from the other room. It was one of her dad's LPs, and she would give anything to go back in time, but her dad was gone, and Aunt Judith had died a few months ago. They had travelled over to the Isle of Man for the funeral, and Cynthia was almost glad that her aunt hadn't been around to see Les make a fool of them at the wake.

'She's a better dancer than you!' Les called out.

Leaving the dishes to soak, Cynthia returned to find Jane struggling to balance on her dad's boots. 'Is that so?' she asked. It was only practice that fixed the smile on her face despite seeing the panic brimming in her little girl's eyes.

She peeled Les's fingers from Jane's wrists so she could take her place. He pulled Cynthia close, and the moment her face was hidden from view, she looked from Jane to the door, and flicked her gaze upwards. It was time to go to the attic.

'Loosen up,' Les told Cynthia, giving her waist a shake. 'You don't know how to enjoy yourself.'

'I am enjoying myself,' she replied stiffly. 'I'm just full after dinner, that's all.'

Les closed his eyes. 'Your dad had great taste in music. Better than today's rubbish. Bloody Osmonds.'

For a few minutes, Les was absorbed in the music of yesteryear, but when the track changed to a slow song, he became aware of Cynthia once again.

'You're my ebony eyes,' he drawled.

Even if Cynthia had wanted to point out that her eyes were grey, Les didn't give her the chance. He clamped his mouth over hers, his tongue forcing its way into her mouth like a serpent stealing her voice. He pawed at her, feeling the softness of her breasts while the rest of Cynthia's body turned rigid.

'Do you know how much I love you?' he slobbered into her neck.

'Yes.'

'You don't love me.'

'I do.'

Les tipped back his head and guffawed. '"I do," she says!' The laughter ended abruptly as he grabbed her hair so she had no choice but to meet his gaze. 'So will you be my wife?'

'Don't do this, Les.'

'You're a stubborn bitch,' he snarled, letting go of her. She tried to move away, but he grabbed her again, pinning her by the arms. 'What happens when you get pregnant again? Do you want another bastard?'

This was one thing Cynthia didn't fear. She had gone on the new contraceptive pill within days of Les showing up with his little red suitcase. Thank goodness the law had changed to make contraception available to unmarried women. She wouldn't subject another child to having a father like Les.

'I don't know why you're so cold,' he continued through gritted teeth. 'You're not normal. Give me one good reason why you won't marry me.'

'You know why,' she said, going against her better judgement by answering him.

'If I knew, do you think I'd keep asking?'

'Because of this!' she said, looking down at the fingers digging into her flesh hard enough to bruise. 'How can you love me when you enjoy hurting me so much?'

Les released his grip, and she wasn't sure if the shock on his face was feigned or not. 'I'm not like some men.

Christ, you're lucky I'd have you. No one else would.' He sneered as he looked her up and down. 'You've let yourself go, Cyn. You could do with asking that sexy mate of yours for some tips. Not that it'd do much good. You always were ugly.'

'Then go,' she said, not quite an order, but firmer than a plea.

He smiled. 'Not only ugly, but cold-hearted as well. Are you happy to pack your daughter off too? Because you know I'd have no trouble getting her. Is that what you want? To be a free agent?'

Les pushed her away with repulsion, and as he turned to refill his glass, Cynthia slipped out of the room. Her instincts told her to run, but she couldn't leave Jane. Nor could she go into the kitchen where there were too many sharp objects and hard surfaces. She climbed the stairs to her bedroom, and as she reached the landing, Les turned the music up to full volume.

Lying down on the bed, Cynthia pulled the pink candlewick bedspread around her. She could feel the thump of her heart as if it were a ticking timebomb, and all the while, Les was downstairs demolishing a bottle of rum. As long as she kept out of the way, there was a chance he would eventually pass out.

And then her dad's LP jumped. The needle was stuck in a groove, and the Everly Brothers repeated the same snatch of lyrics over and over until there was a loud crash.

'You've scratched it now!' he screamed.

'It was only dust,' Cynthia whispered, but it was too late. The damage was done.

She braced herself as she heard the stomp of boots coming

up the stairs. Les didn't bother turning the door handle, and Cynthia curled into the foetal position as the door frame splintered with a kick. Would she be punched or raped first? At least he didn't hit her face these days; that was something.

CHAPTER 20

Jane watched the refracted rays of morning light play across the bedroom ceiling after a night of fitful sleep. On the one hand, she could rest easy knowing her anxiety about Evan hadn't been the product of an irrational mind after all, but that meant her concerns for Ashleigh's safety were real too.

She wasn't sure what had been more disturbing to witness; a young woman's attempts to defend herself with clods of earth, or Evan's cold and controlled response. Jane had stayed up long enough to see the lights across the way go off without the dark silhouette of Evan appearing in any of the windows, but there was no way of knowing how long he would stay away. Whatever his wife was being forced to endure, it wasn't over.

Angry that men like her dad still existed, Jane was determined to help, but there were limits to what she could do as a concerned neighbour. It made her wonder if May had felt the same with her mum. She had been on hand to offer support, but ultimately Cynthia had been the heroine of her own story, and the same could be true of Ashleigh, if only she could be persuaded to believe in herself.

Feeling a sense of purpose that had been missing for months, Jane hurried down for breakfast, before heading up to the attic where the blind had been left open like the lid of a watchful eye. It was just after ten, and she had a clear view into Ashleigh's bedroom. The bed was empty and unmade. The kitchen was empty too, and the mess in the garden had been cleared up. Would the memory be swept away as easily?

Jane regretted not videoing the skirmish on her phone to show Ashleigh. A view of the relationship from another angle might have helped her neighbour recognize how toxic it had become. Or did she know that already? What if yesterday had been the final showdown?

Jane remembered the day Cynthia had decided enough was enough. Eight-year-old Jane had been sobbing into her cup of cocoa as she watched her mum scooping up piles of her dad's clothes and frantically shoving them into the red tartan suitcase open on her parents' bed. The matted blood in her mum's hair was proof, if it were needed, that it had taken immense courage for her to make her stand. When Cynthia had told her daughter that they weren't going to be afraid any more, her words had been the kiss that had made everything better.

An old ache, starting in Jane's arm and running down her back, eventually forced her away from the window. Seated at her desk, she pushed against the chair's backrest and straightened one stiffened vertebra at a time. She may not have evidence from the latest fight, but she had captured

146

other images of Evan and his handiwork. There had to be something she could use.

Jane began flicking through the photos taken in March and worked forward. It might be useful for Ashleigh to look back at how Evan had systematically destroyed their garden, then compare it with how he treated her the same way, but when Jane reviewed the images taken after the tree had been hacked down, she realized she could widen her search for incriminating evidence. The lower part of the house was visible now, and she zoomed in on each photo for a better look through her neighbours' windows.

The living room blinds remained steadfastly closed, but the kitchen gave the occasional glimpse of activity. In one, a silver plant pot had appeared on the windowsill, progressing to another where there was the impression of green shoots poking out from it, and then a pop of pink blossom. It was a hyacinth, but by the time May's cherry tree was heavy with blossom, the silver plant pot lay broken on the patio, the bulb exposed and the plant decaying.

The next photo to grab Jane's attention was taken at the beginning of May, a week before she had unwittingly taken the snap of Evan. The camera lens had caught both her neighbours this time, and they were in the kitchen. The day had been dull, and the spotlights were on to illuminate Ashleigh and Evan in what was obviously another intimate moment that Jane would rather not see. The couple were visible from the waist up, and Evan was bare chested. Ashleigh was thankfully clothed and had her back to the window. Her hand was raised, possibly resting on Evan's chest, although it was difficult to tell what she was doing from that particular angle.

In a flush of fresh embarrassment, Jane flicked quickly to the next photo, which was the one where the flash had gone off accidentally. She stared through her ghostly reflection caught in the window as if she could still see the house beyond with the couple standing so close together. She forgot to blink. Something was off.

Forcing herself to return to the image that had mortified her moments earlier, Jane zoomed in until the back of Ashleigh's head was nothing more than a jumble of pixels, then zoomed out again. She frowned at the straight line Ashleigh's blonde hair cut across her shoulder blades.

When Jane had visited her neighbour some four weeks after this photo was taken, Ashleigh's hair had been halfway down her back. It was possible she used hair extensions, but hadn't Ashleigh said it had always been long? The woman in the photograph had shoulder-length hair. It couldn't be Ashleigh, but whoever she was, her pose suggested she was as comfortable around a semi-naked – or God forbid, completely naked – Evan as any lover might be. Jane groaned inwardly. He was having an affair, and while this might be enough to persuade Ashleigh to end her marriage, what about the poor victim he was lining up to take her place? Were there now two women to worry about?

Zooming out of the photo, Jane's gaze was drawn to the empty flowerbed where Evan would be digging a long, narrow trench within days. What had he buried there? And perhaps more importantly, what became of this unidentified woman?

CHAPTER 21

Ashleigh was sprawled across the new swing seat, feet dangling over the edge, one arm resting against her aching forehead, and her phone clutched to her chest. It wasn't nearly as warm as it had been at the weekend. The air felt oppressive, and she couldn't quite catch her breath. She could do with a glass of water. A couple of paracetamols would help too, but they hadn't been waiting for her when she had peeled open her eyes that morning. She didn't know where Evan had spent the night, but it hadn't been with her.

Gripping her phone so tightly her knuckles hurt, Ashleigh willed it to vibrate with an incoming call, or the beep of a message. She pulled up her sunglasses and squinted at the screen as if force of will could conjure up just one new notification in the two minutes since she had last checked. Nothing.

She had sent Evan a flurry of texts after he had stormed off and had continued to send them well into the night, each one more desperate than the last. Some she couldn't remember sending, but all had gone unanswered.

I'm so sorry. Please come home.

We can work this out.

I don't know what I've done wrong.

Please forgive me.

Where are you?

Who are you with?

Who is she?

There were messages sent via WhatsApp that mirrored her texts, but none were marked with a double tick to show they had been opened and read. And when she had checked Messenger before dawn, it showed Evan as being active four hours earlier, which meant he had been online while she tossed and turned in her sleep. He would know how desperate she was to hear from him, and yet he had remained silent. His cruelty knew no bounds.

Feeling her isolation more acutely than ever before, Ashleigh considered who else she could reach out to. She hadn't spoken to Rose for weeks, nor did she want to, which only left Jess, who would see Evan's departure as good news. Her friend couldn't imagine a love so all-consuming that it ripped a hole in Ashleigh's chest every time she and Evan were apart.

It wasn't healthy, Ashleigh knew that, but if she could flick a switch and turn off her feelings, she wasn't sure she would. She had known Evan since she was a teenager. He had been her rock at a time when the foundations of her life had been disintegrating. Her father's sins were a burden that Evan had helped her shoulder. She was nothing without him. And he knew it.

Ashleigh rose unsteadily to her feet. She had tidied up the mess she had made in the garden as best she could, but she couldn't undo everything. Her shoulders still hurt after Evan had shoved her violently against the living room wall and pinned her there. She wore the same denim shorts as yesterday, and her T-shirt had soil marks that matched the colour of her bruises. The weekend wasn't supposed to have ended like this.

When she had got up early on Sunday, she had been looking forward to helping Evan in the garden. They had spent a lovely day on Saturday, going to the garden centre to buy the swing seat and pick up some plant food for the seedlings in the trough. They were looking forward to eating some home-grown greens in the coming months, but nothing in their garden was destined to thrive, and it was all her fault.

She should never have complained when Evan said he was nipping out for a quick game with his football mates – even though the season had ended. 'Don't make a big deal out of this, Ash,' he had told her when she tried to protest. 'Didn't we agree how important it is to keep separate interests?'

He had made it sound like she was the problem. Perhaps she was. She could have admitted that she had phoned in sick rather than work her weekend shift just so they could be together. She couldn't see the point in spending their free time separately. Unlike Evan, she didn't have other 'interests'. All she could do was let her anxiety build as she waited for her husband to tire of whoever he was with. That was why she had sneaked out to the off-licence to buy three half-bottles of vodka, figuring they would be easier to hide. But she couldn't hide the fact that she had drunk one of them when Evan arrived home far earlier than she had expected.

Vodka gave her the worst hangovers, and Ashleigh's head swam as she stumbled towards the house. She needed a caffeine fix, but she paused at the kitchen door. This was where Evan had been standing when he pointed up to their neighbour watching them from her attic window. 'You're not fooling anyone, Ash. People can see you're the crazy one,' he had said. What did Jane think of her now?

As Ashleigh made herself a coffee, she felt only slightly guilty that she had replaced the decaf in the decanter with proper stuff unbeknownst to Evan. Not that he was around to drink it any more. Except he had to come home eventually, she told herself. It wasn't as if he had packed his bags, having only grabbed his work clothes from the dryer before storming off. That had to be a good sign. Didn't it?

She reached for her phone, and gasped when she saw that Evan had read her WhatsApp messages. He could be staring at the screen right now, and this was the chance she so desperately needed to get his attention. But what to say? Her brain was fuggy, and she didn't know what pleas or promises would make him come home.

Deciding a picture was better than a thousand words, Ashleigh reversed the camera to take a selfie, but there wasn't a filter yet invented that would make her look presentable. That wasn't necessarily a bad thing. Showing her vulnerability might speak to Evan's more sensitive side, if it still existed. But what if Evan wasn't alone? He always said she was being ridiculous whenever she accused him of sleeping around, but he had slept in someone else's bed last night. She didn't want some other woman seeing the photo and laughing at her. She needed to be more creative.

After fishing out two empty vodka bottles from the recycling bin – the one she had drunk before Evan came home, and the one she had downed afterwards – Ashleigh went upstairs to retrieve the last one hidden behind a box of tampons. Working quickly, she poured its contents down the kitchen sink so that she had three empty bottles with their necks pointed at the plughole. This was the photo that would get the reaction she was after, and she posted it on Instagram rather than direct to Evan so that he would realize she was serious this time. Not that Ashleigh considered this the problem that needed solving in their marriage, but if it gave Evan the sense of control he needed over her, so be it.

By the time she had finished her coffee, there were plenty of responses to the photo. She laughed when she saw Jess's.

OMG why didn't you give it to me!!! Only joking. Well done honey.

Others, who weren't in Ashleigh's circle of trust, appeared supportive, but their comments were thinly disguised fishing expeditions for more details. They assumed her drinking problem had been passed on like a family curse. It was what Rose thought, and Ashleigh was surprised her sister hadn't left a comment, even though she had liked the post. And then her phone rang.

'Well done you,' Rose said by way of a greeting.

'Don't say it like that.'

'Like what?'

'Like you don't believe I can keep it up,' said Ashleigh, pouting.

'Maybe I know why you've done it.'

'Which is?'

'For Evan.'

'This isn't about anyone else. It's about me,' Ashleigh said, stealing the sentiment Rose had used in the early days of her own sobriety.

Rose had given up alcohol soon after humiliating her boyfriend at her sister's wedding, and when that failed to win him back, she had pretended being single was her choice. Ashleigh's situation was completely different, as was her relationship with alcohol. She only ever drank when she was anxious, even if she did tend to carry on until she was numb. The anxiety was the problem, but she could see how it might look.

'And what does Evan think about it?' asked Rose.

'He's really proud of me,' Ashleigh said, because she knew he would be.

'Are you sure about that?'

Ashleigh's jaw tightened. 'You've spoken to him, haven't you?'

'Let's just say, I can't imagine there was much vodka left in those bottles when you emptied them,' Rose said with more than a hint of smugness. As if sensing Ashleigh's finger itching to cut the call, she added quickly, 'Look, I don't want us to fall out again. I'm glad you're answering my calls – finally. Why did you answer?'

Ashleigh could ask herself the same thing. It didn't seem to matter how badly Evan treated her, Rose only had to hear the mention of alcohol and she pushed the blame onto Ashleigh, which was what had happened when Ashleigh had left Evan back in May. It was almost as if Rose was praying for the day her sister would replace her as the latest fuck-up in their family tree.

154

There was only one reason Ashleigh had answered the phone. Rose had Evan's ear.

'Maybe I do need to take a long, hard look at myself,' Ashleigh said. She lifted an arm and examined the latest bruises, only to squeeze her eyes shut. She hated that small voice that asked why she was humiliating herself like this.

'If you're serious about getting sober, then you're going to need professional help to sort your head out,' Rose said.

'What, like a psychiatrist?' Ashleigh asked. She was laughing, but she was panicking too. What had Evan been filling her sister's head with?

'Why not? Or some kind of therapy at least. We saw our dad kill someone, Ash. Shit like that takes a lot of processing.'

Ashleigh had been fifteen, and Rose thirteen at the time. They had been dozing in the back of the car, and had felt rather than seen the impact. 'It was an accident,' she said.

'He was drunk.'

'And you should know better than anyone that alcoholism is a disease.'

'I also know how important it is to take responsibility for your own actions,' replied Rose. 'It took me a long time to see that, but I came through the other side, and you can too. But you have to mean it this time, Sis.'

Ashleigh sniffed. All she wanted was for Rose to tell Evan to come home. 'I do mean it,' she said. 'This isn't Evan giving me ultimatums. This is my choice. I'm ready.'

'Good,' Rose said. 'And for the record, I am proud of you for getting to this point.'

Ashleigh could sense her sister making plans for them to attend AA meetings together, and cut off the invitation before it had passed her sister's lips. 'So will you talk to Evan for me? Tell him I'm sorry about yesterday. Tell him it won't happen again.'

A long sigh hissed down the line, like a snake in the grass. 'He's a broken man, Ash.'

Heat bloomed in Ashleigh's cheeks. 'So why am I the one with the bruises?'

'I think we both know why.' There was a pause that neither sister was quick to fill. 'Your relationship is bad for you both,' Rose conceded, 'but this is the first day of the rest of your life. It can be a lonely path sometimes, but you'll always have me. Let go of Evan. Make the break for both of you.'

'What?' Ashleigh said, the disbelief sharpening her voice. 'But I need Evan. I'm not doing it otherwise. What would be the point?'

'I thought the point was that you were doing it for yourself.'

'Oh, go away, Rose.'

As Ashleigh hung up, she was shocked by how much she needed a drink, and it took all of her willpower not to root out the empty vodka bottles for whatever dregs were left. She leant over the sink and stroked a finger across the gleaming stainless steel before bringing it to her lips. Her tongue reacted to the warmth of the alcohol, and her mouth filled with saliva. She took a step closer to the recycling bin, but was stopped by an alert on her phone.

It was a message from Evan. He had booked the afternoon off work and was on his way home.

CHAPTER 22

Jane had her phone pressed to her ear as she left the house. 'I need some advice.'

'Ooh, please say this is about downsizing,' Sheena replied. 'Those apartments I mentioned are still available. They're not too small, the ground-floor properties have gardens, and they're pet-friendly, I've checked.'

'What are the neighbours like?' Jane muttered.

'There are no wife beaters at least,' Sheena said, then gasped. 'Oh God, there I go saying something stupid again. Sorry.'

'It's fine,' said Jane as Benji led them out of the cul-de-sac.

As they reached the end of the road, the dog attempted to pull her around the corner, but Jane crossed the lane rather than go past the all-too-familiar row of townhouses. She needed to create some distance to check her perspective. She didn't want to make any rash assumptions this time.

'Have you heard from your mum?' she asked.

'Repeatedly; in fact, I've not long put the phone down with her. It sounds like Ashleigh and Evan had a right ding-dong yesterday. Is that what you wanted to talk about?' asked Sheena, her reply almost lost amongst other voices, and the beep of a card machine.

'Sorry, are you busy? Should I go?'

'Nonsense,' Sheena said. 'Give me one minute.'

Jane trudged up a steep incline as she waited for her friend to find somewhere quieter. She already regretted not taking the shorter route to the Arno. It was becoming more and more difficult to let Ashleigh out of her sight.

'There, that's better,' Sheena said once the background noises had diminished.

'Ashleigh had to fend him off with a garden fork,' said Jane, immediately picking up where they had left off. 'She was terrified.'

'It's beyond me why she went back to him in the first place.'

'I'm more worried about what he was up to while she was away.'

'Such as?' Sheena asked.

Jane inhaled deeply. 'I was looking back at my photos again this morning, and it turns out the snap of Evan leaning on his spade wasn't the first picture I'd taken of him. There's another one *before* he started digging that bloody hole.'

'Ooh, you mean the grave,' Sheena said, putting on a spooky voice. When Jane didn't respond, she added, 'Sorry, me being insensitive again, but you will look back and laugh at it one day.'

'I don't know if I can.'

'So tell me about this photo,' Sheena said to appease her friend.

'It's another shot taken from the attic window, and you can see straight into their kitchen. I hadn't registered the two figures before. It wasn't as if they were fighting. Far from it.'

'Good grief, this isn't another X-rated episode, is it? You could end up with a reputation – and a restraining order.'

'Which is why I'm wondering what to do next,' Jane replied. 'It isn't X-rated, but it is intimate. Evan is bare chested, and the woman he's standing with is close enough to touch.'

'Eurgh, can't you just delete it?' said Sheena, then quickly added, 'Hold on, why did you say "a woman"? Isn't it Ashleigh?'

'It's hard to tell because she has her back to the camera. She is blonde, but her hair is much too short. I don't think it is Ashleigh. Actually, I'm sure it isn't,' Jane said, firming her conviction. 'Whoever she was, Evan was cosying up with her shortly before Ashleigh left him.'

'It could be *why* she left,' Sheena said, reassuringly jumping to the same conclusion that Jane had reached. 'Did the other woman visit again while Ashleigh was away?'

'It's not like I have a spy cam trained on their house,' said Jane, although the thought had crossed her mind more recently. It would be easy enough to set up, but even she couldn't justify that level of intrusiveness. Not that she wasn't invading their privacy already, but her surveillance over the last twenty-four hours had been motivated by genuine concern.

She had spotted Ashleigh in the garden earlier looking lost and broken, and most recently in the bedroom. The bed had been made and she was blow-drying her hair, which Jane hoped was a sign that she was getting on with her life. But what about the mystery woman? What if she hadn't managed to escape Evan's brutality? Could Jane have imagined the wrong woman lying in the grave he had dug? If only she had taken more interest in her neighbours before Evan covered his tracks.

'I stopped taking photos from upstairs after my camera was stolen,' she continued. 'I was too self-conscious to even use my phone. Evan knows I'm watching now.' She shuddered at the memory of him pointing up at her the evening before.

'Your camera!' exclaimed her friend. 'Oh, my God, he knew you were taking photos, and must have been worried you'd snapped him with the blonde! That's why he took it.'

'I don't know . . .' Jane stopped. Evan could have noticed the flash from her attic window when it went off accidentally, then put two and two together the following week when he caught her with her camera. 'You really think that's why he took it?'

'You're the one who's convinced it was him, and this is as good a motive as any.'

'Your theory does make more sense,' Jane admitted as she reached the park and headed for the rose garden.

'Why, what was yours?'

Jane breathed in the sweet scent of roses on the breeze. The early bloomers added a splash of colour to banish her dark thoughts. It had been ridiculous to think Evan had murdered his mistress and buried her body in the garden. It wasn't as if there had been any reports of a missing woman in the local news, or at least not on any of the online sites Jane had been scouring.

'I have a darker imagination than you, obviously, but I think you're right,' she replied, pinching the bridge of her nose. 'And with any luck, he'll move on, and Ashleigh can bid him good riddance. It's the other woman you have to feel sorry for.'

'Hmm.'

'What does that mean? Do you know something?'

'You know I said I was on the phone to Mum?' Sheena began. 'Well, while we were talking, she suddenly says, "He's back!" She must have had her nose pressed against the front window.'

Jane's heart sank. 'Evan came home? When?'

'Maybe an hour ago? With any luck, he's just picking up his stuff.' Sheena paused, and Jane heard her sucking in her breath. 'I'm getting as bad as you and Mum. Can we just forget about them? Honestly, Jane, isn't this another good reason for looking for somewhere else to live?'

'She can't take him back,' Jane whispered, too preoccupied with the image of Ashleigh getting ready in her bedroom to pay attention to Sheena's questions. Picking up her pace, she had the exit from the Arno in her sights. 'Men like that don't stop until they've chipped away their victim's identity, until they can't remember who they used to be. I can't stand by and let that happen to Ashleigh. She needs to know what he's been up to.'

'I know why you're doing this,' Sheena said as if she could see the direction Jane was taking. 'After what you told me about Les, it's hardly surprising that the lines have blurred between the present and the past. You're angry with your dad – and not just for you, but on behalf of your mum. He did what he did without consequence, and you can see the same thing happening here, but this isn't your battle, lovely.'

'It feels like my battle,' Jane said, choking on her words.

'I know it does, but it's really not.'

CHAPTER 23

Jane raced into the house, leaving poor Benji with his leash trailing as he followed her up the stairs. Almost two hours had passed since she had seen Ashleigh blow-drying her hair. Had she been making an effort because she knew Evan was coming home? Was she back under his thrall? Jane didn't stop moving until her hand slammed against the attic window.

The Jarvises' kitchen and bedroom were deserted, as was the garden, and the living room blinds were motionless, giving nothing away as always. Jane focused again on the upper window. Earlier, the angle of the vertical slats had provided only a composite image of Ashleigh at her dressing table, but Jane's current view was much clearer, revealing a crumpled but otherwise empty bed in an empty room. The tableau reminded her of the evening she had seen more of the Jarvises than she had wanted, but that wasn't what made her suddenly gasp. The blinds had not been opened wider, they were missing. Jane could see the headrail listing at an angle with one end still attached to the frame.

The slats were a tangled mess; evidence that Ashleigh had resisted Evan after all.

Turning on her heels, Jane almost tripped over Benji's leash. She unhooked it from his harness and was on the move again, thundering down the stairs. 'I won't be long,' she called out to the dog before slamming the door behind her.

Jane broke into a jog as she left the cul-de-sac and made two left turns. She checked the cars parked along the road as she approached the row of townhouses. Evan's wasn't one of them, but Ashleigh's was still there. Jane felt sick to her stomach as she pulled open the wrought-iron gate and rapped on the door. A net curtain twitched and a moment later, the door opened.

'Hello, love,' said May.

Jane pressed a hand to the stitch in her side. 'Sorry, have you got a minute?'

'I've got as much time as you'd like,' May said. Her rheumy eyes sparkled when she added, 'That was a bit of excitement yesterday, wasn't it?'

'Excitement I could do without.' Jane glanced towards their neighbour's door and wished she'd had the courage to knock there first, but if Evan wasn't at work, he might still be close. 'Can I come in?'

May led the way through to the kitchen at the back of the house. The fitted units looked dated but were far removed from the Formica cabinets Jane recalled from her childhood. The smells of fried food and cigarette smoke, however, were reassuringly familiar. May put the kettle on and unhooked two mugs from a mug tree.

'I spoke to your Sheena before. She said you'd seen Evan coming home.'

'Those two don't know when to call it quits.'

'I'm so worried about her, May.'

'I'd love to tell you it'll sort itself out, but I have a horrible feeling it's going to get worse before it gets better,' May said. 'But you shouldn't get yourself worked up over it. That girl can hold her own. I didn't rate his chances when she picked up that garden fork, did you?'

May spoke loudly even though the Jarvises lived on the other side of the party wall. It didn't help that the door was ajar too, raising the risk of being overheard, and Jane resisted the urge to close and lock it for good measure.

'His car isn't outside,' she said.

'They went out.'

'Both of them?' Jane asked, relieved that Evan hadn't left his wife battered and bleeding on the bathroom floor. There were countless other scenarios Jane had conjured too, but none included the couple going out together. Unless he was taking her to the hospital? 'Did you see Ashleigh? Did she seem OK to you?'

'If you hadn't seen them at each other's throats yesterday, you'd think they were love's young dream.'

Jane shook her head. She was at a loss to explain what hold Evan must have over Ashleigh for her to tolerate his cruelty, but it needed to be broken. 'I'm wondering if all this trouble is because Ashleigh found out he's been up to no good. Did you ever notice another woman visiting while she was out?'

'An affair?' May asked. 'No, I can't see it. And don't go building your hopes up that she'd be any better off if he left. The cycle would only start again with the next bloke. Some people go looking for trouble.'

Unsettled by May's lack of compassion, Jane said, 'Maybe she thinks the abuse is normal. Did you know her dad was an alcoholic?' She wasn't going to explain how she knew. If May didn't know of the connection between her neighbour and the infamous Robert Martindale, Jane could at least spare Ashleigh that particular shame.

'I suppose it makes sense,' May said as she finished making two teas. 'Sugar?'

'No thanks,' Jane said, taking the mug. She was listening out for the first sign of Ashleigh's return next door, and jumped when May slammed a cupboard door.

'Sorry, this blinking thing won't shut properly,' said May. 'Chris said he'd fix it, but that was months ago. I think I frighten him. I must be the mother-in-law from hell.'

'I hear he adores you.'

'Ah, maybe that's the problem,' she said, tucking her short, sleek hair behind her ear. There was a twinkle of wickedness in her eyes. 'He can't trust himself to be alone with me. It was always the way.'

'Do you want me to have a go at fixing it?'

Jane could see that there was more than one cupboard door hanging crooked. She pulled open the nearest to examine the problem, and as she did so, the door dropped half an inch and the hinges creaked.

'Ah, don't worry. Our Steven can do it next time he's down from Glasgow,' May said of her son. 'He'd probably do a better job than Chris anyway.'

'Better than me?'

With a shrug, May knew she had lost the argument. 'Are you sure you wouldn't mind?'

166

'Not at all. The carcasses look relatively solid except where the screws have eaten away at the MDF. Even if I have to reposition the hinges, it won't take long.'

May's eyes brimmed with affection. 'You remind me so much of your mum.'

'Sometimes it feels like I'm picking up where she left off,' Jane replied. 'I wonder what she would have made of the things going on next door? Do you think she had any inkling there was something wrong?'

'I doubt it. Things were never as bad as they are now.'

Jane sipped her tea. 'I wish Mum was here now to talk some sense into Ashleigh.'

'I wish she was here too,' May said softly. 'Now she was someone who knew how to break free from the cycle of abuse.'

'And you helped her pick up the pieces,' Jane said as they stumbled onto a subject that had been buried for fifty years. 'You knew what went on, didn't you?'

'Oh, I knew enough, although your mum hid more than I could possibly imagine.'

'From the both of us,' added Jane. The stitch in her side had moved to an ache in her heart. 'Do you think she was happy, May?' Despite the good times, it was her mum's lingering death that prevailed in Jane's memory. Cynthia had cried out in terror, day and night. 'I know that's what Mum wanted us to believe, but I can't help thinking she just learnt to hide how scared she was.'

'Scared of what?'

'Lesley Morgan.'

May bristled at the mention of his name. 'I'll admit that man taught Cynthia to pretend things were fine when they

167

weren't, but you can't fake the good times we had once he was gone,' she said, staring at Jane intently. 'She was happy, love. And she wouldn't want to see you worrying about her so.'

'I'm fine, May.'

'Now who's pretending?' she said. 'I know you've been through the mill lately, and not everything in life can be fixed as easily as my skew-whiff cupboards, but if Cynthia were here, she'd tell you to trust your instincts. She'd say she's given you the shoes, but they're on your feet.'

'She would,' Jane said with a nod. It had been one of her mum's favourite sayings.

'And she'd say dance to your own tune.' May was on a roll.

'I don't remember that bit,' Jane said, smiling.

'OK, fine, I've been known to dish out my own gems of wisdom now and again,' May said, giving Jane her hardest stare. 'And my advice to you is, don't worry about getting the steps wrong once in a while, enjoy the dance. You only get one song, and you don't know when it's going to end.'

As she held her smile, tears glistened in May's eyes; a reminder that even those who lived seemingly happy lives had suffered bumps in the road too.

'You miss Billy, don't you?' asked Jane.

'It never crossed my mind that we wouldn't grow old together,' May admitted. She turned away and began mopping up the non-existent drips she had made pouring the tea. Clearing her throat, she added, 'Of course, if he was still here, I'd be complaining about him getting under my feet, or nagging him about fixing these cupboards. Not that he would have been any better at it than me, which is why I was always so blessed to have your mum taking charge of stuff like that.'

'And it would be my honour to carry on the good work,' Jane said. 'I could come back tomorrow if you like?'

'Only if it's no trouble.'

'It's not,' Jane said, grateful for an alternative to standing guard at the attic window.

After they had finished their tea, Jane made sure they swapped phone numbers, which meant no more games of charades, or using Sheena as their go-between. May was showing Jane out when they heard the creak of a wrought-iron gate, followed by the thump of a front door knocking against the party wall. There followed the sound of laughter, and May put her finger to her lips before standing on tiptoe to look through the peephole.

'They're back,' she whispered. 'I can see his car. Oh, wait, he's taking something out of the boot. Looks like a sack. No, it's a bag of compost. And she's got trays of plants.' May turned back to Jane and pulled a face. 'God knows what state the garden will be in when that pair have finished. They're not exactly blessed with green thumbs.'

'I don't understand how they can go from one extreme to the other.'

May came over to squeeze Jane's arm. 'Let them make their own mistakes. You're best staying out of it.'

'You didn't,' Jane reminded her.

'That was different.'

'How?'

May set her jaw. 'It just was,' she said. 'Cynthia was my best friend. I couldn't have stood back even if I'd tried.'

Jane couldn't tell May that she felt the same about a

169

practical stranger. Her mum had gone to great lengths to protect her daughter, and Jane simply wanted to pay it forward. She had to help, whether Ashleigh thought she needed it or not.

CHAPTER 24

1974

'Look what I found,' May said, pulling four tapered candles from her shopping bag and handing them to Cynthia. 'Who would have thought these would be top of everyone's shopping list in this day and age?'

'How much do I owe you?' asked Cynthia, inviting her friend inside so she could fetch her purse from the kitchen.

'Nothing. It's the least I can do since I'm using your stove all the time.'

May's electric cooker was six months old, but not much use during a power cut. The government had brought in a three-day week to conserve depleted coal reserves as a result of the oil crisis, and there were regular power outages. Candlelight had started out as a novelty, but wasn't much fun when it was your only source of warmth as well as light during the cold winter nights. What made matters worse, candles were selling out faster than shopkeepers could stock the shelves. Cynthia didn't consider herself lucky by any measure, but having a gas cooker in 1974 was a boon.

'You do more than enough for me,' she told May, almost embarrassed to admit it. As well as being an emotional crutch, May had been helping Cynthia with childcare after Mrs Lisman followed her family to West Germany where her son was stationed. So much for Henry Simpkin raising his daughter to be self-sufficient.

'The country can't go on like this much longer,' May said as she unbuttoned her calf-length sheepskin coat with its fleece trim. Unsurprisingly, the skirt beneath was as short as ever. May was a follower of fashion, but it was going to take her a while to fully embrace the trend for longer hemlines.

Cynthia, by contrast, cared very little about current styles. Her flared jeans were both practical and unlikely to draw attention from Les. 'It's amazing what you can get used to,' she said as she filled the kettle.

'At least Les is still able to work,' May replied, not picking up on the change of tone. 'It drives me crazy having Billy under my feet all day. God knows what it'll be like when he retires.' She laughed at whatever image she saw of them in the future. 'Can you imagine us as pensioners?'

'If we're still around.'

May threw her coat over a chair and walked across to Cynthia. Gently, she tucked a loose tress behind her friend's ear to expose a pale but unblemished face. The only bruising was visible just above her collarbone.

'Has he been at it again?'

Pulling away, Cynthia busied herself making the tea. She couldn't look May in the eye when she said, 'Maybe I should marry him. It might stop him being so angry all of the time.'

'You know he'll only find another excuse to take it out on you.'

Cynthia had once told May as much, but she no longer recognized herself as the woman who had said it. She hadn't anticipated that Les would turn out to be just as stubborn as she was.

'I lost out on another repair job yesterday,' she said. 'I'd picked it up as a favour for another plumber, but when I turned up at Iris Rigby's, she refused to let a ne'er-do-well like me in the house. She said it wasn't personal, but she was worried about her reputation. I stood on her doorstep like a fool.'

'The cow,' May said in disgust. 'She always was a bit pass-remarkable if you ask me, but that's no reason to give in now, Cyn. To hell with the Iris Rigbys of this world. She's half the mother you are, and you'd be twice as good if you didn't have Les pulling you down. Isn't it time you kicked him out? I'm happy to help you pack his bags.'

'I can't,' Cynthia said, handing May her tea.

'This is your house, damn it. And if you need extra muscle, our Billy knows someone who can rough him up for you. They'd be happy to give him a taste of his own medicine, no questions asked.'

Hiring muscle was such an alien concept that it made Cynthia smile. 'I'll bear it in mind,' she said. 'Now can we change the subject? What happened on *Coronation Street* last night?'

'Still not got your telly fixed then?'

Les had put his foot through the TV a couple of weeks

173

earlier. It was a rental from Visionhire, and Cynthia was too embarrassed to go back to the shop. It wasn't the first one he'd broken.

May was in the midst of telling Cynthia the latest dramatic storyline when they heard the front door thump open. Les stepped into the kitchen a moment later.

'They've bloody well sent me home. I might be off for a while.'

'I thought hospitals were exempt from the restrictions,' said May.

Les took a second or two to appraise their neighbour. His eyes were fixed on May's chest when he said, 'You here again, Trouble?'

'She was dropping off some candles.'

May set down her half-empty cup. 'And now I must be off. Billy's taken the girls to the park, and they'll be starving when they get back.'

'Jane shouldn't spend so much time over at yours,' Les said. 'We don't want to take advantage.'

'It's no bother,' May replied, giving Les a wide berth as she picked up her coat.

After Cynthia saw her friend to the door, she returned to the kitchen where Les was pouring tea from the pot. He was whistling to himself, which she hoped meant his mood wasn't as sour as his breath. He had been steaming drunk the night before and had gone into work late, and not particularly sober.

'When do you think you'll be back at work?'

Les spun around. 'What's with the twenty questions? Don't you believe me?'

'Of course I believe you,' she replied, her heart sinking along with any hope of getting to the truth.

It wouldn't be the first time his drinking had cost Les his job. He had let slip that his decision to leave the merchant navy hadn't been entirely by choice. If he had been fired again, Cynthia didn't know how they were going to cope. It wasn't that she relied on his wage, but if he didn't have money of his own to spend, he would use hers.

'Instead of checking up on me,' Les said, 'maybe you should pay more attention to what your daughter's up to.'

Cynthia didn't reply. She didn't have the strength for another argument.

'We have no way of knowing what goes on over there,' Les continued. 'I don't trust that Billy; he spends way too much time with little girls if you ask me. And May still thinks she's a teenager. You can hear her playing music in the middle of the day. I mean, who listens to the Beatles these days?'

'I can go and get Jane if you like.'

Les leered at Cynthia as he slurped his tea. 'Leave her. If you want to make yourself useful, make me a bacon butty, I'm starving.'

Cynthia felt her legs tremble as Les came closer.

'I've been thinking,' he said. 'If I do get bored and leave, I might not bother fighting you for custody. I'll just tell social services how you pass Jane around the neighbours. She'll be taken into care before you know what's happening. I could probably have that Billy put away, too. Do you want to do that to your friend?'

Cynthia shook her head. She would rather take another beating than do that to May.

'Then you'd better keep me happy,' Les said with a smug smile.

175

CHAPTER 25

Before Jane set to work on May's kitchen cupboards, the polite thing to do was warn the neighbours about the noise.

'Hello,' Ashleigh said, peeking out from behind the half-open door.

'I hope I'm not disturbing you, but I saw your car,' Jane said, tipping her head towards the Ford Fiesta parked further down the road.

The frown forming on her neighbour's brow prodded Jane's conscience, and she broadened her smile by way of compensation. They didn't live on the same street, but of course she knew which car was Ashleigh's even though it was rarely parked outside her house because space on the lane was hotly fought over. It was the kind of thing any stalker worth their salt would have found out.

'I'm doing a bit of DIY for May,' Jane continued, raising the heavy Black and Decker drill in her hands, currently minus the drill bit. 'It could get quite noisy so I thought it best to let you know.'

'I'm sure it won't be a problem.'

Ashleigh went to close the door, but Jane carried on talking.

'The thing is, I know you saw me at the window the other evening—'

'It was something and nothing,' Ashleigh interjected.

'That might be so, but it was upsetting to watch, so goodness knows how you must have felt. Frightened, I imagine.'

Ashleigh bit her lip, then opened the door a little wider. Her smile was hesitant. 'You must have thought I was terrible, waving that garden fork around like a lunatic.'

'Not at all.'

Ashleigh relaxed her shoulders. 'Well, I can promise you it won't happen again. Everything's fine now.'

Jane's eye twitched. 'He's no good for you,' she said, giving up all pretence of having called to apologize for the DIY.

'Please, don't say that. I don't expect you to understand this, but I love Evan, faults and all, and I always will.'

'And does he love you in return?'

Ashleigh flinched. 'Of course he does. You just don't know him like I do.'

'I know it was no coincidence that the thief who broke into my house came from your garden.'

'Why can't you let that go?' asked Ashleigh, growing more agitated. 'You need to leave us alone.'

As Ashleigh began to close the door, Jane slapped her hand against it. She had spotted the bruising around her neighbour's wrists. 'I can't do that, Ashleigh, not after everything I've seen.'

Ashleigh's stare hardened. 'Then maybe you should keep your blinds closed.'

'I'm more interested in keeping my doors locked,' Jane replied. She would carry on talking until Ashleigh slammed the door in her face, and even then she would shout through the letterbox. Ashleigh needed to wake up to the fact that one day she might not be able to fight off her husband's attacks. 'Did you know it was only my laptop and camera that were stolen? I think it was because Evan spotted me taking photos from the attic.'

'So you *were* taking photos of us?'

Ashleigh's cheeks were pink, and Jane reciprocated with a blush of her own. 'No, I was taking photos of my garden. None include you, but there is one with your husband in the background that I think you should see,' she said. 'Here, let me show you.'

Tentatively, Jane withdrew her hand from the door and took her mobile from her pocket. Ashleigh watched without a word as Jane struggled to scroll through her photos whilst juggling the heavy drill.

'I've been updating Mum's garden,' Jane said to fill the silence as she searched for the incriminating photo. 'And that's why I was taking photos as I went along.'

'Your mum was always staring out of her windows too. The tree was in the way back then, but I could still see her in her bedroom. I did wave at her once, but she never waved back. I'm sure she was only looking at her garden too.'

Jane's hand faltered. 'I expect she was, but sometimes it's hard not to notice what goes on beyond our boundary lines.'

'Believe it or not, things were quieter back then. We were happy once,' Ashleigh said, then must have realized how it sounded, and quickly added, 'We're happy now.'

'I know you want to believe that, but I wonder if you'll feel the same when you see this.' Jane tapped her finger hard against the screen of her mobile to open the image of a semi-naked Evan with another woman. 'It was taken a week before my camera was stolen.'

'Then why do you still have it?' asked Ashleigh, her eyes narrowing with suspicion.

'I had everything backed up. Here, look.'

As Jane tried to hand over her phone, Ashleigh recoiled, so Jane had to balance the drill in the crook of her elbow and used both hands to zoom in to the image. Her voice softened as she held it up to her neighbour's face. 'I thought it was you at first. I presume Evan must know this woman quite well.'

It took Ashleigh a few seconds to absorb what Jane was showing her, and then the colour drained from her face. She took the phone in a shaking hand.

'I know it must be difficult when you're being bombarded with conflicting information,' Jane said. 'All I can say, Ashleigh, is that when the person you love and trust is feeding you a warped version of reality, you have to trust your instincts. What do you see?'

Ashleigh thrust the phone back at Jane, her face unreadable. 'I don't see anything. Evan often takes his T-shirt off if he's working in the garden.'

'Even on an overcast day?'

'Look, I don't know what kind of relationships you've had in the past,' Ashleigh replied icily, 'but I don't automatically

179

assume my husband is having an affair with every woman he's left alone with.'

Jane wouldn't be swayed. She didn't trust Evan to keep a single one of his wedding vows, and she suspected Ashleigh didn't either. 'When we spoke the other week, you said Evan was the only one for you, but you didn't sound nearly as certain about his commitment. I think when you look at that photo, you see the same thing that I do. And I never actually suggested an affair, but you did.'

'This is ridiculous,' Ashleigh said, showing some of her earlier grit. 'Haven't you got anything better to do?'

Jane felt the drill slipping from the crook of her arm and managed to catch it. She was losing Ashleigh too. 'I'm sorry if this is upsetting for you, but you'll never convince me that your husband hasn't got a secret to hide.'

Ashleigh had retreated back into the house, but Jane pushed on. If she couldn't reason with the younger woman, she would frighten her into action, and there was an old fear that Jane had never managed to free herself from completely.

'You need to ask Evan what he buried in the garden,' she said. 'And if I were you, I'd think about what could have happened to that woman in the photo.'

When Ashleigh's eyes widened, Jane wanted to believe it was because she finally understood why her nosey neighbour had broken every social convention to reach this point. But then Ashleigh released a short bark of a laugh.

'You still think there's a body buried in the garden, don't you?' she asked. Her jaw was clenched as she struggled to contain her anger. 'Please, you need to stop this, Jane. If you must know, the woman in the photo is my sister, and she's very much alive. Whatever's going on, it's not me with the problem. It's you. Just go away and leave us alone.'

Jane barely had time to blink before the door was slammed in her face.

CHAPTER 26

'We're going to the pub,' Sheena said, grabbing Jane by the elbow and steering her out of St Saviour's. 'And then you're going to tell me what's wrong.'

With their yoga mats held over their heads, they dodged a summer shower to reach the pub. Sheena left Jane to grab a table while she fetched their drinks.

'It's a wonder you didn't just bring over the bottle,' said Jane when her friend pressed a very large glass of white wine into her hand.

'There wasn't that much left in it to be honest,' Sheena said. She sipped her orange juice unenthusiastically as she watched Jane take a long, satisfying swig of wine. 'So?'

'I've fixed your mum's cupboards.'

'I know,' Sheena said, playing along. 'Which is why that first glass is compliments of Chris. He wants to know if he can keep you on a retainer.'

'I was happy to do it.'

'I know,' Sheena said again.

'It got me thinking about doing some kind of odd job

182

service for a living. It'd keep me out of trouble, and I have all the tools and equipment Mum left in the garage.' Aware that she really was turning into her mum, Jane stopped to take another gulp of wine. Her mum would be furious. She had always encouraged her daughter to live her own life, but what did she expect? It was because of Cynthia's secrets that Jane's options were limited. Stretching her neck to loosen the invisible shackles, Jane asked, 'Is there anything you need doing? I'm happy to be paid in wine.'

'I'll give it some thought,' said Sheena. She drummed her fingers on the table. 'So? What did she say?'

'Your mum?'

'You know who I mean.'

Jane shrank from her friend's piercing look. 'I showed her the photo. It turns out the mystery woman was her sister.'

'Oh dear,' Sheena said. 'I don't suppose Ashleigh was too happy about that.'

Jane could feel the wine buzz at the back of her head, its warmth spreading down her body and loosening the knot in her stomach. 'Well, it didn't stop her laughing at me.'

'Wow, that's a bit harsh.'

'Not if some mad woman knocks on your door to tell you she's still convinced your husband is a murderer, only now she's claiming it's his secret lover – who just so happens to be your sister – who's buried in the garden.'

'Oh,' Sheena said, keeping her mouth in an 'O' shape as she reappraised the situation. 'So after we talked about Evan stealing your camera to hide evidence of an affair, you took it one step further.'

'Or one step back. Maybe there is some innocent reason why Evan was half-clothed during a secret visit from his sister-in-law, but that doesn't mean he isn't guilty of something. He dug that hole for a reason,' Jane said, and then snapped her mouth shut. She had to stop with this obsession. It was driving her – and everyone else around her – crazy. 'I don't want to think about it any more.'

'So is that going to be an end to it?'

'It already is,' Jane said. 'When I got home, I went into every room that overlooked their garden and pulled down the blinds, even the one in Mum's bedroom. I can't help someone who doesn't want to be helped.'

'Especially someone who laughs in your face,' Sheena said with a scowl. 'She doesn't deserve your concern.'

Jane took a deep breath and released it with a sigh. 'I shouldn't have let myself get caught up in it all, but I thought it would help me understand what Mum went through. I've been left with a house full of memories that I can't make sense of because most of them aren't mine.'

Sheena wiped the condensation from the side of her glass. 'We all saw it differently. Take me. I thought we had to keep out of your dad's way because he didn't like kids. It never occurred to me that your mum was . . . that both of you were victims of domestic violence. I doubt I knew such a thing existed back then. If it helps, my memories of your house are of us playing pirates in the garden, getting ready to go clubbing, our first dates. *The good times.* They're all there too.'

'I know, but so much has been overshadowed by the bad stuff. Even after all these years, I can still remember that dread I used to feel when I reached home. I never knew what I was walking into when Dad was around.'

Sheena tensed. 'I've just remembered that fight we had. You were supposed to come to ours after school but stomped off home instead. You must have been so mad at me to actually want to go back,' she said, looking sheepish. 'And then you had that bloody accident falling down the stairs.'

'You mean when I broke my arm?' Jane asked as she reflexively bent her right elbow. It had been a greenstick fracture and she had worn a cast for what felt like months, but there had been no lasting damage. So why did she feel the pain now?

'I'm sorry we argued.'

'I can't imagine it was anything important,' Jane said, unable to recall the details of their fight. Most of her recollections about that night were a series of snapshots rather than one fluid memory, and the argument with Sheena had been so inconsequential that it hadn't been worth preserving.

'You've forgotten what it was about?' Sheena asked in mock horror.

Jane thought harder about the spat, and to her surprise, she found herself smiling.

'The Bay City Rollers!' they said simultaneously.

'You wanted to marry Woody, when obviously he was going to fall in love with me,' said Sheena.

'Rubbish, he was mine,' Jane replied. She tried to hold on to the spark of nostalgia, but her thoughts turned to what had come next. The light in her eyes dimmed. 'You shouldn't feel guilty about it.'

'But I did. I used up all my pocket money to buy you the "Shang-A-Lang" single, and a box of Matchsticks,'

Sheena said. 'I can remember being so worried because you were even quieter than usual in the days afterwards, and I didn't know if it was because of me, or because your dad left around that time.'

'He left the same night as my accident,' Jane said. Even after all these years, she was surprised how faithfully she kept to the script that her injury had been an accident.

Sheena's face fell as her innocent recollections were realigned with Jane's reality. 'Did your dad have something to do with it? Is that why he left?'

'Yes,' Jane said, liberating one of her family secrets. 'And if it makes you feel any better, me being in a mood after our fight had nothing to do with my fall. And there were no stairs involved.'

'No, that doesn't make me feel any better,' said Sheena. 'What did happen?'

Jane clenched her jaw. If she opened her mouth now, it wouldn't be words but sobs that escaped.

'It's OK,' Sheena said, noticing her friend's struggle. 'Have you ever spoken to anyone about it? And I mean properly.'

'I told Phil soon after I'd had Megan. He couldn't understand why I was such an anxious mother, and it took us both a while to realize I was only ever anxious when he was there. I didn't know how to trust him with our daughter.' She paused to recall the night she had told Phil about her dad's cruelty. She wasn't exactly sure what she had said, just that she had felt incredibly safe with Phil's arms around her. 'He was great about it,' she added wistfully, only to remember her husband's profile was now on a dating app. She was never going to feel that safe again, and it hurt more than she could bear.

'And why wouldn't he be understanding?' Sheena asked. 'Why wouldn't any of us? Becoming a parent would have been an especially difficult transition in your life, and losing your mum is another. If you ask me, there's a lot going on inside your head that you need to process. It's not healthy to keep it bottled up inside.'

'I suppose.'

Sheena waited, and when Jane refused to continue, she said, 'If you can't talk to me, why not try Phil again? It might help him realize that this isn't something that can be solved with an HRT prescription.'

Jane blinked. She would not cry. 'It's too messy. I don't want to involve him.'

'Shouldn't you let him decide that? He might surprise you.'

Jane shook her head. 'It's too late, even if I wanted to. He's back on the dating scene.'

'He's what? When?' Sheena asked, picking up her drink for a kick of wine, only to realize she was drinking orange juice. She set it down again in disappointment. 'Fine. Never mind Phil. You've still got me, and I'm going nowhere.'

Jane swallowed hard. The pressure building up inside her couldn't be contained forever. She needed to let someone else know that the monsters from her childhood were still there, and by looking away and pretending they didn't exist, she had allowed them to creep closer. 'I– I found something. Well, Phil did actually.'

Before she could continue, Sheena's phone pinged.

'Shit, sorry,' Sheena said. She didn't take her eyes off her friend as she reached for the phone lying face down on the table. Her eyes darted briefly to the screen, and her shoulders sagged. 'Bloody Jamie. I said I'd pick him up from the station. He's been on some training course all day. I'd ask Chris, but his car's in the garage.'

'It's fine. You should go.'

Jane put on a brave face that was well practised. She had come so close to telling Sheena about the secret she guarded up in the attic, and wasn't sure if she should be relieved or disappointed that they had been interrupted. For now, she was the only one condemned to lie awake at night wondering what might have happened if she had gone to May's that day instead of going straight home from school.

CHAPTER 27

1974

Cynthia parked her minivan out of view of the house to give herself a moment to prepare. She steepled her fingers as if in prayer, but her hands shook too much to hold the pose.

'You can do this,' she whispered.

Her words of encouragement fell on deaf ears, and half an hour later, the engine had grown cold. Spring was on its way but the days were still short, and the light was fading when she noticed a couple of boys race past her car. They were school friends of May's son, Steven, which meant he would be on his way home too, shepherding his little sister and her best friend. Jane always stopped off at May's to be told whether she was staying for tea or could go straight home. Today, May would tell her she had to stay there until seven o'clock, which should give Cynthia enough time to do what she should have done five years ago.

Allowing herself no more thinking time, Cynthia drove

the short distance home and parked up. For the first time in a long while, she hoped Les was in. She needed to get this over and done with and would deal with the consequences later.

The house was silent, but a strong smell of smoke alarmed her. She rushed into the kitchen to find a blackened chip pan lying in the sink with the cremated remains of chips floating in a pool of oily water. There were soot stains around the stove, and one of the gas rings had been left on. Cynthia turned it off and went in search of Les, as much a threat to their lives as any house fire.

Les lay comatose across the orange Dralon sofa, his head propped on an arm as ribbons of saliva drooled from his open mouth. How had she ever compared him to Robert Redford? Prodding his shoulder with the tip of her boot, she stepped back onto the purple rug as he attempted to swipe away the irritant without opening his eyes.

'Wake up, Les,' she said, and poked him again.

'Jesus Christ, will you stop it.'

Towering over him, Cynthia had the illusion of power, giving her the courage to persist. 'You need to wake up,' she said, then kicked him. It felt so good.

'What the f—' Les snapped his eyes open and made a grab for Cynthia's leg, but she was too quick. 'What's wrong with you? Have you gone mad?'

'You nearly burnt the house down – again.'

'Yeah, well, I didn't.'

As Les manoeuvred himself into a sitting position, there were creases on the side of his face. They would fade in minutes, unlike the nasty bruise around his swollen eye, which would take longer to heal.

'That must hurt,' she said.

Les touched his face, seemingly surprised by the tenderness around his eye. She didn't ask how he had got it, and wouldn't receive a straight answer if she did. Since losing his job, Les had been barred from every pub in the area for fighting, lewdness, or both. He made trouble wherever he went.

'Want to kiss it better?' he asked.

'No, I want you to leave.'

Les sat back and laughed. 'Ooh, I think she's jealous.'

'I'm asking you politely to pack your things and go,' Cynthia said, grateful that the adrenalin coursing through her veins had kept her voice level.

'And what if I say no?'

'I'll phone the police.'

'No, you won't,' he replied with annoying confidence. 'We both know it wouldn't just be me being hauled off. They'd take Jane away too.'

'I'm willing to take the risk.'

'Wow, really? Do you have any idea what happens to kids in care?' he asked. 'You won't recognize her by the time the system spits her out, assuming she'd ever want to see you again.'

Cynthia held his gaze. 'You're no longer welcome here, and I want you to leave.'

Les bared his teeth, his face turning puce. 'And walk away with nothing? Do you seriously think I'm going to do that, Cynthia? I gave up everything for you, you selfish bitch. Who else was there for you and your brat?'

'I was there!' she hit back. 'You didn't come back to save me, Les. I was quite happy saving myself, and if I did it once, I can do it again. I don't need you. I never did.'

Les looked at her askance. It was as if he actually believed he had been her hero. 'And what about me? Where do I go?'

'I don't care.'

'In that case I'll stay here,' he said, folding his arms.

'Fine, I'll pack for you.'

As she turned to leave, Cynthia could hear the springs on the sofa creak. Fear prickled her scalp as if she could sense his hand reaching for her. He grabbed a handful of her hair, and as he yanked her backwards, a fist smashed into the side of her face. Cynthia was falling, and when she landed on the rug, she turned onto her side and curled into a ball.

As the blows rained down, the pain became too much and Cynthia's mind blocked the messages her body was sending. She had known he would beat her, and the beating would be worse than any other, but it was going to be worth it. She would call the police, if her neighbours didn't do it first, and they would see what he had done. They wouldn't take Jane away. With any luck, they wouldn't even see her.

'Stupid bitch,' she heard Les mutter. He had exhausted himself and was back on the sofa. 'I think you've broken one of my toes.'

Cynthia could feel blood trickling from her ear as she turned onto her front. She raised herself up gingerly onto her hands and knees, and turned her face towards him. 'I want you to leave,' she said.

Les stopped rubbing his foot and cocked his head as if he didn't quite believe what he had heard. She was meant to have submitted by now. Doubt flickered across his face as he touched the bruising around his eye. He really was having a bad day.

Emboldened, Cynthia prepared to stand. She panted through the pain, and didn't realize immediately why Les had started smirking. And then she heard it too. The back door in the kitchen had opened and closed.

CHAPTER 28

While Evan was in the bathroom shaving, Ashleigh sneaked downstairs. She was filling his travel mug with coffee when he appeared, having already made sandwiches for his packed lunch.

'What have you done all this for?' he asked, unable to accept this small act of kindness without questioning Ashleigh's motives.

'Nothing,' she said as she came over to rest her hands on his chest. 'I just wanted to show you how much I love you.'

He kissed her forehead, and kept his mouth pressed against her skin. 'You're like an addiction, do you know that?'

Sensing he was about to pull away, Ashleigh gripped Evan's work fleece and hung on to him. He needed to say he loved her back, but instead he clamped his hands around her wrists. He held the power to snap bones, but she felt the soft pads on his thumbs stroking the bruises that were yellowing after their fight four days earlier.

'I love you too,' he said eventually.

Ashleigh stood on tiptoe, but before her lips could find his, Evan extracted himself.

'No, Ashleigh, I have to go to work.'

She didn't understand. He loved her one minute and pushed her away the next. He left her, and then he came back. He told her it was over, and then he was ripping her clothes off. That was what had happened when he came home on Monday. He had gone upstairs to pack his bags, knowing she would follow. He had ignored her as he shoved his things into a holdall, but in the next moment he was covering her sobs with his mouth, pinning her against the window where they became entangled in the blinds as he lifted up her dress and tore at her knickers.

At least he had stayed, she reminded herself. Evan claimed to have spent Sunday night in his car after their fight, which had immediately sounded suspicious. Where were all the friends he supposedly met up with for football twice a week? Admittedly, he no longer had his best mate, Reece, to watch his back. A few years ago, Reece had become a little too touchy feely with Ashleigh on a night out, and Evan had broken his nose. Ashleigh had also been given a lecture afterwards about being over-friendly, but back then, their arguments hadn't evolved into physical fights.

She liked to think that she was his addiction, but did she hold as much power over him as he would have her believe? What was it Jane had said the day before? 'When the person you love and trust is feeding you a warped version of reality, you have to trust your instincts. What do you see?' She saw someone who hadn't wanted to tell

195

her where he had actually spent the night. Evan would call that paranoia.

Not wanting to sour the moment, Ashleigh pushed all thoughts of the photo her neighbour had shown her out of her mind.

'I want us to have a baby,' she blurted out as Evan reached for his packed lunch.

He turned slowly to face her. 'That's a big step, Ash.'

'We always wanted kids, and it feels like the perfect time. Fiona is being a bit of a cow about me being off work so much. You know she's looking for an excuse to fire me,' Ashleigh told him.

Her boss at the salon had sent a terse email after Ashleigh had missed yet another shift that week. She claimed to be concerned about Ashleigh's welfare, but it was reaching the point where it would be better to jump before she was pushed.

Evan gave her one of his looks, like he was weighing her up. 'Are we ready for a baby?'

Ashleigh thought so. That was why she had thrown away her contraceptive pills within minutes of slamming the door on Jane. She felt bad for having laughed at her neighbour, but it had been a mask to hide her humiliation. She wore another mask in front of Evan. She had to believe the situation was retrievable, even though there was only one way to interpret her sister pawing her husband's naked chest. She was not going to let Rose steal him from her.

'If you think it's too soon,' she said, bowing her head, but not conceding.

'Don't you think it would be too much for you right now? You can barely look after yourself, Ash.'

'I can,' she said to the floor. 'We could just stop taking precautions. Let fate decide.'

'Maybe.'

And that was how they had left it, but as Ashleigh stepped into the garden with a steaming mug of coffee, she was considering how to give fate a helping hand. Stress was a factor when it came to fertility, and when her phone rang and Rose's name appeared, she decided that was one stressor she could do without. Her sister had come to expect daily updates on Ashleigh's apparent battle with the booze. It was possible that Rose was genuinely willing her to succeed, but she suspected it was more a case of wanting to be the first to know when Ashleigh failed. With so many mixed messages, it was hard to tell who she could trust.

One person who had never let her down was Jess, so when Rose gave up waiting for her sister to pick up the phone, Ashleigh relaxed back in the swing seat and called her friend.

'Morning,' she chirped when Jess answered after a second attempt. 'I thought I'd give you a quick ring. It's been ages.'

'Hiya.'

'Sorry, are you in the office?'

'No, I've taken a few days off.'

'The weather's gorgeous, isn't it? I'm out in the garden on our new swing seat,' Ashleigh said. 'I posted a photo, did you see it?' She wouldn't mention the fight. She had to remain positive.

'I've not been on Insta much.'

'I thought not,' Ashleigh said. She had finally got around to sending Jess a lovely bouquet, and had expected her to post something online, but Jess had sent a private thank you instead. Something wasn't right. And then Ashleigh remembered. 'Oh, God, I forgot, didn't I?'

'Yes.'

'It was your follow-up appointment on . . .' Ashleigh wracked her brain, needing to prove she cared enough to remember.

'Yesterday.'

'Please, Jess, don't hate me. There's been a few dramas here, but I didn't want to worry you.' When she didn't get a response, Ashleigh felt a growing sense of dread. How had she forgotten Jess's biopsy results? 'But now you're worrying me. How did it go? Is it bad?' What would she do without her one and only friend?

Jess waited a heartbeat. 'It was fine. I'm fine. It was just a mole.'

'Don't do that to me! My heart was in my throat!'

'Great response, Ash. Straight back to being all about you,' Jess said, her tone remaining dull.

Ashleigh bit her lip. 'You're right. I'm being a selfish cow, but I couldn't have got through the last few months without you. No, actually, the last few years. You're my rock, Jess, and I want to be yours too. Please forgive me.' Not liking the lengthening silence, she added another, 'Please,' for good measure.

'I shouldn't,' Jess replied, but the lilt in her voice gave her away.

'But you will.'

'I always do, don't I? I know it's not your fault. I don't think I'd know what day it was either if I had someone controlling my every move.'

Ashleigh didn't want to hear criticism of Evan right now, not from someone else. 'Ah, ah,' she said. 'We're not talking about me. Tell me what happened. What did the doctor say? Were you nervous? Did Harry go with you?'

There was a groan on the other end of the line. 'Do you mind if we do this another time? Harry took me into Liverpool for a slap-up meal last night, and I've got a stinking hangover. Are you still off the booze, honey?'

'I realize it's a concept you're unfamiliar with, but I feel so much better for it. You should try it.'

'I'm not that bad, am I?' Jess asked. 'I know it was mid-week, but I had reason to celebrate, and not only because of the biopsy results. I've finished my probation period at work, and there's talk of training me up to be a legal secretary. How good is that?'

'That's brilliant,' Ashleigh said, trying not to sound jealous.

It didn't seem that long ago that she was the one with an exciting future mapped out in front of her, but her world had shrunk to the confines of a tiny townhouse and a wrecked garden.

Grateful that Jess didn't want to stay on the line and gloat, Ashleigh finished the call and drained her coffee. High above her head, seagulls soared across a vast blue sky, their angry caws disturbing her thoughts. And then her phoned pinged with a message.

Tried calling. How are you? I could meet you for lunch if you fancy it Rx

Her sister had become an annoying buzz in her ear that Ashleigh would rather ignore, but she didn't want Rose to suspect she was avoiding her, not until she had worked out what to do with the information Jane had obligingly shared. She tapped out her reply.

Sorry, I was on the phone to Jess. Meeting her for lunch so will catch up another time. Off to have a bath and get ready x

Turning her attention to the garden, Ashleigh noticed that the tender stems of rocket and pea shoots that she and Evan had planted on Monday were drooping and thirsty. He had left his wife with careful instructions on how to water them without bruising the leaves, which was ironic when you thought about it. How she wished he would care for her so conscientiously.

With her gaze remaining on the trough, her thoughts returned to Jane, and how convinced she was that Evan had buried something there. What if Ashleigh could find out what it was? And what if that something could help swing the balance of power back in her favour? It might be enough to stop Evan running off with her cow of a sister. Blackmail was an ugly word, but it could be justified if it was used in the right way. Now all she had to do was dig up the dirt.

CHAPTER 29

Wrapped in her dressing gown, Jane went out to hose the garden before the sun rose too high. The last of the gaps in the parterre's segments had been filled with colourful foxgloves, cornflowers and snapdragons, and in the furthest section, Jane had replanted a couple of rose bushes that had outgrown her mum's containers. She was giving them a good soaking when she heard activity from the other side of the hedgerow.

Humming to herself to drown out the noise, Jane pressed down harder on the hose trigger, but she could still hear whoever was working in the Jarvises' garden. She tried to focus instead on what she might do with the day ahead. She could take Benji to the beach at New Brighton, or to Delamere Forest, or frankly anywhere that was far enough away not to see or hear what was going on next door. Oh, God, it sounded like digging.

Leaving the rose bushes standing in puddles of water, Jane returned to the house and climbed two flights of stairs while muttering to herself. She took hold of the chain to roll up the blind, felt the tension in the mechanism match her body, then stopped as she replayed the sound of Ashleigh's laughter. Hadn't she been humiliated enough? Apparently not, as inch by inch, light began to trickle into the room.

Jane crouched down to see the view that was slowly being revealed. There was the patio below her, then the parterre, the hedgerow, the Jarvises' patchy lawn beyond. Raising the blind a little higher, she caught sight of a pair of legs. Ashleigh was lifting shovelfuls of earth from the trough and adding soil to a growing mound.

When she stopped to stretch, Ashleigh tilted her head towards the attic window as though expecting to see her neighbour there. Jane's body jerked with scalding shame, and she was about to pull the blind down again when she realized Ashleigh was waving at her. When her neighbour was certain she had Jane's attention, she motioned for her to come and join her.

'What the . . .?'

Jane raised her index finger to indicate that she would be there in one minute. She didn't allow herself time to consider an alternative response, one where she pretended not to see Ashleigh. She needed to know what Evan had buried, and this appeared to be an opportunity too good to miss.

It was more like ten minutes before Jane reached the side gate to Ashleigh's end-terrace. She would have been quicker, but as she raced to find her trainers, she realized she was still in her dressing gown. The need to change had given her time to consider what else she might need, and she had grabbed an extra spade from the garage.

'Why are you doing this?' Jane asked as Ashleigh led her to the back garden.

'Curiosity,' Ashleigh replied. Like Jane, she was wearing a T-shirt, but had matched it with denim shorts as opposed to the canvas trousers Jane wore.

'So you do think Evan buried something?'

Ashleigh picked up the spade resting against the trough, and considered her response. 'I have no idea what Evan does when my back is turned,' she said. 'Not ever.'

'The photo?'

'I'm sorry I didn't react better, but it was such a shock.'

'And I'm sorry I sprung it on you like I did,' Jane said, ready to forgive. The laugh could only have been a nervous reaction to seeing the photo. 'With all the highs and lows you've been through recently, I imagine it was quite disorienting.'

Ashleigh slid a hand over one of her wrists, but the yellowed bruises remained visible. 'Do you think Evan does it deliberately?'

'Don't you?' asked Jane. 'I assume you're seeing things more clearly given what you're doing now.'

'Just a little. You were right, I didn't know about my sister's sneaky visit, but I shouldn't be surprised. They've been in league for a while,' explained Ashleigh. 'It doesn't matter how bad it gets, Rose will always defend Evan because he's convinced her that I pick the fights.'

'No one deserves to be abused.'

'I can't blame Rose, not really. It's hard not to fall under Evan's spell,' Ashleigh said. Tears sprung to her eyes, and she pressed her lips tight, which served to emphasize her downturned mouth.

'After everything he's done, you still love him, don't you?' Jane said with sickening realization.

'I'm afraid so,' Ashleigh said. She lifted her spade and thrust it into the dark soil. 'But it's time to fight back, if you'll help me.'

Jane looked across to the house next door. If May had the kitchen door open again, she might be able to hear them talking. 'Do you have any ideas what we might find?' she asked in a low voice.

'It's not going to be a body, Jane,' said Ashleigh, reading her mind.

Jane scanned the emptied contents of the trough. It was a mixture of dark mulch and compost strewn with limp leaves and exposed roots. Nothing suspicious so far, but that didn't mean they wouldn't find something to justify the knot tightening in her stomach. 'Then what?'

'I'd rather wait and see,' Ashleigh replied cryptically. 'There's a chance I could be wrong.'

Rather than joining in with the efforts to empty the trough, Jane used her spade as a wedge to prise the timber frame away from the ground. 'There's no base so I think we might be able to lift the whole thing up and out of the way. It'll be easier to dig then.'

Ashleigh worked from the opposite side, and gradually the frame began to move. The trough was crudely made from cherry tree branches and held together with two-inch nails. It almost fell apart as they hoisted it to the back of the garden.

Removing the remainder of the loose soil was easy enough, but soon they hit compacted earth. With the sun climbing high in a cloudless sky, Jane's sweat-dampened hair clung to her neck as they scraped an outline of the pit Evan had dug two months earlier.

'Do you need a drink?' asked Ashleigh.

'Water would be good,' Jane said, but there was no time to rest. 'How long do we have?'

'Evan won't be back until this evening.' Ashleigh was heading towards the house, but stopped to assess their work so far. She chewed her lip. 'What will I do if we don't find anything? Is there a chance we can put everything back the way it was?'

Jane preferred not to think that far ahead. 'I doubt it,' she said, 'but let's figure that out once we've finished.'

'Thank you for doing this.'

Jane pressed her foot against the spade, and as she thrust it into the baked earth, she felt some satisfaction. 'It's my pleasure.'

When Ashleigh returned with plastic beakers filled with iced water, Jane had made a start at one end of the excavation site. She paused to down her drink, then continued with her task. Ashleigh worked from the opposite end, and they matched each other, spade stroke for spade stroke.

It was more difficult to synchronize their efforts when it became necessary to stand in the hole, so they took turns. When it was time for Jane to take a break, she refilled the beakers from an outside tap, and swilled her face with cool water at the same time. They had cleared at least a foot when Ashleigh climbed out, her sweat-sodden T-shirt sticking to her body. Her face was the colour of fresh raspberries, but when she swiped a hand beneath her blonde fringe, it revealed markedly paler skin.

'I think you've caught the sun,' said Jane, then touched

her own face. She had assumed the salty sweat had made her skin taut, but she was burning too. 'I didn't think to put on sunscreen.'

'It's a bit late now,' Ashleigh said, and Jane's response was to shovel more dirt out of the re-emerging pit. They were getting closer, and there could be no delay.

They were at least two feet down when Jane asked, 'Can you remember how deep the hole was before Evan filled it in?'

'Not much deeper than it is now,' Ashleigh said anxiously.

That tallied with the photo Jane had taken, even though she had formed an image of it being much deeper. Thank goodness it wasn't a grave, she thought as a chill ran down her aching spine in spite of the midday heat.

Determined to keep going until they found something, Jane flung the next spadeful up and over the side, but her arms trembled with the effort.

'Do you want me to take over?' asked Ashleigh, the younger woman's impatience showing.

Jane didn't have the breath to answer. She cut the ground again with her spade and managed to plant it two inches into the unyielding earth before her foot slipped. Refusing to admit defeat, she tried again, but once more she was met with unexpected resistance. Her heart had been beating hard as it was, but now she felt it flutter wildly. She thought she might pass out.

Using the edge of the spade, Jane scraped away the loosened clumps of earth before dropping to her knees.

'What is it?' asked Ashleigh, kneeling down at the edge of the pit for a closer look.

Sweat was dripping off Jane's eyebrows and stinging her

eyes. 'I don't know yet,' she said quietly for fear of raising the dead.

Using the sleeve of her T-shirt to mop her brow, Jane blinked hard to keep her vision clear, and began raking through the earth with her fingers.

'Here, use this,' Ashleigh said, handing her a trowel.

Jane set to work, but instead of the metal blade grating against gritty earth, she heard a thunk. She didn't think she had hit rock, or root, or anything to do with Mother Nature. Like an archaeologist on the verge of a discovery, she used the tip of the trowel to gently scrape away more dirt. There was a rustling noise, but despite the bright sunshine, Jane couldn't distinguish between the dark earth and what had made this unnatural sound. She explored the area with her fingertips.

'It's a bin bag,' Jane said. She was grateful that whatever was inside the bag didn't squelch, but it wasn't enough to stop her stomach lurching. 'What if we're disturbing a crime scene?'

Ashleigh jumped into the hole. 'It's fine. Let me take over.'

Jane didn't argue. Her nausea had turned into a pressing need to vomit, and she was still retching in a corner of the garden when Ashleigh climbed out of the hole. Jane turned to find her neighbour wiping loose dirt off her knees with one hand, while in the other, she held a black bin bag at arm's length. The plastic was torn, revealing a silver-grey object with sharp corners.

'Is that what I think it is?' Jane asked.

Ashleigh placed the bag on a small patch of lawn that wasn't bald or covered in soil, and knelt down in front of it. Jane moved closer but didn't dare sit in case her back seized up. She watched as Ashleigh struggled to untie the knot before giving up and tearing the bag open. There were two items inside.

'I'm so sorry, Jane,' said Ashleigh as she laid out the laptop and camera.

CHAPTER 30

When Ashleigh heard Evan's keys in the door, her start sent ripples of rose-scented water scudding to the edge of the bath. This was it.

It had been tricky convincing Jane that she should face Evan alone, but given her neighbour had just thrown up at the sight of the bin bag, she was in no shape to argue. Ashleigh had assured her that she held all the power now, thanks to their discovery. There would be no more fits of rage, no more violence . . . But what if she was wrong? Ashleigh's earlier confidence was wavering. Nothing about her relationship with Evan was ever predictable, and this was her boldest move by far.

'Ashleigh? Are you in?'

Evan sounded more curious than agitated, which meant he hadn't seen the garden yet. If he poked his head into the living room, the blinds were angled to take the glare off the TV as always. It was the view from the kitchen window that would give her away, and he would only be drawn there if he noticed the dirty footprints. She could have made more of an effort to cover her tracks, but what would be the point? It was all going to come out, and it was going to happen very soon.

'I'm in the bath!' she called, and sat up as she listened to his footsteps drawing closer. She pulled her knees to her chest.

'You don't norm—' Evan stopped the moment he entered the bathroom.

As Ashleigh looked up at the man towering over her, she immediately regretted her decision to remain in the bath. She had thought it would be calming, but she had left herself vulnerable and exposed. Her wet hair was scraped back from her face, revealing a stripe of pale skin across her forehead. 'I caught the sun.'

Evan glowered at the drink in her hand. 'I thought you'd stopped.'

Ashleigh responded by knocking back the last dregs of wine before pulling herself up to stand. 'Can you pass me a towel?' she asked.

The veins at Evan's temples throbbed as he turned away without a word.

He was almost out the door when she said, 'The towel? Please?'

Evan grabbed her bathrobe from the back of the door and threw it at her before stomping downstairs. She quickly wrapped it around herself and chased after him.

'It's only one glass, Evan,' she said when she caught up to him in the kitchen. 'And I needed it after the day I've had.'

Evan opened the fridge and lifted a bottle of wine to eye level. There was only an inch or so left. 'One glass?' he asked.

Cold rivulets of bath water ran down Ashleigh's back, making her shudder, but she hid it well. She couldn't show weakness. 'If I'm going to break your rules, I might as well do it properly.'

'They're not my rules.'

'Sorry, I'd forgotten I'm not supposed to notice that you've manipulated me into thinking they're my decisions, and that I'm the one who needs fixing. Well, I have news for you, Evan. I'm not broken.' There was a tremor to her voice that Ashleigh told herself was nothing more than anticipation. 'I know what's good for me and what isn't. Aren't you going to ask what I've been doing today?'

Evan parted his lips as if to speak, but the air expanding his chest came out as a hiss. He tried again. 'I was hoping it wouldn't come to this, but I'm not entirely surprised. It's why I've kept an overnight bag in the boot of the car. I've had enough, Ash.'

This was the point where he would expect Ashleigh to drop to her knees and beg him to stay, but those days were gone. 'I won't let you go to her,' she warned, stepping into his path.

It would take only a gentle swat from the back of his shovel-sized hands to send her flying, but she would take that chance.

'I know who she is now.'

'And so it begins,' he said in exasperation. 'Go on, who am I having an affair with this time?'

'It was odd, don't you think, that Rose knew you'd spent the night away from home before I'd even mentioned it to her? I doubt she was happy when you came back to me, but you're so good at stringing people along.'

He laughed. 'You seriously think I'm having an affair with your sister? You're sick, do you know that?'

Ashleigh didn't have a copy of Jane's photograph to show him, but he would only try to talk his way out of it anyway, like he did every other time she questioned his fidelity. 'Oh, don't tell me. It's me being paranoid again,' she said, mimicking his laugh.

Her behaviour was confusing him. She wasn't going to shout or scream or cry. She didn't need to. Ashleigh had something that would stop him exerting any more control over her, and not only something, but someone. Jane might be nothing more than a nosey neighbour to Evan, but she had become Ashleigh's most crucial ally.

They glared at each other, and when it became a staring contest, it was Evan who blinked first. 'Move out of the way, Ashleigh.'

Bath water dripped onto the floor, but Ashleigh stood her ground. 'No.'

'This is crazy. What's the point in staying?' he asked, his voice devoid of emotion. 'There's nothing left worth fighting for.'

Evan's apparent disregard for her feelings was all part of his strategy. She had seen it so many times before. 'Who said anything about fighting?' she asked. 'I won't be provoked. I won't react no matter how hard you push my buttons. You don't have that kind of hold over me any more.'

'A hold over you? I'm the one who's been trapped. And if you can't see that – if you can't acknowledge that your behaviour has all but destroyed our marriage – then there's no hope for us, there really isn't.'

212

'*I've* destroyed our marriage?' she yelped.

Evan flinched. 'So much for not overreacting.'

'I'm responding like any sane person would if they were being goaded, but hey, let me be the unreasonable one.'

'When you've been drinking, that's exactly what you are. That's why it was so important for you to stay sober, but you were never serious about it, were you?'

'I only drink when I'm scared. *You* scare me, Evan,' she admitted. 'That's the bit that has to change.'

'You're not scared of me.'

Ashleigh allowed a single teardrop to slide down her cheek. 'I'm scared of how much you'll hurt me. Especially in the ways that don't leave bruises. Like sleeping with my sister. Who in their right mind would look at her twice?'

Evan's jaw twitched, a sure sign that his patience was about to snap. It was a dangerous game they played. 'There's nothing going on between me and Rose,' he said. 'And you'd realize that if you hadn't been drinking yourself into a state.'

'I've had one sodding bottle of wine, and not even a full one! I've had better things to do.' Her breathing was laboured, and she sought to regain her composure. 'You still haven't asked what I've been doing, Evan. Go on, I dare you.'

She glanced past him, drawing his gaze outwards to the garden.

'What the hell have you done?' he asked, taking two steps backwards so he could see through the window. 'You've ruined . . .' His voice faded to nothing.

'We found what you were hiding.'

'Why are you doing this?' He couldn't take his eyes from

the mess she and Jane had left, but then his head snapped back. 'What do you mean, *we*?'

'I couldn't have done it on my own,' Ashleigh replied. She had worked through her anxiety, and her pulse had slowed. The worst was over. He knew he had been found out. 'Jane helped. It was her property she was recovering, after all.'

Evan blinked hard. It would take time to adapt to the new version of their life where his one and only priority would be keeping her happy. 'How did she . . . How did you know what was there?'

'Jane was still suspicious about that hole, and it took me a while, but I finally figured it out.'

Evan looked at his wife with utter contempt.

'Don't look so worried,' she continued. 'I've convinced her that you're not a bad person deep down, and she's promised not to report you to the police as long as you behave yourself. You don't really have a choice. It might not be the crime of the century, but I don't imagine your boss would be too happy if you ended up with a criminal record.'

'You bitch,' Evan said as he wiped the sheen of sweat from his brow. 'You absolute bitch.'

When he balled his hand and raised his fist, Ashleigh wasn't scared. It was such a liberating feeling. 'You can't touch me,' she hissed, but her victory was short-lived. She screamed.

CHAPTER 31

Jane lowered herself carefully into the warm bath, soap suds popping painfully against her burnt neck. She needed to wash away the dirt, ease her aching muscles and soothe a particularly weary mind. What a day.

After watching Ashleigh untangle the stolen goods from their plastic shroud, Jane had wished Phil was there to see that sometimes there was a very good reason for paranoia, but her first priority had been to inform the police. It should have been Ashleigh's too.

'I'm so sorry, Jane. I had a horrible feeling this was what we would find,' Ashleigh had said as she laid out Jane's property for inspection. She knelt back on her heels, looking utterly exhausted.

'You shouldn't be the one to apologize,' Jane said, rasping from the vomit that had burned the back of her throat. She wasn't sure if it was the discovery of a buried secret that had made her throw up, or simply overexertion, but she continued to feel nauseous, and it was made worse when she tried to bend down to check her laptop.

Ashleigh noticed Jane struggling and took charge, opening the laptop and wiping muddy smears from the screen. The bin bag hadn't been airtight, and there was extensive water damage. Unsurprisingly, it failed to power up, so Ashleigh moved on to the camera, removing its lens cover and turning it in her hands as if she were a demonstrator on a shopping channel.

'I assume there's no doubt these are yours,' she said.

'I'm afraid not. Do you want to speak to the police first, or shall I?'

'The police?' Ashleigh asked, jolting in surprise. 'I– I was hoping we could keep them out of it. You have your stuff back. Please, take it.' She shoved both items across the grass towards Jane's feet.

'Ashleigh,' Jane said as she looked down at the fragile figure kneeling in front of her. 'Your husband broke into my house and took what didn't belong to him. I suspect it's not the worst crime he's committed, but it is the one he's committed against me. He needs to be held to account, and I'm prepared to stand up to him if it means you don't have to.'

'But look around you,' Ashleigh said. 'He'll know I was involved if the police come knocking, and you can't exactly say you came here without my permission. He'd have you charged with trespassing, not to mention destruction of property.'

'Then what's the alternative? Do you really think we can put everything back, and expect him not to notice?'

'No, of course not. I want Evan to know that we've found his little stash. This is the leverage I've been looking for, Jane. I appreciate none of this puts Evan in a good light, but he's not all bad,' Ashleigh pleaded. 'This is the wake-up call he's needed.'

'After all this, you still think you have a future together? This isn't just about the theft,' Jane reminded her. 'It's not even about the affair with your sister.' She looked pointedly at the fading bruises on Ashleigh's arms. 'Think about what he's been doing to you.'

'He's a weak man, and what he needs is a stronger woman. That isn't Rose,' Ashleigh said, her chin jutting out. 'And lately, it hasn't been me either, but that's about to change. He'll lose his job if you go to the police, and you know he'll blame me. This evidence protects me until I can get Evan to accept that he's the one who needs help. Don't you see? I can make him listen to me for a change.'

Jane wiped her face on the sleeve of her sweaty T-shirt, hoping to clear her vision and see beyond Ashleigh's slight frame. She was determined, Jane had to give her that. 'Is he worth it?'

'Yes,' Ashleigh replied without hesitation. 'I love him too much to give up now, and nothing you say will change my mind. Please, let me do this my way.'

Jane had been finding it hard enough to keep upright, let alone stand up to Evan, but her agreement had been as cool as her bath water had become. Raising herself up, she yelped in pain as she stretched to pull out the plug.

Drying herself off, Jane smothered her sunburnt skin in aloe vera gel and slipped into a pair of jogging pants and a hoodie. She would have preferred pyjamas, but she wasn't sure what the evening would bring. She didn't share Ashleigh's optimism that she could conquer the man who had bullied her, and prayed neither of them would have cause to regret their decision. Hobbling down to the kitchen, she made herself a cup of cocoa; her mum's tried and trusted method of making her daughter feel better.

The recovered goods were languishing in the utility room in the replacement bin bag Ashleigh had given her to carry them home. Jane didn't want to handle them again. Evan wasn't going to change, and she had a horrible feeling the police would be checking the laptop and camera for fingerprints, if not today, then at some point in the future.

According to Ashleigh, Evan would be home very soon, and Jane wanted to see his reaction if he went into the garden to assess the damage. Wrapping a hand around her hot drink to soothe her aching fingers, she trudged back upstairs, but her joints complained with every step, and she was out of breath by the time she stopped at the door leading to the attic. She had climbed that narrow staircase with worse injuries, but she had been much younger then. Now, she couldn't do it.

Drawing a deep breath, Jane let the scent of chocolatey milk tempt her towards the ill-fitting door to her mum's room. She used her foot to help force it open, and echoes of the past came back to taunt her. It was always the noises that lodged deepest in her memory.

The sound of wood splintering had carried up to the attic that afternoon her dad had kicked open the bedroom door to get to her mum. Jane had tried covering her ears, but nothing had ever been able to block out the yelling, the screams, and the crashes. Those noises were the soundtrack to her childhood, but on the night she had listened to her dad's yelling for what would be the last time, she had heard something new – her mum's voice matching his in volume and strength.

Remaining on the threshold of the bedroom, Jane closed her eyes and pictured how the room had looked later that same night. There had been a yellow cellular blanket covering the bed; a red tartan suitcase lying on top; her mum's face, bloodied and swollen; and her dad's personal possessions ready to be packed away.

Jane's eyes snapped open and the world fast-forwarded five decades. The bedroom was empty except for the fractured light leaking through the edges of the closed blind. Dust motes rather than ghosts danced around Jane as she moved over to the window and raised the blind. The glare from the evening sun was strong enough to sting her eyes, but she quickly settled her gaze on the house opposite. Her vantage point wasn't as good as the one from the attic, but it was good enough. The Jarvises' kitchen was empty, as was Ashleigh's bedroom. There was no tell-tale sway of blinds in the living room. All was still.

Jane was standing where her mum would have been when Ashleigh spotted her. Did her mum deliberately ignore her neighbour, or had she been too absorbed in the memories that would haunt her to her dying day? Had she chosen not to fix her bedroom door so it would serve as a reminder? A warning of what happened when you let a man like Les into your life.

Setting down her drink on the windowsill, Jane tilted back her head and let the sunlight play across her closed lids. This time her mind took her to safety, back home to Buxton and a house that had suffered nothing worse than complacency. She willed Phil to materialize so he could massage her tired shoulders. He wasn't a particularly passionate man, but there were displays of affection that were tender and loving; the hand on the small of her back, or the kiss on her cheek before disappearing into his study. In recent years, those touches had felt infuriatingly perfunctory, but she craved them now as she took out her phone. She had given up any right to seek comfort from her estranged husband, but at least she had an excuse to reach out. She tried not to sound too smug when she sent a message explaining that day's find.

She didn't expect Phil to reply immediately as he would be on the commute home, but it raised the question of whether he was going home alone. As far as she knew, he hadn't arranged any dates, but it was going to happen one day. They were fast approaching the point of no return.

Jane rested a hand on the windowsill for support. She understood that he didn't want to be on his own. Neither did she, and more to the point, she didn't want to be with anyone except Phil. With her strength sapped, it was becoming harder to pretend that any of his so-called faults mattered. There was only one reason she was severing herself from her family, and sadly, it was a very good one. She bit down on her lip, and almost cut through the skin when Evan appeared in the kitchen opposite.

He had stepped backwards as he continued to talk, or possibly shout at whoever was out of Jane's line of sight. And then he looked out of the window. If he hadn't seen the hole they had dug already, there was no missing it now. There was no time to gauge his reaction as he disappeared from view again.

Anticipating that the Jarvises' argument might spill out

into the garden, Jane opened a window. As usual, she could hear the birds' evensong above the hum of traffic. Children were out playing, but Jane's blood ran cold when she heard what sounded like a scream. Her phone beeped seconds later, but it was only a message from Phil. He was asking if she had informed the police yet, already interfering in something he knew nothing about, and as she filed away her annoyance for the next time she felt her resolve weakening, there was another message alert. Fear clamped Jane's insides.

They're at it again. Sounds bad. Love May xxx

Why had she allowed Ashleigh to convince her to step away? She dialled May's number.

'What can you hear?' she asked.

'Here, listen.'

Jane imagined May pressing her phone against the party wall, but it was no good. 'The phone isn't picking anything up,' she said, then had to repeat herself more loudly so that May heard her reply. 'What are they saying?'

'There's lots of shouting, but it's hard to work out, even with my hearing aids at full volume. It's stuff like, "How can you love me when you act like you hate me?" That sort of thing.'

'Ashleigh?'

'No, that's him. I did hear her scream though.' May released a loud sigh. 'If it goes on much longer, I'm going to have to call the police again.'

Jane knew all too well how quickly an argument could escalate. But even if the police were called, they could arrive too late, or might not respond at all given there had been one wasted visit already.

'I have Ashleigh's number,' she said. Swapping contact details had been part of their pact. 'Let me see if I can speak to her before we involve the police.'

'Good luck with that,' May said. Before Jane could end the call, she added, 'By the way, what were you up to before in her garden?'

May had seen them in the garden, but it didn't sound like she had spotted what they had recovered.

'She's realized she can trust me,' Jane said enigmatically. 'I'll give her a call.'

With her eyes trained on the Jarvises' kitchen, Jane let the phone ring out, cutting it just as it switched to voice-mail. She tried again, and was wondering how many more attempts she should make when the call connected.

'Ashleigh?' She couldn't be sure it wasn't Evan.

'Hello, Jane.' Ashleigh sounded nasal, as if she had been crying and her nose was blocked.

'I heard a scream,' Jane said, choosing not to bring May into it. 'Are you OK?'

'I'm fine.'

Those two words were a reflexive response, used too often to give the questioner permission to ignore someone's distress. 'You're not fine,' Jane said. 'Don't say you are.'

A slender figure appeared at the kitchen window. Ashleigh was deliberately putting herself on view, but she kept her body at an angle. Her head was bowed and her blonde hair fell in front of her face.

'Please don't call the police,' Ashleigh begged.

Jane squinted as she watched Ashleigh turn towards the window. Her face was deathly pale, but there were darker patches too. From a distance, Jane couldn't be certain, but it looked like bruising, or even blood around her nose. 'Has he hurt you?'

'We had a bit of a disagreement, but Evan's promised things are going to change.'

'He's promised?' Jane repeated, her voice quaking with anger. 'By hitting you?'

Ashleigh pulled back the damp trails of hair sticking to her cheeks. It was blood. 'I know it looks bad, but it was an accident.'

'I don't believe you.'

'I understand your concern, but this is me making all the decisions here. I don't want the police involved, and I know I can't stop you reporting the recovery of stolen goods, but please, give him a chance. He's genuinely sorry.'

Jane couldn't believe what she was seeing as Ashleigh extended an arm. It was like she was on stage and had invited Evan to join her. The villain of the piece appeared in profile. He wouldn't turn in Jane's direction, but his very presence made her want to throw up again. Evan was the embodiment of everything she and her mother had endured at the hands of another man with an uncontrollable temper and a thirst for cruelty.

'Please, Ashleigh, I think you're making a terrible mistake,' she said. The silence on the other end of the line was deafening, and it left Jane cold. 'Even if your mind is set on this path . . .'

'It is.'

'Then promise me one thing. Don't ever let your guard down.'

Ashleigh hung up.

Jane backed away from the window and stood in the middle of her mum's empty bedroom. She had thought she could help Ashleigh because she had seen her mum go through something similar, but that had been a mistake. Their situations felt very different. The two women were very different. Her mum had endured the abuse because she felt she had no choice, but Ashleigh's decision to stay with Evan appeared to be of her own free will. The only common factor the women shared was Jane, and in both cases, her only contribution had been to make matters worse.

CHAPTER 32

1974

With one ear blocked with blood, Cynthia hoped she had mistaken the sound she had just heard. It couldn't be Jane, she was home too early, but Les's reaction confirmed the worst. He raced out of the sitting room and slammed the door behind him, separating mother and child.

'Hello, sunshine,' she heard him chirp.

Feeling woozy, Cynthia hobbled across the room and rested a bloodied hand against the closed door. What terror would she inflict if her daughter saw her like this? She was always so careful to tidy herself up after a fight.

'What's that horrible smell?' Jane was asking.

'Your mum burnt the tea. You know what she's like.'

'Where is she?' Anxiety fractured the little girl's voice as she called out, 'Mum?'

Cynthia had to make a choice. She wanted to protect Jane, but pretending the violence didn't exist only perpetuated the abuse. She pulled open the door and stepped into the empty hallway.

'I'm here,' she called out.

She heard a satchel being dropped onto the kitchen table, followed by some sort of scuffle.

'Oi, come back!' Les bellowed.

Jane darted out of the kitchen so fast that she almost ran into her mum. Cynthia gave a gasp as her broken body tensed for impact.

The little girl's eyes widened in horror. 'Wh-what happened? Are you OK?'

'You were supposed to stay at May's.'

Jane bit down on her trembling lip. 'I didn't . . . I couldn't . . .'

'Your mum's having one of her meltdowns,' Les said, appearing behind her. He was smiling, clearly amused by the sport of it all. 'I don't know about you, but I think it's time we escaped this madhouse. It's going to be just you and me now, kid.'

Cynthia reached for her daughter's hand. 'He's not—'

When the phone rang, three pairs of eyes darted to the little table with the cushioned seat next to the stairs. The trill repeated three times, then stopped.

'That'll be your mate giving you a warning.'

May had only recently had a phone installed, but calls were expensive and unnecessary when you lived within shouting distance. For the times when it was too dark and muddy for their daughters to use their hedgerow tunnel, May and Cynthia gave each other three pips to signal that someone was on their way home. A reciprocal message would be sent to confirm all was well without incurring the cost of connecting any calls.

Jane pulled her hand from her mother's grasp. 'I can ring them back,' she offered.

'Leave it,' snarled Les.

To Cynthia's amazement, Jane ignored her father. It was almost exhilarating to see her standing up to him, until Les lunged at her.

Fortunately for Jane, Les had to get past her mother first, but when Cynthia attempted to block him in the narrow hallway, he had no trouble finding a weak spot; her whole body was a mosaic of injuries. He thumped Cynthia's shoulder hard enough to bring stars to her eyes, but she only cried out when he snagged one of Jane's pigtails. He was pulling their daughter backwards, ready with an open palm to greet her face.

Cynthia struck Les hard on the side of his head with her fist, unbalancing him enough to deflect the slap he had been aiming at their daughter, but he kept hold of Jane's pigtail long enough to spin her around. He made another grab for her, but the little girl jerked her body away hard, then kept falling backwards from the momentum. Cynthia held on to Les's sleeve to stop him going after her, but the damage was already done. Jane smashed into the table, knocking the telephone off its stand with a clatter. Her body twisted, and she landed on the floor with a thump, one arm bent awkwardly beneath her.

The sound of Jane's scream brought both parents to a halt, and in that moment, everything changed. No court would take Les's word over Cynthia's after this. He was never going to take her baby away from her. He licked his lips nervously, clearly thinking the same, then made a move to check on Jane.

'Stay away from her!' Cynthia yelled, placing herself between the two.

Jane had curled into a ball, a pose familiar to her mother, but her damp eyes snapped open at the sound of Cynthia's warning. Cradling her injured arm to her chest, she scrambled backwards until she reached the bottom of the stairs.

'Hide!' Cynthia urged her daughter.

Jane didn't need to be told twice, and scurried upstairs, but when she reached the landing, she faltered. 'Come up too, Mum,' she said, as if a flimsy piece of plywood was ever going to protect them.

'I'll be fine,' Cynthia promised. And she turned to face Les.

CHAPTER 33

When there was a knock at the door just after eleven o'clock, Ashleigh was still in bed. There was a dull ache between her temples from too much wine the night before, but it was nothing compared to the intense pain around her nose. Evan had assured her it wasn't broken, and had given her painkillers before leaving for work. She had tried to get back to sleep, but she knew it wouldn't take Jane long to come nosing.

Tightening the belt of her dressing gown, she didn't bother to check her reflection. She knew she looked a mess, and kept her head dipped as she opened the door.

'Morning,' said Rose brightly.

Ashleigh's head shot up, and she planted her foot behind the door so her sister couldn't force it open. 'What do you want?'

Rose stood with her arms folded across a dark blue hoodie with white stripes down the arms, and matching jogging pants. She wore a baseball cap and virgin white trainers to complete the ensemble. This was Ashleigh's sister playing dress-up, and today she was some sort of life coach or personal trainer for the weak-willed and spineless. The only thing missing was a whistle hanging from her neck.

'You've been ignoring my calls,' Rose said. 'I was concerned.'

'Well, as you can see, I'm fine, so don't let me keep you from your run.'

'My what?' Rose pulled a face. 'I don't do jogging. A long walk is kinder on the joints and good for the mind.'

Ashleigh sighed. 'Then feel free to carry on with your walk.'

'I came in the car.'

Ashleigh looked her sister up and down. 'Oh, right. It's just that you look a bit hot and sweaty.'

'And you look like you've slammed your face into a door,' retorted Rose. 'So, are you going to let me in?'

Ashleigh was tempted to refuse, but she didn't think the impromptu visit had anything to do with a couple of missed calls. Rose hadn't looked the least bit surprised to see the bruising across Ashleigh's nose that had spread beneath her eyes. Evan had obviously phoned her the minute he left the house.

It must have been humiliating for him the night before, being paraded for their neighbour like a wild pony that had just been broken, but Ashleigh had felt wonderfully empowered. All the fear that had kept her body under a permanent state of stress had been transferred to her husband. She would set the rules of engagement from now on.

'I don't want you speaking to Rose,' she had told him that morning. He had been giving her the silent treatment since losing their argument, and it was starting to grate. 'Not about this, not about anything. In fact, block her number.'

'Or what?'

'What do you mean?'

'If I don't comply, what will you do next?' he asked. 'Persuade our lovely neighbour to have me arrested?'

'I was the one who convinced her not to go to the police. You heard me on the phone. I would never let her do that to you,' she said, abhorring the way he twisted her intentions as if nothing had changed.

'She wouldn't be involved at all if it wasn't for you and your stories.'

'They're not stories,' Ashleigh replied as she sat up in bed and explored her sore and crusted nose with her fingers. She had to remind herself that she was not the villain. 'Can't we just forget all that stuff? I want us to go back to enjoying being together the way we were.'

'I can't go back when I don't know what part of us was ever real.'

'What's real is our love,' she said, keeping the focus on the present. 'It's going to be OK, I promise. Now be an angel and get me some painkillers.'

Evan had kindly obliged, but apparently there were some things she was going to have to do herself, like telling Rose to stay out of their lives. Ashleigh left the door ajar and headed for the kitchen.

The blood spatters from the night before had been wiped away, and if you didn't look at Ashleigh's face, you would think nothing untoward had ever happened. Except in Rose's case, you wouldn't see it even if the walls had been dripping with blood.

Rose observed her coldly. 'You've destroyed that man.'

'You mean my husband?'

Pulling off her baseball cap, Rose raked her fingers through her hair. She was the same shade of blonde as her sister, but Ashleigh's hair was longer, and glossier too. Despite Rose's claims to have embraced a healthier lifestyle, her complexion was blotchy, and whatever fad diet she was on had made her face gaunt and her chest concave. Rose had to be delusional to think Evan would ever choose the ugly sister.

'Did Evan send you?' asked Ashleigh.

'No, he didn't want me talking to you, but what I have to say needed to be said to your face. Evan and I are not having an affair.'

Ashleigh didn't believe her, but it didn't matter. 'Then it won't bother you if you don't see him again.'

'You're actually forbidding him from seeing me?'

'It's a joint decision. Evan and I have reached an understanding.'

'Is that what you call it?' Rose sneered. 'You always were a conniving cow.'

When Ashleigh arched an eyebrow, the movement pulled at the overstretched skin around her nose. Her eyes began to water. 'All I'm doing is standing up for myself, but I don't expect you to understand that. You prefer to magnify other people's faults so you don't have to acknowledge your own.'

Rose laughed. 'I think you're describing yourself there.'

'Oh, I know my faults. I've spent the last couple of years having every single one of them pointed out to me, and I've had enough.'

'Your problems with Evan go back a lot longer than a couple of years, Ash. Have you forgotten the way you flipped out at your wedding? If only you'd done it before you exchanged vows, Evan might have had a lucky escape.'

Ashleigh swatted away a tear. 'If I flipped out, it was only because you spent the whole day slobbering over my husband. Not that you'd remember, you were smashed by the time we got to the church.'

'You weren't exactly sober yourself, I remember that much,' Rose said. Her flat chest rose then fell with a huff. 'Most people are allowed a blow-out now and again, but not us. Alcoholism is a disease we inherited, and whether that was nature or nurture doesn't matter. Knowing you have a problem is what counts.'

'You sleeping with my husband is the problem, Rose!' Ashleigh said, careful not to raise her voice too loud. The walls had ears. 'Creating an alternate reality where I'm the baddie and Evan is the poor victim is the problem.'

Rose ignored the tears that scored Ashleigh's cheeks and opened the fridge. There was a bottle of wine cooling in the door, and she took it out to slam down on the worktop. 'No, Ashleigh, this is the problem.'

Ashleigh had bought two bottles of wine yesterday before the dig, anticipating the drama that would follow, but she had drunk only one. *One.* The other was on standby in case she needed to decompress after what was proving to be a very stressful week. It wasn't as if she was back to hiding vodka around the house, and there was beer in the fridge too, which Rose conveniently ignored because those were Evan's.

'Save your lecture for someone who cares,' Ashleigh said.

'And that's your other problem. Not caring,' Rose hit back. 'Evan has fought for you, defended you, made excuses for you. And in response, you've become meaner and nastier.'

Something caught at the back of Ashleigh's throat; it was hard to tell if it was a sob or a laugh. 'Oh, well, if Evan says that's how it is, it must be true,' she replied. 'You don't see it, do you? It's a sport to him. He humiliates me, taunts me, tries to control me.' She could go on, but Rose's constant shaking of her head was incredibly annoying so she went in for the killer blow. 'And when I bend one of his rules, he uses me as a punch bag.'

'You actually believe your own lies, don't you? You're the bully, Ash.'

'You think I could bully Evan? Have you seen the size of him?' Ashleigh said with a snort. 'Or better still, look at me, Rose. Look at my face. You know this isn't the first time, although the bruises are usually easier to hide.'

'Hide them? You love showing them off every time there's a sob story to sell,' Rose replied. 'And can you please stop with the waterworks? You're the only person I know who can turn it on like a tap. Sorry, but it doesn't work with me.'

Ashleigh made her chin wobble, but it didn't seem worth the effort while Rose remained stony-faced. 'When did you get so cold?'

'When I saw through your lies. It's interesting how your bruises were nearly always on your arms and wrists, almost as if someone was fending you off. Evan would never raise a hand to you in anger.'

'Well, he did last night!' Ashleigh said through gritted teeth.

'I don't believe you.'

'Of course you don't, but it's no less true,' Ashleigh said, infuriated because she was telling the truth for once.

She had known Evan's patience would snap one day, and there was no doubt that the intent had been there when they faced off in the kitchen. She hadn't been afraid when she saw him ball his hand into a fist.

'Go on then, hit me,' she had goaded him. 'I know you want to.'

There followed a pregnant pause, and the only sound was the drip, drip of water trickling off Ashleigh's soaking wet hair and onto the floor. And then Evan had lowered his arm. 'No, Ash, I'm better than that.'

The damp bathrobe clung to Ashleigh's cooling skin, but fury warmed her belly. 'Better than *me*? Is that what you mean?'

'Stop. We know where this will end.'

Ashleigh could feel the blood pulsing in her veins. His lack of reaction was infuriating. It was like she wasn't worth the effort; all part of his strategy to erode her self-worth.

'Why are you doing this to me!' she screamed. It was her turn to make a fist.

'Yell all you like. You're never going to get me to hit you,' Evan warned. 'I'll walk away if I have to, and no amount of blackmail, emotional or otherwise, will make me come back.'

Whenever Ashleigh reached this level of rage, it was as if her body was controlled by an unseen force. Spittle flew from her mouth as she lunged at her husband, but she had forgotten about the puddle of bath water she was standing in. As her feet went from under her, she fell forward, just as Evan stepped back to avoid the punch heading his way. She hit the floor with a grunt as air was pushed from her lungs. Her head tipped back briefly, but gravity took over and her face smashed against the tiled floor. Evan hadn't tried to save her, and that had hurt almost as much as the fall.

'For what it's worth,' Rose told her sister. 'I wish he *had* hit you. It might have been the one thing that would bring him to his senses. Why he's put up with you for this long is beyond me. He should never have let you home again after you'd left.'

Ashleigh sniffed back the last of her tears, but the pain in her nose twisted her features into a snarl. 'And why would that be, Rose? So you could take my place?'

'There's something wrong with you, Ash,' Rose said, her finger-pointing making her movements jerky. 'You can't let Evan out of your sight without accusing him of something, even if he's only gone as far as the garden. He encouraged you to get involved, but you turned it into one of your nasty games.'

'Encouraged me? Wow, he's done a good job brainwashing you. For your information, Evan locked me out of the garden.'

Rose shuffled back a step as Ashley leant closer, but she wasn't giving up. 'Because *you* dug up all the flowerbeds.'

'We were building a water feature!'

It was Ashleigh who had come up with the idea, and she had marked out the trench Evan would eventually be obliged to dig. It would have been easier to maintain than the stupid plants he had wasted an entire weekend fussing over, not to mention the hour she had spent pulling them up while he was at work.

'So it wasn't a pond then?' asked Rose, scrunching up her ugly face. 'You just have to destroy anything and everything that brings him a little joy.'

'I didn't touch his precious flowers!'

'What about the cherry tree? You must have been hacking away at it for days. You're nothing if not determined.'

It had been a jealousy-fuelled protest to Evan's alleged trekking expedition back in the spring, and the reminder ignited fresh anger. 'He should have stayed home,' she said. 'Was he with you?'

'What?'

'Did you go off for a dirty weekend together? Because he must have been with someone, Evan hates hiking.'

'Maybe he was just looking for an excuse to get away from you,' Rose replied. She tried to hold Ashleigh's gaze, but she always was the weaker sibling. She looked instead to the bottle of wine she had taken from the fridge. 'I can't believe how stupid I was, thinking you could change. You're still a bitch, whether you're drunk or sober.'

'Oh, please. Don't make out you were ever interested in my welfare. You can't wait to sink your claws into my husband.'

'Believe what you like.'

'Oh, I will. And you still haven't answered my question,' Ashleigh said with a snarl. 'Did you go away together?'

Rose twisted the baseball cap in her hand, uncomfortable under the intensity of her sister's scrutiny. 'For God's sake, no.'

'But you like spending time with him, don't you?'

The stain of embarrassment blooming on Rose's neck gave her away. She was a real and present danger to Ashleigh's marriage.

'So you're not going to deny it?'

'Maybe I do like him. So what?' Rose said, her jaw jutting out as she finally met Ashleigh's gaze. 'And if you don't learn to treat him better, Ash, I might just show him what he's missing.'

Ashleigh's chest rose as she sucked in oxygen to fuel her burning fury. The heat rose higher, and as Rose turned on her heels to leave, all Ashleigh could see was red.

'Don't you dare walk away from me,' she growled.

CHAPTER 34

After the back-breaking work in Ashleigh's garden, it was as much as Jane could do to shuffle to the park and back with Benji the next morning. Her sunburn made her cheeks painfully tight, but she could hardly complain considering how Ashleigh's face must hurt. She was tempted to knock at the house when she noticed that Evan's car was absent from the lane, but she didn't want it to look like she had come to gawp, which wouldn't be too far off the mark.

She had opted instead to give Ashleigh a call once she was back home, then forced herself to wait some more. As midday approached, she could bear it no longer, but when she dialled Ashleigh's mobile, the phone rang out. She was about to cut the call when someone answered. There was no greeting, just heavy breathing.

'Hello? Ashleigh, is that you?'

'Sorry, I thought you'd rung off. Hi, Jane. What can I do for you?'

'Are you busy?'

'Actually, my sister's here. She dropped by for a chat.'

Jane couldn't work out from Ashleigh's tone if this was a good thing or not, but surely the sight of Ashleigh's injuries had brought Rose to her senses. Together they could break the spell Evan had cast over them both. 'I'll let you go then,' she said.

'It's not a problem, Rose was about to leave anyway.'

'If you're sure, but it was only a quick call to see how you were after yesterday. You are OK, aren't you?'

'Couldn't be better,' Ashleigh said, sounding more chipper than she had when she first answered. 'Rose and I have had a proper talk, and I'm seeing things so much clearer now. In fact, I think I owe you an explanation. If it's not too much trouble, I'd like to call around this evening.'

'Of course, if you think it would help.'

'It would,' she replied. 'Shall we say about eight?'

'Perfect, I'll see you then.'

With nothing better to do, Jane spent the rest of the day waiting. She read a book, had a snooze, took Benji for another walk, and generally pottered in the garden. She avoided anything that required disturbing the soil too much. She hadn't recovered from the shock and repulsion of her spade hitting something shrouded in plastic. It could have been a body; it was what had been on her mind the whole time she had been digging. Evan was capable of murder, she was sure of it, and that view was reinforced when Ashleigh arrived at eight o'clock prompt.

'Please, shoo the dog away if he's being a nuisance,' said Jane. She was doing her best not to stare at the vivid rainbow of colours blooming on Ashleigh's face, having already made the mistake of gasping when she answered the door.

'He's no trouble, are you, boy?' said Ashleigh, letting the dog settle on her knee as she relaxed against the sofa cushions.

After the initial shock of her injuries, Jane was surprised to notice there was an unexpected glow about Ashleigh. The sun had bronzed her skin and left a smattering of freckles across her cheeks, albeit accentuated by the bruising. Her honeyed blonde hair cascaded over her shoulders and shone in the low sun streaming through the French doors, which Jane had kept firmly locked despite the fine weather.

'Can I ask what happened when Evan came home?'

'This isn't his doing, if that's what you're thinking,' Ashleigh said, touching her face. 'It was a silly accident. After our dig, I was aching all over so I had a bath, and a bit too much Dutch courage if I'm being honest. I heard Evan arrive home and hurried down to the kitchen without drying myself properly. I wanted to explain what we'd been doing before he spotted the mess himself, but my feet were still wet and when I slipped, I smacked my face on the kitchen floor. It's as simple as that.'

'You didn't argue?' Jane asked. Ashleigh's version of events sounded rehearsed, and whether any part of the account was true or not, there were omissions, May could testify to that.

Ashleigh trailed a finger along the length of Benji's back, making him shudder with pleasure as she straightened the parting in his long, silvery fur. 'We might have exchanged a few words when Evan realized he'd been found out, but after I fell over, he took care of me. The accident gave us a chance to collect our thoughts,' she said, absorbed in her task. 'Things have been going from bad to worse lately, and our relationship had become this bubbling pressure pot, but now it's been released.'

'I can see that,' Jane said with a heavy dose of sarcasm.

'Evan needs to manage his anger better, I know that, and so does he, but I have to take some of the blame too. I'd built myself up into a kind of hysteria.'

'Are those your words or his?'

'I know what you're getting at, but I've been struggling ever since I lost my job at the travel agency. I haven't been able to admit this until now, but I've been drinking more than is good for me. I've been hiding it from most people, but not my sister, who was also an alcoholic.' Her eyes flicked up. 'Sorry, I mean, she *is* an alcoholic, a recovering one. You never really stop, do you? She was the one who spotted the signs before anyone else, and she's been advising Evan on how best to support me.'

'I see.'

Ashleigh was paying close attention to the dog's coat, wrapping long strands of fur around her fingers. 'They weren't having an affair, Jane. If they met behind my back, it was because they were worried about me.'

Jane wasn't fooled. Ashleigh's complexion might be glowing, but her words suggested a woman who had been worn down to a pale impression of herself. 'But if your husband had nothing to hide, why did he steal my camera? I'm sorry, Ashleigh, but it doesn't make sense.'

Ashleigh chewed her lip. 'Maybe he knew how paranoid I'd be if I saw the photos. Especially as he had his top off.'

'Except we didn't know each other back then. Why would he think I'd show you my photographs? An innocent man might take the view that it was low risk, but a guilty one would want to cover his tracks.'

'I don't pretend to understand all of his motives, but I think deep down Evan is insecure. He likes the illusion of control.' Ashleigh's brow creased. She was becoming flustered by Jane's logic. 'Maybe he took your camera because he didn't like someone taking his photo without permission.'

'It would be excessive by anyone's standards to break into a neighbour's house if that were the case. He could have simply asked me to erase the photos. You must see there's more to it than that,' Jane said softly. 'And you seemed pretty convinced he and your sister were having an affair yesterday. What's changed?' She looked pointedly at the bruising across the bridge of Ashleigh's nose and beneath her eyes.

'Whatever he's done, he's sorry now, and I love him enough to forgive him. I don't expect you to understand when you've never been in this position.'

'Actually, I do know what it's like to accept domestic violence as the norm. My father was a bully and a drunk, and my formative years were spent never questioning why I had to make myself invisible. He terrified me. And all these years later, he still terrifies me,' Jane said, unable to ignore the decades-old fear that had resurfaced during her mum's last days, and lingered still.

'I'm sorry for you,' Ashleigh said, 'but that's not been my experience.'

'Are you sure about that?' asked Jane. She saw Ashleigh twitch in response, but pushed on. 'You must have had a difficult childhood, too.'

Benji yelped. 'Oh, I'm so sorry,' Ashleigh said while attempting to rub the dog's back. 'My fingers got tangled in his fur.'

Not willing to be consoled, Benji leapt from Ashleigh's lap and disappeared in the direction of his bed in the kitchen.

'It's fine, no harm done.'

Ashleigh checked her watch. 'Maybe I should—'

'I hope you don't think I've pried,' Jane said. Now that she had brought up Ashleigh's childhood, she couldn't let it drop. 'But I am aware of your dad's conviction.'

'We can't have any secrets in this day and age, can we?' Ashleigh observed dryly, but at least she didn't ask Jane to explain how she had stumbled upon the information. 'For the record, just because my dad was a drunk, didn't mean he was also abusive. He was good fun to be around.'

Jane was tempted to challenge her, but it was a valid point. This wasn't Jane's story, it was Ashleigh's.

'He was what my sister called a high functioning alcoholic. Mum had a drinking problem too, and if anyone was responsible for the accident, it was her. She was meant to be the nominated driver that day, but she treated it like a competition to see who could get drunk the fastest so the other would have to drive,' Ashleigh said. 'And I'm not excusing either of them, but it's fair to say that my family has a habit of using alcohol to solve problems. Rose recognized I was doing the same, and it's time I accepted it too.'

'Will your sister be helping you?'

Ashleigh looked down at her watch again. 'Probably not.'

'She must have been shocked when she saw your injuries this morning.'

'She's had worse herself when she's been on a bender,' Ashleigh said. Without the dog on her knee, she couldn't stop fidgeting. Her discomfort was obvious, less so the cause. 'But to answer your question, she's proud of what I'm doing, but we both recognize that we're too alike to be able to support each other.'

'Could it be that you still don't trust her, Ashleigh?'

'I do want to believe her. I want to believe them both.'

'But?'

'I'm sure it's nothing.'

'Sorry, do you need a tissue?' asked Jane, seeing Ashleigh dab at her glistening eyes.

'No, it's fine, I'm being silly.' She sniffed, then straightened the watch on her wrist. 'Evan wants to help me, and it makes sense that he'd take advice from Rose. That would be reason enough for them to message each other all the time. Wouldn't you say?'

'It's one explanation. Have you seen any of their messages?'

Ashleigh shook her head quickly. 'But just as I was leaving to come here, I saw her name pop up on his phone. It's probably nothing. I have to stop obsessing about these things,' she said, more to herself than to Jane. 'You don't have to worry about me, Jane. And I'd be ever so grateful if you could forget all about what's happened recently. We are where we are, and that's the only part of our lives we can control.'

Jane envied anyone who could put the past behind them so easily. 'I suppose . . . If you're sure there's nothing I can do to change your mind,' she said. Feeling suddenly bone-weary, she had to stifle a yawn. 'Sorry. Yesterday really took it out of me.'

'You do look exhausted.'

Jane glanced at the clock, as conscious of the time as Ashleigh. 'I might have an early night.'

'Me too. The last few days have been draining, and I just want to switch off. The doctor prescribed me some sleeping tablets a while back, and I've avoided taking them so far, but not tonight.'

'You don't have to rush off,' Jane said when she saw Ashleigh about to rise.

'No, I won't keep you. I just wanted to say thank you for looking out for me. I know I've said hurtful things about you being at the window, but I've come to find it reassuring. And don't worry about Evan catching you. It'll do him good to know he's still being watched. If he puts a foot wrong, you have my permission to call the police.'

'I will,' Jane said, unsettled that Ashleigh was already preparing for that eventuality.

CHAPTER 35

1974

With their daughter out of sight and out of his reach, Les shoved Cynthia against the wall. Crushing the collar of her overalls in his fist, he lifted her so she had to stand on tiptoe.

'I make the rules in this house,' he said, baring his teeth.

His face was so close that Cynthia could see the individual bubbles of spittle foaming at his mouth.

'Are you listening to me?'

Cynthia's mouth was set in a grim line. Les wasn't going to bully his way out of this one.

'No one is leaving,' he continued. 'Not me, not you, and not Jane. And don't even think about taking her to hospital. No one is going to know about this. OK?'

They had both seen Jane's arm twist as she fell, but it was her scream that had left no doubt about a more serious injury. She would need hospital treatment, and Cynthia was going to make sure she received it.

Les waited for Cynthia to agree, or at least acknowledge that she had heard him speak, but her expression remained blank. He let go of her collar, only to clamp his hand beneath her chin, his fingers and thumb pressing into her cheeks to force the words from her mouth.

'I said, OK?'

Still, she would not speak.

'You're a nutter,' he said, spitting in her face before slamming her head against the wall.

Cynthia had had her head smashed enough times to know that the pain ought to have been excruciating, so it was odd that she didn't feel it. Nor did she cry out, which was the final insult to Les, and he stormed off to the kitchen.

This was where Cynthia would normally retreat, but the threat Les posed went beyond what harm he could do that day. He had struck out at Jane this time, and that was a precedent that couldn't be allowed to go unchecked. It would not become the new norm in their lives.

Stalking into the kitchen, she found Les filling a glass with water. His hands were shaking, and he slurped noisily. It was the first time Cynthia had seen him shaken.

He turned at the sound of her laughter. 'What's so funny?'

'I don't think you realize that the more you try to prove how strong and clever you are, the more stupid and pathetic you look. You're a little boy throwing a tantrum. That's why I'm laughing.'

Les flung his glass at her, but she dodged it easily, moving without impediment despite her injuries. This riled him more, and he glanced around for another weapon, something heavier, harder, sharper. Cynthia did the same.

Within her reach was an old jam jar full of oddments.

She registered a spanner and a screwdriver amongst felt-tip pens and a ruler before her eyes snapped towards the knife resting on a chopping board. Les had noticed it too. Knives were usually kept hidden away in a drawer, but he'd been cutting up potatoes to make chips.

Les was closer to the knife, and he lunged towards it. There was no time for Cynthia to flee, he would only catch her if she tried, so she barrelled straight towards him. As she rammed into Les, his fingers glanced off the handle, sending the knife spinning across the worktop.

Cynthia tried to block him again, and when Les elbowed her out of the way, she refused to bend. The numbness that protected her from pain had become her superpower. She grabbed his shirt to twist him around, then pushed with enough force to send him reeling backwards. He tried to catch his fall, but his hand slipped on the wet Belfast sink. There was a loud thwack, and he went down like a hanged man in a noose.

CHAPTER 36

Despite Jane going to bed early, sleep refused to come. Unlike Ashleigh, she didn't have sleeping tablets to switch off her thoughts, and as time trickled from one day to the next, she debated which was worse: the cruel mind games Ashleigh endured, or the unconcealed brutality her mum had suffered. She didn't fully understand either's torment because she couldn't see the full picture. She had heard rather than seen what had happened to her mum, whilst with Ashleigh, she was relying on her view from the attic window.

She tried to use logic to fill in the gaps, treating each situation like a mathematical equation, but she kept coming up with errors. Ashleigh's behaviour had so many inconsistencies. She had accepted Evan and Rose's explanation of their relationship, and yet she clearly didn't trust them. She had evidence to prove her husband was a thief, but was using it to make her abuser stay rather than force him to leave.

In contrast, there was no doubting that Cynthia had

wanted Les out of the house, but here there were anomalies too. The version of events Jane had grown up believing didn't fit with the evidence that had come to light more recently. And what was that evidence? A box of miscellaneous items linked to her dad, and a small suitcase. Even now, she would be hard pressed to explain what had gone through her mind when Phil had broken the seal on her old den, but it had been enough to put her whole life on hold. Her family thought she was irrational. She *wanted* to be irrational because the alternative was unthinkable.

Tossing and turning from one side of the bed to the other, Jane became tangled in her thoughts as well as the bedlinen, and flung off the solitary cotton sheet that weighed heavily on her. It was one o'clock, too soon to give up on sleep, so she stared up at the ceiling and repeated the breathing exercise her yoga teacher had taught her. Breathe in. Breathe out. Let go.

When her thoughts were finally ready to release her, she drifted towards sleep. And then, a hot flush rose through her body.

'For God's sake,' she cried out, jumping out of bed to open a window. The night was still, and the air dense with summer heat that did nothing to cool her.

There was no reason to believe she would catch a breeze from any other window, but she found herself climbing the narrow stairs to the attic, careful to avoid the creak on the third step. There was no barricade at the top, no suitcase balanced on an old army trunk to block the line of sight to her den, nor was there that sense of safety she had felt as a child when reaching her refuge.

The half-closed blind provided just enough ambient light

for Jane to reach the window without stubbing her toe. She raised it fully to open the window, and the smell of grass filled the air, but the heat was no less oppressive. In the houses opposite, she spied a light in an upstairs window. It was three doors down from the Jarvises' where there was a young family with a new baby. No mystery there. The house directly opposite was in darkness. All was quiet, or so she thought until a shadow moved across the frosted window in the Jarvises' bathroom.

Rubbing the grit from her eyes, Jane looked again, but stillness had returned, and she turned away. Ashleigh wasn't the reason she had dragged herself up to the attic at two o'clock in the morning, but her steps were leaden as she went to her desk to select the pen with the sturdiest nib. Wielding it like a sword, she crossed the room to the secret den that had once been a place to escape the monsters, but now contained them.

She used the makeshift tool to score through the outline of the false panel, leaving jagged edges of lining paper. With a final jab, she poked through the hidden spyhole, discarded the pen and with just one finger, removed the panel with an ease that belied the emotional strength the act required.

The air smelled musty and unnervingly familiar as she leant forward for a better look inside. Half hidden in the gloom was the box Phil had rummaged through, and next to it, the dark shape of a suitcase. She didn't need more light to know that its cover was red tartan.

Jane had stared at that crisscross pattern for what seemed like hours on the night her dad had disappeared. With her eye pressed to the spyhole, she had listened to every thump and crash, heard her mum's repeated demands for Les to leave, and longed for the sound of the front door slamming behind him. What she hadn't expected was the squeak of the wrought-iron side gate. The fighting had stopped, but she wasn't convinced that the danger had passed, and it was some time later when the attic light came on. She had released a whimper when she heard a creak on the third step.

'It's all right, it's only me,' her mum had said as she removed the panel. 'You're safe.'

Crouching down so they were at eye level, Jane's mum held a mug of cocoa to coax her little girl out, but the comforting aroma of warm chocolate wasn't enough to disguise the metallic smell of blood.

Her mum set down the drink so she could check her daughter. 'How's your arm?'

'I can't move it. It hurts.'

Her mum stroked a trembling thumb across Jane's red and crusted eyes to wipe away fresh tears. 'May's going to take you to hospital.'

Fear gripped Jane's heart. 'No, Mum. I want you to take me.'

'I have to stay here.' Cynthia's smile wobbled, but she managed to hold it long enough to reach her eyes. 'Please, Jane, you've been so brave. Can you try a little longer? For me?'

Jane stared at the dried blood around her mum's swollen left ear, matted in her hair and staining her overalls. 'But you're hurt too.'

Cynthia rested a palm on the side of her head and winced. 'If I go with you, people will start asking questions about what happened. They might think I can't look after you. Do you understand?'

'I'm sorry,' Jane said, her lip quivering. 'Is it my fault? I know I was supposed to ask May before coming home, but me and Sheena had a fight. I didn't think.'

'Jane, none of this is your fault. Do you hear me?'

Jane nodded.

'And don't you worry about me, I'll mend. We both will,' her mum said, trying not to grimace as she straightened up. She rummaged in a nearby crate and picked out an old headscarf to make a sling. When it was tied securely around Jane's neck to support her injured arm, Cynthia picked up the mug of cocoa. 'Now drink this before it gets cold.'

Jane took a sip, her eyes never leaving her mum's face. 'Where's Dad?'

'Gone.'

Her mum had the weirdest smile as she moved the red tartan suitcase, unzipping it to take out the old bedding that had been stored inside.

Jane almost spilled her cocoa when she realized her mum was demolishing her barricade. 'You can't do that. What about next time?'

'There isn't going to be a next time.'

Jane forgot all about her sore arm as she trailed after her mum down the stairs. 'But how do you know Dad won't come back?'

'Trust me,' Cynthia said as she dumped the suitcase on her bed and flung it open. 'We're not going to be afraid of him any more.'

They had tried so hard to live by that mantra in the years that followed, but her mum's songs and silliness hadn't dispelled their fears completely. They had simply been locked away in a suitcase that wasn't much bigger than the carry-on luggage allowed on modern day airlines.

It was remarkable how the tales they had told back then had endured for fifty years, like how Sheena believed Jane had fallen down the stairs, even though it was May who had fabricated that particular fib on the way to the hospital. At least Jane had been party to that lie, unlike the story of her dad hitching a free passage on the next ship out of the Mersey, travelling the seven seas and sending his daughter the occasional present until he bored of his old life. That one had been sold to her as a truth, but it only held up as long as Jane didn't look for the flaws in the logic, or peek inside the suitcase she now knew he had never come back to collect.

She didn't doubt it still contained all those essentials her dad would have needed for his travels, not when it was sitting alongside a box containing gifts that had perpetuated the lie she had been sold. Jane had no way of knowing where the suitcase had been lurking during the time she had refused to give up her den, but by the following Christmas, when she had rejected the last present from her dad, her mum had sealed away all her secrets, thinking they could be forgotten.

Jane reached inside the box and rummaged blindly until her hand wrapped around the plastic dome of a snow globe. The water level inside had dropped over time, and when she turned it over, she felt the fake snow hitting the sides in thick clumps, but she was more interested in its underbelly. It was too dark to read the three words written on a tiny gold sticker, but she knew what it said. Made in China. She had told everyone her dad had sailed to the other side of the world based on this information, and she had never thought to question it until very recently.

It was when her mum was dying that Jane first noticed the unravelling threads in the story that had been so carefully woven. Despite all her promises, Cynthia was afraid that Les could still hurt them. Jane had wanted to dismiss her mum's distress as confusion, but there was no confusion on the day Phil had taken it upon himself to ransack the attic in search of family heirlooms.

Seeing him hold up the snow globe, then spotting the hidden suitcase, had sparked connections in Jane's mind that terrified her. Her husband had thought she was over-reacting, but he simply hadn't realized what she had been reacting to. In an instant, Jane had known that whatever had happened to her dad, whatever her mum had been trying to hide, it had the power to destroy her family. Jane had to protect them, and she had used the only weapon to hand: the flaws in her marriage that gave her the perfect excuse to separate Phil and Megan from any harm that might come their way. Phil had to leave, and she had to stay. It had been that simple.

Jane threw the snow globe back in the box, and it landed softly on her dad's overcoat. It had been cold that night, and logic dictated that he wouldn't have left without it. Nor was he the type to have sneaked out by the side gate.

Her mum's final warning came back to haunt her.

'He's still here.'

CHAPTER 37

Ashleigh heard the mattress creak, and snapped her eyes open as Evan swung his legs off the bed. He leant forward to rest his head in his hands, and released a groan.

'Bad night?' she asked.

'Not great.'

When Ashleigh had returned home from Jane's the night before, Evan had been slumped asleep in front of the TV. He had already finished off the curry she had made specially for him, and judging by the empty bottles on the coffee table, he had also given in to the temptation of the cold beers in the fridge. She had bought the beers at the same time she had picked up the wine Rose had tried shaming her with. That bottle was still intact. Not a drop had passed her lips since falling flat on her face in the kitchen. Was that only two days ago? It seemed longer. So much had happened since.

'Did you notice what time I went to bed?' Evan asked.

She stared at his arched back. He was still wearing the T-shirt he had changed into after work, minus his jogging pants. 'It was after me,' she said, wrinkling her nose. It was taking forever to heal. 'Why? Can't you remember?'

Evan didn't answer.

'Sorry, can't help,' she said. 'I took a couple of sleeping pills when I got back from Jane's and was out like a light.' Ashleigh yawned into her pillow. 'God, I'm ridiculously tired. Maybe I'm pregnant.'

'Already?' he asked, his head jerking in her direction. 'When did you come off the pill?'

'A few days ago.'

'Then I'm guessing not.'

'We could try,' she said, reaching over to stroke his back.

Evan moved away from her ever so slightly. 'I'm tired too,' he said.

Ashleigh scowled: had Evan been scratching that particular itch elsewhere? 'In that case, why don't you get some fresh air?' she said. 'You must be dying to sort out the garden after the mess we made.'

'I can't be bothered.'

'Please, Evan. I want you to be happy,' Ashleigh said, trying to sound genuinely concerned. 'I tried to tidy things up, but you're so much better at that sort of thing than me. It really is an eyesore.'

Evan didn't respond, which was better than another refusal.

'I promise I won't interfere. I'm happy to stay in bed,' she said with a yawn.

'I suppose it might clear my head.'

Ashleigh watched Evan reach for his phone on the bedside table as he stood up. A blush rose to his cheeks, and from the rapid tap of buttons, she guessed he was busy deleting messages. He knew his wife regularly checked his phone, but it was too late. She had already seen the exchange that had taken place while she was en route to Jane's. Rose had asked if her sister had left yet and whether she could come around. Evan's response had been immediate, telling her it wasn't safe.

Ashleigh hadn't known her husband was in the habit of punctuating his messages to his sister-in-law with a kiss, but she had taken some comfort in his rejection of Rose's advances, even if his response was motivated by caution.

'Can you open the blinds before you go?' she asked, lifting a hand, then dropping it again as if she were too feeble to complete the task herself.

Evan did as he was told, and twenty minutes later she could hear him working in the garden. She was lying flat out on the bed, arms extended across the full width of the mattress, her head turned so she could watch the house opposite. The attic window had been a half-closed sleepy eye for days, but now it was wide open, and as she listened to the scrape of loose earth being shovelled into the trough, she wondered if Jane was watching. Ashleigh feigned sleep, until she drifted off into dreams of a life where Rose was no longer a threat, where Evan gave his soon-to-be-pregnant wife all the attention she craved, and where everyone forgot how bad things had needed to get before they could get better.

CHAPTER 38

It was the sound of a spade slicing through soft earth that woke Jane with a jolt. She had fallen asleep at her desk, her head resting on folded arms that stuck to the keyboard as she tried to move. It took a while to work out that the noise that had disturbed her hadn't followed her from her dreams, but came instead from the open window flooding the room with morning light.

Too stiff to straighten up properly, Jane hobbled over to the window and spotted Evan working in his garden. The trough was back in its usual place, and he was refilling it with dark earth. Jane's heartbeat thrummmed against the back of her throat. She was always going to look at Evan with a spade and see a gravedigger, but she could clearly see Ashleigh fast asleep in their bedroom.

Jane turned away and rested her back against the windowsill to survey the room. She had been looking for bodies in all the wrong places, as was apparent from her internet search history from the early hours of the morning. It wasn't the first time she had tried to trace Lesley Morgan, having embarked on a new quest each time technology made the world a little smaller, but never had she been so desperate for proof of life. All she had needed was one hit on Google, but it was time to acknowledge that she was more likely to find her dad much closer to home.

If Jane understood her mum's warnings, and Les was still here, where was the body? Jane could take a sledgehammer to the attic walls, but she didn't think it was necessary. She couldn't guess what had been going through her mum's mind that night, or in the subsequent fifty years, but she would never have let Jane continue to play in the attic after her dad had vanished if there was a corpse nearby. Admittedly, her mum had sealed up the den within the year, but the family skeletons hidden inside didn't include her father's remains, she was certain of that.

Knowing the search must continue if she was ever to find peace, Jane went downstairs to make a cup of tea. She followed Benji out through the back door, but while the dog headed towards the garden, Jane went straight to the side gate and gave it a good rattle. Had it been the wind that had made it creak that night? Was it even the same gate?

No closer to the truth, Jane poked her head inside the garage that had been converted into a workshop by her grandfather. It was home to a collection of carefully curated tools and equipment, and Cynthia would never have tainted it with Les's presence. Jane moved on to the patio that was made from the same yellow paving stones as those in the rest of the garden, all of which had been laid in 1974. It was an easy date to remember because so much had happened that year. She had been eight. Her dad had vanished, and her mum wanted to add the sunshine back into their lives.

As Jane sat at the patio table and sipped her tea, she told herself it was perfectly normal to while away the morning wondering where her dad's body might be buried. *Might* being the operative word. Her internal debate was far from settled, but instinct told her that his disappearance had been too swift and too final for a man who took pleasure in intimidation. She tapped a paving stone with her slipper.

Burying bodies under the patio was a well-worn trope and felt too obvious, but Jane's gut told her she was approaching the truth. You only had to look at the contrast between the work her mum had put into modernizing the house and compare it to the garden and the garish Seventies paving stones. It wasn't bad taste that had made her mum leave the garden untouched, nor had it been pure nostalgia that had stopped Jane digging it up after she died. The family secret had been passed on to the next generation with no explanation, and instinctively, Jane had known she must protect it.

'Too late,' her mum had said. Had she meant it had been too late to warn Jane of the truth? Too late to fix things? And was Jane destined to commit the same mistake with her family?

As if she had conjured Megan from the ether, her phone rang.

'Hello, sweetheart,' Jane said, cradling her mobile to her ear.

'Hi, Mum.'

Her daughter sounded deflated, not quite the life raft

Jane had been hoping for, but concern for Megan overrode all other fears. 'Are you OK?'

'I'm fine. Are you?'

'Yeah,' said Jane, matching the lie.

'What have you been up to?'

'Not much. You?' When her daughter didn't answer, Jane wasn't going to be fobbed off a second time. 'What is it? What's wrong?'

Megan paused, then exhaled loudly, 'I'm just worn out by this impasse you and Dad have reached.'

'Try being me,' Jane said with a mirthless laugh as she surveyed the garden. Benji had been sniffing around, but heard the sound and came to join her. Jumping over the box hedging that outlined the rays of the sun design, he was as determined as ever to avoid the garden's centrepiece.

'God, I wish I was you,' Megan said, the dullness in her voice replaced by frustration. 'I wouldn't let this bloody stupid charade go on a second longer. It's pathetic. Dad says he's fine, but he's not. He's heartbroken, Mum, and *you* did that to him.'

'I know I did,' Jane replied as she stood up. Her groan was in part from sore muscles, but there was pain from the hurt she had inflicted on her family too. 'I wish I could explain, but the truth is, I haven't completely worked it out myself.'

As she spoke, Jane stepped onto one of the paving stone paths. In the cold light of day, the design looked more like a spider's web than a sunset, and Jane was the one it had trapped.

'Are you saying you've destroyed your marriage without knowing why?' demanded Megan in her ear.

With Benji following, Jane reached the curved edge of the central sun, but could go no further. 'All I can say is that it has nothing to do with your dad.'

'It has everything to do with Dad! You can't walk away from a thirty-year marriage and claim it has nothing to do with him. I don't understand. What is it you're not telling me?'

How Jane wished she had asked the same of her mum. She squeezed her eyes shut so she didn't have to look at the awful paving stones, and thought back to how the garden had looked before the makeover. The original patio had been made from large grey flagstones, and beyond that was the working garden her Great Aunt Judith had created. Jane could remember picking summer fruits when she was very young, but not all the land had been worked. One section had been little more than a piece of wasteland.

Jane's brow knitted together as this elusive memory grew in substance. Her dad had smashed up the old Anderson shelter, leaving a deep pit that, in the eyes of a child, had become a boat, a battlefield, or a mountain to climb. In her mind, Jane overlaid a map of the old garden on top of the sun design. The hairs on the back of her neck stood on end despite the sun on her face. She opened her eyes.

'Oh, God.'

'Mum? What is it?'

'I can't . . .'

Jane was staring at the exact spot where there had been a hollow big enough to accommodate two little girls. Or the body of an adult. It was now obscured by an eclectic mix of planters that covered the centrepiece of her mum's design like sunspots. It was as if Cynthia had needed the added reassurance that those paving stones weren't going to move.

'Please, Mum,' Megan said, her tone as gentle as a kiss. 'What can I do to help?'

'You can't do anything,' Jane said as her whole body began to shake. 'I'll be fine in a minute.'

'What if I come over?' Megan suggested. 'I'm supposed to be working tomorrow, but I'll see if I can get someone to cover for me.'

'Absolutely not!' Jane snapped out of her trance. 'I don't want you here. I don't think I could cope . . . It's not you. I just need some time.'

'You've had time, and it hasn't helped. You don't have to go through this all by yourself,' Megan said. 'We're here for you. Me *and* Dad.'

'I'm sure he's far too busy picking new dates,' said Jane, needing to remind them both that Phil had closed off that particular option.

'Dad isn't as interested in finding someone else as he's been making out. He'd want to help, I know he would. All you have to do is ask.'

'It's not that simple.'

'Yes, Mum, it really is. Ask him.'

Jane dismissed the suggestion, but when she was left alone with her thoughts, she continued to grasp her phone tightly. She stepped gingerly onto the circle of paving stones as if testing her mettle to go it alone. It was no surprise that Benji refused to follow. Did he know she was walking over a grave? She staggered back onto the path.

Returning to the safety of the patio, Jane opened the list of contacts on her phone to scroll past names of old friends in Buxton who might welcome a call but were more comfortable sharing recipes than theories about murder. She paused on May's name. She was the only other surviving witness to the events of that night, but Cynthia wouldn't have involved anyone else in her crime, especially her best friend and a mother of two. Jane's next option was Sheena, but she was at work, and in truth, there was only one person Jane wanted to open up to, and she had already scrolled past his name.

She prayed Megan was right, but when Phil didn't answer her call after eight, nine, ten rings, she hung up.

With horror, she realized it was Saturday morning. What if Megan was wrong about him not dating? Phil could be sharing breakfast with some faceless woman at that very moment. She pictured him checking his phone and giving his companion a look of apology for the interruption.

Jane tipped her head back and watched a magpie flit from one rooftop to the next, until the threat of tears subsided. She was about to pick up her empty teacup when her phone rang. It was her turn to consider ignoring the call, but her need to speak to Phil was greater than any fear of embarrassing herself.

'Sorry, I didn't mean to disturb you,' she said before Phil had the chance to speak.

'You're not disturbing me. I was putting out the rubbish, that's all.'

It was one of the few household chores that Jane had never had to remind him to do, especially after a Friday night takeaway. 'What did you have?' she asked.

'Indian.' Assuming this information would elicit some surprise, he added proudly, 'I've acquired a taste for lamb jalfrezi and onion bhajis. Megan is horrified. It's not on her list of healthy options for the over fifties, but it gives me the illusion that I'm not as averse to change as people think.'

'People like me?'

'Some men buy motorbikes and leather jackets. I've ventured into the dangerous world of poppadoms and lime pickle.'

Jane's smile quivered. She could spend the rest of the day talking such silliness, but that was a privilege she had surrendered. 'I wasn't sure if you were with someone else.'

'Ah, no. It might take a while to build up the nerve for that sort of thing,' he replied, nimbly avoiding the word 'date', as Jane had done.

'I'm sorry for how I've treated you, Phil. You've done nothing wrong.'

Phil thought for a moment. 'I'd beg to differ, but I've had enough of arguing.'

'So have I,' admitted Jane, her voice catching.

'If you want my opinion, and you know you're going to get it anyway, we're just two people who care deeply for each other, but have forgotten how to show it,' he said. 'Or am I mistaken?'

Emotions bubbled inside Jane's chest. 'No, you're not. But I'm still sorry,' she began, 'because even though you've summed up the problem with our relationship perfectly, it doesn't make things better. If anything, it makes it harder for me to say that even though I do still love you, Phil, I can't come home. I needed to tell you that, and I think, at last, I'm ready to explain why.'

When Phil didn't respond, Jane couldn't tell if it was because he was shaking his head in dismay, biting his tongue in frustration, or cursing her under his breath. His silence told her only one thing. She couldn't do this over the phone.

'Are you busy? Do you think you could come over here? There's something I need to show you.'

CHAPTER 39

When Jane reached the attic, she turned to wait for Phil. He was wearing Bermuda shorts and a colourful Hawaiian shirt that Jane didn't recognize, and certainly wouldn't have let him buy. Despite the questionable attire, she had wanted to hug him as soon as he had climbed out of the car, but Phil had greeted her with the gentlest touch on her arm. He had judged that she needed to be handled with care, and he was probably right.

At the top of the stairs, Phil glanced over at the window. If he was expecting her to mention the latest developments concerning her neighbour, he would have to wait. There were worse crimes.

'Over here,' she told him.

As they stood shoulder to shoulder in front of the cubby hole door, Phil scratched his beard. 'It was no coincidence that we started arguing within minutes of me finding that box, was it?'

'No.'

'Is it still there?'

She could feel the warmth of Phil's skin so close to hers, and yet she shuddered. 'Yes, and not only the box.'

Phil nodded thoughtfully. 'Shall I?' he asked, extending his hand towards the cut-out hole in the plywood.

'Please.'

Once the panel was removed, they both crouched down. Jane could see yellowed Sellotape marks scarring the inside walls. Below the spot where one poster had been, she had carved Bay City Rollers in capital letters. Underneath, Sheena had coloured in a series of red hearts that had faded along with their schoolgirl crushes.

Unable to look at the box and suitcase Phil dragged into the light, Jane watched Benji sniff inside the now empty cubby hole. If he was a cadaver dog, he found nothing to alert his handler.

'This used to be my den,' she explained to Phil. 'Although a better description these days would be a panic room. Mum built it.'

'So your dad wouldn't find you?'

Jane nodded. 'She didn't like me using it after he'd gone. I didn't exactly forget about it, but it was a place I chose not to revisit.'

'Until now.'

Phil pulled the box towards him, but unlike his last rummage, he treated each item inside with a touch of reverence. As well as the snow globe, there were colouring books with writing in a foreign language that young Jane hadn't recognized at the time.

'Your dad was in Germany?'

When Jane gave a noncommittal shrug, Phil continued rooting through the box. Beneath the old overcoat he had coveted the first time he had seen it, there were boots, gloves and a scarf. Phil sat back on his haunches as they turned their attention to the suitcase. There was a padlock that kept secure the zip that ran along three sides.

'Do you have a key?' he asked.

'No, but I came prepared.'

As she went to straighten up, Jane put her hand on Phil's shoulder as leverage, and almost couldn't bear to let him go. Making it to her desk, she picked up a pair of bolt cutters and handed them over.

While her husband worked, Jane remained standing. Her fear mixed with the must in the air and made it hard to breathe as Phil snapped the shank of the padlock.

He turned, sensing her unease. 'Are you ready?'

At first the zip wouldn't budge, and even when Phil managed to pull it down to the first corner, it stuck again. Despite Jane's previous prevarication, waiting to see what was inside felt interminable, and she was about to fetch the Stanley knife she had on standby when Phil's persever-ance paid off and all three sides were open. He flipped back the tartan cover as if revealing a magic trick that would explain why their marriage had gone into freefall.

There were no surprises for Jane, and her heart dropped. The case contained exactly what she had thought they would find, although she hadn't expected her dad's clothes to be folded quite so neatly. She had a vision of her mum desperately shoving handfuls of shirts into the case, but it must have been a trick of the mind. Only Jane had been panicking that her dad would reappear at any moment.

If she dared to pick up one of the paisley patterned shirts, she imagined it would smell of cheap cologne and stale beer, but her greatest fear was what lay hidden beneath. Every muscle in her body tensed. She was getting closer to the truth.

'So this was your dad's suitcase,' Phil said, giving his wife a quizzical look. 'But why would your mum keep it?'

'I'd say the more pertinent question is, why did my dad leave it behind?'

Phil moved his head from side to side as he considered the conundrum. 'After beating up Cynthia and breaking your arm, Les was probably expecting a visit from the police.'

'Even so,' she said.

Phil prodded at a pair of socks. 'I still don't understand what this has to do with you not coming home.'

'Keep looking.'

'For what?'

When Jane had followed her mum down from the attic, there had been a collection of things on the bed waiting to be packed, things that were even more essential than an overcoat and a pair of boots for a man embarking on a new life.

'Just look,' she said, clinging to the last vestiges of hope. Not everything fitted with her working theory. The colouring books were from another country, she reminded herself.

Sensing his wife's growing anxiety, Phil gently peeled away the layers to uncover a pair of slippers, two belts, a shaving set, and a tub of Brylcreem that might still contain the imprints of her dad's fingertips. At the very bottom were the things that Jane hadn't wanted to find. She clamped a hand over her mouth as Phil lifted up a folded leather wallet and a passport.

Opening the passport briefly, Phil set eyes on his father-in-law's face for the very first time. A frown formed deep ridges across his brow. 'So . . . He didn't set off on his travels across the world. Not easily, at least.'

Jane fought to contain the shockwaves rocking her body. 'Or at all.'

'What are you thinking?' Jane asked after they had retreated to the kitchen.

Phil took the cup of tea she pressed into his hand. 'It's odd, I'll give you that,' he said, resting his back against the edge of the worktop.

Jane took up a similar position directly opposite. 'It's more than odd, Phil. It's terrifying.'

'I wish I'd stopped to think how upsetting it must have been for you to see me pulling out your dad's things. I'm sorry, Jane. I should have been more sensitive.'

'You might have been a bit distracted by me telling you our marriage was over.'

'Ah, yes, there was that.' He offered a sad smile. 'So explain it to me. What made you take one look at your dad's suitcase and decide you couldn't come home to Buxton?'

'Isn't it obvious?' she asked, more of a plea than a challenge. She didn't want to have to say the words, but it was too much to expect Phil to reach the same horrifying conclusion when, until recently, she had refused to acknowledge it herself.

'I'd rather hear your thoughts, Jane. The life you describe with your dad is completely alien to me, and the only memories I have of this house are good ones, with you and

273

your mum. I literally can't imagine what it was like for either of you leading up to the time your dad . . . Tell me what happened on the night he disappeared. You can add the context. I can't.'

Jane held Phil's gaze. He had deliberately referred to her dad as disappearing, *not* leaving, which meant he was at least opening his mind to other possibilities. But he made a good point. It was for her to set out the facts as she knew them. She raised her teacup and took a small sip to moisten her lips.

'On that last night, I'd come home earlier than I was supposed to, and walked in on them fighting. Mum was already battered and bleeding,' Jane said, closing her eyes only to open them immediately when a picture formed. 'I don't know why Dad had kicked off, he rarely needed an excuse, but I do remember him threatening to leave and take me with him. And he would have done it too, just to hurt Mum. He thought it would be easy convincing everyone she wasn't respectable enough to bring up a child.'

'Because she was an unmarried mother?'

'Mum had had a run-in with social services before. They'd turned up at the hospital when I was born, thinking they could persuade her to give me up for adoption. She was seventeen, there was no father on the scene, and she didn't have maternal support – my Great Aunt Judith was living in the Isle of Man by this point. They told Mum she wasn't fit to look after me, but she didn't give in to the pressure, and my granddad made damn sure she took me home with her.'

'Good for him,' said Phil. He stared down into his teacup when he added, 'But was it a real threat? I mean, Cynthia did go on to bring you up on her own without any inter-ference from the authorities, didn't she?'

'Only because Dad didn't report her,' said Jane as a cold shudder ran down her spine.

Jane was drip-feeding her husband the information, and thought she saw a flicker of realization behind his eyes, but typical of Phil, he gave little away.

'And why do you think that was?' he asked.

Jane told Phil everything she could remember, from her fight with Sheena right up to the point where May whisked her off to the hospital. 'By the time I came home again, Mum had finished clearing out Dad's things, and the suit-case was nowhere to be seen. I assumed he'd been back to collect it, or Mum had forwarded his things on. I never really questioned it, but deep down, I was always terrified that he would come back. Actually, no,' she said, correcting herself, 'I was scared he hadn't left.'

'Go on,' Phil said, forcing Jane to make the connections he couldn't yet see.

'While I was hiding upstairs, I'd been waiting to hear the front door slam, but I only ever heard the creak of the side gate.' She shook her head. 'That wasn't Dad. He liked to make a big entrance, and he was the same with his exits. I don't think he left, Phil. *He's still here.* Doesn't that sound familiar?'

'It was what Cynthia kept saying.'

Phil hadn't been able to get much time off while his mother-in-law was dying, but he had visited when he could, and had witnessed her distress as she spoke those words over and over again.

'But she was delusional,' he continued. 'Some days she

thought she was a young girl. Other times, when she was becoming agitated, it seemed like she was reliving her life with Les.'

'I'd presumed the same, but . . .' Jane set aside her tea. 'There *had* been confusion, but not all of it was on Mum's part. We had this one particular conversation when she was almost coherent, and I think I missed the one chance I had to have a proper talk with her.'

'What did she say?'

'That she was sorry, and scared that she'd left it too late. I thought she was talking about the years it took her to kick Dad out, but later in the conversation, when she was telling me to hide, what if she knew she was in the present? What if she wasn't asking *me* to hide, but to hide *something*?'

'The suitcase?'

Jane shook her head imperceptibly. 'Not just the suitcase. I'd been working in the garden that day and had dirt beneath my nails. I don't think she liked the idea of me digging out there. I'd spent weeks trying to show her photos of the things I'd planted, but she turned her face away every single time. Whatever she wanted me to keep hidden, I think it's in the garden.' Jane came to a juddering stop when she saw the horror she felt reflected in her husband's eyes. 'Oh, Phil, if only I'd stayed at May's like I was supposed to, Dad would never have hurt me, and Mum wouldn't have been forced into an impossible position.'

'She had to make him leave.'

'And when he wouldn't . . .'

When Jane's breath hitched, her husband set down his cup and came over to wrap his arms around her. She pressed her face against his chest. There were so many emotions to wrestle, but it was the smell of the man she had loved for three decades, a mixture of deodorant and sweet sweat, that threatened to overwhelm her. She forced down the lump stuck in her throat. She had to speak the unspeakable.

'I think my dad died that night. I don't know exactly how, and I don't want to, but I have to face the possibility that Mum disposed of the body while I was at the hospital with May, or maybe later when I was in bed. There was a ditch in the back garden where the old Anderson shelter used to be. Mum spent weeks, if not months, laying those paving stones over it, and she never lifted them again except for the odd repair.'

'Jesus,' whispered Phil. She heard him swallow hard. 'But even if she did kill him, why the hell wouldn't she go straight to the police? She'd been beaten. So had you. It would have been a clear case of self-defence.'

'I don't know. Maybe she didn't think she could prove she had no other choice when she killed him, in which case it would be manslaughter at best,' she said. 'And this was the Seventies, remember. Coercive control wasn't recognised like it is now, and Mum had a reputation for being a strong, independent woman. She would have gone to prison while I would have been placed in care. Whatever happened that night, she must have felt that she had no choice.' When Phil's embrace tightened a touch, she lifted her head. 'She did what she did to protect me, and now I have to protect her.'

Phil's eyes widened in disbelief. 'Wait. You've just told me there might be a body buried in the garden, and your plan is simply to ignore it?'

'Mum did.'

'And you think you can live like that?'

Jane managed a bitter laugh. 'Clearly not,' she said. 'I think there was a reason I looked at my neighbour digging a hole and immediately jumped to the conclusion he was burying his wife. I was projecting my fears rather than admitting what my subconscious was screaming at me.'

'But you could be wrong. What about the presents you received? Those colouring books were from Germany.'

'It's one anomaly, Phil, in amongst so much damning evidence,' she said. 'The only way to know for certain is to locate my dad, or his body. And personally, I'd be happier living with an untested theory than risk being proven right.'

'Are you sure about that?'

'No,' she said, grateful that Phil was there to push her closer to a decision. 'I know I have to do something, but I'm struggling to decide what that should be. I could go to the police, but I dread to think how that conversation might go. "Hello, it's me again, the woman who imagines buried bodies in people's gardens. Well, you're not going to believe this . . ."'

'You have a point,' Phil conceded. 'But for what it's worth, I think you've been incredibly noble, if not a little reckless dealing with this by yourself. At least now, whatever happens next, you won't be alone.'

Jane slipped gently from Phil's grasp, reasserting the distance she had to put between them. 'I can't involve you in this. What if I'm right? Can you imagine the scandal back at school if or when it comes to light?'

Phil wiped a hand across his face. 'Frankly, right now I'm struggling to imagine any of this.'

278

It didn't pass Jane's notice that he hadn't disagreed about the potential damage to his reputation. 'I chose to go it alone to protect you and Megan, and I stand by that decision. I appreciate you coming over, I really do. I didn't want to open the suitcase alone, and you have helped me see things more clearly.'

'You're sending me away again?'

The sight of Phil's eyes glistening was almost enough to break her. Jane was tempted to plead with him to be patient, that she would figure a way out of this mess, but there was a very good chance she wouldn't. 'You should find someone else,' she said. 'Someone less complicated.'

Phil surprised her by laughing. 'You do realize that my foray into online dating was simply a ruse to get you back? As was the threat to undo all your good work in our garden. That bleeding heart plant of yours is doing just fine.'

'You lied?' This was a version of her husband that was as unfamiliar to her as his Hawaiian shirt.

'There was only one bleeding heart left to wilt, and it was mine,' he admitted, tapping his chest. 'I know I haven't been the husband you deserved, but I would like the chance to change that.'

'All those things I said about our marriage . . .'

'Were true,' Phil interjected. 'I expected life to continue as always, but that isn't going to happen for many different reasons, so we adapt together. To be clear, I was never going to go on any dates. I was trying to shock you into a response, Jane, that was all. Which seems ridiculous now that I know what you've been dealing with.' He was still smiling when he added, 'I take on board your wish to keep me out of this, but with all due respect, you can bugger off. I promised myself that if you ever gave me a second chance, I'd do better by you. My job isn't as important as you are. Not even close.'

When Jane inched towards Phil, he moved forward too, and they met halfway. She would send him away again, but not yet. For one last time, she would allow herself to revisit the love she and Phil shared, and her breaking heart soared when he kissed her.

CHAPTER 40

'Are you sure you don't want a glass of wine?' asked Sheena in a way that suggested she thought her friend needed a drink.

'Sparkling water is fine,' Jane told the barman, who had hesitated with their order. The yoga stretches had loosened her tense muscles, and she wanted to enjoy the sensation of being able to take a full, deep breath without any stimulants.

'So?' asked Sheena once they were seated. 'What's going on?'

'Why do you think something's going on?'

Sheena raised an eyebrow. 'Oh, maybe because it looked like you had joined the class on a satellite link with a noticeable delay. At one point you were stuck in the chair pose like you were settling down for the evening.'

'I've been talking to Phil,' Jane admitted, having become accustomed to having her defences pulled down, or some of them at least. 'He came over at the weekend.'

Her friend's eyebrow remained resolutely arched. 'The *weekend*? As in a sleepover?'

Jane would have loved to return Sheena's wide grin, but couldn't. 'Before you get any ideas, it doesn't mean we're getting back together, but we have reached a new understanding. Phil's slowly figuring out the post-menopause, post-losing-Mum me. We both are, and . . .' Wanting to offer something closer to the truth, she added, 'I've stopped being angry at him for not recognizing what I'm going through when I'm the one that's hidden so much.'

'Now there's a lesson we could all learn,' Sheena replied. 'I bet Megan is over the moon.'

'She doesn't know. It wouldn't be fair to raise her hopes.'

'So let me get this straight. You and Phil have kissed and made up, but you're not getting back together – even though it's been obvious for a while that's what you wanted.'

'It's not about what I want, or what Phil wants for that matter. It's complicated.'

'What's complicated?'

Jane and Phil had spent hours debating what to do next, and the only thing they had agreed upon with any certainty was what not to do. Digging up the garden by themselves was potentially disturbing a crime scene and might land them in trouble with the police. She could sell up, but what kind of life would she have waiting for the axe to fall, or to be more precise, for the spade to break the ground when the new owner did some gardening? Locking up the house and leaving its secrets for the next generation wasn't an option either, because the next generation was Megan. So that left two choices: she could persuade the police to dig up her family's murky past, or she could prevaricate further. Phil had agreed to the latter, if only because he would prefer to wait for the school holidays so he could give her his undivided support. Jane remained adamant that she wouldn't involve him at all, but that was an argument for another day.

'It's the house,' she told Sheena cryptically. 'Too much has happened there for me to walk away.'

Sheena watched Jane take a sip of sparkling water. 'You're giving up your marriage for the sake of a house you haven't lived in for the last thirty odd years?' she asked. 'And you're supposed to be the logical one? I dread to think what sense you'd make if that was wine.'

Jane smiled. 'Just as muddled, I suspect.'

'This can't be what your mum would want,' Sheena persisted. 'Didn't she put anything in her will about what she expected you to do with the house?'

'It was distinctly lacking in detail,' Jane said, but she could understand why. It would have been an interesting day at the probate office to receive a confession as part of Cynthia's last will and testament.

'What about my mum? Cynthia might have talked to her about stuff like that.'

'I don't imagine Mum told her everything,' said Jane. Even though May had been to the house that night, Cynthia had sent her straight off to the hospital with Jane, keeping both of them out of the way while she cleaned up. 'It wouldn't help.'

Sheena leant forward, staring intently. 'Are you sure about that?'

Jane bit her lip. 'Not really.'

'OK, then, let's go,' Sheena said, picking up her yoga mat from beneath the table.

'You want to go right now?'

'Why not?'

The reason was apparent when May answered the door in her nightie and dressing gown.

'Has something happened?' she asked, looking past her unexpected visitors. 'Someone else hasn't disappeared, have they?'

'Who's disappeared?' Jane asked, her heart stuttering as both May and Sheena glanced in the direction of May's next-door neighbour. 'Ashleigh?'

'No, her sister,' May said. 'Didn't she tell you?'

'I haven't seen her for a few days.'

'Jane's been distracted,' Sheena explained as she slipped past May. 'And we're not here about the bloody Jarvises.'

Jane was left to offer the apology. 'I'm sorry it's so late. We could come back tomorrow.'

'Nonsense, come in. I was about to make myself a cocoa. Do you still like them?'

A few minutes later, Jane was perched on the edge of an armchair, her hands wrapped gratefully around a hot mug despite the evening heat.

'Right then, what's this about?' asked May.

'Jane won't admit it, but she and Phil have got back together,' Sheena jumped in, 'but she's insisting they stay separated because she doesn't want to part with the house. And now we have to exorcise some ghosts so she can skedaddle back to Buxton. Not that I want to lose her again, but my God, she's miserable at the moment, and someone needs to talk some sense into her.' She stopped to acknowledge her mother's hard stare. 'Fine, I'll leave it to Jane to explain.'

May turned to her daughter's best friend. 'How can I help, love?'

Unsure where to begin, Jane went back to the first time she had started to have doubts. 'One of the last things Mum said was that time had run out for us, like she had something important she should have told me.'

May gave her a gentle smile. 'Oh, love, I wouldn't set any store in what your mum said. It wasn't the Cynthia we all knew and loved lying in that bed.'

'Her fear was real though. You heard how she kept telling us Dad was still there?' She watched for May's reaction when she added, 'She never really escaped him, did she?'

May considered the question for a moment, giving nothing away. 'Tell me what you want to know.'

'What do you remember about the night my dad disappeared?'

'Everything,' May said with a note of resignation, as if she had known the question would come one day. She sat back against the worn cushions and blew across the surface of her mug as she gathered her thoughts. 'But to understand fully, you need to appreciate what had been going on around that time. I guess you know Les had lost his job, and he was happy to be a layabout while your mum worked herself to the bone. More than anything, she worried about you being home alone with him when he was drunk, which was why you spent so much time here. I didn't mind at all. You were a quiet little thing, and that was a novelty in this house.'

When May gave her daughter a sidelong glance, Sheena rolled her eyes.

The love between the pair made Jane's heart clench. She swallowed hard as May picked up her story again.

'I wasn't working, but being a housewife in those days wasn't as easy as it is now with all your gizmos and gadgets. To get through my chores, I liked to play my records. I was a proper Beatles fan, sneaked off regularly to see them play long before they were famous,' she said as if she hadn't mentioned it many times before. 'After I got married and had kids, I missed all of that, so I'd grab a duster and dance around the living room like I was back in the Cavern.' The light in her eyes dimmed. 'That day your dad left, I'd had my records on while I was out cleaning the front step. I came in to fetch clean water when he appeared behind me.'

'Les?' asked Sheena.

'I'd left the door open, and he'd marched straight in. He suggested we should have a private party. He was always making innuendos,' May said, the words on her tongue were as repugnant as the idea. 'He was a good-looking man, Les, but he thought a lot of himself. He expected every woman to fall for his charm, and a lot of them did.'

Jane had never thought of Les as a charmer, although her mum must have been dazzled by him once upon a time.

'Not me, though. I saw how he treated my Cynthia,' May said to Jane. 'And I knew he had a temper, so I was civil but firm when I asked him to leave. He kept ignoring me, and that's when I threatened to ring your mum. It didn't matter where Cynthia was working, she always made sure I had a contact number in case of an emergency.'

'And did you phone her?' It was Sheena again, and a frown had replaced her earlier spark of amusement.

'Les said it would be better if no one knew. He made it sound like we were getting up to no good, and I was worried how your dad would react if he found out Les had been trying it on,' May said. 'I'm pretty sure he would have punched Les's lights out, or at least tried.'

Jane blinked as a half-forgotten memory resurfaced. 'But someone did hit Dad. He had a black eye the last time I saw him.' She had presumed at the time it was her mum.

May raised one hand into a fist. Her jaw was set firm with an anger that hadn't diminished over the decades. 'I'd never struck someone before, and I can tell you now, it felt good.'

'*You* hit him?' asked Sheena.

'Too right, I did. There's only so long you can be polite about such things.' Her eyes narrowed at the memory. 'He'd got me in a dance hold and started swinging me about. I was too busy telling him to leave to notice how the sneaky bugger was manoeuvring me into a corner. When he tried it on, I punched him.'

'I'm so sorry,' said Jane, aghast. It hadn't crossed her mind that her dad's intimidation had extended beyond her family.

May's lips puckered, and the wrinkles around her mouth deepened. 'I grabbed my sweeping brush to fend him off, and it was like poking a tiger. He wasn't pretending to be a charmer any more. I'd never seen anger like it, and especially not directed at a woman. It was as if there was nothing behind those green eyes of his.'

'Did he leave?' asked Jane, feeling sick at how far her dad might have taken things.

'Yes, he left,' May said. She hunched her shoulders, and sought out the warmth of her drink. 'I'd been quite naïve up until that point. Stupidly, I'd assumed he must have had some redeeming qualities for your mum to put up with him, but that man was bad to the core.'

'Did Mum know it was you who hit him?' asked Jane.

'Oh, yes. I was on the phone to her as soon as I'd chased Les out of the house. I had this horrible feeling he was going to take it out on her, and poor Cynthia was mortified. She felt responsible, like she had somehow enabled him to treat women like that, but I told her she wasn't to blame for any of it. He was.' Cocoa slopped from May's mug, and she wiped it away. 'Anyway, it was enough to convince her to finally kick him out.'

'So it wasn't because he broke my arm?'

'No, love. Cynthia had already decided what she needed to do, but maybe seeing him hurt you made her all the more determined.'

'It took more than determination. He could always silence Mum with his fists,' Jane said. She was quiet for a moment as she thought back to all those times her mum had taken the punches. It was only seeing Les turn on the people she loved that had tipped her over the edge. 'Did you ever see my dad again?'

May blinked away her own memories. 'What's going on, love? Why do you ask?'

'Because I was always terrified that Dad wasn't out of our lives for good, despite what Mum said. And in the end, she couldn't hide how she thought the same.'

'I worried about it for a long time too,' admitted May. 'I stopped playing my records, and never answered the door unless I was expecting someone. People used to think I was hiding from the rent man.' She tried to raise a smile from Jane, but her face fell when she recognized the importance of the question. 'There was a rumour going around the pubs that someone had done him in.'

'But he couldn't have been bumped off. What about Jane's presents?' Sheena reminded them.

'I wouldn't be surprised if Mum got that snow globe from Woolies and just pretended it was from him,' Jane said, turning to the only person who might know. 'What do you think?'

'I don't remember a snow globe. What other gifts were there?' asked May, needing the prompt.

'Colouring books from Germany.'

'Oh, erm, yes,' May said guiltily. 'They were from Mrs Lisman. Her son was in the army, and the family relocated over there for a while. She'd looked after you when you were a baby, and kept in touch.'

'You knew?' asked Jane. 'Didn't you find it odd that Mum was giving my dad credit for someone else's presents?'

'Cynthia wanted you to have something to show off to the other kids who had dads, that was all.'

'I don't think it was the only reason,' replied Jane. 'You said there were rumours. What if someone did kill him?'

May looked away briefly, but her voice was strong when she said, 'There were times when I wished him dead.'

When she offered no more information, it was Sheena who broke the silence. 'Does any of this help?' she asked Jane.

'A little. I still can't quite believe I'm in this situation.'

'What situation? I still don't understand,' said Sheena.

'It's . . .' Jane started.

'Complicated,' Sheena finished for her.

'Too complicated to sort out tonight, and you have a long drive home,' May said to her daughter, making a point of checking the clock on the mantel.

'And an early start tomorrow,' Sheena conceded.

When they set down their drinks and stood up, May

289

took hold of Jane's sleeve, but she was looking at Sheena when she said, 'Night then, love.'

Sheena gave her mum a peck on the cheek. 'Night, Mum.' She was about to leave the room when she realized Jane wasn't following. 'Do you want me to drop you off?'

'She'll be fine,' answered May. 'You go.'

Sheena narrowed her eyes, but headed out anyway. 'I'll catch up with you both tomorrow,' she warned, clearly having worked out there was more to the story.

When they heard the door slam, Jane dropped down onto the sofa. Would she ever hear that sound and not wish with all her heart that Les had just left them alone?

May sat down next to her and took hold of her hand. 'Come on, you need to tell me. Why all these questions?'

It was apparent Jane wasn't going to get her hand back until she gave the unedited explanation for her late-night visit. 'I found Dad's suitcase, May. It was hidden in the attic, and it had everything inside. His clothes, his wallet, his passport.' She turned to see the colour drain from May's face. 'And I can't stop thinking that I never actually heard him leave. I heard the creak of the side gate, but it must have been the wind. Subconsciously I knew Dad wouldn't have sneaked off like that. He would have slammed the front door. And even if he had left, he would have come back again, or at least tried.'

'Oh,' May said, wrapping a second hand around Jane's. 'I see.'

'If he didn't leave, it means he's still there, just like Mum kept saying. You know what I'm getting at, don't you?'

'He died,' May said in a strangled whisper. She had to take a couple of deep breaths. 'He died that night.'

290

'I believe so, yes,' Jane replied gently. 'At the moment, it's just a guess, but I think there's a reason Mum never lifted those awful paving stones in the garden for fifty years.'

'Oh, Lord. I did wonder,' May said, her voice sounding distant all of a sudden. 'She was forever looking out at the garden.'

'Ashleigh said the same thing,' Jane said with a sigh.

'I'm surprised she'd be interested in anyone except herself,' May muttered.

The condemnation of May's neighbour sent a ripple of concern through Jane. 'Should we be worried that her sister has gone missing?'

'No,' May said firmly. 'As I told the police, I saw her leaving Ashleigh's around midday last Friday, and she seemed fine to me. I'm sure she'll turn up eventually.'

'But it must be serious if the police are involved.'

'Which means you don't need to be,' May said, her grip on Jane's hand tightening. 'Keep away from Ashleigh, love. That one's bad news.'

Jane wasn't in a position to argue. She didn't have the strength to embroil herself in another crisis, even if she wanted to, but May's lack of sympathy bothered her. 'Did you ever think Mum was more trouble than she was worth?'

'Never.'

'But some people do think women bring it on themselves by staying. It must have been frustrating to see Mum simply accept what Dad was like.'

The pressure being applied to Jane's hand was making May's entire body shake. 'She didn't accept it, and neither did I.'

'Sorry,' Jane said, regretting the challenge. 'I know you were a good friend, and I'm glad you hit Dad.'

May puffed out her chest. 'Then you should know I hit him again, and harder.'

'But you said you didn't see him again . . . I don't understand.'

May looked down at her bony knuckles and relaxed her grip. She patted Jane's hand. 'It was me who used the side gate that night. Knowing what Cynthia had planned, I was worried when I didn't get the return signal to my three pips, so I nipped around to check. Straight away I could hear your mum and dad yelling at each other, so I'm guessing you didn't hear me arrive – I know they didn't. I'd sneaked along the side of the house, and they still didn't notice when I came into the kitchen.'

Jane gasped. 'You saw what happened?'

'Les was reaching for a knife – he was going to kill her. I couldn't let that happen.'

'Oh my God,' Jane said. 'What did you do?'

'I hit him with a frying pan. I hit him hard.' Her eyes were rimmed with tears. 'Oh, God, Jane. What if it was me who killed him?'

CHAPTER 41

1974

Cynthia circled Les's crumpled body on the kitchen floor, her eyes never leaving him as she picked up the knife they had fought over. Above the sound of her panting, she could hear only one other person breathing hard. May.

It had all happened so fast, and Cynthia hadn't registered her friend's arrival until Les had hit the floor. May held the iron skillet poised for a second strike, but the first had hit its mark with surprising efficiency. He hadn't seen it coming.

'Is he dead?' asked May, her voice trembling.

Cynthia leant over the body, and as she held her breath, she couldn't be sure if Les was holding his. Time stood still, and then she saw his chest rise and fall.

'Unfortunately not,' she replied with forced bravado.

She didn't want May to see how scared she was. The adrenalin rush was dissipating, and there was only so long her body could hold back the pain. May, the person she had come to rely on more than anyone else in the world, had become an accomplice, although it was as yet unclear what their crime might be. Cynthia might wish Les dead, and often had, but he needed to survive, if only for the sake of her friend.

Keeping the tip of her blade aimed at Les's chest, Cynthia went over to May. 'Let's get that away from you,' she said, levering the skillet from May's grip and setting it back on the stove.

'What are we going to do?' May asked, her whole being quaking as the enormity of what she had just done hit her.

Cynthia looked down at her tormentor and considered every possible outcome. Les had no obvious signs of injury except a tiny trickle of blood from his nose. Assuming he did wake up, he might be concussed, and would need medical attention. The police would be involved, and social services too.

'You should leave,' Cynthia told May.

'No way.'

Cynthia was already ushering her friend back out the way she had come. She kept hold of the knife, but closed the door behind them in case Les regained consciousness and overheard them talking.

It was late afternoon, cold and dark, as the two friends huddled together outside. 'He didn't see you,' Cynthia whispered. 'So whatever happens, you don't have to be involved.'

'Involved? What do you mean, involved?' May continued to shiver uncontrollably.

'If Les won't leave, I'll have to call the police. I can say I hit him with the skillet because he was attacking me.'

'He *was* attacking you.'

'Yes, but not you. I know you were only defending me, but Les won't make life easy for either of us if he knows you were involved. For every accusation we make, he'll find a way of dodging it, you know he will. Doing it my way is simpler.' *If he wakes up*, she kept thinking. He could have a bleed on the brain and die. She could be charged with murder. But better her than May.

'Have I made things worse?'

As Cynthia gave May a hug, her broken ribs cried out in pain. 'I'd probably be dead right now if it wasn't for you.'

'How's Jane? Where is she?'

'Upstairs in the attic. She's safe for now, but I might need you to look after her,' Cynthia said, her voice wobbling. She pressed her lips together. 'She fell, and I think she's hurt her arm. Even if I can get rid of Les, I can't show up at the hospital looking like this. The more we can get through the night without any questions asked, the better.'

'Do you want me to take her now? Billy's due home soon, he can look after the kids.'

Cynthia considered her options. She couldn't bear to think how Jane was coping, especially if her arm was broken, and it killed her not to agree. 'No, May, you need to go back home so it looks like you were never here. I'll phone you as soon as I can.'

May wasn't ready to abandon her friend, but a groan from the other side of the door forced them into action.

'Go. Now!' Cynthia hissed.

Before hurrying away, May looked to the blade in Cynthia's hand. 'You keep hold of that.'

295

With the creak of a gate, May was gone. Cynthia wiped sweat from her palms before holding the knife out in front of her as she returned to the kitchen.

CHAPTER 42

'I heard Les coming round before I left, I'd swear to it,' May said. 'But what if that noise had been his death throes?' Her eyes were watery, her skin deathly pale. 'I couldn't care less if I killed him or not, but to think my Cynthia buried him to protect me, then kept the secret for the rest of her life. I couldn't . . .' Her words choked her.

'You didn't kill him,' Jane said, giving May's hand a squeeze. 'You thought at the time he was waking up, and he probably was.'

The two women looked at each other as they realized this alternative was no less chilling. Neither of them knew what Cynthia had planned when she had returned to the kitchen, knife in hand. If Les had still been alive, he may have attacked her again, but it was also plausible that she had killed him in cold blood to stop him inflicting more hurt on them all. That could explain why she had to hide the body.

'You won't tell Sheena yet, will you?' asked May. 'I don't want her to worry.'

'Not if you don't want me to.'

It would be hard to keep things from her friend, but Jane knew how May felt. Wasn't she putting off telling her own daughter too? Hadn't Cynthia done the same? They were all strong women, and their greatest weakness was their need to protect each other.

'And we could be worrying for nothing. We don't know how Dad died. Technically, we don't even know *if* he died,' Jane added, clutching at straws if only to ease May's distress.

'Then we need to find out.'

'It might be better if—'

'Better if you picked up where your mum left off?' May guessed. 'I don't want to face the same wretched death as your mum, knowing I'm leaving behind an unmarked grave for someone else to find. Do *you*?' There was fire behind her eyes when she answered her own questions. 'Not on your nelly. Les has outstayed his welcome, and something has to be done about it.'

It had been obvious from May's haunted expression that their talk had ripped open old wounds to cause fresh pain, and Jane feared that prolonging the ordeal might kill her. May had said something needed to be done, but what? Phil was coming over at the weekend so they could revisit their options, but after two sleepless nights in a row, Jane could take it no more, and on Friday afternoon, she called her old friend PC Hussein on impulse. With a little persistence, he had promised to call in at the end of his shift for what she had described as a little chat.

Unable to sit still and wait, Jane took Benji out for a long walk. They had avoided the hottest part of the day, but it was still uncomfortably muggy, and after an hour or so, sweat was trickling down her back, soaking her T-shirt. She would need a shower when she got home, although she was cutting it fine before the constable's arrival.

She was almost at a run as she crossed Oxton Fields, but when she turned into the familiar tree-lined lane and spotted Ashleigh coming out of her house, she slowed down to a snail's pace. There was a taxi waiting, and she hoped her neighbour would disappear into it before noticing her.

According to the news, the police were continuing their search for Rose Martindale, but given how Ashleigh looked to be going out on the town, Jane could only presume she knew something the public didn't. Jane tried not to feel guilty for being preoccupied with her own problems, but when she saw Ashleigh pause to put her keys in her clutch bag, she picked up speed again.

Benji was walking ahead and gave a sharp yap that made Ashleigh turn towards them. When Jane lifted her hand in greeting, there was a second's delay before Ashleigh offered a beaming smile that threw Jane slightly.

'Hello, there,' said Ashleigh. She wore a tight dress that was designed to be short, but was shorter still on her tall frame.

'You look nice,' Jane replied, now close enough to see the sparkly eyeshadow and eyeliner flicks that had been drawn to sharpened points. If the bruising from the week before was still there, it was hidden well. 'Going somewhere special?'

'To see my friend, then out clubbing, I hope.' She gave a nod to the taxi driver who hadn't been able to park up and was blocking the road should another car need to pass. 'I should go.'

'I heard about your sister. Have there been any developments?'

Ashleigh had taken half a step, but stopped, her shoulders sagging. 'No,' she said. 'I'm worried Rose has gone off on a bender. It was inevitable, I suppose, but still surprising. She seemed fine when she called around last week.' Tears glistened in her eyes. 'Something must have upset her.'

'I'm so sorry. I hope she turns up again soon.'

The taxi driver beeped his horn. 'All right, I'm coming!' Ashleigh shouted, and when she rolled her eyes, it wasn't clear if it was Jane or the driver that was irritating her. 'So anyway, my friend is dragging me out to cheer me up.'

'Have fun.'

Ashleigh had a mischievous smile when she said, 'Oh, I intend to.'

Jane was relieved to be on her way: Ashleigh's behaviour was erratic, almost as if she didn't know what emotion to settle on, or what mask to wear. Jane pushed that last thought to the back of her mind. May's dislike of her neighbours was rubbing off on her.

Reaching home, Jane managed to change her top, but she didn't have nearly enough time to cool down before the doorbell rang. Insisting PC Hussein join her for a cold drink, she dropped ice cubes into two tall glasses of elderflower and mint cordial.

'Much appreciated. It's been another hot one, hasn't it?' said the PC. 'I can't wait for this weather to break.'

'The garden could do with some rain,' she said without thinking. How was that going to look when he found out what was there? Taking a breath, she added, 'Shall we go into the sitting room?'

'Sure, lead the way.'

'Have you been busy?' Jane asked when they were seated.

'The usual, but as I mentioned, this is my last call, so I'm off home after this,' he replied, which she took to mean he was hoping Jane's problem would be quickly sorted. He was in for a shock.

'I appreciate you taking the time to see me.'

'Technically, I'm already off the clock,' he admitted. 'It didn't sound like you wanted an official visit. You said you needed to run something past me?'

'Yes,' Jane said, grimacing. 'Yes, I did, didn't I?'

She was starting to regret her rash decision to do this on her own, but she hadn't wanted to wait for Phil to arrive, or ask him to cancel the governors' meeting that evening. It was better if he wasn't implicated, but sitting in her mum's recliner, she felt so alone.

'So,' the police officer asked patiently, 'how can I help?'

Jane surreptitiously wiped a trickle of sweat crawling down the side of her face. She imagined he thought her a bumbling fool, and she hadn't even got to the crazy part yet. 'Remember when I was convinced that Evan Jarvis had buried his wife in the garden?'

The constable laughed. 'Hard to forget,' he said, only to realize that Jane hadn't intended it as a joke. 'Sorry.'

Jane wasn't sure she could continue. How was she going to convince him this wasn't another flight of fancy? 'I . . . I saw something in that house that I'd experienced myself. My father was abusive, you see, and in my early childhood, I saw, or heard, how he treated my mum,' she began. 'She would send me up to the attic, to stay safe while she took the punches: it became normal to me.'

The police officer put his glass down on the floor. 'That must have been terrifying for you,' he said. 'I can understand now why you might have thought the worst about your neighbours.'

'I did apologize to them. Well, to Ashleigh. We've become friends of sorts,' Jane explained.

'Really?' PC Hussein asked, frowning. 'Well, I guess she appreciates having you look out for her. Is that why you wanted to talk to me? Is it about Rose Martindale?'

'Do you know what's happened to her yet?' said Jane, aware that she was allowing the conversation to veer off at a tangent, but it was easier meddling in other people's lives than sorting out her own. 'Ashleigh says she might have gone off on a drinking binge.'

'I'm sorry, I can't comment,' he said, before adding, 'besides, I'm not directly involved.'

'I saw the appeal for information.'

'Did you happen to see Rose last Friday?' the PC asked.

'Friday? I thought she'd gone missing at the weekend.' Jane had caught only the tail end of the local news earlier. Rose's car had been found parked as normal in her street, and there were no obvious signs of disturbance at the house.

'She was reported missing last Saturday after failing to meet up with a friend, but there haven't been any sightings of Rose since she left her sister's house. That would have been around midday on the Friday.'

'Oh,' said Jane, as she thought back to the events of that day. 'I phoned Ashleigh when her sister was there, but no, I didn't see Rose.'

Friday had been the day after they had uncovered Evan's secret stash. Jane had phoned Ashleigh late morning, but it was her visit on Friday evening that suddenly came to mind. Jane could see her neighbour sitting where PC Hussein was now, the shadows beneath Ashleigh's bruised eyes deepening each time she looked down to check her watch. She was worried about a message Evan had received from Rose just as she was leaving the house. She didn't trust her husband.

'Have you questioned Evan?' Jane asked hesitantly.

'Why do you say that?'

The sweat on Jane's brow prickled her skin. She had been restless that night, and had woken up in the attic on Saturday morning to the sound of Evan refilling the trough that had once again been placed over the grave-shaped trench.

'Ashleigh suspected he was having an affair with her sister, but I expect you know that,' she said, only to see surprise on the young officer's face. 'I'm sure she's mentioned it to whoever's investigating. Unless . . .'

PC Hussein leant forward. 'Unless what?'

'Unless she's too afraid,' Jane said, drawing each word out slowly. She wouldn't fall into the trap of accusing Evan of burying a body a second time, not while she had a skeleton of her own to uncover. She pulled her thoughts away from the Jarvises' garden, over the hedgerow, and across the yellow paving stones to the spot where the old Anderson shelter had been. She couldn't catch her breath.

'What is it, Mrs Hanratty?'

'I didn't call you over to talk about the Jarvises,' she said. 'I want to report a missing person. His name was Lesley Morgan. He was my father.'

CHAPTER 43

Ashleigh tugged down the hem of her dress as she tumbled out of the taxicab. Lights glowed from one of the town-houses, and she gravitated towards it. She had known Evan would wait up for her.

Forcing her key into the keyhole, she couldn't figure out why it wouldn't turn, then spluttered with laughter. This was the house with the crying baby. Ashleigh had smiled at the new mum the other day, wondering if they would become friends when Ashleigh got pregnant. Not that she had any chance of conceiving while Evan refused to touch her, but never mind. It was probably for the best.

It took a couple of attempts before Ashleigh unlocked the correct door, her keys jangling so loudly that there was little point pretending to keep quiet. Once inside, she slammed the door shut and kicked off her heels with a loud clatter, a little peeved that Evan hadn't stayed up after all, but as she stepped into the unlit kitchen for a glass of water, a disembodied arm reached out towards her.

'Shit, Evan! You scared the crap out of me. What are you doing lurking in the dark?'

'Waiting for you,' Evan said, handing her a glass.

When Ashleigh's sight adjusted to the dim light from the digital display on the microwave, she fixed on Evan's expressionless face. 'Worried about me?'

'No, I'm more concerned about being woken up by someone smashing their fist into my face.'

'I've never—'

'You have, albeit only once,' he bit back. 'But after all the attention my black eye drew, you made sure to hit lower. Apparently you do have self-restraint when it suits you.'

'Do *you*?' she challenged.

'Drink your water.'

Ashleigh felt the weight of the glass in her hand. 'If I've ever hit out, it's because you push me to it, just like you're trying to do now. Christ, Evan, can't you leave me in peace?'

'Tried that,' he said.

With her free hand, Ashleigh thumped her fist against his chest. It was like punching iron. 'Ow,' she cried out, shaking her hand. She glared at him as if he had hurt her deliberately.

Evan sighed. 'I know this is where you start screaming about how this is all because you love me so much, but can we not do that? I'm exhausted,' he said, sounding as if the simple effort of talking was too much.

Ashleigh sipped her water then left it on the nearest countertop. The kitchen had borne witness to one too many fights lately, so she sloped off to the living room. She sat down on the sofa and waited for Evan to follow.

'Why are you being like this?' she asked when his silhouette filled the door frame. 'I haven't been out for ages. And if I drank too much, it was only to keep up with Jess, you know what she's like.'

'I know what you *want* people to think she's like, but can we stop pretending? Jess hasn't got the drink problem. You have.'

'Oh, piss off. You're not going to stop me having a good time just because you love being miserable.'

'I'm beyond caring what you do, Ash, because after tonight, I'm not going to be here. I'm leaving you.'

Ashleigh wasn't sober enough to follow every nuance of Evan's statement, but if this was a threat, it wouldn't work. 'Oh, really?'

'If you and your neighbourly friend want to report me to the police, go ahead. I'll deal with the consequences. You can't blackmail me into staying.'

With all the focus on Rose's disappearance, Ashleigh had almost forgotten about the theft. 'Don't worry about that,' she said.

'I'm not. I want this part of my life to be over. There's no way back for us. You've broken every promise you ever made,' he said, his voice a whisper.

She could point out that he had broken vows too, but for once, she wasn't in the mood for an argument. She was willing to move on from his affair with Rose.

Evan shifted from one foot to the other, her silence making him nervous. 'We've run out of options. You're not interested in anyone except yourself. You don't even care that your sister's missing for God's sake.'

'I don't know why Rose's disappearance had to be

reported in the first place. Her clean-living friends don't remember the drunk who'd book an all-inclusive holiday just to get the free booze.' She jutted out her chin and tried not to let her head wobble drunkenly.

'You seem to be the only one who isn't worried,' said Evan. 'What really went on between you two? You were the last one to speak to her.'

Ashleigh snarled. 'Was I? Don't say you weren't messaging her all day every day because I know you were.'

'Sad as it may seem, the only thing Rose and I talked about was you.'

Evan's quiet but disapproving tone was enough to make Ashleigh want to scream. 'I'm sure the truth will come out eventually,' she said smugly.

'As long as it's not your version of reality. What did you say to her, Ash?' Evan persisted. 'Did you throw our so-called affair at her too?'

'Stop talking about my bloody sister,' Ashleigh hissed.

'Fine, this is pointless anyway,' said Evan coolly. 'I'm done.'

As Ashleigh jumped up, her shin caught on the edge of the coffee table and she let out a yelp. 'No!' she cried at the top of her voice. 'Don't do this! Please! Stop!'

'No, Ashleigh, *you* stop!' Evan bellowed. 'I've never raised a hand to you, and I never will!'

Ashleigh's chest heaved as her eyes flicked past Evan towards the hallway. He followed her gaze to the party wall. There had been enough sour looks from their eavesdropper in recent weeks to suggest May had started to question the narrative Ashleigh had been peddling, and Evan's latest outburst wouldn't help. He had learnt her tricks, but Ashleigh wasn't about to back down now. She grabbed the edge of the table and pushed it onto its side with a howl. It landed on the rug with a disappointing thud because Evan had got into the habit of clearing anything away that might be breakable. She spun around to face him, but he had gone.

She rushed into the hallway. 'Don't you dare!' she yelled, reacting too quickly to think about how that might sound to their neighbour. She lowered her voice. 'Where do you think you're going?'

Evan was at the front door. He kept his back to her. 'Away from you.'

'You can't do this,' she said, scrambling to grab his arm as he reached for the door handle. 'If you leave now, I'll tell the police everything. You'll be banged up before you know it.'

He gave their home one last cursory glance. 'I'll take that risk. It has to be better than *this* prison.'

'But you love me. You do, Evan. You've always said how you're addicted to me.'

Evan peeled away the fingers digging into his flesh, revealing a pattern of bleeding half-moons from Ashleigh's false nails. 'Not any longer.'

Ashleigh stepped back, fury twisting her features. 'Fine, go if you want. It makes my life easier.'

When Evan closed the door softly behind him, Ashleigh glowered after him. She was comforted at least that he couldn't go running to her sister. If Rose knew she had missed the opportunity she had been waiting for, she would probably turn in her grave.

CHAPTER 44

Jane had spent the entire weekend on edge, so when she heard a loud rap on the window as she passed May's house on Monday afternoon, she jumped out of her skin. Her heart was still hammering as May came out to speak to her.

'Has Phil gone?' the older woman asked.

'He left late last night.'

'So, erm, I don't suppose there's been any word from the police yet?' May continued, revealing what was obviously the true reason for stopping Jane.

'The constable I spoke to wasn't back at the station until today, so he's probably just filling in the paperwork now. And they'll conduct a database search first, I should imagine.'

Jane could already tell them not to bother looking in the public domain, and she doubted there would be evidence of Les paying taxes or claiming his pension either. There was only one place left to look, but she understood there was a process to follow. The next step would be a visit from detectives before any order could be given to break ground.

'It shouldn't take this much time,' May replied as if the police had taken months instead of only three days. 'They will come, won't they, love?'

'I hope so,' Jane said, not sounding as confident as she would like.

PC Hussein had listened with interest to her blow-by-blow account of the night her dad had disappeared as well as the more recent discovery of the suitcase containing all his worldly possessions. She had chosen not to mention the squeaky gate, or any involvement from May whatsoever. Nor had she specifically mentioned the theory that her mum had killed her dad and buried him in the garden. The constable had already laughed when she mentioned the last time she had reported a buried body, and she hadn't been able to put herself through it again. Surely she didn't need to. Wasn't it obvious what must have happened?

PC Hussein hadn't felt it necessary to examine the suitcase himself. If Jane had verified that its contents belonged to her dad, that was good enough for him. He had promised to log the missing person information when he was back on duty, and they would take it from there.

But what if she had left too much open to interpretation? Could her ramblings have confused him?

'If they don't get a shift on,' May told her, 'I'm coming over there to start digging myself.'

Jane smiled. 'You and me both.'

'I don't know about you, but I won't get a proper night's sleep until this is over,' fretted May, who looked as if the years had finally caught up with her.

'I shouldn't have involved you.'

'It had to be done, but I do wonder what the world will make of it. I just hope they'll think kindly of my Cynthia. And of me.'

'Now, May, we've talked about this,' Jane said sternly. 'As far as anyone else is concerned, the last time you saw Dad was that afternoon when you gave him the black eye. He wasn't there when you called around later to take me to hospital. And as for me, I didn't hear anyone else when Mum was fighting off Dad. And that's the truth.'

'A lie by omission is still a lie,' May said, her knuckles turning white as she gripped the gate. 'I was there when she was getting beaten, and I'm the only one who saw Les try to pull a knife on her. If I killed him, I'm more than capable of defending my actions, and I want to explain Cynthia's too. If we're going to tell her story, we have to tell it well so that people know what a beautiful and courageous woman she was.'

Jane's heart swelled. May had been, and still was, her mum's truest friend, which was all the more reason for Jane to protect May from herself. 'We'll see.'

'We certainly will,' said May with a smile that disappeared as she glanced down the road. Her weary eyes narrowed. 'Now here comes someone who's good at telling stories.'

The scathing remark was directed at Ashleigh, who was striding up the lane. Wherever she had been, she hadn't taken the car.

'Don't look at me like that,' May said under her breath. 'She's not all sweetness and light.'

Jane was at a loss to explain why Ashleigh left May so

cold. She would agree that their neighbour could be abrupt, but given her history, it was hardly surprising. Her hardened exterior was a defence mechanism. 'Her sister's still missing,' she reminded May.

'Did you know Evan's gone AWOL too? They had an argument on Friday night, although it was more like the early hours of Saturday morning,' May said, speaking quickly as Ashleigh approached. 'I don't say this lightly, but if you ask me, she's the troublemaker. Evan isn't as tough as he looks, I heard him crying once. Maybe more than once. I'll tell you about it some time.'

Jane wasn't sure she wanted to know and was grateful that Ashleigh was there to cut short the conversation. There would always be those who apportioned blame to the victim, but things were never as simple as they appeared. No matter what you saw or heard, unless you lived through it, you couldn't understand what motivated people to do the things they did. Of all people, May should know that.

'Hi, love, how are you?' May greeted Ashleigh.

Ashleigh's response was more of a grunt. 'Fine.'

'Any news?' asked Jane.

'You tell me,' Ashleigh asked, sniffing the air. 'You're more pally with the police than I am. I assume it was something you said that made them take me back in for more questions.'

Benji had been resting with his chin on Jane's foot, but he scurried behind her, winding his leash around her legs and giving Jane a temporary distraction to gather her thoughts. The only police officer she had spoken to was PC Hussein, and there was only one thing Jane had said that could have led them to re-interview Ashleigh – Evan's alleged affair with Rose.

'I'm sorry, I only mentioned something in passing,' she explained, careful not to repeat the gossip in front of May. 'I presumed you would have told them already.'

Ashleigh rolled her shoulders. 'Whatever. It's been a long day. Personally, I still think it's too soon to start digging into every aspect of Rose's life. Or mine. She'll turn up any day now with a tan and a stinking hangover.'

'They will find her,' Jane assured her.

Ashleigh took out her front door key. 'I suspect you're right,' she said sombrely, but she didn't look happy about the prospect at all.

CHAPTER 45

Ashleigh applied a slick black line across her upper eyelid as she listened to her phone ringing. The call from an unrecognized number stopped only long enough for the caller to hit redial. There was another pause, another redial. Having spent the day before with the police, Ashleigh guessed today had been Evan's turn.

Moving on to her other eye, Ashleigh stroked the pencil deftly along the line of her lashes then finished with a flick. Only when she was satisfied that it matched the other perfectly, did she pick up the phone.

'What the hell, Ash?' Evan demanded.

The face reflected in the dressing table mirror held no expression. 'Is something wrong?'

'Yes, something's wrong!' There was a tremor in his voice, suggesting he was about to burst into tears. 'You told them I killed Rose.'

'No,' she said firmly, 'I explained my suspicion that you were having an affair, and that Rose knew I'd be out that night because she'd heard me make the arrangements with

Jane. I just thought it worth considering that she might have headed back this way later on in the day. I never actually suggested she reached our house.'

'Oh, but you're more than happy for the police to think that.'

Ashleigh sighed. 'I'm sure you can talk your way out of it, you're pretty good at playing the innocent.' The corner of her mouth tugged upwards. 'Unless there's incriminating evidence to catch you out? I take it you're not phoning from your mobile because the police have it? Oh dear.'

'I didn't see Rose at all that day. She suggested coming over while you were out, but I said no. I crashed out in front of the TV and didn't move all evening.'

'Too afraid I would catch you in the act?'

She imagined his jaw twitching when he said, 'There was nothing going on.'

'Oh, come off it, Evan. Rose was in love with you, anyone could see that. Did you enjoy stringing her along? That poor cow kept her bed warm for you—'

'Don't talk about Rose like that,' Evan snapped. 'I didn't sleep with her, Ash. I wouldn't even take up her offer of a spare bed the other week. I knew it was asking for trouble spending the night under anyone's roof because you're *that* paranoid.'

'So Rose did offer then? I bet she was gutted when you came back to me. And once we'd made our pact . . .'

'You mean when you tried blackmailing me into staying?'

'Oh please. It must have killed Rose to know you'd never be hers.' Ashleigh made sure her voice was etched with pain when she added, 'Maybe she did kill herself?'

'She wouldn't do that.'

'You sound pretty confident. Is it because you know what actually happened?'

'No, but my guess is you upset her enough to make her want to get as far away from you as possible,' he replied. 'She'll come back when she finds out the police are blaming me for her disappearance. *She* wouldn't stitch me up for something I didn't do.'

'And if she doesn't come back?' When Evan didn't answer, Ashleigh continued to paint a future that didn't look too bright for him. 'I hope you've paid the rent for your little bachelor pad in advance. I can't imagine you'll be able to afford it for much longer if you lose your job over this.'

'I'll face whatever comes next,' he said, sounding surprisingly optimistic. 'And it'll be worth it just to know you're out of my life. I can't tell you how good it feels to come home at night and not worry about what I'm walking into.'

Evan had refused to give Ashleigh his new address when she messaged him about forwarding his mail, but he had let slip it was a B&B somewhere in New Brighton. 'I bet you don't even have your own bathroom.'

'It's still better,' he said. 'I can actually buy a new shirt or have a haircut without being accused of doing it to hit on other women. All that time I felt responsible for how angry you'd get, but you lit your own fuses, Ash. You never needed much of an excuse to destroy everything I cared about, be that my family, friends, or even the garden. I mean, who gets jealous over a fucking lawn?'

'I was killing the weeds,' she said.

'By pouring bleach all over the grass? I should have realized then that you were insane.'

'And whose fault is it for driving me crazy?'

'I don't know, and I don't care. Once Rose is found, I'll be free of all your drama.'

'Then it looks like this has worked out well for both of us,' she replied, picking up a tumbler of vodka and raising it in a silent toast. 'I can go out when I want, drink what I want, and do what I want.'

The vodka was a quick pre-drink before the proper pre-drinks with Jess, followed by a meal out. Ashleigh didn't care if it was a school night as she had an extended leave of absence from work – her boss had backed down from threats of firing her when she heard about Rose. Jess had warned she needed to be up early the next day, but Ashleigh saw that as a challenge. She would have no problem keeping her friend out late.

'And the best part,' she added after swigging her drink, 'is that I don't have to come home to your whiney voice telling me what an awful person I am.'

'But you *are* an awful person,' Evan said. 'And I can't believe it's taken me this long to figure it out. I don't think for a second that Rose has killed herself, but if she has, I will blame you.'

'Well, I blame you!' Ashleigh said, her eyes flaring. 'And who do you think the police are going to believe? I've shown them photos of my bruises.'

'I know, and I've admitted I caused them,' Evan said calmly. 'But don't be surprised if the police aren't as gullible as your friends. They know that kind of bruising is consistent with someone being restrained. You might find it more difficult to explain my injuries, however. I have photos too, Ash.'

'Liar,' she hissed. She had checked his phone constantly, and he didn't have another camera, but she didn't like his tone of voice. She took another sip of her vodka to calm her thoughts, then stiffened. Jane had a photo of her sister inspecting Evan's bare chest. 'Rose took them?'

'It was her idea to record my injuries. And the police won't need to wait for her to show up to get them. Good old cloud storage, eh?'

Ashleigh had to stop herself from launching her glass at the mirror. 'Your injuries could have been self-inflicted.'

'Except they weren't. Unlike all those scratches you got when you crawled through a hedgerow to steal our neighbour's things.'

'That was your fault,' she snapped back. 'You made me do it.'

Evan drove her mad at times, especially when he tried to talk her down, or worse still, removed himself from the situation. She was sure he did it to wind her up even more, but two months ago, he had tried a different tack.

It was the weekend she had set him to work digging the hole for her fishpond, or water feature, or whatever excuse she had given for pulling up all his flowers. He kept asking specifics about what it was meant to look like, implying that she was making it up as she went along. That was when she had finally lost it.

'Do you have to pull apart everything I suggest?' she had yelled at him while he stood in a two-foot-deep hole that served no purpose. She had only come out to see if he wanted a beer.

Evan put down the spade, careful to keep it out of Ashleigh's reach. 'I just—'

'I can't do anything right!' she said, tears trailing down her cheeks as she stormed off.

Evan caught up to her in the kitchen, where she was opening her second bottle of wine that day. 'Come on, Ash, you can't keep behaving like this,' he cajoled. When she didn't answer, he threw in his trump card. 'You do know there are people who can see you throwing tantrums.'

'What do you mean?'

He had nodded in the direction of Jane's house. 'I've seen her taking photos. God knows what she makes of us.'

'Of me, you mean,' Ashleigh snarled, but it got her thinking. How long had their neighbour been watching? How much of the desecration of Evan's garden had she seen?

Ashleigh had tried to tell herself it didn't matter, but she hadn't liked the idea that someone might hold information that could be used against her. It was becoming harder to control her temper, and there were times when she would have gladly killed Evan. Her greatest fear was that one day he would push her too far; that was why she took such care curating the correct story. She was the victim, and she didn't want evidence to exist that proved the contrary.

Evan's warning had made her nervous, and after he had gone to work the next day, she had tried to drink her worries away. It was only when Jane had walked past the house on her dog walk that the perfect opportunity for Ashleigh to take back control had presented itself. She hadn't given a thought to the mad bat having bloody cloud storage.

'Why are we even having this conversation?' she asked him now. 'My sister is missing and all you want to bang on about is a bloody camera being stolen?'

'I'm banging on because you're the one who mentioned it to the police yesterday,' Evan said. 'Well, it's backfired, Ash. With any luck, it's made them realize that nothing you say can be trusted.'

'You think?'

'What if I can prove it couldn't possibly have been me who broke into Jane's house?' he asked. She could hear his infuriating smile down the line. 'I knew I'd have to defend myself if I left you, so I've been checking the CCTV footage at work. Not only do I show up throughout the day of the robbery, but my car is there in the car park the whole time. The police have a window of opportunity for the break-in, and now all they need to do is cross-reference it to the footage. They could be looking at it right now.'

'But you're the one who buried the stuff in our garden!'

'I did it to cover *your* tracks! But I'm tired of doing that. You're not worth the trouble.'

'Go to hell, Evan!' Ashleigh screamed. There was an explosion of glass as her tumbler smashed into the mirror.

CHAPTER 46

Two more days had passed without the expected knock at the door, and although Jane hadn't reached the point where she was ready to start digging as May had suggested, she saw no harm in preparing the ground for the inevitable excavations. It wasn't as if there would be any evidence to disturb above ground.

'What are you doing?' Phil asked his out-of-breath wife when he phoned during his lunch break.

'Clearing space just in case the forensics team ever show up.'

She had her phone wedged between her chin and shoulder, and continued to drag, roll and push a large terracotta pot containing a dwarf peach tree onto the patio.

'I might dig up the box hedging too,' she added as she straightened up and looked across the garden. 'I don't want them trampled over, although I've no idea what I'll do with them afterwards. Those paving stones are never going down again.'

'Can't you wait until the weekend? I can help then.'

'It's not that big a job, and I'm almost done. Clearly you never saw me moving boulders around our garden. That rockery didn't appear by some seismic shift.'

'I did see you, but damn it, Jane, do you have to do everything on your own?' he asked. 'If you want me to be more involved, you have to leave some room for me to be of use.'

'Fair point,' she conceded with a rueful smile.

Since admitting to Phil that their marriage wasn't as broken as she had wanted him to believe, they had been tentatively reconfiguring their relationship into one that might serve them for the next thirty years. For the most part, it had been Jane leading with the demands for change, and this was the hardest Phil had pushed back so far.

Her husband was quiet for a moment. 'You're going to carry on, aren't you?'

'I have to,' she admitted. 'We could be overrun by people in white hooded suits at any moment.'

'We? As in us?'

'Me,' she said, correcting herself. 'It's not too late to back out. I could start using my maiden name so the press doesn't associate me with you.'

'Not a chance, Mrs Hanratty. Whatever comes of this sorry mess, it'll be worth it if it means you get to come home again.'

'I wish I was back there now,' she admitted.

'It'll all be over before you know it, and in the meantime, I'll come across as often as I can. I was thinking of asking Megan to join us this weekend,' Phil suggested. 'It's not fair to keep her in the dark.'

The idea of telling their daughter about the harrowing

ordeal her grandmother had been forced to endure made Jane's stomach flip. 'She's going to be horrified.'

'No, she's going to be happy that we're rebuilding our relationship, and as for the rest, she'll handle it better than you think. Like me, she'll be relieved to have answers after months of not understanding what you were going through. We need to regroup and be a family again before the media circus comes to town. Assuming, of course, there is a story to tell.'

Jane admired his optimism, but she had to agree that it was time to bring Megan into their circle of trust. 'OK, invite her.'

After promising to call Phil if there were any further developments, Jane went inside to wash her hands and quench her thirst. As she debated whether to opt for pain-killers, or a walk to stretch her stiffened limbs, the doorbell rang. Finally.

Clutching a tea towel like a security blanket, and flanked by her trusted dog, Jane went to answer the door. She was expecting plain clothes detectives, but her visitor wore a pretty summer dress with puff sleeves and a tear-stained expression.

'Oh, love, what's happened?' asked Jane, beckoning Ashleigh inside. 'Is it your sister?'

Ashleigh declined the offer of Jane's tea towel to mop the tears streaming down her face. 'Still nothing. Oh, Jane, it's unbearable.'

'Come in. I'll get you a tissue.'

While Benji sloped off to the sitting room, Jane took Ashleigh into the kitchen. Above the floral notes of her neighbour's perfume, there was the sour smell of alcohol. She poured Ashleigh a glass of water.

Ashleigh hiccupped. 'Evan's left me.'

Jane did her best to look surprised. 'I'm so sorry,' she said automatically. 'Or should I be?'

'I know – you probably – think it's for – the best,' she said, her words punctuated by tiny sobs. 'But just because – we don't live under the same roof. Doesn't mean – he can't get to me. He'll just – finds new ways.'

Jane waited until Ashleigh had finished slurping her water. 'What's he done?'

'I should explain – about the other day. If I seemed angry, it was because I was scared. I knew there'd be trouble – if I told the police about him and Rose. I was supposed to believe him – when he said there was nothing going on.'

'But you didn't believe him, did you?' asked Jane, recalling Ashleigh's less than convincing performance on the night Rose had disappeared. 'You were worried they were sneaking behind your back.'

Ashleigh's bloodshot eyes fixed on Jane's face. 'I think they were together while I was here. When I got home, something wasn't right. Evan practically pushed my sleeping tablets into my hand, and the next morning I couldn't lift my head from the pillow.'

Jane pressed her palm against her chest. She didn't know if she should mention Evan filling in the hole in the garden the next morning. It felt unwise to start theorizing with someone who was already distraught. Unless Ashleigh harboured similar suspicions.

'Do you think Evan had something to do with Rose going missing?'

Her neighbour swept the tissue across the puddles of mascara under her eyes. 'I don't dare to think,' she said.

'But if you know anything, or saw anything, you will tell the police, won't you? I can count on you, can't I, Jane?'

Ashleigh's trembling smile, combined with the coldness of her stare, made the hairs on the back of Jane's neck stand on end. 'Of course.'

The smile grew more confident. 'The thing is, I sort of need a little favour.'

With May's warnings ringing in her ears, Jane said, 'Go on.'

'I had to explain to the police how we found the things Evan stole from you. I figured it was best telling them before you did,' she said with a snort.

'That's good. Isn't it?'

'It should be, but Evan's far too devious to be caught out. It's my own fault for thinking I could use the theft against him. He's trying to fabricate a defence.'

Now that Ashleigh wasn't sobbing, Jane noticed her words were ever so slightly slurred, and the stale smell of drink wasn't all that stale. 'What kind of defence?'

'An alibi. He has CCTV from work to convince the police he couldn't have been anywhere near your house at the time of the break-in.'

'But he works for Royal Mail. Wouldn't he be out and about anyway?' It was how she presumed Evan had been able to get back home during the day without being missed.

'He works in one of the big distribution centres, and now he's management, he doesn't leave the site.'

'Then how—'

'Before you go jumping to conclusions,' Ashleigh cut in, 'keep in mind what I said about Evan being in management. All he has to do is switch that day's recording to another day.'

325

'I'm sure the police would know if he tried to do that.'

'I'd rather not take that chance.'

Jane took a deep breath and puffed out her cheeks as she exhaled. 'Sorry, but I don't follow where I come into this.'

'We need to be smart, Jane. What if you were confused about when the burglary took place?'

Jane wafted her T-shirt to drag some cool air over her damp skin. 'But I'm not confused.'

Ashleigh's stare hardened. If her eyes weren't so bloodshot, it would be difficult to believe this same woman had been sobbing her heart out two minutes earlier. 'You're not following,' she said impatiently. 'What if you were to tell the police you were confused. What if, say, you hadn't used your laptop or your camera for a day or two? They could have been stolen long before you noticed. Possibly during the night. I mean, thinking about it, that's what must have happened.'

'No, I'm quite sure of when they were taken, and I really think you're worrying for nothing. It's not as easy as it might seem to switch files. The CCTV recordings will more than likely be date stamped, and even if they're not, the files themselves will have metadata.'

As Ashleigh glanced away, Jane caught the eye roll. The abrupt change in demeanour was unsettling, and Jane was tempted to suggest Ashleigh go home and sober up, but she had learnt from a young age not to provoke a drunk. Ants crawled down her spine. Why was she comparing Ashleigh to her dad?

'You don't have to get all technical, Jane. Let's just say the files can be passed off as the wrong day,' Ashleigh persisted.

'If the CCTV isn't date stamped, my photos are. I know exactly when my things were stolen, Ashleigh, and I'm not about to lie to the police,' Jane said more forcefully than should be necessary.

There was a flash of anger behind Ashleigh's eyes that quickly disappeared when she noticed Jane flinch. Her lip protruded when she said, 'Can't you see what I'm going through? You say you want to help, so help me. I want the police to concentrate on looking for Rose, not mess about with this silliness. I don't understand how you could be so mean.'

'It has nothing to do with being mean,' Jane said sharply, refusing to let Ashleigh intimidate her. She shouldn't feel that way. 'And I'm sure in the scheme of things, the theft hardly matters. The police will be far more interested in finding Rose.'

'It matters to me. If Evan can get away with stealing from you, he can get away with anything.'

'If he had gone missing from work that day, the CCTV will prove it,' Jane said, surprising herself by framing Evan's guilt as a possibility rather than a fact. 'Are you saying it's possible he didn't steal my things? Is that why you're so upset?'

'Don't be stupid!' Ashleigh spat the words at her, but when Jane recoiled, she began to wail again. 'Sorry, I didn't mean to snap.'

There were no tears this time. Either Ashleigh was all cried out, or this was all for show. It was becoming easier to see through Ashleigh's mask even though Jane wasn't sure what lay behind it. 'Who else could it have been?' she asked, thinking out loud.

'No one! It was obviously him!'

As Ashleigh stepped forward, Jane was forced back, acutely aware that she was being hemmed into a corner of the kitchen by someone who was becoming more and more volatile.

'You have no idea what he's capable of. He needs locking up,' Ashleigh said while tearing her tissue to shreds. 'He'll come back, you know. Do you want that? Would you be happy living that close to a killer?'

'A killer?' Jane asked. 'But you don't know Rose is dead.'

Ashleigh's chest rose and fell steeply. 'Don't I?'

It could be old ghosts playing games with her, but Jane recognized the danger in every heavy object and sharp kitchen implement. The blood in her veins turned to ice, but she made a play of wafting a hand in front of her face. 'Sorry, I'm having a hot flush. Let's go outside.'

She moved towards the back door, but Ashleigh blocked her. 'Why does everyone walk away from me!'

There was the scrape of claws as Benji came running out of the sitting room, but he went straight past the kitchen. And then the doorbell rang.

Thankfully, Ashleigh couldn't block both kitchen exits, and Jane darted into the hallway. 'I won't be a minute.'

Fearing she was being pursued, Jane's scalp tingled as she recalled that painful tug on her pigtail as her dad grabbed her. Reminding herself that she was no longer that child, she stopped in her tracks halfway between the silhouetted figures at the front door, and the woman in the kitchen she no longer felt obliged to help. She wouldn't be bullied again. Not in this house.

Returning to the kitchen, Jane found the back door ajar.

The room was empty except for the torn confetti of a tissue left damp with crocodile tears. She looked out to the garden just in time to catch Ashleigh crouching down and forcing her way through the hedgerow. Coincidentally, it was exactly where the chicken wire had been trampled over on the day of the break-in. Ashleigh knew the route very well.

CHAPTER 47

Jane was in a daze when she answered the door to a smartly dressed woman who introduced herself as Detective Inspector Morris. The young man next to her was Detective Constable Hartnell, but their names drifted over Jane's head. There was too much to process after Ashleigh's bizarre behaviour, but she had a feeling the detectives' arrival was connected.

'I don't suppose you're here about Lesley Morgan, are you?'

'Lesley who?' asked DI Morris.

'My—' Jane stopped and swallowed back her disappointment. The police had other priorities, and she must do what she could to help find Ashleigh's sister. 'Never mind. Would you like to come in?'

'I believe you spoke to one of our officers last week in relation to Rose Martindale's disappearance,' began DI Morris once they were inside. The detective was sitting forward on the sofa with her arms resting on her knees whilst her colleague sat back with his legs crossed, notepad in hand. 'And we'd like to ask you a few more questions.'

This was where Ashleigh wanted Jane to lie for her. But why? Jane glanced at the closed French doors, and instead of picturing the shadowy figure of Evan slipping into the house, the slender form of a woman took shape. Had Ashleigh been the thief all along?

'Mrs Hanratty?' asked the DI.

Jane blinked hard. Ashleigh was right about one thing. Jane was stupid. She should have listened to May: Ashleigh and Evan were as bad as each other. 'Sorry, yes. Where would you like to start?'

'We gather you have some knowledge of the family that might help us with our enquiries. More specifically, Ashleigh and Evan Jarvis.'

'Yes, although I wouldn't say I know them very well, if at all,' she added with a wince.

'But Mrs Jarvis has confided in you?'

'I suspect she told me what she wanted me to hear.'

DI Morris had startling blue eyes that were cold and intense, and Jane was grateful to be on the right side of the law. 'Do you want to explain what you mean by that?'

'I'm not sure if I can, but I can tell you everything I know,' Jane began. 'Most of my observations have been from afar, and I saw Ashleigh Jarvis as a woman in distress. I thought I could help her.'

'And how long have you known her?'

'I became aware of the Jarvises about two months ago. It was the same day someone broke into my house and stole my laptop and camera.'

'We've seen the report of the break-in,' confirmed DI Morris. 'Go on.'

Jane explained how she had gone to warn her neighbours

about the burglary later that day. 'While I was talking to May Jones, Evan arrived home from work. Soon after he went inside the house, we could hear him arguing with Ashleigh. He accused her of being twisted,' she said, and was shocked to find she might agree with him. What had triggered the argument?

'And this would be the altercation reported by Mrs Jones?' asked DC Hartnell, referring to his notes.

'Yes, and I'm beginning to wonder if the two events were related.' Jane could imagine Evan walking in to find Ashleigh playing with the new toys she had stolen from Jane. Suddenly, she felt as angry as Evan had been. 'I know Ashleigh's told you we found my stolen property buried in their garden. I haven't touched them since we dug them up. Do you need them?'

'Actually,' said DC Hartnell, 'we're more interested in what you know about Mr and Mrs Jarvis's relationships with Rose—'

'Hold on a moment,' DI Morris interrupted. 'Mrs Hanratty, are you certain about when your things went missing?'

Jane set back her shoulders. 'Absolutely. I'd been using my camera that morning and transferred the photos onto my laptop. They're both water-damaged, but I'm sure some of the data will be recoverable. If not, the photos on my cloud drive all have date stamps. As you'll be aware, I suspected Evan had stolen my things because he'd seen me taking photos from my attic window and didn't like it. But Ashleigh tells me he has a convincing alibi. Is that true?'

DI Morris gave the briefest of nods, then asked, 'She's spoken to you about it?'

'She was here when you knocked and was quite upset – enough to rush away again.'

'We didn't see her leave,' said DC Hartnell.

'You can get through the hedgerow between our gardens. Funnily enough, it's how the thief accessed my property too.'

Jane watched as DC Hartnell jotted something in his notepad. She would love to know what his notes said about her. Were the detectives impressed that she had been right to suspect her neighbours of being involved in the break-in, or had they laughed at her like everyone else for jumping to the conclusion that Evan had buried his wife in the garden? Now a second woman had gone missing, and once again, Evan had filled in that damned trench. Jane would happily ignore her suspicions to avoid further humiliation, except for one thing: unlike Ashleigh, Rose hadn't been found.

'It might be useful if I showed you the view from upstairs,' she suggested.

'Why not,' said DI Morris.

The attic space felt cramped once all three were gathered at the top of the narrow staircase, and while the two detectives eyed the window, Jane was drawn to her dad's suitcase. Even if the officers were too busy to concern themselves with a cold case, it would do no harm to mention it.

'I hope you don't mind, but while you're up here, can I show you something quickly?' she asked. 'This suitcase belonged to my dad, and we found it hidden behind this false panel, here.'

DI Morris looked to where Jane was pointing while DC Hartnell inched closer to the window.

'It has all of my dad's belongings inside. His wallet, passport, *everything*,' Jane said. It was enough to pull DC Hartnell's attention back to her, and both detectives frowned. 'I explained to PC Hussein last week, I haven't seen this since the night my dad disappeared in 1974. It was my mum who packed his things after a particularly violent argument. He was abusive, you see. We never heard from him again, not ever. His name was Lesley Morgan.'

'Ah,' DI Morris said, recalling Jane's opening gambit. 'Then I think we should make a note to chase things up back at the station,' she said. 'But I'm afraid, for now, we need to concentrate on finding Rose. Is that OK?'

'I understand,' Jane said, and was heartened at least when DI Morris took one more curious look at the suitcase.

'I suggest you don't touch it again until we've taken a look,' she cautioned before joining her colleague at the window.

'You have a pretty good vantage point from up here,' observed DC Hartnell.

'Better than I realized. I was only ever interested in the garden, but the camera picked up more than I intended.'

'Ashleigh tells us you have a photo of Evan with Rose,' said DI Morris. 'We need to see that.'

'Of course,' Jane said, already at her desk. As she opened her laptop, she added, 'I thought it was Ashleigh at first. They do look alike.'

'Yes, we noticed that too,' the detective replied.

'I wasn't paying any attention to them at the time, but my flash accidentally went off, so it's possible Evan noticed me. And he definitely saw me taking photos when he was digging a trench in the garden. I sent that photo to PC

Hussein a while back. Have you seen it?' DI Morris's blank expression answered the question for her. 'It's why I thought he stole my camera and laptop.' She stopped scrolling through her albums. 'Except he didn't steal anything.'

DI Morris shrugged. 'Evan does admit he buried your things in his garden.'

'He does?' Jane replied, grateful to the detective for offering up this small gem of information. 'Do you think Ashleigh knew they were there?'

'She says not, and Evan has confirmed he didn't tell her,' DI Morris replied.

'I suppose that does make sense. Ashleigh didn't seem sure about what we'd find when we started digging. I'm glad it wasn't a complete performance, but I'm afraid she did handle the evidence quite a bit, probably to cover the fact her fingerprints were already on them.'

DC Hartnell glanced over his shoulder. 'You think it was Ashleigh who broke into your house?'

'What changed your mind?' added DI Morris.

'When Ashleigh was here earlier, she wanted me to change my story so it looked like Evan could have broken in the night before. She was quite forceful, to the point of being threatening, which made me realize Evan's alibi must be solid,' Jane said. 'It has to have been Ashleigh who stole my things, but I haven't got the faintest idea why.'

When the detectives offered no theories of their own, Jane concentrated on finding the photo of Evan and Rose. Turning the laptop to show them, she explained how Ashleigh had initially dismissed any suggestion of an affair, then had an apparent change of heart that led them to dig up the garden. She mentioned Ashleigh's confrontation with

Evan later that evening, and everything she could recall of the following day when Rose disappeared.

DI Morris folded her arms across her chest. 'Did you invite Ashleigh around to your house on that Friday night, or did she suggest it?'

'It was Ashleigh. I'd phoned that morning to see how she was after her fight with Evan.'

'And this would be the phone call you mentioned to PC Hussein. You thought Rose was still there?'

'Ashleigh said she was just leaving.'

'Did you hear Rose in the background?' When Jane shook her head, DI Morris added, 'And are you absolutely certain you didn't see Rose at all? Ashleigh claims they stayed in the kitchen.'

'I don't keep a constant lookout,' Jane said, laughing uneasily.

DI Morris looked disappointed. 'And that evening, what time did Ashleigh arrive here?'

'Eight o'clock.'

'How did she seem?' DI Morris asked.

'Well, her face was bashed in. She insisted she'd slipped on wet kitchen tiles because she was in such a rush to explain to Evan what we'd found in the garden.'

'Why didn't you report the recovery of your stolen items straight away?' asked DC Hartnell.

Jane bit her lip. 'Ashleigh was so certain it would be better to handle it without the police – she convinced me she could use the proof of Evan's alleged crime as a bargaining tool, so he would have to stop hurting her.'

'Clearly that didn't work,' DC Hartnell said under his breath.

'Back to Ashleigh's visit on Friday evening,' DI Morris said. 'What did she tell you about her conversation with her sister?'

'Nothing specific, I don't think. I got the general impression that theirs was a complicated relationship. She mentioned how Rose had been an alcoholic, and was convinced Ashleigh was too. She said she and Rose were too alike to be able to support each other.'

'Do you know if she accused Rose directly of having an affair with her husband?' asked DI Morris.

Jane pressed a hand against her forehead. 'She didn't say, but Ashleigh gave a lot of mixed messages that night. She claimed Evan had convinced her there was no affair, but in the next breath, she was worried about him and Rose being in constant touch with each other. Did Ashleigh tell you Rose had sent Evan a message that evening? She'd seen her sister's name come up on his phone just as she was on her way out to see me.'

'We know there were messages that day,' DI Morris said, exchanging a look with her colleague.

DC Hartnell closed his notepad. 'Could we have a copy of the photo?'

'Sure, you can take it now. I've got a spare flash drive somewhere,' Jane said, setting to work. 'In fact, you can have the whole album.' She took a deep breath. She couldn't let them leave without telling them her final fear. 'You might want to look at the other photo I mentioned, the one where I thought Evan was burying Ashleigh after she'd gone missing.'

'Sometimes it's good to remain suspicious,' DI Morris said generously.

'As long as you're not afraid to look a fool,' Jane said. 'Take another look out of the window.'

Jane tried to slow her breathing as she watched the detectives gaze out across the adjoining gardens to the row of townhouses.

'Do you see the trough in Ashleigh and Evan's garden?'

'Yes,' DI Morris replied, squinting her blue eyes.

'Evan put it over the trench that had been there, the one where Ashleigh and I dug up my laptop and camera the day before Rose went missing. The hole we'd left was roughly the same dimensions as the trough, but two feet deep,' she said. 'After Ashleigh's visit on that Friday night, I was restless, and came up here at around two in the morning. The lights were out across the way, and I can't swear to it, but I might have spotted someone moving about in the house.'

'And you thought that was odd?' replied DC Hartnell.

'I don't know,' Jane said a little too sharply. She was still working it out for herself. If Evan needed to conceal a body, surely he would do it under the cover of darkness then finish the job when it got light. That would explain why he was still up. Certain that her logic was sound, Jane continued. 'But after falling asleep at my desk, I woke on Saturday morning to the sound of Evan in his garden. The hole in the ground had been filled, and the trough was already back where you see it now.'

'And where was Ashleigh?' DI Morris asked, pulling her attention away from the window.

'In her bedroom. She'd told me she was going to have an early night and take some sleeping pills. She still looked to be out for the count.'

'So let me get this straight. This was the morning after Rose went missing?'

'Yes.'

The two detectives stared at Jane askance. 'And once you heard about Rose's disappearance, you didn't think it was suspicious that her brother-in-law had been filling in a grave-shaped hole in his garden?' asked DI Morris.

'You have to see it from my perspective,' Jane said. 'For a while now, I've imagined bodies buried everywhere.'

CHAPTER 48

1974

By the time Cynthia re-entered the kitchen, Les had managed to crawl across the floor to the table. He was heaving himself up to stand when he heard the back door closing, and turned towards the sound. As he wiped his nose, he smeared blood across his face, giving his smile a ghoulish quality.

'So you and your mate think you have a plan?'

'I don't know what you're talking about,' said Cynthia. The knife in her hand made her feel invincible, and she spoke with the authority of someone holding all the power. 'You attacked me, Les. And when I saw you reaching for a knife, I pushed you away and you fell over. When you tried to get up again, I smashed you on the head with the skillet. Remember?'

Les tried to laugh, but his face creased in pain. 'I'll make sure you both geh . . .' He frowned. His tongue wasn't working properly. Nor were his hands as he tried to steady himself. 'Get you l-locked . . .' His sneer vanished as his facial muscles slackened. His legs went from under him, and for the second time that night, he dropped to the floor. He started to fit, but only briefly.

Cynthia waited until all was still, then approached his motionless body. Les stared up at her with unseeing eyes. She nudged him with her boot, but he didn't so much as twitch. She kicked him harder, panicking now. He didn't move.

Dropping the knife, Cynthia crouched down next to him. 'Wake up, damn it. You bastard, wake up,' she said, shaking Les with desperation and rage, but she already knew he was dead. She sat back on her haunches. What was she going to do now? What could she do?

She was in no rush to call 999. Les had no need of an ambulance, and Cynthia didn't want the police. They would charge her, if not with murder, then manslaughter, or something, and she would lose Jane after all. And that was assuming they believed she had acted alone. It would kill May to stay silent while Cynthia took the blame, but speaking up would get her into worse trouble. Her best friend would be faced with an impossible dilemma.

Cynthia leant over Les so her face was inches from his. 'I won't let you do this,' she told him through gritted teeth. 'You've taken as much as you're ever going to get from us, do you hear me?' She wiped a hand across her damp cheeks. For five long years she had stayed strong, but this was too much. 'I'm not crying for you. You don't deserve my tears. No one is going to mourn you, Lesley Morgan. No one is going to even know there's a grave.'

Jumping to her feet, Cynthia ignored the pain from her

bruised and battered body. She had to work fast. Jane might notice the silence and come downstairs. May could reappear with Billy. Or someone else might have heard enough to warrant a call to the police after all. And even if she wasn't interrupted, there was still Jane quaking up in the attic. She wanted so much to tell her they were safe.

After locking the back door, Cynthia grabbed the jacket Les had flung over a kitchen chair. It had his wallet inside, and as she hurried up the stairs to her bedroom, she made a mental note of all the other things that needed to disappear. There was his big overcoat, his shaving gear, his passport, the rest of his clothes. She stopped in the middle of her bedroom. The suitcase. She couldn't take it without Jane seeing her, but that was fine, she told herself. She could pack while Jane was there, and if her daughter asked, she'd tell her she was going to send her dad's things on.

Pulling the pink candlewick bedspread off her bed, Cynthia bundled it in her arms and raced back downstairs. She would hide Les's body in the pantry for now, then phone May so she could take her daughter to hospital. Cynthia would have more time to bury the body that way. Her plan was set, but despite her confidence, she stopped at the kitchen door and listened. Why was she still scared? Had she done enough to keep them all safe?

CHAPTER 49

Twenty-four hours after her most recent visit from the police, Jane stood at the attic window, eyes trained on the house opposite. Ashleigh had tried phoning several times, and when Jane didn't pick up, she had sent a text offering profuse apologies for becoming overwrought, attributing her heightened emotional state to her understandable stress. Jane had replied politely that the police had all the evidence that proved the break-in had happened as originally reported. There had been no further communication.

As Jane waited for the next chapter in the Jarvises' lives to unfold, she kept her phone pressed to her ear, enjoying the simple pleasure of listening to her daughter's voice, even if she was only complaining.

'Can't you just tell me now why you and Dad want to talk to me?' Megan asked above the hum of her Land Rover's engine. 'A few more days isn't going to make that much difference.'

'It might,' replied Jane.

Megan groaned dramatically. 'You do realize I'm not

going to be able to sleep for days. Can you at least give me some warning about how bad it is?'

'There's going to be a storm to weather, but we'll get through it,' Jane promised. 'Now can you concentrate on your job, *and* your driving?'

The background noise changed pitch as the Land Rover's engine idled. Megan had stopped the car. She didn't make a sound, not so much as a breath. And then. 'Mum? Are you ill? Is that what this is about?'

'God, no!' Jane said in a rush. 'It's nothing like that, not at all. It's . . . There's a lot I've had to process, and undoubtedly more to come, but I've finally accepted that I don't have to do it on my own. That's what Sunday is about. Please, I can't say any more. I want the three of us there together.'

'But you and Dad are OK? You're actually speaking to each other?'

'We're doing more than OK,' Jane said, needing to give her daughter something.

It was nice to have the reminder that there were some sparks of joy to be found amidst the darkness, but before the worry lines on Jane's forehead had a chance to soften, a figure clad in a white crime suit appeared in the Jarvises' kitchen. She stifled her gasp.

'So I'll see you on Sunday then?' Megan said.

'Yes,' Jane managed. 'I love you.'

'Love you too, Mum.'

Jane shoved her phone into her hoodie pocket while her eyes remained trained on the figure, presumably DI Morris, giving orders as more people in white suits appeared, some inside the house, others from around the side entrance.

344

Soon the garden was teeming with them, and a forensics tent was erected around the trough that Evan had built.

DI Morris came out to stand at the kitchen door and glanced up at Jane as if she expected her to be there. She briefly raised her hand in greeting, and Jane was only vaguely aware of her arm lifting to return the gesture. The detective had listened to her, and with a flip of her stomach, Jane knew they would find Ashleigh's sister very soon. What the hell had Evan done to her? Poor Rose. If only Jane had been able to do something, but once again she had remained on the periphery while unspeakable crimes were taking place.

The flash of anger gave her a jolt, and she glared down at the spot where she believed another body was buried. She hated her dad for torturing her mum, not only during his life, but after his death. His hold on their lives had to stop, and it had to stop now.

Benji yapped in excitement as Jane dashed downstairs and out to the garage, where she selected a chisel, a mallet, a pickaxe and a spade before returning to the bright sunshine. The tools made a loud clatter as she dropped them onto the cleared circle of paving stones, making Benji scuttle back to the house.

Getting down on her knees, Jane chiselled away at the pointing between the paving stones, breaking fingernails as she dug out the shards. Before long, sweat was dripping off her face to leave dark patches on the faded and mottled squares of poured concrete. She could hear activity from the other side of the hedgerow, but she didn't stop until she had loosened the paving stones enough to start lifting them.

Rising to her feet, Jane's head began to spin, and her dizziness was exacerbated by the wobble of the loosened foundations. She pulled off her hoodie and used it to wipe her face before swapping the mallet and chisel for the pickaxe. Raising it high over her head, she smashed it down between the joints in the paving stones, then paused to catch her breath and listen out for any raised voices. No one from across the gardens appeared to care what she was doing.

One by one, Jane prised up the concrete slabs to expose a layer of sand and hardcore. Her shoulders ached, and sweat stung her eyes as she used the spade to reach a solid crust of earth. She needed the pickaxe again and grunted as she hacked away at the excavation site, not knowing how far down she would need to dig.

She could remember the vast hollow she had played in as a child, but it had been gradually backfilled with garden waste over the years. She didn't think it had been that deep on the night her dad went missing, although it was possible her mum had dug down first. Whatever Cynthia had done, she was patently better than Evan Jarvis at concealing a body.

It was back-breaking work, but Jane carried on until she was rewarded with the sight of black soil. The saltiness of her sweat made her throat dry, and she began to gag at the thought of what she was surely about to find. Forced to take a break, she drank some water then revisited the garage to fetch a hat and a pair of garden gloves, although it was too late to save her blistered hands.

As she stepped out of the garage, she didn't notice the figure approaching the side gate until PC Hussein called out.

'Mrs Hanratty?'

Shit, she thought. 'Oh, hello, officer.'

'Have you got a moment?'

'I'm in the middle of some gardening. What's this about?'

The constable dipped his head as if to keep a low profile. The entire neighbourhood would be on high alert due to the police activity at the Jarvises', and the arrival of a uniformed officer at Jane's house wouldn't go unnoticed. 'Could we go through to the back?' he suggested.

'Erm, you've caught me at a bad time,' she said, too exhausted to think up a better excuse to keep him away from her handiwork.

'I only need a minute, and don't worry,' he said with a smile. 'It's me that's in trouble.'

'Sorry?'

He nodded again towards the garden. 'Shall we?'

Reluctantly, Jane led PC Hussein through to the back. Benji raced up to greet their visitor, and for the moment at least, the police officer was more interested in the dog than anything else.

Jane indicated to a patio chair that faced away from the garden. 'Please, sit down.'

Despite her best efforts, PC Hussein glanced over his shoulder, but it was unclear if he registered the uprooted paving stones as his gaze travelled beyond the boundary to the neighbouring gardens. 'Thanks,' he said.

'Can I get you a drink?'

'I'm fine, but go ahead if you need one.'

Jane wiped the fresh beads of sweat running down the side of her face and picked up the water bottle she had left on the table. She sat down and took a sip to prise her tongue from the roof of her mouth.

'I owe you an apology,' the PC said, leaning forward so that he didn't have to raise his voice any louder than necessary. 'When I saw you last Friday, I was on my way home and looking forward to my first weekend off in a while, but I thought some of the information you'd given about Rose Martindale might be important, so I called it in.'

'I saw them erecting the tent. They must be pretty sure they're going to find her.'

The officer returned Jane's grim expression. 'I imagine we'll know soon enough.'

'And what about Evan? Has he been arrested?'

Her visitor looked uncomfortable. He wouldn't be allowed to tell her anything, of course. 'The matter is in hand.'

Jane rubbed her arms. Would Ashleigh be shocked? After their last encounter, Jane wondered if she would even care. 'DI Morris said I'd have to go to the station and give a formal statement. Does that mean I'll be required to give evidence in court too?'

'Let's take it one step at a time, shall we?' PC Hussein replied. 'I'm not here about that, Mrs Hanratty. It's about your father.'

After days of tortuous anticipation and deafening silence, the thought hadn't occurred to Jane that the police might have progressed that particular investigation. Their assistance was a tad late. Or was it? PC Hussein wouldn't be on his own if they needed to extend their search. Could this nightmare be over?

'Have you found him? Is he still alive?' she asked. She didn't particularly care one way or the other, as long as there was proof that he had lived beyond 1974.

'I'm afraid I don't know,' PC Hussein said, quashing Jane's hopes. 'With everything else that's been going on, it completely slipped my mind to file the report. I got a right earful from DI Morris about it.'

'Oh, I see. It's OK.'

'That's kind of you, but I wanted to apologize. I'm still learning on the job, but I wanted to let you know that it's filed now,' he said. 'Our enquiries are ongoing, but strictly between you and me, I can see your father had quite a record.'

'A police record?' Jane asked. It shouldn't surprise her. It was just a shame he hadn't been locked up for his crimes.

'As long as your arm,' the PC said, tapping the side of his nose. 'Lots of cautions, and an alleged sexual assault in Glasgow that didn't get to trial. But not so much as a speeding ticket since you said he went missing.'

'I see.'

'I've been told to ask you about the suitcase you found,' he said, tugging at his collar as if the memory of the conversation with his superiors made him uncomfortable. 'Do you think you could show it to me now?'

'It's still in the attic,' Jane told him.

As they stood up, he narrowed his eyes. 'You hadn't been expecting us to find him, had you?'

Jane shook her head, then quickly moved to block PC Hussein's view as he turned back to the garden. 'The French doors are locked, so we need to go through the kitchen.'

The PC wasn't listening. He stepped around her. 'Mrs Hanratty . . . What have you been doing?'

Jane decided there was nothing more to lose, and squared up to him. 'My dad's disappearance might be some cold case that's barely worth your time, but it's taken over my entire life. I don't know what happened to him, but I need to find out.'

The constable looked from Jane to the excavation site. 'You think that's where he's buried? Why didn't you say any of this before?'

'Given how I misread the situation when Ashleigh went missing, would you have listened? What's done is done, and I can't wait another day.'

'I'm afraid you'll have to,' he said, reaching for the radio receiver pinned to his uniform.

With her hands on her hips, Jane addressed the police officer as she might an recalcitrant student. 'I'm going to finish what I started.'

Breaking ground on what might be her dad's unmarked grave had allowed Jane to take control of her own destiny, and no one was going to wrestle it back from her, not even the police. She strode past PC Hussein and grabbed the pickaxe with a renewed sense of urgency.

PC Hussein followed, intending to confiscate it, but he withdrew his arm quickly as Jane swung the pickaxe downwards. 'Mrs Hanratty, you can't do this.'

'Of course she can.'

May was approaching from the hedgerow, pulling at a long bramble shoot that had stuck to her cardigan. The scratches on her hands suggested she had fought her way through hardier stems.

'Mrs Jones, I really don't think you should be here.'

'If you want to make yourself useful, go back to the Jarvises. Sounds like there's a bit of commotion over there.' Coming alongside Jane, she added, 'I think they've found something.'

Goosebumps pricked Jane's arms, and she fought the urge to cry for a woman she had never met while May continued to glare at the police officer.

'I'm not leaving,' said PC Hussein, taking hold of his radio again.

'Suit yourself,' May replied, picking up the spade.

'Please, ladies. Could you both just . . .' His words fell away as he watched Jane strike the earth a second time.

'If we don't find anything,' Jane said as she wrestled the head of the pickaxe out of the ground, 'then we don't have to waste police time.'

PC Hussein had his hand on the call button of his radio, but paused when he heard her gasp. Jane had snagged something that refused to crumble. All eyes stared into the hole.

Hooked around the tip of the pickaxe was what looked like a rag, but as Jane tugged, it became obvious that it was part of a much larger piece of fabric. The decayed weave had an impression of raised swirls, and although it was the colour of dirt, Jane knew the cloth had once been pink candlewick.

With a gentle tug, the fabric tore, and there was a small avalanche of soil that revealed what might be the curve of a stone. Except this one was white and had distinctive cranial ridges. Cynthia's words reverberated around her daughter's brain: *He's still here.*

'Drop the pickaxe and step away,' PC Hussein said, but the handle was already slipping from Jane's grasp. 'This is now a crime scene, and neither of you are to touch anything else. Understood?'

Jane and May nodded in unison, but they remained frozen to the spot, and the inexperienced constable had to be satisfied with moving the tools out of their reach instead. He began speaking rapidly into his radio as he stepped towards the patio, never taking his eyes off the two women.

'Oh, May,' Jane said as tears mingled with the sweat trickling down her face.

'What must my Cynthia have gone through?' May rasped. 'And all because of me.'

'We don't know that.'

'But we might soon enough. I know you think you can keep me out of it, but I won't let you. I never wanted to take a life, but if it were a choice between that man and your mum, I'd choose her every time, and I don't care who knows it.'

'In that case, you might want to start with Sheena,' said Jane, as she spotted her friend walking in from the side gate.

Sheena stopped behind PC Hussein who was too busy speaking into his radio to notice her. Jane and May couldn't hear what he was saying, but Sheena's expression turned from surprise, to shock, to horror.

'For God's sake, you can't . . .' PC Hussein began when he saw Sheena slip past him.

'What's going on?' Sheena said. She tensed as she looked from one shocked face to the other, then finally down to the exposed skull. She recoiled, almost tripping over loosened sods of earth in her strappy sandals. 'Fuck.'

'It's my dad,' Jane said huskily.

'Fuck,' Sheena repeated, her high-pitched voice on the verge of hysteria. 'Mum phoned me in work, said I should come over, but I never dreamt . . . I drove like a maniac down the M53. I thought something had happened to you.'

She looked up and stared wide-eyed at her friend. 'This is . . . This is . . . Bloody hell, Jane.'

'There's a lot we need to tell you,' Jane admitted, looking to Sheena's mum for agreement, but May was watching PC Hussein.

'Do me a favour, love,' May said to her daughter, who was on the opposite side of the pit. 'Move yourself over just a step.'

'What are you doing?' Jane asked in a low voice, having realized May was attempting to block herself from the police officer's line of sight.

'I wouldn't worry about him,' Sheena said as she stepped to the left. 'All hell has broken loose by the sound of it. Someone on the radio was telling him they'd found a body, while he was trying to explain he had one too.'

'So they have found Rose?' asked Jane, her voice wobbling.

'I'm guessing,' Sheena said, as they watched May stoop down to get a closer look at what they had uncovered. She shuddered. 'God forbid there are any more bodies being dug up today.'

May reached over to an area around the top of the skull, and knocked away a clod of earth.

'Can you see anything?' asked Jane.

'Not yet. But surely I hit him hard enough to break his skull.'

'What?' exclaimed Sheena, only to be silenced by her mother's glare. Much more quietly, she added, 'Fuck, Mum. *You* killed him?'

'Will you stop swearing! I'll explain later,' May said, her firmness belying the shake in her hand as she tugged at the half-buried remnants of the bedspread covering the other side of Les's skull.

Nothing happened, so May tugged harder. Earth crumbled, and as the fabric disintegrated, she lost her balance. Jane made to catch her, but May landed with a thump on the ground. As Sheena went to leap over the open grave to get to her mum, PC Hussein grabbed her sleeve.

'Don't do that,' he said. 'Is she OK?'

'I'm fine,' May answered, although her face was deathly white. She looked to Jane who had crouched down next to her. 'Do you see?'

'Yes, May, I see.'

The skull was almost completely exposed, but as Lesley Morgan stared up at them, only one eye socket was empty. The other had the handle of a screwdriver protruding from it.

CHAPTER 50

Ashleigh had been offered a drink and opted for a hot, sweet tea. It was for the shock. They had found Rose, and Ashleigh had been given the grim duty of identifying the body, confirming that the clothes her sister had been found in were the ones she had been wearing when Ashleigh had last seen her. They had asked about a missing baseball cap that May had seen Rose sporting, but Ashleigh couldn't recall it. Again, it was the shock, she told them, but that hadn't stopped them asking questions, and now she was stuck in a tiny interview room facing two police officers.

'What exactly did you and Rose talk about that Friday morning?' asked DI Morris.

'I've told you everything I know.'

'If you could just go through it again, please.'

Ashleigh looked pointedly to the duty solicitor sitting next to her in his polyester suit, but he made no objection to her being forced to repeat everything. Even though it was Evan who had been arrested, she was still being interviewed under caution, and it had seemed wise to have legal counsel, but this man was useless.

'Rose wanted to tell me how amazing I was doing keeping off the booze,' Ashleigh began.

'And what time did she arrive?' asked DC Hartnell.

Her statement was lying on the table right in front of him, and Ashleigh fought to keep the frustration out of her voice when she said, 'Just after eleven.'

She waited for another interruption, and when it didn't come, she put herself back in the moment, recalling the last ever conversation she would have with her sister. Her chin wobbled. 'Rose offered to take a step back. She understood how I needed to begin my recovery in my own way. She knew me better than anyone.' Choking up, Ashleigh reached for a sip of her tea, but her hand was shaking so badly that it splashed onto the table. 'I'm so sorry. This is . . . This is just too awful. I can't believe what's happened.'

When her solicitor offered nothing better than a tissue to ease her suffering, Ashleigh snatched it from him.

'I appreciate this is difficult, but if you could try to carry on,' said DI Morris.

The detective's tone oozed sympathy, but Ashleigh knew how to spot faked emotion. 'I'll try,' she croaked, sniffing back snotty tears.

'Who broached the subject of Evan's alleged affair?'

'It was . . . It was Rose. Evan had already told me nothing was going on, and I suppose Rose just wanted to reassure me too. She knew how fragile I was, and she said she would never do anything to hurt me.'

'You didn't challenge her about it?' DI Morris asked, her sharp blue eyes searching Ashleigh's own.

'I wanted to believe her.' Ashleigh hiccupped a sob. 'I wanted to believe them both.'

'And how was she when she left?'

'She was fine. Relaxed,' Ashleigh said, and this time the crushing sense of loss brought real tears. She pressed her fingers against closed eyelids, but all she could see was the blood. So much blood, and Rose's slackened features as she lay on the kitchen floor. You can't get more relaxed than dead.

Ashleigh shouldn't have lost her temper, she knew that, but what had Rose expected after more or less admitting that she wanted to steal her husband? The wine bottle was in Ashleigh's hand before she had a chance to think through the consequences. She had brought it down on the back of Rose's head with a sickening crack, a sound she would never forget.

The speed at which her sister dropped to the floor had made Ashleigh laugh. It was an involuntary reaction, as had been the urge to pick up the bottle in the first place. In many ways, her anger was a monster she had no control over, and when it took over her body, she would retreat to a safe space in her mind where she became little more than an observer. Inevitably, she had returned from her mental bolthole, and when she realized what she had done, a plaintive sob issued from deep inside her. She couldn't say if it was for Rose or herself.

She had inspected the wine bottle in her hand for signs of damage, but the loud crack hadn't been glass breaking. Meanwhile, a viscous sea of red was pooling around her sister's head, and as it spread out across the kitchen tiles, Ashleigh scooped up Rose's baseball cap before the blood could reach it.

Rose's eyes were open, and there was no need to take her pulse. Ashleigh had killed her sister. How on earth was she going to explain this away?

Rose had pushed her beyond what any rational person could be expected to endure, and all because the selfish cow had wanted Evan for herself. Together, they had begun a campaign to convince Ashleigh that she was a paranoid alcoholic, when all the time they were carrying on behind her back. It was classic gaslighting, and if Ashleigh had to convince a jury of that, she would, but as the blood on the floor cooled and congealed, it struck her that she wasn't the one who ought to be judged.

She thought long and hard before taking a single step, and when her plan was formed, she dropped the baseball cap onto the worktop, skirted around the corpse, and raced upstairs. She took off her dressing gown and stripped down to her underwear before gathering a pair of disposable gloves and the hair cap she wore for her deep conditioning treatments. She wasn't sure a surgical face mask was entirely necessary, but it completed the look.

Heading back down, she collected the plastic sheeting Evan had left in the front room after making a start painting over the replastered wall. It would have his fingerprints all over it, but not hers. Working fast, she searched Rose's pockets and removed her sister's mobile phone and a set of keys before rolling her onto the sheeting. The transfer went surprisingly cleanly, but dragging the dead weight through to the front room was quite the workout. She didn't like using the room as her sister's temporary resting place, but there was nowhere else to keep Rose out of sight of Evan, or her ever-vigilant neighbours until nightfall.

Sweat ran down her back as Ashleigh fixed the plastic shroud in place with duct tape, then rolled Rose in a dust sheet like a giant spring roll. Concerned that it still looked like a cadaver, she placed toolboxes and paint pots on and around the body. For good measure, she moved the dining table and chairs that Evan had stacked in front of the bay window back to the centre of the room, creating an assault course should he go nosing.

Once she was satisfied, Ashleigh closed the sliding doors between the two reception rooms and returned to the kitchen to tackle the mop-up exercise. She used strong bleach on every surface, including the bottle of wine. She wasn't too concerned about missing the odd spot or two. It wasn't as if she were trying to conceal the crime, just the evidence that incriminated her.

When she was done, she shoved the gloves, hair cap and mask into a bin bag. She considered putting the wine in there too, but it would be such a waste so she returned it to the fridge, resisting the urge to open it there and then. There was too much to do, and it had to be done with a clear head.

Ashleigh was about to get dressed when Jane rang. She considered ignoring the call, but when she saw Rose's phone lying next to hers on the worktop, she had second thoughts. What if the police were able to track Rose's movements from her mobile signal? Would they compare it with Ashleigh's, and know that Rose should have been in the house at the time Jane phoned? Ashleigh adapted her plan accordingly.

Her initial idea had been to invite herself around to Jess's that evening, ensuring that she was out of the house, and more importantly, Evan was left on his own. She would have an alibi, he wouldn't. The problem was, Jess would only drone on about her wonderful boyfriend and amazing job. Lonely Jane was a much better option.

Confident that her neighbour wouldn't have seen her strike Rose as they had been clear of the kitchen window, Ashleigh caught her breath and answered the call. It wasn't difficult to pretend that Rose was standing next to her, and when she directed a smile into thin air and said all was well between them, Jane swallowed every word.

Ashleigh kept the call short, and was soon on the move again. She picked up Rose's baseball cap and raced upstairs to change into a tracksuit with a white stripe that was very similar to the one Rose had been wearing. Before she put it on, however, she shrugged into a light summer dress that would remain hidden beneath the tracksuit until the time was right. Once dressed, she tied her hair in a knot at the top of her head and put on the baseball cap so that a casual observer would think she had shorter hair. The bruised nose was more problematic, but after applying thick layers of foundation and concealer, Ashleigh was satisfied that she could pull off an impersonation of her sister.

Before setting off on the next stage of her plan, Ashleigh added her dressing gown and pyjamas to the bin bag. There was no need for a special trip to the tip, which might need to be explained later, as their wheelie bin was due to be emptied early the following week. If all went well, Rose wouldn't be found for weeks, if not months. She had no idea how easy it might be to establish a precise time of death, but surely the longer the body was left to decompose, the better.

Making sure to leave her mobile in the kitchen when she left the house, Ashleigh pulled down Rose's baseball cap as she passed May's window. Her heart was pounding. She didn't know where Rose had parked her car, and could be walking in the wrong direction. There was the added jeopardy of bumping into Jane on one of her dog walks, but her luck held out. Too tense to feel any relief at finding Rose's car, she struggled to pull on the fresh pair of disposable gloves before opening the door and sliding carefully behind the wheel to avoid shedding any fresh DNA.

It was a short drive to the street where Rose lived in a two-up two-down terrace. It had none of the character of Ashleigh's house, but they shared a similar problem with parking. Rose often resorted to leaving her car further up the road, which suited Ashleigh's purposes. She wanted to keep away from any neighbours who might recognize the car and fancy a chat with her sister.

Before getting out, Ashleigh took a look at Rose's messages on her mobile, something she had been dying to do since taking possession of her sister's phone. She had seen plenty of messages Evan had sent to his sister-in-law on his phone, but the ones he left for Ashleigh to root through were usually brief and anodyne. She had assumed he had deleted their more intimate exchanges, but scrolling through, she could see that Rose had been equally secretive. From the long list of calls between the pair, it was obvious that they preferred to talk, and that had included a fourteen-minute conversation that morning, shortly after Ashleigh had given her husband explicit instructions to cut Rose from their lives.

Ashleigh's suspicions were justified, but it was frustrating not to find more tangible proof of their deceit. She hoped for some fresh insight when she tapped out a message to Evan, careful to use the wordings and salutations that her sister preferred.

Spoke to Ashleigh. Convinced her there's nothing going on but we need to talk. She's going to see Jane tonight. I'll come over then Rx

Although she didn't want to spend more time than was absolutely necessary in Rose's neighbourhood, Ashleigh waited for a response. It came in less than a minute, but rather than a message, Rose's phone began to ring. Evan was under the illusion it was still necessary to cover his tracks. She cancelled the call.

Her final task before heading home, was to check through Rose's other messages. Her sister didn't have a great social life because she religiously avoided people who drank, so it was a little annoying to discover she was supposed to be meeting a gym buddy that evening. It wasn't a problem. If anything, cancelling the arrangement would make it appear that Rose had had a better offer. She skimmed through the exchanges between the pair so that the reply tallied with their ridiculous keep-fit regime.

Sorry to bail out at short notice but family emergency. Will see you tomorrow at the gym to explain Rx

This time she didn't wait for an answer and powered down the phone. She didn't think to check Rose's photos at the time, or else she would have seen the neat little record of Evan's injuries. They were a devious pair.

Locking up the car, Ashleigh decided it was too much of a risk to sneak into Rose's house. She walked fast out of the street, then broke into a jog as she entered Birkenhead Park. When she was sure she wasn't being observed, she dived into a rhododendron bush to strip out of her tracksuit. She untied her hair, and put her clothes and Rose's baseball cap into the carrier bag that had been scrunched up in her pocket. The only thing she needed to keep for now was the phone; everything else was dumped in her wheelie bin when she reached home. It was only when she was standing beneath a scalding hot shower that the full force of what she had done hit her. She had cried until she was hoarse, lamenting the loss of her sister, her failed marriage, and her errant husband.

Now, as she told the detectives how convinced she had been that Rose was making them worry unnecessarily, tears slipped unchecked down her cheeks. 'I would give anything to have her back safe. I'd even forgive her about the affair with Evan,' she said, hitching her breath. 'What is it about that man that made us both fall under his spell?'

'Do you need a break?' asked DI Morris.

'No, please, go on,' Ashleigh said, sensing she could win the crowd. She took another tissue from her solicitor and blew her nose. 'I need to know what happened as much as you do. Has Evan admitted what he did to her?'

'He says he didn't see Rose at all that day.'

'But you know they were messaging each other, right? Of course she went to see him. Rose knew I'd be out of the house. Maybe they argued. Evan had been forced to choose, and he had chosen me. He loved me, and she would have been devastated. Maybe she turned up drunk. I love my sister, but Rose would get nasty with drink, ask anyone

363

who knew her before she sobered up. I should have seen it coming. She was obsessing over how much I drank, but I guess it was because she was struggling.' Ashleigh gasped back a sob. 'Poor Rose.'

'The pathologist should be able to determine if she had been drinking from the autopsy,' DC Hartnell told her helpfully.

'Thank you,' replied Ashleigh as if they were doing her a personal favour.

It was a shame the autopsy had to happen so soon. After all of Ashleigh's careful planning, Jane had opened her big mouth and told the police about Rose and Evan's alleged affair far sooner than she would have liked, speeding up the investigation. She hoped two weeks had been long enough for the body to rot, and at least her wheelie bin had been emptied. All of the incriminating evidence would be incinerated by now. She remained confident.

Meanwhile, Evan had no defence. When he had come home from work the day Rose died, Ashleigh had been making a curry. To accompany his favourite dish, there was naan bread, and homemade raita with the extra special addition of Ashleigh's crushed-up sleeping pills. Evan was already a little woozy when she had left the house, although apparently awake enough to respond to the final message Ashleigh had sent on her sister's behalf on her way over to Jane's.

Has she gone out? Can I come over? Rx
Don't come. It's not safe x

Satisfied that this last text would be Evan's undoing, Ashleigh had removed the sim card from Rose's phone so she could add it to the rest of the trash in her wheelie later. Her husband's fate was sealed, and she would love to know how he was trying to explain himself to the police. He couldn't even remember her cajoling him out of his stupor that evening to get him up to bed, and he had remained deep in sleep while Ashleigh completed her final task of burying the body and backfilling the hole before crashing out around two in the morning. Little wonder she had needed that lie-in the next day while Evan worked in the garden.

Ashleigh's body shook with another sob that reverberated around the interview room, but when she covered her face with her hands, she allowed herself a small smile. However uncomfortable this interrogation was for her, it would be so much worse for Evan. 'I just want this to be over,' she said.

'Are we done?' asked the solicitor, speaking up for her at last.

'Nearly. Do you think you could answer a few more questions, Ashleigh?' DI Morris asked softly.

Ashleigh nodded as she mopped up her tears.

'So tell me, did your sister know about you stealing your neighbour's property?'

Ashleigh suppressed a gasp. Rose had been murdered and they were asking about Jane's stupid camera? She looked to her solicitor.

'My client doesn't have to answer that. She hasn't been charged with anything.'

DI Morris glanced at the scratches on the back of Ashleigh's hands, sustained from her latest battle through the hedgerow after Jane had turned against her, but then she shrugged. 'Fine, moving on. How did Rose react when she saw your bruised face?'

'I told her I fell,' Ashleigh mumbled, refusing to make eye contact. She wanted them to think she was covering for Evan. All they had to do was press her a little further and she would spin another tale, but annoyingly, the detective didn't take the bait.

'Was she, say, as concerned about you as she had apparently been about your husband's past injuries?'

Ashleigh blew her nose to cover her annoyance, but she had been prepared for this line of questioning. 'She was a very caring person, but a little gullible. She fell for Evan's stories.'

'About?' asked DI Morris innocently.

'Evan told her I assaulted him, but it was only to deflect from the fact that he was abusing me.' Ashleigh stopped, her face a picture of anguish to illustrate how deeply the slur hurt. 'Evan told me about the photos Rose took, but the man plays sport and treats his body like a battering ram. He often injured himself.'

'I see,' DI Morris replied. She let out a long sigh that suggested she was running out of steam, but just when Ashleigh thought the ordeal was over, the detective asked, 'So how did Rose seem when she left?'

'You've asked me that already.'

'OK, let me frame it a different way,' DI Morris said, tilting her head as she observed Ashleigh. 'Why do you think Rose went home after leaving you, and was so distracted that she left her shopping in the boot of her car?'

The discovery of the groceries was one of the reasons the police had taken her disappearance more seriously from the start. It was another oversight, but manageable. 'I've already told you I don't know.' When the detectives continued to wait for an answer, she added, 'She was upset about losing Evan, I suppose.'

DC Hartnell checked the copy of her statement in front of him a little too theatrically. 'You said previously, and again today, that Rose was relaxed.'

'That was how she *appeared*,' Ashleigh replied. They would have to try better if they wanted to catch her out. 'Look, I don't like speaking ill of the dead, but even you must realize how two-faced my sister could be.'

'You didn't like her then?' DI Morris asked.

Ashleigh leant forward. 'I loved my sister.'

'But you didn't socialize that much?'

'We didn't exactly share the same interests, unless you include Evan,' she replied to remind them who they should be grilling.

DC Hartnell shuffled his papers, settling on one page in particular. 'Can you recall the last time you were in Rose's car, if at all?'

Had they found something? Ashleigh chewed her lip, then stopped in case it made her look nervous. 'Sorry, I don't remember.'

DI Morris sat back in her chair and folded her arms across her chest. 'We found a long blonde hair on the driving seat. We'd like a DNA sample to see if it was yours.'

Cold sweat pricked the nape of Ashleigh's neck. She should have tied back her hair before dressing up as Rose, not afterwards. A rogue hair must have come loose. 'So what if it was mine? We hugged that day, and I'm always shedding hair.' It wasn't fair that they were treating her like a suspect over such a minor detail. She turned to her solicitor. 'Do I have to take a DNA test?'

Before he could answer, there was a knock and another officer stepped into the room to hand DI Morris a slip of paper. She read it and passed it to her colleague before turning to Ashleigh. 'Is it fair to say you weren't into fitness in the same way that your sister was?'

'What?' Ashleigh said, feeling suddenly hot. 'I'm sorry, but it seems like you're deliberately throwing questions at me to confuse me.' She glared at her solicitor, prompting him to sit up straight.

'My client's right,' he said. 'And if you're not going to charge Ashleigh with anything, I suggest we leave it there.'

'You make a very good point,' DI Morris said in a way that Ashleigh didn't like. 'Did you know your sister wore a sports watch, Ashleigh? A Fitbit, to be precise.'

Ashleigh gripped the edge of the table. The police were goading her, but she wasn't going to snap. Yes, Rose had a stupid watch to count her steps; she would go on and on about how far she walked without actually getting anywhere. Surely it didn't matter if she hadn't been as active that day – she could have been in bed crying all afternoon for all the police knew. 'So?'

'We've been able to access the stored data.'

'Are you presenting new evidence?' asked the solicitor.

DC Hartnell pushed the slip of paper across the table so Ashleigh and her solicitor could read it. The numbers made no sense.

'As you will see, the watch monitored your sister's heart rate,' DI Morris explained, pausing for a look of satisfaction when Ashleigh blanched. 'Given we found it tight around Rose's wrist, and the data shows the battery was working days after she went missing, we can safely assume the watch tracked your sister's heart rate right up to the moment of death.'

'Eleven twenty-six,' said DC Hartnell, and in case there was any doubt to his meaning, he added, 'in the morning.'

Ashleigh's fingernails thrummed with pain as she held on to the unyielding tabletop. 'No, this can't be right,' she said.

DI Morris's features softened as if she were back on Ashleigh's side. 'You need to tell us what really happened when Rose visited you, Ashleigh. We know you spoke to Jane Hanratty at eleven fifty-one, and told her your sister was there with you. But Rose was already dead by then, wasn't she?'

'No.'

'We'll have to wait for the autopsy results to corroborate our findings, but I expect that to be a formality, and you will be charged.'

'No,' Ashleigh said again. 'No. NO!' She slapped her palm against the table hard enough to make the cold tea splash over the sides of her plastic cup. There was a scrape of chairs as the two detectives rose to their feet.

Ashleigh glowered at them. 'It's a lie! This is a set-up!' she yelled then spun towards her solicitor who had pressed his chair against the wall. 'You said I was here voluntarily. Well, I want to go. Now!'

'I'm afraid that won't be possible,' said DI Morris, raising her voice to Ashleigh's level, but without the temper. 'Ashleigh Jarvis, I'm arresting you on suspicion of the murder of Rose Martindale. You do not have to say anything—'

Ashleigh started talking over her. 'Evan set me up! Are you stupid? Are you all stupid? You can't do this!' She looked again to her solicitor, imploring him. 'Can they?'

Hot tears scorched Ashleigh's cheeks. Real tears. It wasn't fair. Why didn't anyone ever listen to her?

EPILOGUE

Two months later

As Jane stared out of the attic window, she marvelled at the rays of sunlight cutting holes in the pewter sky. It was odd how she had taken so little notice of the vast space above the rooftops before, but she was learning to change her perspective.

As she lowered her gaze, she noticed that Evan's kitchen door was open, and a couple of workmen were busy laying decking across timber footings that stretched the length of the house. It wouldn't be long before the wound left after the exhumation of Rose Martindale's body would be completely hidden from view.

The same couldn't be said for the scars in her mum's garden. The sun design had been removed in its entirety during the police investigation, but the imprint left in the exposed earth was clear to see. It would take time for the wildflowers Jane had sown to take over, but she gave the site only a cursory glance. She had been released from its thrall.

After decades of waiting, her dad had finally left home. She hadn't attended the interment. Lesley Morgan would be no more than a footnote in the history of her family. He didn't define Cynthia Simpkin's life, and he wouldn't define Jane's.

'Mum!' Megan yelled from the hallway. 'We're off to the tip. We shouldn't be long.'

Jane let herself be drawn away from the view, and as her footsteps echoed across the floorboards, dust bunnies retreated to the far corners of the empty room. The false panel had been sealed permanently into place, and the joins were invisible this time. There were no hiding places left, which was as it should be. There were no more threats, and no more secrets.

'Leave all the heavy lifting to your dad,' she shouted down to them.

'You're forgetting whose daughter she is!' Phil replied with a laugh.

A moment later, Jane heard the front door slam behind them. If ever there was a sound that marked closure, that was it, and as she left the attic, she had no intention of ever returning. She closed the door on the landing, and shifted her attention to her mum's bedroom. The door frame had been completely replaced so that the new occupants wouldn't curse every time they forced the door open. Gently, she touched the newly painted timber with a fingertip. It was almost dry.

'All better now,' she whispered, hoping her mum could hear her, and that it would bring her the peace she had denied herself for all those years. Jane felt a shiver as if Cynthia's voice was just out of hearing. 'I'm proud of you too, Mum.'

She was about to go downstairs when her phone pinged with a text from Sheena.

I'll come over straight after work, so don't go sneaking off! S x

Jane couldn't leave without saying goodbye to her friend. With Megan's help, she had made up two large hampers for Sheena and May, filled with all kinds of indulgences. Sometimes friends needed a little help looking after themselves. She tapped her reply with none of her usual hesitation.

I was thinking, we should go on holiday together. Just us two and your mum. Xx

She was halfway down the stairs when an answer came back.

What a fabulous idea, I'll bring brochures! x

A shadow moved across the hallway, and when Jane looked towards the front door, her smile faltered. There was a figure looming on the other side of the frosted glass, blocking out the light as they reached up to ring the doorbell.

As Jane opened the door, the gasp escaped before she could stop herself. 'Oh. Erm, hello.'

Evan had his chin pressed to his chest, and his shoulders were hunched. 'I'm sorry to disturb you. If you're busy, I could come back.'

Benji almost shot past Jane to greet their visitor, but she swept him into her arms. Holding him close, she managed to recover her composure enough to be polite. 'No, it's fine.'

'May said I should come over,' he explained. 'She said you're leaving.'

373

'I'm going home to be with my family,' she said. She could feel Benji's tail thumping against her side. The little dog's excitement was reassuring, and she lowered her guard. 'It's time to look to the future, and I want this house to find new life with a new family. I've managed to find a tenant, and they want to move in as soon as they can.'

She had been quite particular, and was looking forward to handing over the keys to a young woman who had escaped an abusive relationship with her three children. The arrangements had been made through a charity, and the rent had been set at an affordable level to cover basic maintenance costs. Someone was getting a fresh start, and the wrongs of the past were being healed.

'Renting was so much easier than trying to sell up,' she added.

'I can imagine,' said Evan. Having houses as notorious as theirs would put buyers off, but not necessarily the ghouls who would be lining up for viewings if they went on the market.

'My husband and daughter are helping me with the clear-out. They've taken a car-full to the recycling centre, and shouldn't be long. The furniture's staying, so there's only a small amount I'll need to take back to Buxton, like Mum's tools.' Now that Jane was talking, she couldn't stop. 'I'm looking at setting up my own business. A sort of odd job woman. My mum taught me so much, and I'd like to put those skills to good use.'

'The more I hear about your mum, the more respect I have for her.' Evan's voice had a tremble that was unexpected in a man of his stature and strength.

'Not everyone shares your view.'

Although there was a presumption that Cynthia had killed Les in self-defence, there was speculation on social media that he must have been unconscious or severely debilitated for her to aim the killer blow with such precision. The inquest might provide some answers, but no one was ever going to know what had happened in the moment she stabbed Les with the screwdriver. All Jane knew for certain was that her mum was braver than she could ever have imagined.

'I shouldn't worry,' said Evan. 'I'm sure your mum's story won't divide opinion nearly as much as mine.'

Jane's eye twitched. She hadn't wanted to stray onto the topic of Evan's situation, even though privately she had devoured every word that had been written on the subject. Ashleigh's arrest had come as a shock, and Jane had immediately suspected a terrible miscarriage of justice. She knew her neighbour wasn't the person she purported to be, but her original view of Evan held fast, and she had waited for him to be charged too. He couldn't have been an innocent victim in all this. Could he?

'I'm sure the court case will settle the matter,' she said.

'And I'm aware you'll be a witness, unless Ashleigh has a change of heart and admits what she did,' he replied. 'But I'm not here to apply any pressure, if that's what's worrying you.'

It had crossed Jane's mind. 'I can only tell them what I know.'

'If it helps, I don't think your testimony will be the deciding factor. The police have overwhelming evidence that Rose died that morning in our kitchen. I'm horrified that I came home and didn't notice a thing, but Ash must have drugged me with her sleeping pills. Thankfully, the police think so too,' Evan said, catching Jane's eye. They both knew it was convincing everyone else that remained the challenge. 'The worst thing is knowing I was tricked into covering over the hole where she'd hidden Rose's body . . .'

Evan stopped abruptly and took a couple of breaths. He blinked hard before continuing. 'I can't believe Rose was in our garden all that time. She didn't deserve to die.'

'I'm so sorry,' said Jane, her heart pulling in ways she never expected. 'You must have cared a lot about her.'

'Not in the way you might imagine,' he said, managing a wry smile. 'We weren't having an affair, but we were friends. I was still deeply in love with Ash, as mad as that sounds.'

'It doesn't sound mad. She had me fooled,' Jane replied, any lingering doubts about Evan falling away. Most of her preconceptions had been constructed through Ashleigh's words and deeds. May had been right to send him over. They had all been manipulated, but this man most of all. 'Look, would you like to come in?'

It was a surreal moment to beckon inside the man she had once locked her doors against, but as she listened to Evan's footsteps following her into the kitchen, there was no tell-tale prickle of fear on the back of her neck.

'Tell me about the real Ashleigh,' she said when they were seated at the kitchen table.

Evan sipped the glass of water Jane had set in front of him. 'It would be easy to suggest she had two sides, but it was more subtle than that. She could be generous, loving and passionate, but only if you kept her at the centre of your world, and for all those times that I didn't, she took it out on the things she saw as competition for my interests.'

'Like Rose?' asked Jane.

Evan closed his eyes briefly. 'I never imagined it would get that far. Sure, she was jealous whenever I was out of her sight, but she took it out on stuff first, like the garden. I never could have believed how dangerous she would become. I should have left her long ago.'

'Why didn't you?'

'It's hard to explain,' Evan said, pausing to formulate his words. 'I loved Ash more than was good for me, she was . . . addictive.' He pressed a hand to his cheek, rubbing away the embarrassment. 'For too long, I clung to the hope that we would get back to the way we were in the early days, although I'm not sure our relationship was ever healthy. The biggest warning was at the wedding, when she and Rose ended up in a drunken cat fight in the middle of the dance floor.'

'Goodness.'

'But after that, Rose got her act together, and Ash managed to control her drinking for the sake of her career. Until she lost her job. After that, being a part-time receptionist wasn't enough of an incentive to stay sober, and it didn't help that I'd been promoted around the same time.'

'She told me she drank, but made it sound like you and Rose had browbeaten her into believing it was a problem.'

'That's Ashleigh. Part lie, part truth. Part good, part bad. Rose described her best. She said Ash couldn't distinguish between love and hate because both caused her pain. Out of everyone, it was Rose who saw what was coming, although her fear was that Ashleigh would leave me for dead one day, or have me locked up for abuse. That's why she wanted to photograph my injuries. And that's why I had my top off in that picture.'

'Oh, I see,' Jane said, wincing with shame. 'I can't tell you how many times I've regretted ever sharing it.'

'I didn't know you'd taken it, but I can see how it would look,' he said. 'I wouldn't feel too bad about it; if it hadn't been the photo, it would have been something else to trigger her. It was the alcohol that transformed Ashleigh's insecurities into anger, and she convinced me it was my fault. So, I became the shock absorber in our marriage. It was what I was built for.'

'That's not how a marriage is supposed to work.'

His nod was almost imperceptible, as if the concept was one he hadn't completely accepted. 'I'm sure you know by now that it was Ash who stole your things. I don't suppose you would have let me into the house otherwise.'

'Ashleigh tried to bully me into changing my story about the robbery so your alibi wouldn't hold,' Jane said. 'Her behaviour shocked me, but if I'm honest, I'd seen glimpses of someone I didn't like very much before then. There comes a point when you have to stop making excuses for her. I know sometimes hurt people can hurt people, but she knew what she was doing. She was calculating.'

'Well, I'm sorry for involving you,' said Evan. 'I didn't realize how far she'd go when I pointed out you might have photographic evidence of what she'd been doing. I couldn't believe it when I came home to find your laptop and camera on our coffee table. Ash was passed out on the sofa, and her arms were covered in scratches from the hedgerow. I woke her up and told her she needed help, and that was when she lost it.'

Jane was nodding. 'I heard some of what was said.'

'I bet you did,' Evan said sadly. 'Ashleigh knew she was playing to an audience. She'd scream at me to keep away, ask me why I was treating her the way I did, and all the while she was the one throwing punches or anything else she could lay her hands on. I can only imagine how difficult it must be for you to make sense of all her lies.'

Jane could agree with that. Ashleigh was an actress, and everything she did appeared to have been staged, from the way she struggled to unlock the front door, the view into her bedroom, and of course, the fight in the garden. 'What really happened that time she made it look like she was fending you off with a garden fork?'

'I play football for a local team, which Ashleigh hated, but she'd already cut me off from the rest of my family and my closest friends, and I couldn't give up this last piece of me. In May, when we'd agreed she could come home, it was on the condition that we keep our separate interests. The first time I went out, I tried not to worry that it was a late one. I needed the reassurance that she was really OK with it,' he said with the saddest laugh. 'She wasn't. I came home and found her drunk, but when she realized I was sober, it took the wind out of her sails, and we managed to avoid a fight.'

Jane blushed, realizing that must have been the occasion when she had unwittingly become a voyeur. Ashleigh had wanted her to see them, but only because she had been expecting a fight.

'So when I went out again the next weekend, she was spoiling for something. And that was the fight you saw in the garden,' Evan said. 'She wanted everyone to know what a victim she was, so she took the show outside.'

'And to my shame, I fell for it.'

'Most people did.'

'Except May,' Jane said. 'I couldn't understand why she was so cold towards Ashleigh.'

'I couldn't ask for anyone better fighting my corner, although I think it took a while for her to decipher all those mixed messages coming through the walls,' he said.

Jane picked at the fluff on her yoga pants. 'I should have trusted her opinion more, and your wife less.'

'May has been a good friend.'

'My mum thought so too. They went through quite a lot together, as I'm sure you know.' May had ignored Jane's advice and told anyone who would listen about the part she had played that night, but at least she was no longer in the frame for Les's death. Jane had a niggling suspicion that had been Cynthia's intention all along.

From the hallway, there was the sound of keys in the door, and Benji raced out of the kitchen to greet Phil and Megan.

Evan pushed his glass away. 'I should go.'

On impulse, Jane grasped his hand. 'I know May has her family, but with Ashleigh's trial, and the inquest into my dad's death, she's going to have a tough time. I won't be sorry to leave this place, but I feel awful leaving her.'

Evan returned her grip, his touch impossibly gentle. 'I promise I'll keep an eye on her. We'll get through this, Jane. All of us.'

By the time Phil walked into the kitchen, Evan was standing, and Jane's husband had to crane his neck to meet their visitor's gaze. 'Hello,' he said without his usual smile. He turned to Jane. 'Is everything OK?'

'Yes, of course it is,' she said, smiling to let him know he could relax.

Megan appeared over her father's shoulder, equally anxious. 'Mum?'

'It's fine, you two. This is Evan,' she said, introducing him as if they had only just met. And in many ways, they had.

1974

Cynthia stood in the middle of a freshly laid circle of bright yellow paving stones, her arms folded and her feet planted firmly despite what lay beneath. It had taken a couple of months to transform the garden, starting on the night she had dragged a corpse wrapped in a candlewick bedspread out of the house.

The hollow left by the Anderson shelter hadn't been particularly deep, but she had been too afraid to dig down in case the noise disturbed her neighbours. A more pressing problem had been finding sufficient topsoil to cover the makeshift grave. She had scavenged as much as she could from the compost heap before digging up the old vegetable patch the next day. Her greatest fear had been that a fox or a sudden downpour might expose her secret, but at last, she had what she hoped would be a more permanent solution.

'It's lovely,' said May, approaching from one of the paths

that led to the epicentre. 'I was saying to Billy, it looks like a sunset.'

'Sunrise,' Cynthia corrected.

'New beginnings?'

'I hope so,' she replied, although there would be some practical limitations. She would never be able to move house, nor would she want to invite another man to share her life again. Les would continue to exert some control over her, but no one else need know that, especially not May.

Her friend was a force of nature, as had been proven on the night that Les had died. If she hadn't been there, Cynthia would be dead, Les would be in prison or on the run, and Jane would be in care. In Les's world, that would have been a win.

Having May arrested for his murder would have been the next best thing for Les, and that was something very much on Cynthia's mind when she had returned to the kitchen with the bedspread that night. The way Les's lifeless body had moved as she rolled him onto the pink candlewick had made her retch, and she had stepped back for a moment to take some deep breaths, giving her time to consider her next move. And that was when she caught sight of the screwdriver in the old jam jar.

Willing to do anything to protect her friend, Cynthia had knelt down in front of Les, bringing her hands together as if in prayer. She aimed the screwdriver at one lifeless eye before closing hers, then rammed it into his skull. She just about made it to the sink before throwing up, but the deed was done. No one would ever know that May was responsible for Les's death. Not ever.

'He won't dare come back,' May was telling her, 'and if he does, I'll give him more than a whack over the head with a skillet.'

Like most people, May had speculated over where Les had slunk off to. Cynthia had suggested he'd gone off to sea, and she would add weight to that theory in the coming months with imaginary letters, or the odd gift to Jane. It would be a fine balance between proving he was still alive, and not making her daughter too afraid of his possible return.

The rap of knuckles against glass interrupted Cynthia's thoughts. Jane and Sheena were at the attic window, waving at their mothers.

'How long before they grow too big for that den of theirs?' asked May.

'I'm going to seal it up long before then,' Cynthia said. It would make a better hiding place for Les's things than her dad's old army trunk, but that wasn't the only reason. 'I'm worried Jane will never stop wanting to hide.'

'It'll take time, but she'll learn not to be afraid. She's tough, like her mum.'

Cynthia didn't feel tough, or brave. Even if she could keep the body hidden, she wasn't foolish enough to think she could keep her secret forever. Jane would need to know about the legacy she would eventually inherit, or else she was going to be in for a nasty surprise one day. And that was why Cynthia was intent on keeping the red tartan suitcase. At some distant point in the future, she would open it up in front of her grown-up daughter and explain herself. But not yet, and not for a very long time.

Until then, Cynthia would be grateful for each and every

sunrise, and she would devote the rest of her life to undoing the harm Les had caused. Jane would be happy and confident again, and if the damage inflicted during her formative years meant that she retained a certain level of mistrust, surely that was a good thing. There were always people who had something to hide.

Acknowledgements

I loved writing this book for many reasons, not least because it was the perfect form of escapism during the pandemic, allowing me to throw myself into a world I could control. It was no coincidence then that I created a main character who was my age, although I might have taken my research a little too far by going through the menopause at the same time. Thankfully I didn't face quite the same challenges as Jane, but I did spend almost as long looking out at my neighbours during lockdown. I hope they didn't notice.

Setting part of this story in the seventies also allowed me to dip into half-forgotten memories. The working garden Jane recalls was written with my Nan and Grandad's garden in mind. It held untold adventures for a little girl living in a terraced house with only a backyard, and one of my favourite things back then was playing in a deep hole where an Anderson shelter had once stood. Make of that what you will!

Of course, it wasn't only my memories I relied upon,

and I would like to thank everyone who helped me build a broader picture, and in particular my mum for sharing her memories of power cuts, and Pauline and Pete Hewitt for regaling me with stories of sneaking off to the Cavern, and also inspiring me to add a reference to purple and orange colour schemes. Pauline is one of the Ladies who Lunched to whom this book is dedicated. They are the loveliest group of friends I'd ever want to spend lockdown with, and our Zoom calls got me through. The reference to egg coddlers is especially for you; Sue Jones, Karen Sutton, Pat Gibson, Kath Woolley, and Pauline of course.

This book is set in Oxton, Birkenhead and I was grateful for the help of the Oxton Society who do amazing work bringing the community together. Thank you especially to Paul Smith for allowing me to join one of your historic walks, and I only wish I could have written whole chapters on the history of the village.

Thank you as always to Hannah Schofield at LBA Books for your continued support and for helping me take the kernel of an idea and shape it into a compelling story. And another very big thank you to the team at HarperCollins. To Kate Bradley for helping me plot out the book and giving me the confidence to start writing it, to Chere Tricot for all of your insightful edits and patience, and to the wonderful Martha Ashby for making me dig deeper than ever before with this book. I hope it meets your exacting standards!

To my family as always, and my daughter Jess, who allows me to glimpse over her shoulder as she expands her horizons. Maybe one day I'll write a book about your travels, if you don't beat me to it!

And of course, the biggest thank you goes to my readers. The life of an author can feel isolating without the occasional hello from someone who has read and enjoyed one of my books. You spur me on. Thank you.

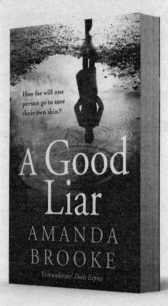

**When a fire destroys the Empress Theatre,
a devastating tragedy unfolds.**

Amelia's mother lost her piece of mind forever when she
left her daughter alone for a few life-changing moments.
The dance school lost their beloved teacher, Hilary,
who died saving the lives of her young pupils.
Karin lost her memory, and the answers she
desperately craves.
Claudia lost the one thing that would have
made her perfect life complete.

As local reporter Leanne picks over the embers of that
night, what seemed like a straightforward case of negligence
becomes something else entirely: somebody is lying – each
person has lost something, but one of them has sold
their soul . . .

There's a murderer in their midst. . .

@thewidowsclub
In response to unprecedented media interest, we confirm that the murder victim was a member of our group. We will not be commenting further.

When April joins a support group for young widows, she's looking for answers after her husband's sudden death. What she finds instead is a group in turmoil.
Set up by well-meaning amateurs, the founders are tussling for control of the group, illicit relationships are springing up, and new member, Nick, seems more than a little bit shady . . .
But the most dangerous secret of all? Not all members are who they seem to be. And they'll go to any lengths to hide the truth . . .

She died.
You're next.

Ten years ago, Jen's cousin Meg killed herself after failing
to escape an abusive relationship.

Now, Meg's ex is back and Jen's domestic abuse helpline
has started getting frightening calls from a girl who knows
things about Meg – details that only the dead girl or the
man who hurt her could have known . . .

As Jen starts to uncover the past, someone is determined to
stop her. Can she save this young woman from Meg's fate?
Or is history about to repeat itself?